INNOCENTS OF MARBELLA

Sharing the gospel is the power of God at work! Romans 1:16

R.C. MOGO

Black Rose Writing | Texas

First printing

ISBN: 978-1-68513-482-2 (Paperback); 978-1-68513-532-4 (Hardcover)
PUBLISHED BY BLACK ROSE WRITING
www.blackrosewriting.com

Printed in the United States of America
Suggested Retail Price (SRP) $22.95 (Paperback); $27.95 (Hardcover)

Innocents of Marbella is printed in Minion Pro

*As a planet-friendly publisher, Black Rose Writing does its best to eliminate unnecessary waste to reduce paper usage and energy costs, while never compromising the reading experience. As a result, the final word count vs. page count may not meet common expectations.

"A historical novel filled with faith, suspense and a touch of romance, Innocents of Marbella had me holding my breath until the last page. R.C. Mogo's debut is masterfully-crafted, drawing readers into medieval Europe through intricate details, fascinating characters, and a powerful plot."
–Anna Daugherty, author of award-winning novel *Outside of Grace*

"R.C. Mogo delivers a stunning historical fiction debut that reads like a blockbuster on pages! I couldn't put this one down!"
–Cam Torrens, award-winning author of *Stable* and *False Summit*

"R.C. Mogo's writing is vivid with crisp descriptions and complex, well-crafted characters. Innocents of Marbella will keep you glued to the page and surprise you with unexpected twists. I highly recommend it!"
–Travis Tougaw, award-winning author of *Foxholes* and *Captives*

TRIGGER WARNING

Please be advised that this novel contains narratives involving trauma and abuse, which some readers may find distressing or triggering. Reader discretion is advised.

For Dad

You diligently reminded me of my self-imposed deadline.
I overshot it by only five days.
And five years.
Now it will diligently remind me of you.

INNOCENTS OF MARBELLA

Marbella, Granada, 1440

Inside the forbidden office chamber, the odor of charred wood curled around Mary. Hundreds of book spines glimmered across the shelves. A Portuguese coat of arms gleamed above the hearth snapping with flames. "The fire's lit. He will return."

Her African accomplice, Hadiza, shook her head, reminding Mary that they did not speak the same language. None of the children did. Even the oldest boy spoke a different type of Arabic.

Master Diogo meant for it to be that way.

Mary crept close behind Hadiza, who was five years older at twelve. Wherever Hadiza went, Mary followed—even places they did not belong. They began pulling open drawers in his desk, silent and deliberate as if moving in a dream. A constant thought echoed in her mind: *go back to your bedchamber.*

Mary involuntarily wrinkled her nose. She shook her head, a desperate attempt to ward off the next twitch. Master Diogo disdained her for this, but most days, she could not resist the urge. So often did she shake her head and twitch her nose that Hadiza had created a hand-sign for horse. Through these hand-signs, she had also convinced Mary that finding this item in the most dangerous place would help them escape the dark tower.

The fire crackled. Or was that creaking wood? Mary whimpered.

"*Hasaltu aleyh*!" Hadiza exclaimed in a whisper. She held out a thin wooden case and pried it open, revealing a neatly folded, off-white fabric, its frayed embroidery the color of an azure sky at high noon—at least, Mary's recollection of the sky.

Had they risked everything for this tattered cloth?

Footsteps rumbled over wood in the hallway. The girls dove into the shadows under the desk. Mary's chest tightened.

The door swung open, its iron hinges juddering.

Mary buried her face into Hadiza's neck.

"Two little innocents, missing in the night." Master Diogo's singsong voice slithered on the shadows.

Hadiza drew Mary back. She did not seem afraid. Mary shook her head to stop her need to twitch, but it happened anyway. Hadiza hooked her hand in front of her face, wobbling her head like a whinnying horse. They shared wavering smiles, Mary's vision blurred by tears.

Master Diogo's sleek boots came into view. Hadiza slung her arm through Mary's, shut her eyes, and closed her dark fingers over the cloth.

In a silent flash of light, Hadiza's arm fell away. The case clattered to the floor. Darting her gaze about, Mary pressed both of her hands to her mouth, swallowing a cry. Hadiza was no longer there.

Hadiza was gone. Hadiza was gone? Hadiza was gone! Mary was by herself under the desk.

She was alone.

Master Diogo stooped, his dark eyes penetrating her hiding spot. The hearth blazed behind him, his eyes just shadows. His cheekbones jutted like a jester mask. The veins in his hands writhed like worms as he picked up the empty wooden case.

It popped shut—Mary flinched.

He flicked two fingers at her. "Out."

Her legs shook as she crawled from under the desk. She stared down where her nightdress hung to her bare feet, gold hair dangling around her face.

"Where is the relic? That was given to me in Jerusalem when I was your age."

Mary tried to swallow, but her throat convulsed, locked.

"Where is the other innocent?"

Mary rubbed a tear off her cheek. "She touched it and then... disappeared."

When she peeked up at him, his black gaze bored into her. "The Moorish girl?"

He seemed to believe her. But how? She barely did herself.

One thing she did believe was that Hadiza would not abandon her or the others. Before she thought better of it, she whispered, "She shall return with the whole of the Royal Guard."

He went still. He placed the case in a drawer and pushed it closed. His smile caused creases to form around his mouth. "I am afraid if this innocent goes to the Guard, she will be taken back here, straightaway."

Mary's nose wrinkled once—twice—and she shook her head. "What do you mean?"

Master Diogo's black eyes glittered. "The Guard is on my side."

CHAPTER 1

Nantes, France, 1440
The City of Grieving Parents

When the church requested Zahra interpret the interrogation of a man who had murdered countless children, who was she to refuse? Though she feared being in the presence of a killer, her fear of the church's wrath was even greater. Her fitted wool kirtle gown felt too tight as she stood before the polished doors of the Council Chamber, flanked by knights in full armor. Her work here today couldn't save the ones he already took, but if he confessed, it would prevent him from doing it again.

A knight stood beside her, his armor jangling. "Mademoiselle, you should not fear. You will not need to speak to it."

Zahra thought that a rather strange comment. "'It,' monsieur?"

The knight's crooked orange mustache gave him a quizzical expression. "The demon inside him."

She looked away, suppressing the urge to roll her eyes. Having been raised these last ten years by a brilliant Catalan scholar, Zahra never subscribed to beliefs she could not verify herself. Rumor was that after Joan of Arc's execution, one of her top military leaders, Gilles de Rais, began kidnapping and sacrificing children to demons. He and his accomplices were arrested in his chateau, where the evidence of their crimes made seasoned constables retch their suppers.

The knight cleared his throat. "Your complexion is rarely seen in these halls, mademoiselle. You by any chance descended from that fellow with all the gold? Master Musa or something?"

"Monsieur, I am more likely to be related to the demon."

His mouth dropped open. Zahra clenched her teeth and chided herself for failing to filter herself, again. It was just that she received the question of her origin even more often than marriage proposals—and many men sought betrothal to a Moor whose dark skin resembled someone descended from the famously rich Mansa Musa. It was a thoughtless assumption people made about her. Much like their assumptions about the existence of God, angels, and demons. In a world mired in superstition, Zahra found it difficult to filter her speech to hide her unbelief.

The only supernatural force in her life was the hum and clack of her worry stones. When rolled in her palm, the vibration of the scuffed black lodestones had a mysterious effect on her. It soothed her, but also dredged up painful memories of leaving Raha behind in Marbella. So, she rolled the stones to keep front of mind the wrong that she had done to her little sister. Weltering in shame was itself a daily comfort.

Others thought the habit strange, but today, the stones were a necessity. Zahra could not be at ease in the presence of men. They were all bent on violence, submission, and power. And this particular man, Commander Gilles de Rais, answered to his basest whims. The child murderer. And considering what she had learned of the investigation so far, murdering them was not the worst of what he had done.

She offered the knight a tight-lipped smile. "Just a jest, monsieur. I am from Marbella, Granada."

The knight twisted around, seeming to notice something beyond her. "The cleric has arrived, mademoiselle."

A sharp sensation spiked through her stomach. "Do I simply repeat everything they say?"

"You don't have to say a word to them, lass. Just listen. If you understand whatever language they speak, you tell us afterward if anything unusual was spoke about. We will report it to the bishop. Ready?"

Instead of answering him with the truth—which was no—Zahra pointed to her upper lip. "Monsieur, forgive my saying but your whiskers are a bit uneven."

His mustache fanned out as he pressed his lips together. "My wife needs more practice."

Zahra mustered a smile. "She has done a better job than I could."

The knight pulled open the double oak doors. "Your husband is clean-shaven, then?"

A muggy gust of air emerged from the dark Council Chamber where the interrogation would take place, and she resisted the urge to turn and run. "Should any man suffer being tethered to me, he would need to live as a wildebeest, I suppose."

He snorted and led her inside the oval-shaped chamber. Battles raged between knights in the paintings that decorated the walls. Four lanterns flamed at each of the cardinal points. The infamous killer of children, Gilles de Rais, sat in a plain wooden chair, his wrists and ankles chained down. As the knight guided her nearer, the killer's torn black stockings came into view, and his once regal doublet appeared tattered. His gaze groped Zahra, lingering too long on her organza neckline.

She stepped backward—but the knight held her in place. Her mouth dried. She circled the stones, their vibration coursing through her palm.

"Where is Francois?" Gilles spoke to the knight, his upper-class accent stained by disdain.

The knight nodded to the armored *valets* beyond the doorway. Their swords clamored against the steel cuisses that protected their thighs as they escorted another man into the chamber. This must be the cleric who would conduct the interrogation, Francois Prelati. He had promised to extract a confession from the accused. His thick silk robes swayed around his ankles as he passed by her.

"*Je vous salue,* Commander." *I salute you.* The cleric spoke with an Italian accent as he bowed.

Gilles nodded like a king receiving his subject. "Tell them of my innocence, Francois."

Prelati pressed a hand to his heart. "It pains me to tell you this, Commander. But you are possessed by a demon who only speaks the language of the east."

Gilles' face paled. His fingers clenched over the arm rests. "Francois, no."

Pitying wrinkles formed around Prelati's eyes. "If I speak Arabic to the demon, it will respond to me in kind."

Gaze darting about, Gilles leaned forward, whispering. "Dear friend, do not do this to me. If they think I am possessed—listen, the charge will not hold. I shall roam free in mere—"

"*Balash.*" *Enough.* Prelati's command of her native language, Arabic, was admirable. "The evidence against you is too strong. But worry not. You may yet be freed. Do your part… *shaytan.*" *Demon.*

The knights looked among one another, not understanding the language. If the French commander replied in fluent Arabic, even Zahra might be convinced of his possession.

Gilles de Rais sagged. He blinked several times, as if holding back tears. "*Ma tureed aqool?*"

What, you want, I say?

Those present gasped. Zahra looked between the two men. Yes, it was Arabic—but at a proficiency she could teach anyone in a matter of months.

The Italian nodded in her direction. "This woman is Mademoiselle Zahra Sabunde. She was hired by the church to interpret our conversation. Say hello, demon."

Gilles slid his gaze to her. He bared his teeth in a chilling smile. "*Marhaban.*" *Hello.*

She clenched her fist and the stones grated against one another.

"He is possessed!" A younger knight cried out.

A fine tremble started in her knees. Was Arabic their code language? She had an urge to tell the knights at once—but fear paralyzed her. Perhaps it would be best to wait and see if they exchanged any secrets. Then she could tell the knights what the men had said.

Prelati's hand shifted under his sleeve. "If this interpreter relays any of what I am about to say to you, I will be arrested. Should that happen, I have a blade that I would bury into her gut. Then all three of us would die inside this chateau."

Her blood drained into her feet.

A toothy grin split Gilles' cheeks. Prelati continued. "Listen carefully, Gillie. You must not, even under threat of excommunication, reveal my part in this. Even if they string you to the stake with flames licking your knees, you stay quiet. I have a plan. Do you understand?"

The child killer's upper lip curled, trembling, red veins sprouting in the whites of his eyes.

Prelati leaned close to Gilles. "We have friends in Madeira. You'll be safely tucked away there to enjoy the rest of your days. But only if you stay quiet."

Their faces were inches away from one another. Droplets of sweat dotted Gilles' forehead. "And Pitou? Henriet? They, not tell?"

He seemed to struggle to find the words in Arabic. Prelati lorded over Gilles like a slave master about to crack his whip. "I have taken care of their silence. Worry only about your own."

"How, I live, Francois? They think, I am demon."

"Demons can be exorcized. Out!" Prelati slapped Gilles' forehead, causing him to groan. His chin dropped to his chest and his black hair hung like the final curtain on a play.

Liars! The urge to cry out the truth stuck in Zahra's throat. Her stomach lurched at the thought of being stabbed. Could Prelati actually break Gilles de Rais out of jail? More likely, he was lying to give the man hope. After the trial, Gilles would be executed for his crimes against children. And that was that. No need for her to interfere.

"It has left!" Gilles' announced in French. "Oh, thank you, Lord. It made me do horrible things—so terrible!" He wept without tears.

"What was said, woman?" The knight with the crooked mustache turned to her, his voice like street grit.

Before she could muster a lie—or the truth that would get her killed— Prelati spoke up. "I exorcised the demon. Did you notice he has also confessed? That is what you asked for, is it not, monsieur?"

The knight continued to stare at her. She fluttered a nod. Apparently satisfied, he waved at a young *gros valet,* assistant to the knights. "Escort them back to their drivers."

Zahra darted from the Council Chamber. Prelati scuttled around the knights, robes rustling, and caught up to walk alongside her. Tension rippled through her body at his closeness. Surely, he would not harm her since she had stayed quiet. She hoped.

Prelati smiled, his upper lip curled like he wanted to bite something. He spoke Arabic in quiet tones. "Remember what happened to our hero, Joan of Arc?"

A mere nine years ago, the martyr had burned at the stake.

She focused ahead like a horse with blinders, crossing the foyer's mezzanine. The marching of the knights' metal solleret boots echoed that of her heart against her breastbone. She could not muster a word, her limbs weak. She reached the split staircase and cut in the opposite direction—but Prelati seized her hand. Hidden inside his silk sleeve, the hard edge of his blade pushed against her shaking palm.

He bowed and kissed the back of her hand. "Simply put, mademoiselle, do not be a hero. Heroes always die."

• • • • •

The two smooth stones circling in Zahra's palm emitted a mesmerizing murmur like the distant voices of chanting monks. Mere hours after her encounter with the pair of killers, a German notary, Hans Bauer, was meeting with Lord Raymond to evaluate Zahra for marriage. Despite her age. Despite her heritage. Despite her liking.

Lord Raymond would never force her to marry, but he still harbored the naïve hope that she would wed and have children. Since he had selflessly helped her get out of Marbella undetected when she was young, she did not wish to rob him of his hope.

She stood next to her maidservant in the drafty great hall of their home, the *Manoir des Cieux*. It was dark by now, but light shined from the soot-stained hearth, illuminating the lofty ceilings. Warped wooden beams sagged under the weight of the roof. Faded tapestries lined the stone walls, haunted by flickering oil lamps.

Isabelle's Breton whisper tickled Zahra's ear. "This might be the one, dear."

Zahra sent her a sideways glance and replied in fluent Breton. "You say that every time, *sittati.*" *My lady.* "And every time, I am relieved you are wrong."

Isabelle uttered an un-lady-like snort. Her skin was like pale pink lilies, her copper hair hidden underneath a white bonnet. "Here's my latest theory on the madness of you not wishin' to marry. You're just waitin' for a Moorish man with skin like *akajou satenn dahlia.*" *Mahogany satin dahlias.*

Zahra choked back a laugh. "Your theories, while perpetually wrong, are quite more fun than the truth."

Isabelle nudged Zahra with her shoulder. "There's my sweet child. You have been scraping those stones all afternoon."

Zahra closed her eyes, unable to forget the Italian cleric's threatening grip on her hand. She had decided not to burden Isabelle or Lord Raymond with what had transpired inside the bishop's Council Chamber, especially not what was said between the two men.

Were they men, or criminals? Child murderers. Monsters.

But she had to think of them as men. To let that *man* walk free was understandable—to let a monster was not. She rolled the stones to grind her guilt out like a mill separating the chaff from the grain.

Isabelle tufted the soft organza on the neckline of Zahra's fitted gown. "Once again, with your tresses pinned up, you confuse men lookin' for a bride."

Isabelle reached for the chalcedony pin holding Zahra's coiled braids in place. She threw her arms up and ducked out of reach. "Notar Bauer is already here to propose, *sittati*. I doubt my hair will confuse him."

The sanctity of the state of her hair was deep-rooted. An intricate hairstyle signified importance. She wore the unmarried woman's braids, but the high-pinned style told a deeper story of her heritage and the status she once held in Marbella. Although she was grateful to Lord Raymond for taking her to France and giving her a home, here she was only the adopted daughter of a scholar.

From nine to nineteen years old, Lord Raymond had educated her in linguistics, law, medicine, and of course, theology. But try as he might to convince her, Zahra remained unmoved by his belief in a creator. Having grown up in the spiritually diverse village of Marbella, she had seen many different religions made up by people longing for meaning. And in France these last ten years, she had seen enough variations in a single religion to know there was no divine artist who had masterminded it all.

"What is taking them so long?" Zahra strode toward Lord Raymond's study chamber, the hem of her heavy brocade gown sweeping her ankles.

Isabelle scurried behind her. The Notar Bauer's German accented voice filtered out of the door hanging ajar. "...marrying a Moorish queen."

Zahra sidestepped the opening, pulling Isabelle beside her. Her mother had always said Zahra had decent hearing—but excellent overhearing.

From inside the study, Lord Raymond's tone was long-suffering. "Notarius Bauer, Zahra would not qualify as a 'Moorish queen.'"

"Princess, then. Why did she run away from such status?"

"She was young, had just lost her mother, the queen, and learned that she was to be married to the king in her mother's place."

"Married to her mother's husband? Would that not be her...father?"

Lord Raymond sighed. "Not her biological father. Her mother was a *qayna*, an elite slave. They met after Zahra was born."

An incredulous laugh burst from Bauer. "The queen was a slave? And had a bastard daughter?"

Zahra whispered to Isabelle, "There were *two* bastard daughters."

"Go on, tell him!" Isabelle prodded her toward the door.

She pushed back and glared. "To what end, *sittati*?"

Her maidservant's eyes darkened. "Some people just need a tellin' to."

The German exhaled a sound of realization. "When his wife passed, he wished to marry her daughter? Perhaps he had a deviant proclivity."

Wood creaked. Lord Raymond's voice lowered. "Careful there. That is my daughter you speak of."

Silence hung. Bauer cleared his throat. "Are you aware if Mademoiselle Zahra brought wealth from Granada?"

Lord Raymond uttered a scoff. "Should you not ask her yourself while courting her, Notarius?"

"I do not wish to insult her."

"But insulting me is just fine?"

"Her royal ties to Granada are certainly valuable. But can she call on them? Does she even correspond with her stepfather, the king?"

Zahra's cheeks burned. Isabelle whispered, "This is not the one."

Lord Raymond's voice seemed to change—his tone lighter, more playful. "You are interpreting at the trial of Gilles de Rais?"

"You know I am."

"You might chance upon Zahra at the Dukes' chateau. She has been hard at work translating the written testimonies for us these last few months."

"What need does she have of work?"

"Who said she had need of it?"

A sharp sound of disbelief erupted from the German.

"I see you are skeptical of Zahra's worth. Let me ask you this, Notarius Bauer." Lord Raymond's tone deepened, and his words grew measured. "How many languages do you speak?"

"Six."

"That is five fewer than Zahra speaks. All your money could not buy you that talent."

"I could buy this little manor, though, couldn't I?"

Isabelle muttered a mild Breton curse under her breath. She nudged Zahra, and whispered, "When he walks out, give him the Gourmelon."

She wanted to send the man crashing to the ground? Zahra felt ill even considering executing the Gourmelon, a scrappy method for a woman to trip a man and bring him to his knees. She examined Isabelle's face for signs of jest. The woman was as serious as a siege.

Lord Raymond's tone cut. "Notarius Bauer, I bid you luck interpreting the gruesome details of this case, next week. And you will need more than luck to catch Zahra's attention."

Bauer laughed without humor. "Professor, I thought I might marry into royalty. Not mediocrity."

His German accent, once charming, now grated. Isabelle's fierce eyes were like the sky before a tempest storm.

A chair inside the chamber rubbed over wood, and boot steps headed in their direction. Zahra ducked behind the open door as the German emerged.

Notar Bauer wore expensive wool clothing and had buoyant hair like a llama's mane. Isabelle curtsied to him, offering a cheeky smile so full it narrowed her eyes to slits. "Have a perfectly joyous evening, Notarius."

He kept walking as if she did not exist. Zahra grabbed for her apron, but the woman bounded like a sprite out of reach, following Notar Bauer. She executed the Gourmelon—not the standard foot-out trip, but she hooked her shoe in front of Bauer's shin, affixing his stepping foot behind his other leg. Unable to plant his foot forward, he slammed onto his hands and knees.

Zahra drew in a sharp inhale. Isabelle snapped her fingers. "Oh, heavens! We must get this floor repaired."

Bauer's teeth bared. "You tripped me."

Three servants rushed to his side, helping him draw to a stand. Lord Raymond stepped out of his office chamber; his thin gray hair fluffed up like a ruffled duck. "What is the commotion?"

Isabelle uttered a high-pitched hum. "This floor, m'lord, it's a hazard, I keep tellin' you."

"Your insolent servant tripped me!" Bauer snatched a silver-tipped cane from his squire, his bushy hair wobbling. He held it up, the whites of his eyes pronounced. "Kneel, woman."

He meant to strike her. Zahra gripped her stones. Should she say something to distract him? Although tucked safely behind the door, her intervention could put him on better behavior.

Wiser to let Lord Raymond handle it. Notaries had money, influence—and he had cause to have Isabelle arrested, should he pursue it. Whatever Zahra might say could seal her maidservant's fate and be the end of her tenure at the manor; or worse, the end of their long friendship. Zahra sent her a pleading look.

Isabelle's friendly mask fell away like wet paint under a stiff rain. "I wouldn't kneel for you if you were my executioner."

Zahra pressed her hand to her chest. Bauer caught sight of her. His face reddened. "Execution sounds very fine."

"You would have to get a legal education to work that one out, Notarius." Lord Raymond jerked his thumb toward the manor doors. "Perhaps if you wander the streets of Nantes, you might find a law professor. Good day."

"All I would need is a lawyer." The German whipped his cloak on and turned.

His manservants pushed open the manor doors. The courtyard beyond was dark but had many sounds—fluffy beech leaves rustled in the wind. Horses scuffed their hooves and nickered.

And a child's voice pierced the air. "Do not touch me!"

CHAPTER 2

It was not only the shrillness of the child's voice that thrust Zahra into a run—it was the language spoken, Amazigh, that of her mother's people in Morocco. Gripping her skirt, Zahra hustled past the slick herringbone drive and through the dark meadow. Lanterns bobbled near the edge of a canal that lined the manor grounds. The figure of a girl in a white gown came into view. Her skin was dark like Zahra's.

Men surrounded her, speaking in placating tones. "You might fall over the edge."

"Put down the weapon."

"You are safe, child."

The girl brandished a sword with great difficulty. The tip of the weapon rested on the ground, unless the men neared her, at which point she heaved it into the air, sending the men scattering back. The girl threw glances over her shoulder, appearing to work up the courage to jump.

"You could die." Zahra's voice cut through the commotion. The men whipped around and held their lanterns toward her.

The girl stilled. She panted in breaths laced with whimpers. Perhaps eleven or twelve, her bare feet shifted in the grass. She gazed at Zahra with eyes like the night, sparkling with the promise of tears.

She reminded Zahra of her little sister, Raha. She spoke past a lump in her throat. "You will not fare well if you go over that ledge."

"I am protected." The girl held out what looked like a napkin.

Zahra stepped between the men holding out lanterns. "What is that, *saby*?" *Little one.*

The girl's chin jutted. "It is a divine cloth."

Was the poor thing delirious? What if she thought she could fly with that rag? "May I know your name?"

Still gripping the hilt of the sword, the girl took a step toward Zahra. The sword thudded to the grass. Her entire body shook, the light linen nightgown not suitable for a Nantes October evening. "Hadiza *ammughen n 'Isa, tazwara nnegh.*"

Zahra blinked. The girl was obviously native Moroccan, which would almost guarantee that she was of some Moorish faith.

Lord Raymond spoke up from behind them, interpreting the girl's words for those present. "The child calls herself Hadiza, daughter of Jesus, our Savior."

• • • • •

Lord Raymond had tried picking Hadiza up to carry her into the manor, but she had cried in protest. Only Zahra could calm her. Taking charge of a lantern, Zahra took the girl to her bedchamber. The girl sank into Zahra's bed, falling asleep with that worn cloth tucked against her cheek.

Zahra set the lantern on the night table. Out the window, the Erdre River glittered under moonlight, hugged by the silhouettes of chestnut trees.

Isabelle burst past Lord Raymond, who stood under the arched doorway. "The little dear screams like a nightjar!"

Zahra laid a wool blanket over the girl. Isabelle trudged through the chilly bedchamber and leaned to peer at her. Her worry lines smoothed into a soft smile.

Lord Raymond clasped his hands behind him. "Isabelle, would you say it is unusual for a Moor to believe Jesus is the Messiah?"

"No time for your ponderblooping, m'lord. This child needs warmth."

Lord Raymond chuckled.

Isabelle crouched before the hearth and fussed for the tinderbox. Soon a bright flame sparked to life.

Zahra set her worry stones down on the night table. For a fleeting moment, she considered offering them to the girl, to help ease her fear as they did for Zahra. "She is just trying to survive in a Christian land."

"She was blessed to have you show up when you did," said Lord Raymond.

A sense of accomplishment swelled in Zahra's heart, but the thought of her little sister swept it away. The girl whimpered as she slept, her face buried into the earthy wool blanket Zahra used as a pillow.

Lord Raymond's troubled gaze settled upon the child. "My cousin Margaret in Albi has need of a young servant."

Isabelle chuffed like a meerkat. "The one they call Mean Mizz Madge? This girl needs love, m'lord."

Lord Raymond nodded. "I wish I could spare you to watch after the child, but I am afraid I cannot."

"Aye. I reckon you cannot. But Mean ol' Madge…" Isabelle muttered.

"I can take her." Zahra did not sound as confident as she had intended.

Lord Raymond tapped his lips with a finger. "What if you helped Isabelle with cooking and the like? To free her up to care for the child?"

Isabelle stifled a chortle. "May the Lord protect our stomachs."

Zahra put her hands on her hips. "If I can learn to speak eleven languages, I think I can learn to cook."

Isabelle waved at Zahra in apology.

Lord Raymond winked. "Pay her no mind, *mi corazón*. I wholeheartedly believe in you."

"To cook, or to care for a child?"

Tension rose like a thick fog. Hadiza shuddered in her sleep. Lord Raymond cleared his throat. "Cooking is a safe way you can help. It doesn't hold a life in the balance."

Because leaving a child in her care would be much too risky.

The air went out of her. Her sister had been only six when Zahra abandoned her. They had planned to swim in fan mussel cove after their mother's funeral the next morning. But Zahra had left before morning came. She wondered often about Raha's reaction when she had awakened to an empty spot beside her on the bed. Had she searched the palace? Rooted through the foliage surrounding the cove? Called out her name?

Embarrassed by a wave of emotion, Zahra crossed the room and gathered linens from the cabinet. "You are right, my lord."

Isabelle clucked at Lord Raymond. "You open old wounds."

His shoes scuffed as he stepped further into the bedchamber. "You have so much on your mind, helping with the trial. I would worry you might—"

"Forget about her?"

"That is not what I meant, *mi corazón*." Lord Raymond looked at Isabelle.

Isabelle placed a hand on Zahra's back. "You let fear take over at times, dear. You cling to those stones, grindin' them like an overworked mill."

The stones beckoned her from the night table. These two did not even give her credit for putting them down? She had tried many times to cast them into the ocean, but she could not let them go. "I left Raha when she needed me most. I cannot be trusted."

Lord Raymond sighed. "Not a soul would blame you for leaving Marbella. You experienced something no nine-year-old should."

Heat burned from Zahra's neck into her face. Lord Raymond was a genius beyond his time, a gifted scholar, philosopher, and writer, yet he churned out utterances that paralyzed her with shame. She half-turned with the linens—where should she put them? — and Lord Raymond stepped in her path, warmth in his eyes.

"'If you have faith as small as a mustard seed, you can say to this mountain, 'Move from here to there,' and it will move. Nothing will be impossible for you.' Jesus said that. You can tell your fear to move out of the way."

Zahra forced a smile. Did he know what he asked? For her to believe in a magical creator lurking invisibly among them. It was too much. "I can teach her French, my lord."

Lord Raymond smiled, but his eyes were sad. "She shall be blessed to have you as her teacher."

After Lord Raymond left, Isabelle pulled Zahra into a hug with all the musty linens bunched between them. Zahra closed her eyes. The memories of the night before she left Marbella flickered like shadows. Her mother had always said Zahra possessed an extraordinary memory, but an astonishing ability to forget.

Isabelle spoke quietly in Zahra's ear. "I have a new theory, care to hear it?"

Zahra groaned.

"Alright I'll tell you." She pulled back and looked at Zahra, worry and love pooled in her eyes. "You don't wish to marry because of what happened to you."

Zahra took a deep breath to ensure she could speak without her voice shaking. "See? The truth is far less fun."

Isabelle gave her an earnest look. "We can work on the chores and watch the girl together, can't we, dear?"

Zahra nodded. "Perhaps we can even teach the girl to cook."

Isabelle uttered a chortle. "We?"

Zahra popped the pile of linens up between them. "These have mold."

Isabelle buried her face in the sheets and inhaled. "Drat."

She snatched them from Zahra, grumbling as she trudged out of the bedchamber.

Zahra genuinely loved that woman. But what good would come of rehashing the past? Zahra did not wish to lick old wounds. She wished only to climb into bed.

Perhaps tuck the blanket a little higher over the girl's shoulders.

• • • • •

In the middle of the night, a scream startled Zahra awake. Something scampered low across the floor. A metal hinge squeaked.

The space in the bed beside Zahra was empty. She flipped the covers and stepped onto the cold stone floor. "*Saby*?"

Zahra approached the dim embers of the hearth and the small iron door leading to the nook typically used to store extra firewood, but it was often left empty. Zahra crouched and rapped her knuckles against the door. "Hadiza, you have taken my favorite hiding place."

The small door eased open. Hadiza peered out, trembling. "I had a nightmare."

The girl's eyes held the depth of a midnight sky. They stared at one another for a time, until Zahra finally replied. "What was it?"

Hadiza dropped her gaze to that ratty cloth clutched in her fist. Just when Zahra felt certain the girl would utter something of great import, her skinny shoulders sagged. "I am sorry I took your hiding spot, *anisa*."

Zahra smiled and leaned to look deeper into the nook. "Not sure I could fit any longer."

The girl uttered a short giggle. Her cheek pressed against her knees, which swam in the linen nightdress too large for her. "I fit well."

Zahra stared at Hadiza. She was only about four years younger than Raha would be today. Zahra's throat tightened. "*Saby*, if you ever feel afraid, you may hide there as long as you like."

A crease formed above the young girl's brow. "You will not tell about it?"

"Never. When I was young, I had a world of hiding places. Some were even in plain sight, but invisible. I told no one about them."

Hadiza's lips parted in wonder. "Did you always feel safe?"

Zahra bit her lip, recalling the moment ten years ago when she had tearfully begged Lord Raymond to take her out of Marbella, to take her with him to France. She gestured for Hadiza to follow her. "Let me show you something."

Rubbing her eyes, Hadiza ambled toward the bed. Zahra guided her back under the covers and sat beside her. She scooped up the worry stones from the side table and presented them in her palm. They were black with gray symbols carved in them, and their irregular shape caused a mesmerizing sound when rolled together.

"Is that coal?"

"Hold them, and you will see they are not like coal."

Hadiza sat up and set her cloth down to take the stones. Using both her hands, she pulled them apart, and touched them to one another. They snapped together. She gasped, pulling it apart to let it pop together again. She grinned. "They are magic."

Zahra smiled and shook her head. "They are lodestone. They are attracted to one another, and iron. It is its nature."

Bringing the stone close to her eyes, Hadiza traced some of the symbols with her fingertips. "What is carved here?"

"That one says, *Suae Fortunae*, and the other says, *Faber*. It means, 'Artist of your own fortune.'"

The girl's eyes lifted. She gazed at Zahra as if trying to read her thoughts. "I do not understand."

Zahra gently reclaimed the stones and began rolling them in her palm. A glassy hum rose between them. "It just means *you* decide. For example, I control my fear like this."

Hadiza lay her head back on the pile of wool blankets and smiled. "It sounds pretty."

Zahra offered them to her, and childish delight crossed Hadiza's face as she practiced rolling the stones in her small hand. Her innocence and easy joy reminded her of Raha. She wondered if, after all these years, she had held onto that joy. She clenched her fist.

In that moment, Hadiza peeled open Zahra's hand and placed the lodestones in her palm. "Perhaps you need these more than I do, *anisa*."

The corner of Zahra's lips twitched between a smile and a grimace as she rolled the stones, realizing she had begun to shake. Thoughts of leaving her sister alone—their mother having just died—made her feel sick. These stones were the only thing that helped.

"I have my own way to feel safe." Hadiza plucked up her tattered cloth and held it out. "This was touched by Jesus Christ himself. It holds power. It saved me."

Without touching it, Zahra examined the cloth, tilting her head, peering at its loose threads, and browning edges. "Saved you from what, *saby*?"

The girl tightened her fingers around the cloth and turned onto her side, curling up under the blankets. "It does not matter now. I am free."

As Zahra dozed off alongside Hadiza, she wondered if the girl had not had a nightmare at all but recalled a terrible memory.

• • • • •

The Château of the Dukes of Brittany was a depressing, many-steepled fortress entwined by a stinking river. Clouds gathered over Nantes as if attracted to the despair in the mucky streets below.

Zahra's remorse over not informing the authorities about the conversation between Francois Prelati and Gilles de Rais waned over the following week. The trial would begin tomorrow, and he would most certainly be convicted and executed.

Perched at a small beechwood desk, she read the last of the testimonies of mourning parents and organized them by date. Their stories weighed on her heart, but she had learned long ago how to put her emotions on ice when needed. Often it seemed they were best kept that way.

Isabelle was off working in the kitchens alongside the chateau staff to prepare a meal just for the four of them. It was quite unlike the palace in Marbella, where all guests dined like kings among royalty while being served hand and foot.

Hadiza stared out the window. Isabelle had pulled the girl's black hair into a smooth bun. She looked like a doll in a powder blue servant dress. She held her little 'Jesus' cloth out, letting the breeze tug it along like it was dancing.

Zahra resisted the urge to tell her to get away from the window, lest she be seen. She had chosen not to inform anyone of Hadiza's presence here. Considering their similar complexions, they would assume Zahra had an illegitimate child, and she may no longer be invited to assist.

"This means 'friend.'" Hadiza announced in Arabic, lacing her fingers in front of her. Like most children, Hadiza failed at nimble segues, interrupting the peaceful silence with a lesson in her made-up hand-language.

"And this means 'morning.'" Hadiza put her fingers in a circle in the air above her head. "This is 'evening.'" She lowered the circle closer to mid-chest.

Zahra bunched her fingertips together near her own lips, replying in French, "This is 'food.' This is 'pain.'" She lightly bumped her shoulder twice with her palm. "And this is 'toy.'" She placed both her fists together and twisted them back and forth.

Hadiza's mouth dropped open. "You have been watching me!"

Zahra continued shuffling papers into piles. "I pick these things up."

Hadiza grinned, revealing the cute gap between her front teeth. The poor girl seemed to revere her. Zahra was not the best role model. She tended to be impulsive. She followed through on bad decisions to save pride. And she was rather peculiar about men; she lacked any attraction toward them at all.

"Did you know that this is 'Jesus?'" Hadiza drew the symbol of a cross on her heart.

They had determined that Hadiza was not faking her devotion to the Christian savior, Jesus Christ. Her belief was whole-hearted. Hadiza could lead a happy life here in France. She could marry the son of a blacksmith or farmer, have beautiful children, and live a simple life under the protection of the manor. She could even teach the people of the village these hand-signs. It could become its own kind of language.

"And this means 'mother.'" Hadiza rubbed a loose fist in a circle over her heart, her eyes glistening.

Zahra avoided the girl's gaze. Hadiza had not yet opened up about where she came from. She hid some great secret. But didn't everyone?

"*Anisa*, are you going to be my mother?"

Zahra finally looked over at the girl. "*Saby*, have you ever accidentally hurt a pet or an animal?"

Hadiza's eyebrows gathered together.

"Zahra!" Lord Raymond's commanding Catalan accent echoed down the hallway. "Pack up, we are finally getting a break!"

Hadiza lit up at the sound of his voice and scampered across the room.

Lord Raymond beamed as Hadiza approached him. It was impossible not to love him, with his child-like joy. The long, honorable robe suited him. He loved God, and he looked like one of the apostles rushing to tell the good news.

"The duke has invited us to stay in his castle in Clisson. To thank us for all our hard work on the case." Lord Raymond set his leather satchel down and leaned to rummage through it, leather buckles creaking.

"Don't the witnesses testify tomorrow?"

"Indeed, but our job is nearly done. Read this last witness testimony, would you?" He handed her a pile of small papers.

Zahra's fingers closed over the delicate vellum, striped with lines of tiny cursive. "Whose is it?"

"One of the men they arrested in the chateau. There is still uncertainty as to his involvement. Claims he was held there against his will."

Zahra read the title. *Testimony of Stephen Kempe, son of English merchant, John Kempe.*

Lord Raymond said, "Prosecutor Chapeillon requested that Kempe be barred from testifying. I wish to understand why."

"Dare I ask?" Zahra perked an eyebrow.

He showed his palms. "Call it a hunch. We could jot into the trial tomorrow, but the duke's carriage shall arrive sometime after midday."

Zahra hummed agreement, already lost in the Englishman's testimony.

I, Stephen Kempe, swear before God and the court that the statements I am about to make are true and correct. On the evening of September eighth of the year 1440, I was held against my will in the residence of Gilles de Rais, the Château de Machecoul. While imprisoned for a week, I never met the Commander de Rais.

Zahra said, "He never even met the commander. That alone disqualifies him from testifying."

Lord Raymond hung his cloak. "Wait until you read the whole testimony, *mi corazón*. Then pass your judgment, mm?"

Hadiza had returned to the window, where she danced her cloth in the wind, her mind among the clouds it seemed.

"Haddy, recite to me." Lord Raymond spoke in slow, enunciated French. "John, chapter three, verse eight."

While Zahra had spent the last month teaching her French, Lord Raymond put Hadiza onto the 'Good Book.' Not surprising. Hadiza believed this cloth, infused with the power of Jesus, had assisted her escape from some terrible place. Zahra did not press her, supposing the girl would open up whenever she was ready.

Perhaps Zahra was not ready.

Hadiza's eyes darted sideways, then she hooted like an owl. "'The wind blows wherever it pleases.'"

A broad smile spread Lord Raymond's mouth. That was the face of a man who would have liked to have grandchildren. Zahra found that she herself was grinning at Hadiza much the same way. She cleared her throat, returning to the deposition.

Francois Prelati ordered my imprisonment.

Zahra's fingers crept to the stones sitting on the table beside her, closing over them as she recalled the Italian's repellant grip on her hand.

He demanded that I summon a demonic spirit. When I refused, he threatened me.

Hadiza danced her cloth on a breeze and continued reciting. "'You hear the sound, but you cannot tell where it comes from or where it is going.'"

When his threats upon me did not yield results, he brought a child before me, and threatened the boy's life.

"'So, it is with'—" Hadiza screamed. "My cloth!"

Zahra's eyes snapped up, her heart racing from the disturbing testimony coupled with Hadiza's piercing scream.

Lord Raymond dove to grip the girl's apron ties as she bent far out the window.

Zahra leapt to pull her back inside. She scolded in sharp Moroccan Arabic. "We are five floors up!"

Hadiza rung her hands, her brow furrowed. "Please, may we find it? Before someone thinks it rubbish? I cannot bear to lose it, *anisa* Zahra."

Her voice trembled, moisture gathering in her eyes.

Lord Raymond plucked Zahra's coat off the rack and raised his eyebrows. "Nice day for a courtyard stroll?"

• • • • •

A two-pronged staircase leading into the chateau was clogged by a sea of somber men and women shuffling up. Zahra and Hadiza emerged from a more obscure lower-level doorway. The inner courtyard boasted regal white tufa stone and flamboyant gothic ornamentation. For several days now, grieving parents provided testimony against Gilles de Rais and his accomplices. They looked like the dead approaching the gates of the underworld.

Hadiza scurried in an ineffectual frenzy around the flowerbeds and between elm trees. Better that she burned the energy. Looking toward the chateau, Zahra shielded her eyes from the sunlight. Lord Raymond was supposed to wave at them from the window, but she could not see him. Zahra followed Hadiza deeper into the orchard, where plum and pear trees dangled plump fruit.

"Are you lost, mademoiselle?" A man's English accent caught her attention.

She began rolling her stones as her gaze landed on a handsome older gentleman standing in line, his hat in his hands. "No, sir. Thank you."

"Not here to provide a statement, are you?" He peered at the sapphire hem of her gown peeking out from her cloak. She approached respectfully, not rude enough to bellow across a courtyard to a man.

Zahra curtsied. "I am assisting in the investigation, sir."

The man's bagged eyes widened. He seemed unaware that he crushed his hat in his fist. "My wife does not know I have come here. She still thinks our girl will return home."

His eyes were rimmed red, dark bags swollen. The turmoil he exuded was so stark, she dropped her gaze. "My deepest sympathies, sir."

The man squinted. "I have never heard of a woman investigator. Are you taking our testimonies?"

It was not his place to ask, but she pitied him. "Sir, I evaluate testimonies of the accomplices to help decide if they should be included in the trial."

"Is one of them Stephen Kempe?"

Zahra blinked. "As—as a matter of fact—"

"He *should* be included. I would know—Stephen is my degenerate brother, wrapped up in all of this." He shuffled along as the line moved.

Zahra kept pace with him, curious to discover how much hate a man would need to have for his brother to wish him to be part of a trial that could amount to his execution. "Sir, your brother has not been arrested, like the others."

"Found it!" Hadiza's voice rang out in the distance. Her shoes clapped over stone as she approached.

He shook his head. "They haven't yet proven he was involved. But I know he was. He is the reason our Mary is gone."

Hadiza bumped into Zahra and waved the cloth. Her eyes widened. "Mary? I know a Mary!"

"Haddy!" Zahra clutched the girl's shoulders. "My sincerest apologies, sir."

The man's bearded lips pressed into a sad smile. He switched back to French. "You tell your friend hello for me."

"Oh, I cannot. She is in Marbella."

"Marbella!" The man's forehead wrinkled. "That is quite a journey from here."

Zahra tipped toward Hadiza. "*Saby*, did you say Marbella?"

Hadiza lowered her gaze, shoulders tight.

She was shutting down. Zahra had given her enough time. She addressed the man in French. "Monsieur, I believe she is confused since I am from Marbella."

Hadiza's eyes snapped up. "I am not confused. That is why the cloth took me to you. I think… you are supposed to help them."

"Them?"

Hadiza spoke so quietly Zahra had to strain to hear her over the breeze. "The other children."

Stones fighting for space in her palm, Zahra grasped Hadiza's shoulders and turned her away from the man. "Good day to you, sir."

"And to you, mademoiselles." The man inclined a nod and watched them as they hurried toward the shady orchard.

"*Saby*, if there were other children in danger, why did you not mention them?"

Hadiza's head bent low as they walked in the shade of old elm trees. "I was afraid."

Zahra gently squeezed Hadiza's shoulders with her arm. "Did you truly come from Marbella?"

Hadiza nodded. A tear fell over her cheek.

Was it even possible that this child had traveled from Zahra's hometown, only to appear at her doorstep in Nantes? When Zahra had fled the village of Marbella, she had the help of Lord Raymond and those who managed his travel. Hadiza had been alone.

"Where in Marbella?"

Hadiza sat on a stone bench with mold creeping up its legs. She peeked up at Zahra. "At the palace. Where the *malik* Jabir and *malika* Raha live."

The names sliced through her. Zahra sank down beside Hadiza, placing her hand on her forehead to control her sudden dizziness. Raha had become queen?

And why wouldn't she have? Zahra had disappeared days before her marriage to the *malik*, so who better to take her place than her little sister? It sickened her to think it could have happened soon after Zahra ran away—Raha had been three years younger. Hopefully, Jabir at least waited. How old would she be now? Sixteen. She was probably every bit the loving ruler their mother had been. The elm arched above rustled in a breeze, littering large brown leaves around them.

"*Anisa* Zahra." Hadiza's voice cracked. "We must go back to Marbella."

A lump formed in Zahra's throat. She admired Hadiza's bravery—but it was misguided. "Haddy, that is a long, dangerous trip. And once there, we would not have the power to do anything."

Tears trembled on the edge of Hadiza's eyes. "They are my friends. They expected me to come back. But I abandoned them."

Zahra recalled the moment she and Lord Raymond had passed through the shady village of Cordoba in their escape from Marbella. She had planned to tell him to go back—tell him she couldn't go through with this abandonment of her little sister. But before she could utter the words, the memory of that ugly night had resurfaced. That was the first of many chances when she had chosen not to return to Raha.

"Almost losing this..." Hadiza held the cloth out to Zahra. It passed gently from Hadiza's hand into Zahra's. "Made me realize I need to give it to you."

She ran her thumb over it. It was surprisingly soft. It had small holes and tears, its hemming well worn. "I cannot take this, Haddy."

"I believe this is why He brought me to you."

"Come, now. Why would that be, *saby*?"

"*Anisa*, you can figure anything out. Jesus touched this cloth. That means it has the power of God in it. Learn how to make it work."

Zahra could not bring herself to crush her by claiming none of this magic was real. She tucked the folded cloth into an embroidered leather pouch she used for coin and her stones. The girl flung her arms around Zahra. Startled, she did not properly return the hug before Hadiza dropped to lean back into her hands.

Her dark, curious eyes roved the rustling leaves above them. "One time, a butterfly got stuck in a puddle. I ripped its wing trying to help it. It could not fly again after that."

Hadiza's non-sequitur was an answer to Zahra's question from earlier.

The sensation of Hadiza's tight, spontaneous hug still lingered around Zahra's waist. She sighed. "Sometimes we are not suited to care for something, because we might end up hurting it."

CHAPTER 3

"It is October 16 in the year of our Lord, 1440."

Lord Bishop Malestroit initiated court proceedings in Latin, his voice echoing off the domed ceiling. He stood in his majestic *mitre* in an elevated booth alongside other clergy members.

Zahra and Lord Raymond sat near the back of the audience hall filled with Breton villagers elbowing for a view. The chamber smelled of beechwood and sweat.

Notarius Hans Bauer, with his quivering bouffant and ruffled chemise, sat near the witness box in a tufted parlor chair. To blend in with those grieving, Zahra wore a charcoal gown with a square neckline. She hid her stones between her clasped palms.

"Today, we shall hear direct testimony from witnesses."

Bauer interpreted the bishop's opening statement with effortless confidence.

"Prosecutor Chapeillon, the first witness."

The prosecutor descended from the upper booths. He smoothed thick fingertips over his thinning hairline as he examined a parchment. "I call Monsieur Henriet. He has admitted to committing the following crimes with the accused: murder, dismembering, burning, and inhuman treatment of infants."

Bauer repeated the crimes in Breton. An off-key symphony of pained wails rose from members of the audience. Zahra blinked back moisture that threatened to gather in her eyes.

"Immolation damnable of the bodies of these infants, which were offered to demons as a sacrifice. Brutal debauchery."

Bauer stumbled over the words, gulping down a thick swallow. Henriet emerged from the back door, shuffling in chains, escorted by armed soldiers in jupon coats and steel helmets. Vitriol erupted from the Bretons, some of whom had to be held back by the guards.

Henriet testified against Gilles de Rais. He explained how he acquired children for the commander. He offered grisly details about the depraved things done to them. He revealed how de Rais disrespected their bodies once deceased. He explained how they burned them, and scattered the ashes into the cesspit, moat, and other hiding places.

Another man testified. His story resembled Henriet's, yet had further details, painting a picture of unbridled wickedness.

The third man's particularly candid testimony detailed Gilles de Rais' horrific use of ceiling hooks and his penchant for beheadings. At this detail, appearing rather pale, Notarius Bauer rushed out of his chair. The angry Bretons would not let him pass the bar, shouting for him to retake his seat and fulfill his duty.

He vomited on the floor. The court went silent. Zahra pressed her hand to her abdomen, a wave of nausea coursing through her.

Bauer wiped his mouth with his frilly white sleeve. "Forgive me, bishop. I cannot proceed."

This time, people stepped aside as he raced to the exit. He stopped short as his gaze landed on Zahra.

Lord Raymond said, "You caught her attention, after all."

Bauer's lips pinched together. He brushed past them and banged the door open. Zahra slid a look to Lord Raymond, who suppressed a smile.

The bishop removed his spectacles, rubbing his eyes. "I fear we cannot continue today without an interpreter."

"Zahra." Lord Raymond whispered and nudged her with his elbow. "Volunteer."

Her blood rushed. She could not stand before these people and interpret this filth! She whispered back. "Half those men on the entresol know Breton."

"You know they cannot lower themselves to interpret."

The people grew restless, roaring for something to be done. Someone bumped into Zahra. Lord Raymond steadied her. She hissed, "What about us going to Clisson?"

Lord Raymond shook his head. "'This is the way—walk in it.'"

Isaiah. Lord Raymond's favorite book.

A man shouted, "*Kentoc'higomp hor bugale!*" *We will avenge our children.*

Fists shot up, demanding action from the clergymen perched on high. The short wall dividing the courtroom creaked under the weight of the crowd surging forward. The bishop shouted for order. They began bumping one another. She gasped, pushing against a man's back so she would not be crushed. Lord Raymond wrapped his arm around her shoulders. The soldiers closed in, threatening the people in French. But they were unafraid.

They had lost their children. They cared for nothing other than justice.

"*Me a raio!*" *I shall do it.*

Zahra's declaration in Breton seemed to capture the attention of some, who twisted toward her. She pushed between bodies and repeated the phrase. Zahra broke out from the crowd and leaned against the wooden bar that separated commoner from clergy. The unrest abated.

The bishop replaced his spectacles, peering at her. "Zahra, daughter of Lord Raymond Sabunde." He sent a glance to the man she called her father these last ten years. After a long pause, he exhaled. "The court appreciates your assistance. As you know, we interpret for the bereaved parents of Nantes to prove that we seek the vigorous justice they deserve. Please sit."

Tension charged the silence. A soldier pulled up the wooden railing bar. Zahra looked back at Lord Raymond, who smiled, his eyes misty.

She walked around the puddle of reeking vomit and settled into the tufted chair near the empty witness box.

The bishop raised his hand. "Proceed, Monsieur Chapeillon."

The prosecutor's voice had lost its vigor as he leaned tiredly into a wooden divider, reading the parchment. "We call Stephen Kempe, fourteenth-born son of John and Margery Kempe."

Zahra repeated the announcement in Breton, but her voice gave out. She cleared her throat. The red-rimmed eyes of the people bore down on her like a weight. She wet her throat with a gulp. On her next attempt, she was able to speak.

"Louder hence, mademoiselle." The bishop frowned. She swallowed again, clutching the stones in her lap. She was glad to have them, but she did not dare roll them.

Chapeillon continued. "Blood extensively covered Monsieur Kempe when apprehended among those in the Château de Machecoul. The blood was not his own."

After she repeated it, gasps erupted from the villagers. Zahra recalled what little she had read of Monsieur Kempe's testimony, his frightening experience with Francois Prelati, and her chance meeting with his brother. The one who claimed he was degenerate.

Monsieur Kempe strode in from a side door, not the prison chambers like the others. He kept his fitted cloak strapped as if he did not plan to stay long. It was difficult to miss the resemblance to his older brother, tall with wheat-colored hair and moss-green eyes. However, Monsieur Kempe was perhaps only thirty, shaven clean—and noticeably the better for it. The wooden steps creaked as he entered the box for witnesses. The chair creaked as he sat. He did not seem to notice Zahra as his guarded gaze shifted furtively over the seething throng in the gallery.

Oddly, Chapeillon spoke to Zahra in Latin. "Interpreter, I shall briefly address the public in Breton, so no need to relay unless I speak directly to the witness. Understood?"

Although she did *not* understand, Zahra nodded.

Chapeillon faced the people. "On the 15th of September of this year, Monsieur Kempe was found among the men scattering like roaches throughout Château de Machecoul. Question of his involvement is still being investigated."

Kempe's jaw flexed, his gaze fixed on the prosecutor.

Chapeillon turned suddenly. "Monsieur Kempe, did you see the Baron Gilles de Rais engaged in illegal behavior?"

Kempe parted his lips to answer—but halted as Zahra interpreted. She could feel his gaze on her. She finished speaking, and he turned back to Chapeillon. After a long pause, he said, "No."

Murmurs circulated.

Master Chapeillon huffed a disbelieving laugh. "You did not see Gilles de Rais in his own Château?"

"I saw his men." The Englishman eyed Zahra, apparently put off by her interruptions. "Francois Prelati imprisoned me there. He committed many atrocious acts in my presence."

"Monsieur Kempe, this trial is for Gilles de Rais. Should there be a trial for this other person, we may certainly invite you to provide testimony at that time."

Kempe voice was a growl. "*Should* there be a trial?"

"Mademoiselle, there is no reason to relay these outbursts." At Chapeillon's glare, she clipped her mouth closed. Her inexperience was showing.

The bishop rapped his gavel and spoke in English. "Monsieur Kempe, you are giving testimony, not arguing with the prosecutor. Proceed with your answer."

Kempe's nostrils flared. "Prelati demanded that I summon a demonic spirit. When I refused, he brought in—"

"How convenient!" The prosecutor exclaimed, startling Zahra. She did not even have time to interpret what the witness had said. Should she stop Chapeillon mid-sentence? She thought better of it as he rallied on. "Given your stature, you certainly could not be subdued easily. How old are you, Monsieur Kempe?"

After she interpreted, a stale silence descended on the court, while it looked as though Monsieur Kempe wished to bridge the divide and deliver the prosecutor to his maker. His tone was measured and lethal. "Seven and twenty."

The prosecutor slapped his hand on the table and threw it up into the air. "Exactly! Why should they seek you out? The commander was only after children."

Zahra rushed to relay all of this for the people, but Kempe did not wait for her to finish. "They did not 'seek' me out. I went to the Château myself looking for Prelati—"

"Do you have any testimony regarding de Rais himself?"

The veins in Kempe's temples stood out. "Prelati was employed by the accused."

"We are only hearing directly about de Rais." Chapeillon pointed a thick finger at Zahra. She stuttered to a halt. He approached Kempe and dropped his hand upon the edge of the witness box. "Since you have been party to the most heinous crimes this country has ever seen, and possibly will ever see, you will need to provide more compelling testimony if you wish the court to be merciful if and when your trial comes."

Before Kempe could reply, Chapeillon turned to the people. "This man's father was a respected, wealthy merchant in Bishop's Lynn. He is afraid to testify to the truth because it would tarnish his family's good name. And of course, he fears death."

Zahra opened her mouth, but hesitated. Since Chapeillon spoke in Breton, she did not need to translate. What was occurring here? Was the prosecutor hiding information? Manipulating the truth? Lying to the people?

"Lord Bishop, I move to strike this testimony from the record. He clearly has no information."

Zahra could no longer resist the urge to speak out. "It is standard practice for testimonies to be heard in full before being stricken."

All eyes turned to her.

"Mademoiselle." The bishop leaned forward; eyes narrowed upon her. "If you interfere in this proceeding again, I shall have you thrown out. Do you understand?"

Zahra's ears rushed as she nodded. She searched the crowd for Lord Raymond, but he was absent. He had likely left for Clisson without her.

The prosecutor cleared his throat. "Monsieur Kempe has been rumored to be a summoner of spirits. It seems hardly reasonable to accept his testimony. Perhaps it would even be in our best interest to charge him for malevolent magic."

Zahra interpreted this into English for Kempe. His eyes widened. He did not allow her to finish, speaking forcefully. "The horrors I beheld in that castle—"

"Some say he is not divining spirits, but demons!" The prosecutor spoke over him.

But Kempe kept on. "—would chill your soul."

Chapeillon continued as if Kempe were not speaking. "This particular skill was likely the reason—"

"Prelati not only took part in the wickedness—"

"—de Rais wanted him there in the first place!" Chapeillon grew louder.

"—but he was its mastermind!" Kempe's voice thundered.

The crowd melted into pandemonium; fathers raged; mothers wept; others rushed out of the nauseating courtroom.

The bishop clacked the gavel. Face puffed, he spoke above the cries. "Scribe—strike this man's testimony from the record. Monsieur Kempe, you are to be held in contempt, pending possible charges of maleficium this very night. Bailiff, detain the son of John and Margery Kempe, who would be heartbroken if they were alive today. Court is dismissed."

Several soldiers approached Monsieur Kempe, blades drawn. The Englishman stood, bristling. They bound his wrists in an iron cuff, and escorted him to the inner chambers, where the other reprobates were held. The people of Brittany filtered out of the court chamber. One man sobbed into a handkerchief as he staggered out. A woman leaned into her husband as he guided her toward the doors, her eyes distant and bloodshot.

The bishop took the stairs and approached Zahra. "Mademoiselle."

He must have come to scold her for interfering. She began rolling her stones, unable to lift her gaze.

"You should be proud of the excellent work you have done today. You have served the people of Nantes well."

She looked up. His eyes wandered to nothing, as if he struggled with the chasm of immorality they witnessed on this dark day.

• • • • •

Zahra walked alongside a soldier in jupon armor. He escorted her through the residential tower. Lord Raymond had left for Clisson without her, a rare opportunity she would not have wanted him to miss. She was looking forward to the time alone with Hadiza and Isabelle, just ladies. Despite the harrowing day, the bishop's words had encouraged her. She had done something good for these grieving people.

Unbidden, an image appeared in her mind of the angry Englishman being led off in a shackle. She had not done much for that fellow, had she?

There was little she could do. If Chapeillon had committed some kind of act of corruption in the courtroom, she was powerless to uncover it. Were she to pursue it, she could be targeted as a threat.

As they turned the corner, Zahra shook off the negative thoughts. The anticipation of Hadiza's cheerful chatter and Isabelle's cushy hugs warmed her.

The torch mounted near the chamber was snuffed. A chill curled around her ankles.

The soldier lit their way with a lantern. She held up a hand before he could open the door. A man's hushed voice emanated from the chamber. She leaned close to listen, her heart racing.

"The master will not be happy to hear you were arrested." It was a Frenchman with a gruff voice.

"Do I look arrested, Pierre?"

Francois Prelati. Zahra's breath hitched and she jolted backward a step, bumping into her escort. She spun around. The guard held the lantern up near his face and grinned. The door behind her scraped open. A hand clapped over her mouth before she could scream. A heavy arm strapped around her, pinning her arms down. He dragged her inside.

"Mademoiselle Sabunde." The Italian cleric who had just last week threatened her with a knife to the gut stepped into her view.

She let forth a muffled scream. The man holding her chuckled gruffly, his chest reverberating against her back. She struggled to inhale, his meaty hand stifling her nostrils.

Prelati leaned in. "Your servant girl has something my colleague wants."

Zahra shook her head fiercely, looking between the two men. She writhed, unable to loosen his hold.

Gaze roving among the lot before him, Prelati's tone deepened. "Apparently it was not enough that I got him a lovely girl for Christmas. Gordy, has your father at least been happy with her?"

The man holding her—Pierre—said, "Her face twitches."

"*Per la miseria*!" *For misery's sake.* "Her face twitches. Who cares!"

The man named Gordy stepped forward, still holding up the lantern. "He wants the relic." He spoke in English with a strong Portuguese accent.

"Not my problem. Send my regards to your father." Prelati shifted his gaze to Zahra, and that same biting smile curled his upper lip.

"Remember my advice, mademoiselle—I suggest you do what these men tell you. Good night, gentlemen."

Prelati turned with a flourish, scooping his mantle over his head. He closed the door quietly behind him.

Gordy stepped toward her, black stringy hair framing his sharp cheekbones. "The relic was not on your servant girl. It is not in this chamber. And it was not on your maidservant."

Pierre swung her around. She stumbled to her hands and knees. A decorative painting hung askew. A shattered vase lay in the corner, bed covers lumped across the floor. Even the table had been overturned, testimonies on vellum spilled.

Light from the fire shined on a woman sprawled on the floor, her copper tresses spread over the stone like octopus tentacles. Her eyes were wide, dull, and unblinking.

Isabelle.

CHAPTER 4

"*Sittati!*" Zahra dove beside Isabelle. She pressed a shaking hand to Isabelle's face. Her skin was cool. Mottled purple marred her temple. Zahra choked back a sob, combing strands of Isabelle's hair back.

Pierre, a bison-like man with a muscular hump and small eyes, appeared to be chewing on something small between his yellowed front teeth. "Where is the relic?"

She cowered, covering Isabelle. "Where is the girl?"

"Is she asking about the *Berberita*?" *Little barbarian girl.* "Tell her she is back where she belongs," said Gordy.

Zahra climbed to a stand and stumbled over a blanket. She snatched the broom Isabelle had left leaning in a corner and shot her heel into its base. The wood splintered, the bristles falling away. She brandished the jagged end like a spear.

The men shared a glance and laughed. Pierre withdrew a long, curved blade that reflected the lantern light. "The relic."

She had no chance in a fight against two men. She regripped the stick. "Monsieur, I swear I do not know of any relic. Let me ask Hadiza."

Gordy stepped toward her. "You shall never see the girl again."

Pierre closed in. "Little one thought she was safe with you, didn't she?"

Thump thump.

A pulsing sensation coursed through Zahra's body. It centered in her heart—or was it her stomach? Was she going to faint?

As Gordy stepped forward, she jerked back. If she screamed, they would dive on her. As Pierre grew near, she swiped her stick at his blade. It fumbled from his hands, but he caught it again. As he swung, she dashed around the overturned table—into which his blade lodged. Gordy stepped into her path.

Her heart pummeled her ribcage as she gasped for air. She would not survive.

"The relic." Pierre held out his hand.

"I have... no relic!" She swung at him again.

He swiped his blade at her stick. It tumbled out of her hands. She backed up and rammed into the wall.

Pierre advanced on her—but jerked to a halt.

A hiss pierced the air.

A snake as thick as the trunk of a dogwood tree slithered from the shadows and lifted its head. Thrice the length of a man, it was large enough to strike the ceiling. Pierre, eyes wide, dropped into a defensive position. Gordy fell onto his bottom and scrambled back toward the door.

Its vibrantly colored hood splayed, fangs exposed, scales flexing in the dim light.

"Out! Out!" Pierre swiped his blade at the beast. A normal snake might have reeled back, but this one just flashed its fangs. Gordy threw the door open and ran, his boots pounding down the hallway.

As the cobra struck at Pierre, he yelped. He lashed out with his sword. The snake evaded gracefully. The blade sparked on the stone floor. Its fangs clamped into Pierre's leather boot. It whipped its body, his leg thrashing about.

Zahra took her chance and edged out the door. The cobra loosened its grip on Pierre, raised its head, and faced her. Its otherworldly eyes locked onto hers. She flattened against the wall, measuring each breath. The snake's forked tongue slithered from between its jaws and back in again.

Pierre panted, rolled over, and stood. He pounded down the hallway after Gordy. The snake pivoted gracefully and sped after him.

Zahra choked back a cry and hastened the opposite way.

• • • • •

Zahra led the Guard back to the chamber. Lord Raymond, in Clisson, would not even hear of this until tomorrow. The assailants and cobra were gone. After she described what had happened, the guards had exchanged wary glances.

Standing in the hallway, she stole a glance. Isabelle lay still among the destruction. Isabelle's once rosy cheeks were gray and sunken, never to pucker into a smile again. She turned away, struggling to breathe.

The knight of the Château Guard appeared beside her, his mustache now shaved too high above his upper lip.

"Found this down the hall." He held out the broken broom stick.

"That was... I thought it could save me."

"But it was a snake."

"Pardon, my lord?"

"You claimed it was a snake that saved you."

"Oh. Ultimately, yes, it was a snake."

One of the guards knelt beside Isabelle's body. He murmured something to the other guard, and they both glanced in Zahra's direction.

Then he closed Isabelle's eyes and prayed over her.

• • • • •

Neither the soldiers nor the knights believed Zahra's story. Master Prosecutor Chapeillon, who had been awoken by the tragedy, was also skeptical. The bishop was too elevated in position to be bothered. Apparently, a slain servant, a missing Moorish girl, and a tale about a snake were not matters of great import.

They interrogated Zahra in the egg-shaped Council Chamber. Its normally vibrant paintings were bathed in eerie shadows from the lanterns flaming at the cardinal points. Its curved walls had several doors, but only one had a *gros valet*, an armored servant of the knights, posted beside it.

They questioned her for about an hour before leaving her alone with the *valet*. Zahra sat at a small, polished desk used by scribes to record clergy meeting details. Her worry stones whirred as she circled them in her palm. How could she sit here, waiting, useless while those men had Hadiza? Did they even care about her? They could at least interrogate the men who knew Prelati. What if they knew of a place he would hide a child? A shiver overtook her at the thought that Hadiza could endure what befell those children in the testimonies.

Could Hadiza be at this very moment in the hands of Prelati, who Zahra had allowed to roam free? Could she have been taken to the infamous castle, Château Machecoul? Perhaps the men had taken her to one of their homes in Nantes? Or another city?

The truth was they could have taken her anywhere in France—or beyond. Every minute that passed made it less and less likely that they would ever find her. Zahra's chest tightened as she recalled the moment Prelati had threatened her. If she had told the knight the truth when it mattered, Prelati may have attacked her—but Hadiza, and perhaps other children, would be safe.

She clamped the stones still and stood, gathering the courage to approach the young *valet*.

Zahra curtsied. "Monsieur, do you know anything about the search?"

He clenched the hilt of his sword. "I do not know the details."

She looked down at her stones. "I am most worried about the girl."

His armor rattled as he gestured behind him. "No offense meant, mademoiselle, but the man responsible for all the missing children is here."

Her teeth dug into her lower lip. "The commander?"

The *valet* nodded. "As well as his accomplices."

All those evil men were locked up just behind that door. Dare she set foot in there? She eyed the young valet, working up her courage. "Monsieur, is the Englishman back there too?"

He nodded, his visor snapping shut.

"Do you stand guard in case they try to escape?"

When he revealed his eyes again, amusement shone in them. "They are locked in gaols, in separate chambers which are also locked. They cannot escape, mademoiselle."

That was what she wished to hear.

Based on what Stephen Kempe had been able to say in court, and what little she had read of his testimony, it was obvious he had been hunting Prelati down. He might know where the man lived, or something else that could help. However, if she were caught unlawfully questioning a prisoner, she would be in a great deal of trouble.

But it could not be more trouble than what Hadiza was in.

"I should like to speak to the English prisoner."

The *valet* blinked. "Mademoiselle, I cannot allow that."

Zahra's heart thudded against her chest. "You described a very secure situation, monsieur."

"It is not allowed."

"I have Lord Bishop Malestroit's blessing, I assure you."

He shook his head.

She stepped forward, pinning him with a glare. "Were you or anyone you know impacted by the actions of these vile men?"

The *valet's* eyebrows stitched together, emotion plain upon his face. That was answer enough for her.

"Monsieur, I am the interpreter for this trial. I may be able to gain vital information from him. Give me five minutes."

The *valet* gazed into her eyes for a long time. He straightened and nodded. Turning his back on her, his keys rattled. "Follow me."

Zahra released her breath. She ran the stones over one another. The lock clacked, and the door scraped open. He stepped in, armored boots echoing into the deep corridor. Although she had the sudden urge to call it all off, she stepped over the threshold after him.

After passing several iron-studded doors, he turned to unlock one. It seemed to stick, and he threw his weight behind it to pop it open. He had to step aside to allow her to pass by him. An oil lamp hung high on a hook, its light fighting the shadows.

"I must return to my post outside. When you finish, go to the end of this hall and knock."

Zahra stepped inside, her blood rushing. The scent of burnt flint hung in the air. A tall silhouette lingered at the corner of the cell. She could not tell which way he faced.

From the doorway, the *valet* added, "I am sure I do not need to say this, but… do not get near the bars."

Zahra frowned as he pulled the door closed with a muted clunk. She tightened her fingers over the stones to halt them.

She was now alone with a man who had been found bloodied amongst killers. Despite her previous rush to speak to him, she found her words stuck. She looked around her for a seat of some kind—but gasped when she saw the shadow of a person standing at the end of the room. She froze, waiting for her eyes to adjust.

"It is my coat."

Stephen Kempe's deep voice cut through the dark. Zahra's heart slowed as her eyes adjusted to the low light, and indeed—the figure was just a large black coat hanging on a hook outside of the bars. It looked just beyond his reach.

She strained to sound casual. "May I get your coat for you, Monsieur?"

"What do you want?"

She swallowed and circled the stones at her side. "Monsieur Kempe, my servant was just murdered, hours ago, and a child dear to me was taken."

Even obscured as he was, his attention weighed upon her like a boulder. "And?"

She cleared her throat. "I hoped you might provide some information on where she might have been taken. Anything."

He stepped forward, half his face illuminated by the lantern light. His irises seemed to spark in the dark. "You think I am in with all the murderers and child abductors in France?"

Realizing her blunder, she held up her hands placatingly. One of the stones slipped with a clatter. She dove to grapple for it as she yammered. "Of course not, monsieur. To be honest, you are my last chance. I am desperate."

His eyes roved over her when she straightened again. How must she appear? She wore the same charcoal gown from the trial hours earlier, her dark hair pinned in a high, plaited bun, likely tousled from the day's events. His voice held the bluntness of finality. "I cannot help you."

She took a step forward. "Prelati was involved."

Kempe tipped to get a better look at her past the bars. "How?"

"He was in my bedchamber—looking for some 'relic.'"

Kempe's eyes narrowed. "When?"

"Just a few hours ago."

His jaw flexed, chin lowered. Shadows cut his features like a two-toned grisaille painting. He was furious. Deadly.

Hope leapt in Zahra's heart. "Yes—Prelati is free, while you remain locked up. We must have him arrested at once. Where might he take a young girl?"

The Englishman seemed to weigh her words. "Get me out of here."

Zahra froze. "That is not what I came here for."

"It is the only way I will help."

A pit formed in her sternum. "You would withhold vital information?"

Silence hung between them.

Helplessness tore through Zahra. She closed her eyes and clenched her teeth. "Monsieur Kempe, why did you not argue against the accusations?"

He exhaled a bitter chuckle. "You think these people are interested in the truth? I told them the truth, and they shall hang me in a fortnight."

Zahra shook her head. "You could admit guilt and claim repentance. I have seen—"

"You have not seen this beast, interpreter. They will make an example of me. And now I understand why. Prelati."

Zahra did not understand—and she did not care. “Then do something good with what time you have left. Tell me what you know of these men. Please. Anything.”

Kempe’s eyes smoldered with purpose. “Get me out of here. I can find her.”

Allured by his confidence, Zahra took a small step forward. “How?”

“I possess the means.”

She searched his face. “The accusations made about you ‘divining spirits.’ They are true?”

“To some extent.”

“You would use magic to find Hadiza? Oh.” She turned away, pressing her hand to her forehead. This man was insane. “I am sorry to waste your time, Monsieur Kempe. But I do not believe in magic.”

His eyes flashed. “Godspeed. By the time you get desperate enough to come back, she will be much further away—if alive.”

Zahra resisted the temptation to throw her stones at him. “I would not even know how to get you out of here.”

Kempe shrugged. “Use your feminine wiles.”

Her eyes widened. “Excuse me?”

“Plenty of men would fancy a Moorish woman.”

Zahra reeled back. The gall! Who was he to say such a thing to her? “For that comment alone, monsieur, I should claim first row at the gallows.”

During the silence that followed, a thread of guilt weaved through her for uttering such cruel words. He glared, glancing at the door, as if daring her to walk out. “Then I have nothing for you, interpreter.”

Against her better judgment, she stepped forward and clutched one of the cold iron bars. “You would let a child die?”

“Many children are dying.” His tone was harsh. “I have no confidence you would put any good use to whatever information I gave you.”

“You do not know me.”

"I know you well enough. You know several languages. Which means you knew Chapeillon was shutting me up in there. You were easily silenced."

She flushed. "I had no power."

"No power? Or no courage?"

Her throat constricted. Of course, a man would tell her to exercise 'courage,' which would get her labeled a witch, put on trial, and hanged, or worse. Something Isabelle might have said sparked in her imagination. *"What help would you be to anyone, dear, if you're locked up?"*

A muted bump resounded from the end of the hallway. Zahra jumped back from the bars and whisked around. Footsteps sounded. This conversation with the Englishman had gone nowhere, and now she would be caught. Or worse, what if Gordy and Pierre had returned?

The lock rattled. The *valet* would know the chamber door was unlocked, so it must not be him. Zahra backed up several paces. The door dislodged with a clunk. She backed into the wall. Beside her hung the Englishman's coat. She slipped behind it. With her dark skin, and deep charcoal gown, she might be able to remain hidden, as thick as the shadows were.

A small tear in the back of the coat allowed her to see Chapeillon peeking around the door. His eyes skimmed past her as if she were invisible. She held her breath.

"I was told the interpreter was in here."

Kempe remained still. "She failed to convert me to the Moor faith."

Zahra rolled her eyes. She allowed herself a slow exhale. His coat had the earthy scent of smoky pine and applewood, as if he spent time in the forest by warmth of fire.

Chapeillon chuckled and shoved the heavy door closed. "Those animals are persistent, are they not?"

Kempe turned to face the prosecutor. "Not as persistent as you pederasts. You have the worst punishment coming, yet still you cannot resist."

Chapeillon's gaze roved casually over the Englishman's accommodations. "Monsieur Kempe, I assure you, I do not harbor that particular appetite."

"Then why protect Prelati?"

Chapeillon sauntered deeper into the small chamber. Zahra could no longer see his face as he tilted his large head. "One word: power."

The prosecutor's openness with Kempe was telling. He knew the Englishman was not long for this world. Her stomach turned as she realized neither would she be, should he discover her in here. A gray hunting spider scuttled over the wool. She jerked back, pressing her lips tight. If that thing jumped on her…

Kempe approached the bars. "I see you have the keys. How did you manage that?"

Chapeillon stepped backward. "I ask, and I am given, Monsieur Kempe. That is the nature of power."

The two men faced one another; Kempe towering. He leaned quite close to the bars, eyes hard upon Chapeillon. "That what you hope will happen, here? You will ask, and be given?"

Chapeillon's lip twitched into a peculiar smile. "A man is nothing without hope."

Zahra was uncertain what the men were speaking about, but the tension between them was unmistakable. She held her breath for fear she would be heard.

Monsieur Kempe gestured to his cell gate. "Well?"

Zahra's eyes widened. Master Chapeillon's 'appetite' was not for children, like those men on trial, but for something else. And Monsieur Kempe attempted to lure him into his cell.

The prosecutor appeared gripped with indecision as his fingers clenched and unclenched the clinking cell keys. He uttered a sharp laugh. "You are a beautiful sight, even though you wish to crack my head open."

Kempe's eyes darkened. "Compliments from a corrupt sodomite."

Chapeillon's upper lip curled, showing his teeth as he spoke. "Perhaps if your brother begs, they will allow him to bury your body instead of burning it. Are you on good terms with James these days?"

Kempe's adam's apple dipped in a swallow. Silence stretched. Zahra pled silently that he would leave and not find her lurking in the shadows. Pleading to whom, she did not know.

Monsieur Kempe's voice was a low burn. "The blood of children is on your hands."

Thump thump.

That blood-rush feeling again. Was she going to be ill? She was stuck, unable to do anything except experience the strange thrumming sensation that centered in her lower-sternum and radiated outward.

Kempe leaned away from the bars. "What is happening with your skin?"

The ring of keys hit the stone floor. Chapeillon held out his hands covered in shiny, leprous bumps. He dropped to his knees and drew up his sleeves. It had spread up his arms. He let forth a wail that the *gros valet* would certainly hear.

"Interpreter. The keys." Kempe's commanding voice snapped her out of her paralysis. She swept his coat aside, ran past the prosecutor, and snatched the keys off the floor. Shaking violently, she chose one at random—wrong one.

"You!" Chapeillon staggered to a stand. Her leg muscles locked up. Flesh sagged over his eyes. His face looked like melting wax. "Witch!"

Chapeillon pitched toward her. She dropped her lodestones and threw up her arms in defense. He jerked to a halt, his hands a mere inch from her. Kempe had a fistful of Chapeillon's tunic, his arm outstretched between the cell bars. The prosecutor suspended in motion for a fraction of a second. Kempe yanked him backward. The back of Chapeillon's head hit the iron with a resounding clang. He slumped to the floor.

Kempe crouched and reached through the bars to extract the ring of keys from Zahra's frozen grip. If she learned nothing else from this terrible day, at least she now knew she was utterly useless in a fight.

A bang echoed from the end of the hallway. Kempe tested key after key. Metal hinges squealed as the cell door swung open.

He passed by her and whispered, "Not too fast on your feet, are you?"

Zahra snapped back, "Not so easy using your feminine wiles, is it?"

Kempe sent her a glare as he pressed his ear against the door. Footsteps pounded down the hallway. Behind them, the diseased prosecutor sagged awkwardly against the bars, unconscious.

Monsieur Kempe pressed his shoulder into the door. The *gros valet* called out. "Everything all right, Master Chapeillon?"

Kempe lifted a finger to his lips. After a few moments of silence, the handle rattled. Kempe held it closed with his weight leaned into it. The *valet* cursed under his breath and grunted, the door shook. A beat passed, and Kempe hauled it open. The *valet* stumbled into the chamber. Kempe used the young man's forward momentum to throw him to the floor. A cacophony of crashing armor rang out.

The *valet* fumbled to retrieve his weapon, but Kempe disarmed him and headed for the door with the poor fellow's sword in hand. Zahra dove near the *valet's* floundering legs, grappling for her stones.

"Halt!" The *valet* snatched Zahra's arm.

The breath went out of her. She yanked back but could not dislodge his grip. She looked toward the corridor, expecting Kempe to help her.

Instead, he did not even spare her a glance as he left.

CHAPTER 5

Time seemed to slow as Zahra ran through ways to stop Kempe from leaving her behind. The *gros valet* uttered a cry. He had just seen Chapeillon's unsightly skin condition. His grip on her arm loosened.

Zahra jerked her arm free and dove into the narrow hallway. "I heard about Mary!"

Monsieur Kempe emerged from a different prison chamber down the hall, its door hanging wide open. "What did you say?"

"Where are the keys?" Her voice came out sharp and shrill.

Behind her, the *gros valet* flew out of the cell chamber and crashed to the opposite side of the narrow corridor. "Halt, you both!"

They turned and ran. They burst into the Council Chamber, where the knight with the crooked mustache widened his eyes. He ripped out his sword.

Kempe blocked the knight's first blow with the *valet's* sword, a clang ringing out. A short exchange of blows took place before the knight disarmed Kempe, clearly the superior swordsman. He shoved Kempe so hard he flew into a chair, which demolished beneath his weight. Kempe groaned as he rolled onto his side. The knight kicked the sword out of his reach. Kempe stumbled to a stand with a new weapon: a broken chair leg. He backed up, breathing hard, stopping near Zahra.

The knight eyed Kempe, holding his sword at a practiced angle. "I met your mother in Leicester when she was in prison. I wish you no harm, lad."

The *valet* charged in, his tone fearful between labored breaths. "My lord, Master Chapeillon has an unholy affliction upon him. He needs medical attention."

The knight flashed his teeth in frustration. Clanking and rattling echoed from the dark hallway. He pointed his sword at Monsieur Kempe. "A storm raged three weeks 'til your mother was let out. Is that what we are dealing with here, son?"

Kempe regripped the leg of the chair. "Do you wish to find out?"

A sinister laugh echoed from the corridor. A man emerged, arms flinging wide, his face split by a grin. "I always find a way."

The *valet* pointed his sword at the man. "Gilles de Rais!"

Monsieur Kempe and Zahra shared a glance and broke into a run. Gilles de Rais was tight on their heels. He had chosen the child killer as a distraction? "You released him?"

Kempe blasted through one of the double doors and held it open a crack. She raced through. "Not for long." He slammed it shut and rammed the chair leg through the doors' iron rungs. Gilles de Rais rammed against the blockade.

The muffled voice of the disgraced Commander filtered through. "Let me out, Monsieur! You will have riches! Countless women! Please! *Ulgh—*"

The doors strained against the splintering chair leg caught between the rungs.

It wouldn't last long, but perhaps long enough.

She sped like a frightened hare over the mezzanine level of the great hall. They burst into the chilly night air and fled down one side of the forked staircase.

The courtyard only had a few foot soldiers guarding its perimeter. Lord Raymond's driver, Bernard, paced beside his carriage. He saw Zahra and took his hat off to get a better look. Relief burned in her chest. She pointed. "Hurry!"

The foot soldiers reached for their swords.

She called out to them in French. "Master Chapeillon needs a medic! He has contracted *infestantibus lepra.*" *Aggressive leprosy.*

The whites of their eyes flashed, hands paused at the hilts of their weapons.

She and Kempe reached the carriage.

"Stop them!" A war-cry erupted back at the doorway. The knight with the crooked mustache leveled his sword in their direction. The foot soldiers drew their weapons and gave chase.

"Where we going?" Bernard scrambled up to the driver's perch, fumbling for the reins. In a single, swift motion, Kempe overtook Bernard's space, grabbed the reins, and whipped them. The horses set off, jolting her inside the carriage.

Kempe said, "We follow the river West."

• • • • •

The carriage creaked as it sped alongside the Loire River. Zahra kept peeking out, expecting riders to emerge behind them. This chariot would not be as fast as an experienced soldier on a single horse.

What was she doing? In the span of an hour, she had gone from respected interpreter to outlaw. The dark river rushed as if racing them. She imagined diving in to let the cold grip her. That would be preferable to Lord Raymond watching her hang.

Zahra shivered in one of Isabelle's spare cloaks that smelled of gardenias. Images of her beloved friend's gray face haunted her. Emotion clouded her eyes. She fumbled to find the pouch with her worry stones, her hands trembling.

Her private moment interrupted, Kempe opened the cabin door from the outside and swung into the carriage while it was still in motion.

Zahra struck a tear off her cheek and folded her arms. "This will all be for nothing if you fall to your death, Monsieur Kempe."

He settled into the bench across from her. "Speak."

A spider crept over the shoulder of his white tunic. "A vile thing is on you."

He brushed it off.

She jerked her feet up. "Now it is in the carriage with us!"

"You said, 'I heard about Mary.'"

Zahra curled her legs under her, gathering her skirts and tucking them under her calves. "That is the only reason you helped me. I knew I should not have broken you out."

"Broken me out?" Monsieur Kempe leaned forward, laying the entire weight of his gaze on her. "You did not plan any of that."

Zahra cleared her throat and searched the cabin floor for the eight-legged insect.

Kempe sat back again, watching her. "Can you explain Chapeillon's disease?"

She shuddered at the memory of the prosecutor's expression of horror as lumps formed over his cheeks and ears, his flesh sagging below his jawbone. "Shouldn't I be asking you? After all, you have been publicly accused of malevolent magic."

Zahra did not believe any such thing—but the Englishman's expression darkened. "Tell me what you know of Mary."

She resisted the urge to roll the stones in her palm. "Hadiza came into our lives a month ago. She claimed she had escaped from a place where other children were being held. And… I am not sure that I believed her." A flush of shame mounted from her neck into her cheeks. Like Pierre had said, Hadiza had thought she was safe with Zahra. How wrong she was.

Silent, Kempe displayed the patience of a Donatello masterwork in ivory. She cleared her throat. "Before the trial, I met a man who told me his brother Stephen was wrapped up in the case. And he mentioned his missing daughter, Mary."

Kempe exhaled. "James was there to provide a statement?"

"He believes Mary will not return."

Stephen's jaw flexed, and his voice hardened. "What do you know of Mary?"

Zahra's throat felt scratchy and dry. Monsieur Kempe could have escaped without her. By helping her, he risked returning to his death sentence. All for what she was about to say. She feared to utter it aloud.

"When your brother said her name, Hadiza recognized it. Said that she knew a Mary."

Kempe's stare intensified. "And?"

"The way she said it—"

"Mary is a very common name."

The smooth stones began running over one another, emanating a glassy buzz. "I know! But we are in France—where the name would be 'Marie.' And Hadiza is from Morocco, where the name would be 'Maryam.' Yet she claims to have known this girl in Marbella, where the name would be 'Maria' or 'Marya.' So, it seems likely—well, fairly possible—that the 'Mary' she spoke of was English. And there are few English girls in Granada."

Zahra was out of breath by the time she finished speaking. Monsieur Kempe leaned back and closed his eyes. Her gaze fell as she strained to recall more. Perhaps she had caught a detail that might help. "When I overheard the men speaking, Prelati asked if they were happy with a girl. Which sounds as if—"

"As if these men trade children like sacks of grain." His shoulders were rigid, and shadows gathered in his eyes. His gaze dropped to the stones rolling in her palm.

She clenched her hand, crossing her arms again. "Monsieur, I am sorry it was not something more definitive."

Monsieur Kempe cast her a dismissive glance. "Do not bother with apologies. After I help you tonight, I shall forget we ever met."

• • • • •

Zahra rode alone. Kempe had returned to the driver perch to guide Bernard over poorly formed roads and pathways winding through the black forest. They ended up in a crumbling manorial village south of Nantes. The carriage drew to a halt in front of a tiny wattle and reed home, clawed at by shadows of creeping thistle.

Monsieur Kempe jumped down, his weight jostling the entire chariot. "Stay here."

Zahra shoved the small window curtain aside. "You are leaving us?"

Kempe held up two fingers as he continued walking. "Two minutes."

He turned away and crossed his arms, shoulders tucked forward. He must be cold after the river-side drive without a coat. He rapped quietly on the door.

Bernard approached the small window, standing outside the carriage. Lines of tension ran across his face. He spoke in a whisper. "'Moiselle, I waited for hours to learn what happened."

His voice had the slightest of quivers. She forced herself to look in his eyes. "Monsieur Kempe is helping me find little Hadiza."

Bernard removed his hat, his eyes glistening. "And Madame Isabelle?"

Zahra dug her teeth into her lip. She shook her head. Bernard sank against the chariot and lifted his hat to hide his face as he wept.

An attractive, olive-skinned woman answered the door to the small house, holding up a candle. "Stephen!"

The woman drew the door open, revealing her wool robe and a tousled red braid. Kempe's wife? She could not make out his words, but she noticed he did not embrace her or step inside the house.

A man appeared behind her—the bearded fellow Zahra had met in the courtyard. Kempe's brother. Hostility pinched his face. He pushed the door, but Kempe stopped it with his hand. The men argued.

Zahra climbed out of the carriage. As she drew near, the two men spoke harshly to one another.

The elder brother's tone mocked. "I thought you put all that behind you, brother?"

Monsieur Kempe appeared impassive. "Not your concern. I shall be on my way once I have my belongings."

"'Tis my concern when my child is involved."

The woman's high voice penetrated the tension. "Stephen, a lady travels with you? Who is she? Do come in, *cara*."

All eyes turned to Zahra.

Recognition flickered in James' eyes, his anger lines smoothing. "You are the woman from the courthouse." He squinted, looking between them. "You knew him all along?"

Zahra stilled the stones behind her back. "No, monsieur! We met while he was in—"

"We cannot stay." Stephen cut her a look, and she bit the inside of her cheek.

Concern etched over the woman's brow. "Stephen, dear, where is your coat? Get inside to warm up a bit, would you?"

"He is not stepping foot in here, Merla."

Merla's lips pursed. "James Richard Kempe, open this door or your bed tonight shall be as cold as the Loire."

The bearded brother deflated, stepping aside. Merla beckoned Zahra. Hesitating, she looked back, and saw Bernard inside the carriage, his forehead pressed into his fist, likely praying.

Stephen's eyes followed her as she entered his family's home. Merla's soft brown eyes were kind, framed in lines of sadness. "Stephen, *tesoro*—be as stubborn as you like, but in or out. Firewood's scarce these days."

He ducked inside, shutting the door behind him. Merla had called him *treasure* in Italian. Their small home was well-maintained, its sturdy buttresses and trims painted white. Four stools hugged a thick oak table, the kitchen only steps away. A single door led back to what was likely their bedroom.

"Sit. What is your name, *cara?*" *Dear.* James' wife must be Italian. Merla placed a blanket around Zahra's shoulders.

"Zahra." She smiled as she perched on a stool near the fire. Merla reminded her of Isabelle, maternal and warm.

"Welcome, Zahra. My, you are a radiant beauty." She shot a sly glance in Stephen's direction as she hung the kettle over the flame. "I'll be right back, *cara.*" She took her candle with her into the small back room.

Zahra self-consciously ran her fingers over her hair, checking it was not tousled. James hovered in the middle of the home. His eyes had dark circles under them. "Brother, I have a Godly duty to tell you again: it is clear scripture that we are not to contact spirits."

Monsieur Kempe replied in a low voice. "I am uninterested in a Lollard's interpretation of scripture."

Lollard? Perhaps James was a follower of that controversial preacher, Wycliffe, who dared to preach a different doctrine than the Church espoused. That might explain their being in France in such humble conditions. At the trial, Chapeillon had mentioned Kempe's father had been a wealthy merchant.

Merla reappeared, hoisting a weighty leather bag into Monsieur Kempe's arms. She also offered a wool coat with aged stitching. "Keep it if you like."

James snatched the coat before Stephen could take it. "Listen well, little brother. Do not speak our child's name as you engage with the devil. You have done enough harm."

Kempe stiffened as if he might strike his brother. Instead, he stepped back, threw the door open, and left. James slammed the door after him.

Merla ground fragrant herbs in a stone pestle, tears threatening to fall. The scent of fresh thyme lured Zahra to stay. But she knew she could not. She stood and folded the blanket. "Madame, I am grateful for your kindness. But I must rejoin Monsieur Kempe. He is helping me find a child."

James stepped toward her, his voice low. "Do not accept his help. If anything, he is the cause."

Merla's pestle dropped into the mortar with a loud crack. "James!"

"The cause?" Zahra looked between them.

James' lips trembled as he spoke through gritted teeth. "My brother thinks he consorts with spirits. But they are demons. And he did it under my own roof, while my child was home!"

Merla accepted the folded blanket from Zahra, speaking quietly. "Stephen loves Mary. He would never do anything—"

"If you know what is good for that child you are looking for, you will abandon any thought of asking for his help. And run. Run far from him!" James pivoted and disappeared into the back, slamming that door, too.

Merla blinked moisture from her eyes. "James is usually not like this. Our daughter went missing about eleven months ago." Her voice strained through what sounded like a closing throat. "And he has—well, he connected Stephen's… spiritual activity to it, somehow."

Zahra spoke without thinking. "It could not be related. None of it is real, Merla."

Merla set the blanket down and plucked the bubbling kettle from the hearth. Steaming water filled a small mug full of fragrant, crushed herbs. "Stephen and James' mother was a special woman. She had Stephen while on a spiritual pilgrimage. She dragged him throughout Israel, stuck by her side like a shadow. And…" She set the kettle down. "He has a gift. He has been able to know if a child has passed."

A chill crawled up her spine. Zahra resisted the urge to explain the many ways Monsieur Kempe could have tricked them; namely, he could have done the harm himself. She shook the thought.

"Deuteronomy eighteen, ten. 'Do not call forth the spirits of the dead. It is detestable to the Lord.' That is why we do not ask him to find out about our baby girl. But…" Merla bowed her head. "I take one step after the other hoping she might show up on our doorstep one day."

Zahra's heart ached. She blinked back tears. "Perhaps she will."

Merla returned a tremulous smile. "Stephen used to call her 'Rabbit' because she would wiggle her nose like a wee bunny. Used to bother us. What wouldn't I give to see that little twitch again."

Zahra brushed a tear off the corner of her eye with a fingertip. For some reason, the chilling conversation between Prelati and his men sprang to mind.

Merla cut into Zahra's attempt to recall it. "What child are you looking for?"

"Raha." Zahra flushed, stuttering. "I—I—misspoke. The child's name is Hadiza. She is my… my friend."

Merla placed her hand on Zahra's shoulder. "I hope you find her, darling. And whoever Raha is, too."

• • • • •

Zahra emerged from the cozy Kempe home, the chill biting through her cloak. She carried a soft piece of bread wrapped in a napkin, as well as James' coat over her arm.

Monsieur Kempe stood beside the carriage like a shadowy wraith.

"Ready?" He sounded annoyed.

She held out the heavy wool coat. "Merla insisted."

Kempe glanced toward the house where Merla peeked through the cracked door. He accepted the coat from Zahra, his cool fingers briefly grasping hers—an accidental touch. She clenched her fingers to herself and stepped back. Monsieur Kempe held the coat up to Merla in thanks before he swung it on.

Bernard sat in the carriage, arms crossed—snoring. She stepped onto the ladder to climb in, but Kempe approached, his voice a burn in the dark. "Interpreter, we must walk where we are going."

Halfway up the ladder, Zahra turned. Their eyes were level. The frigid air puffed between them. Her heart skipped a beat. Why should they need to walk anywhere? She placed the bread next to Bernard on the carriage bench.

Kempe headed off past the path toward the dark forest. He lifted his collar to ward off the cold. He seemed like a dangerous person to be alone with in the forest. Her heart skittered like a fleeing animal. She hated the dark. She wished to be home at the *Manoir de Cieux*, curled up in bed. Only the thought of finding Hadiza spurred her into the gloom after Monsieur Kempe.

"Should we ask Merla for a light? I cannot even see my own hand in front of me."

The moist brush crunched underfoot. With one hand, Zahra held the front hem of her gown off the ground. Her eyes played tricks; it looked like shadowy figures moved between the trees. She clicked her worry stones and rolled them like a steady stream.

His silence unnerved her.

"Monsieur Kempe, your brother is correct in that, according to your Bible, it is forbidden to communicate with spirits. I seem to recall several verses. Numbers, Deuteronomy, Acts—"

"A scholar in 'my' Bible, are you?" Kempe's tone mocked.

"My tutor, Scholar Lord Raymond de Sabunde, has a proclivity to make all Biblical study de rigueur. In both Greek and Latin, no less."

"Yet he failed to teach you to speak plainly."

"I just mean—he required me to read it a lot. I also have an excellent—ehm, well, never mind." Zahra realized she was flaunting her education. Perhaps Kempe's mother had gone on religious travels with him instead of having him educated. "Monsieur Kempe—since we are in this together, now—would you tell me what happened in Château Machecoul?"

When he was arrested, he had been drenched in blood that was not his own. And she had not read his full testimony to know what happened after Prelati attempted to coerce him to summon a demon. Through the dark, his eyebrows were drawn. Did he not like to talk about it, or would the truth of what happened frighten her? It was dark and she hadn't the faintest idea what he planned do to her out here. She could fling the stones at him. She tapped them together, the subtle magnetic snap satisfying.

"What is your deal with the rocks?"

Took some nerve to ask her that in such a tone. "They are lodestone, from Greece. They are slightly magnetic, as is their nature. And on them is carved, 'Master of one's own destiny.'"

He finally slowed down a bit as they entered a small, dark clearing. The hem of her skirts clung to her calves, a chill shooting up her legs. He faced her, peering through the shadows. "You play with stones to remind yourself that God does not direct your steps?"

When he put it like that, she appeared quite the heretic, didn't she? She swallowed, pulling open the small leather pouch to place them inside. "No, monsieur, I 'play' with them because they soothe me when I am nervous."

"Then I would keep them out."

A premonitory tingle coursed over Zahra's skin. Monsieur Kempe knelt in the clearing. From his leather satchel, he pulled out small carved statues and placed them in a circle. He extracted a blade and stabbed it into the soil in the middle of the circle. He bowed his head, and prayed quietly in Latin, his rich voice calm and rather beautiful. He called upon a lonely, roaming spirit to assist them.

It unsettled her, but she also found it absurd. This was how he intended to locate Hadiza? She chided herself for being here. She had already closed her pouch, and she would not give him the satisfaction of her pulling the worry stones out again. She tipped her head back to gaze at the sky. The tall trees swayed as if in a worshipful trance.

His haunting prayers halted.

A hand rested on her shoulder. Bernard? She turned—but no one was there. A shriek caught in her throat.

Kempe's eyes had gone all-white, his expression blank. A spindly-fingered hand crawled out of his mouth like a spider. The protruding arm extended to the ground from Kempe's gaping jaw. She clapped her hands over her mouth to hold in a scream. She backed up several paces and rammed into a tree. "Monsieur Kempe!"

Her cry seemed to snap him out of a spell. The hand disappeared. Kempe stood and backed away from the items. He commanded, "Show yourself."

An unnaturally dark pocket of shadows clung nearby. Something was there, but when she tried to focus on it, her vision blurred.

"I need not show myself," it said, "for you see me every day."

The disembodied voice sounded like two or three people speaking at once, each at a different pitch. Who—or what—was it? She trembled with the desire to run. Whatever that thing was, it was meant to be run from. She edged behind Monsieur Kempe so if that thing had eyes, it could not look upon her.

Kempe straightened, his voice holding authority. "Spirit, you are bound to answer my questions truthfully."

The shadow undulated in a way that was both mesmerizing and repulsive. "What questions?"

"A girl was abducted tonight. Where do we find her?"

The trees froze as if time had stopped. Steam hung in front of her lips.

It replied at such a low register, she could not make it out. Then, the voice spoke directly into her ear. "The child shall be taken back to Marbella."

The shadow launched itself at them. More specifically, at Zahra. It moved so fast that it was upon her before Kempe could react. She sprawled onto her back, her scream echoing as she crossed her arms over her face.

Nothing was there.

Starlight cut through the clouds and the trees resumed their swaying. Voice high, she said, "What happened?"

Kempe's chest rose and fell. He did not seem to have expected any of this. "I thought it was going to go inside of you. But it did not."

Zahra's knees shook as she climbed to a stand. "Go inside of me?"

Kempe's gaze roved the surrounding forest.

She clutched his coat. "Could it still be here? You look like you think it is still here."

"Cease your chatter."

They stood scanning the darkness. Her senses had sharpened, her pulse pounding in her ears.

"Who is she?" Its growl seemed to roll over the forest floor in a deep rumble.

Zahra clutched her chest, feeling faint.

Kempe glanced back at her, frowning. "She is nobody."

It chuckled. A shiver overtook her. She clung to Kempe's side.

A flicker of light caught her attention. A small flame, without a source, illuminated the circle of items in the dirt. They were gemstones, talismans, and tiny sculptures of beasts. The intricately carved hilt of the blade buried in the earth glinted. Nearby, a patch of velvety wild roses reflected the flames. The heat intensified as the fire grew. There was no smoke.

"Step through this fire to find the child."

Zahra's lungs constricted. "What?"

The voice had changed, somehow. Soothing and reverberating in her skull. Kempe narrowed his eyes upon the flames. "Go. The fire is an illusion."

She spoke through gritted teeth. "We can get to Marbella by boat!"

"I thought you were in a rush?"

She stared at the fire, its heat tingling her face. "You are mad if you think that is an illusion."

Lifting his palm toward it to feel its heat, he nodded. "It is convincing for a reason."

"I shall not."

Kempe shrugged. "It is your choice."

And there it was again. Her choice. What would she choose? Of course, she would never stop searching for Hadiza. Would she? At the very least, she would never stop advocating for children like Hadiza. For children like Mary. For the unnamed ones, passed between depraved men. For the ones whose twitching caused problems.

Zahra gasped. "Monsieur Kempe!"

She faced him and clutched the front of his coat. He looked between her hands and wild eyes.

"Merla mentioned Mary had a twitch. The Frenchman in my bedchamber said the girl's face twitched. The same men took Mary!"

A gleam entered Monsieur Kempe's eyes. The roaring flames reflected in his irises. His skin had a warm hue in the firelight. Sharp shadows accentuated his jawline and adam's apple. With his hair loose, he looked like an angel overlooking his battalion, ready for war.

Zahra gestured behind her. "Let us go charter a craft. We could be there in two weeks if the weather is good."

Kempe shook his head. "No—we go through the fire."

"You may do as you wish, monsieur." She let go of his coat and backed up a step. Heart racing, she flicked her gaze to the fire. If she ran, would that thing chase her? Would it try to 'go inside' her again? These thoughts would haunt her for life.

Zahra turned to bolt—but Monsieur Kempe grabbed her arm. She whipped around and they locked eyes. His gaze was intense, a hard line between his eyebrows. "Consider it, interpreter."

"What are you doing?" She jerked at her arm. But Kempe was much, much stronger.

"It will not harm you."

"Then you jump in it! I shan't touch it!" She dug her heels into the soil.

Kempe grabbed her other arm. "Do you see there is no smoke?"

The deafening flames were far more persuasive. She tried to pry his grip open with her nails. Impervious to her clawing, he drew her nearer to the fire. He meant to put her in it! Heat prickled her skin. She kicked his shin. But it was like kicking an oak. If she tried to bite one of his hands, she would have to shift her weight forward. That would make her far easier to throw into the fire. "Please Monsieur Kempe! Stephen! Hear me! You are insane! I will burn!"

Zahra sank back toward the ground as he dragged her. Flames licked her shoes, the soles of her feet scalding. A glint of metal caught her eye—the blade. Zahra twisted and bit his hand. Tendons crackled under her teeth.

Kempe uttered a growl of pain, releasing one of her arms. She snatched his blade out of the ground and swung at him. He jumped back, then grappled for the blade.

Zahra sliced a clean cut across the palm of his hand. He roared in pain, closing his bloody palm into a fist. She was finally gaining some of her power back.

Or so she thought.

In a horrific moment of clarity, she realized he had not thrown her into the fire by now as a twisted attempt at kindness. After the cut, he effortlessly yanked her and hurled her in.

Zahra flailed, swallowed by the blaze.

CHAPTER 6

In the months before her mother died, Zahra learned of the lever that could kill everyone.

On the floor of their mother's bedchamber, the Solar, she and her sister played the pebbles game, *gebet'a*. Their mother Ghaliba performed her prayers on the rug nearby.

On the shiny flagstone floor, Raha sat with her dark legs crossed, her feet dirty from their hiding game of *kayf-taghfa* earlier. Those dirty feet irritated Zahra because she had to help her clean them in the bath. Was she not old enough to wash her own feet? She was just lazy.

"Ha!" Zahra scooped up the last of the pebbles, winning the game.

Raha growled and dove on Zahra, prying at her fingers. She was strong for her size. Instead of allowing Raha to get them, she threw them.

"Girls." Their mother's stern voice carried. The pebbles bounced, several sliding under the door of the forbidden lever chamber. Only their mother had the key.

After they apologized for their behavior, Ghaliba showed them where the key was hidden. The girls fought for the best position in front of the door.

"One day, when you rule Marbella, you may need it."

The iron door of the lever chamber swung open. Inside, an intricate network of taut cords and pulleys ran parallel to one another like harp strings. A wooden bar cinched all the cords, connecting them to a single lever on the wall. A large, messy tangle of ropes hung nearby.

Raha placed her hands on her hips. "That is it?"

Ghaliba chuckled, resting her hands on each of their shoulders. "If you pulled that lever, a great big fire would burn in every room and corridor. Soon after, the whole tower would collapse."

Zahra and Raha looked at one another with wide eyes.

They held hands and stepped forward. Ghaliba spoke sharply. "You only enter the lever chamber if we have been raided. And you can only pull the lever if the tower is empty. The rope ladder is for the brave one who pulls the lever."

That night, they rested beside one another to the sound of their mother's soft breathing.

Raha whispered, "Zaza, are you going to be queen?"

Zahra propped up on her elbow and smiled. "Yes, when Uncle Yusef becomes king, I will become queen. And we shall have lots of beautiful children."

Raha did not return the smile. "Would you make sure I am out of the tower if you have to pull the lever?"

Zahra playfully demurred, as if uncertain.

Urgency entered Raha's tone. "Promise me, shackee kahtee."

Zahra smiled at Raha's cute pronunciation of *shaqiyqati*. My dear sister. Looking into her baby sister's dark eyes, she realized her worry was genuine.

Zahra cupped Raha's full cheeks in her palms. "Promise. I would never leave you behind."

• • • • •

The flesh-flaying pain cemented Zahra's hatred of Monsieur Kempe. He had been wrong—the fire burned. Soon, she would be nothing but ash. How she had wasted her life.

Why did burning alive feel like drowning?

She opened her eyes, vision blurred. Bubbles expelled from her mouth.

An invisible current weighed down her cloak, gown, and lace-up boots. She divested herself of the cloak and kicked. Sunlight streamed down around her.

Bursting above the surface, Zahra sucked in a rough breath, salt on her tongue. To unlace her shoes, she had to dunk under again. Cool water rushed between her toes. Thrusting her arms and legs, she broke the surface again. She sucked in a wet breath. She twisted hither and yon, searching for land. A mountainous coastal village with a sprawling white palace bobbed in the distance.

Marbella.

A wave slapped her in the face. She choked on water, arms flailing. Her arms stroked, pulling her toward the shore. She gained mere inches.

An undercurrent lured the layered skirts of her gown. Despite her efforts, she submerged. Her arms burned with the effort to swim. Somehow this did not push her nose above the water. The surface seemed to drift further out of her reach. She thrashed her legs, but it made trivial impact. The lack of air made her limbs harden like wood. Panic swelled in her chest.

The deep fizzed in monotone.

Something hard slithered around her torso and hauled her above the surface. She sucked in a rough breath, clutching the strong and wonderful arm that kept her afloat. The man's chest supported her back, his jaw against her temple. He treaded water for them both. She rested her head back on his shoulder and relished the act of drawing air. She jerked her legs to assist.

"Rest a moment."

Stephen Kempe.

Zahra twisted to look at him. He had followed her! She renewed her effort to tread. She tried to wrestle from his arm. "Release me!"

"And let you sink like a stone?"

"You let me burn!"

"I must tell you three things before we part ways."

She twisted her shoulders, grunting.

His strength far surpassed hers. "I shall release you when you are on the boat."

Boat?

Kempe turned them. A fishing boat dipped in the current, its sail tied down. Inside the vessel stood two men shielding their eyes from the sun, watching them. He swam them toward the boat. Her legs and skirts swayed in the current like jellyfish tentacles. Once again, she proved to be useless.

Kempe did not even seem out of breath. Had he somehow known they would end up under water? Zahra seethed.

The Moorish fisherman squinted down at her, his arms crossed. "Where did you swim from?"

She reached out a hand. "I shall tell you anything you wish to know. Please help."

He hesitated, looking between the two of them. A playful glint glimmered in his eyes. He leaned down, palm splayed. He gripped her outstretched arms with rough fingers, and Kempe hoisted her over the gunnel. Once on the vessel, the fellow released her. Gown clinging to her legs, she stumbled, dumping onto the deck. She slumped over a pile of fishy netting, panting.

The other fisherman, a sunburnt Arab, wore a navy *shemagh*; fabric cinched to his head with a rope. "Leave the *uroubi.*" *European.*

Zahra looked like she belonged here. Kempe did not. What more motivation did they need to leave him to fend for himself in the Alboran Sea? And shouldn't she allow it, having been thrown head-first into an inferno?

Despite how he had wronged her, she would not be the cause of his demise.

"The *uroubi* is with me."

The two men turned to her. She lay inert like a seal, catching her breath. The Arab gripped a gutting blade. The Moorish man's large nose crinkled. "With you? In what way?"

Still breathless, Zahra struggled to a soaking wet stand. Her legs shook as she straightened her posture. Her dress was as heavy as the

Sphinx of Giza. "I am the daughter of *malika* Ghaliba bint Bashkuwal, and this interrogation insults me. I have spared this unarmed man. Aid him, or I shall ask *malik* Jabir to feed you to the wolves."

She held no real power, and her voice quavered.

The two men looked at each other. They bent over, working together to help Kempe into the fishing boat. Kempe climbed over, and the creaking craft jostled like a toy.

Zahra flung her arms out to balance herself. Her waterlogged underskirts constricted her legs, and she toppled. Fortunately, one of the men caught her arm with a sturdy grip.

Kempe again. She tugged free from his grasp and clambered off, using various guideposts to walk without falling. Mast post. Thick rope. Bucket of fish guts. She dropped onto a bench.

Kempe wiped wet hair off his forehead and nodded to the men. They kept back as if he were venomous. He rested a hand on the mast pole, catching her eye. "We have to talk."

Something was different about him. Perhaps because it was her first time seeing him during the day, outside. Sunlight glimmered on the ocean, revealing that his eyes were not a dull moss color, as she had thought, but more of a pale green like the gemstone, aventurine.

The Arab held the curved scaling blade across his chest in open threat. "Is that English? Who is this? Your slave?"

"That man is no slave." The Moorish fishman stood with his arms crossed, employing admirable balance in the middle of the wobbly craft.

Zahra needed to explain who Kempe was. But all of this was incomprehensible. She fumbled for her stones in the wet pouch, thinking of how far she had come. How did they get here so fast? How did they get here, period? "Slaves in Europe are not as they are here."

The Moor bared his teeth in a grin. "Please tell us how they are different, *anisa*." *Miss.*

The question was a threat. If she refused to answer, they could toss him overboard. Her, too, for that matter.

Zahra coughed, feigning that she was still catching her breath. The satisfying buzz of the stones was muted by moisture. She slid her gaze to Kempe.

His ivory tunic could be seen as slave's attire. The soaked material clung to him, revealing his muscular build, which could have been developed by years of hard labor for a so-called 'master.' But the Moorish fisherman did not refer to Kempe's physical appearance. There was something else un-slave-like about him. Was it his confident posture? His incisive gaze? His vigor?

That was it.

Zahra turned to the fishermen. "In Europe, slaves are not castrated, as they are here."

The Moorish man chortled. The Arab's eyes squinted to the size of raisins. "*Imra'atan.*" *Woman.* It sounded like a curse. "Biko, you can take them to the *malik* if you like. I do not have time for this. They have scared away all my fish."

The Moor named Biko plodded to the stern to release the sheet and trim the sails. Tension quivered in the thundering canvas, catching a breeze.

Her beautiful Marbella neared. Abundant vegetation blanketed the mountainous coast. The sprawling palace perched at the edge of the forest had five towers of differing heights like a hand waving. The sandy beach ran right up to its wall. Tension riddled her shoulders and neck. She was minutes from facing people she had years ago abandoned. They thought she had left because she had been afraid to marry the *malik* Jabir. Dare she tell them the true reason?

Smoothing her waterlogged hair, she repositioned the pins Isabelle had meticulously placed for her the morning of the trial. Her mouth tucked in a firm frown as she fought a wave of guilt.

Barefoot, Kempe stepped over the pile of netting and sat beside her. "Zahra, I need to talk to you before we get separated."

Zahra turned her back to him. The Moorish fisherman watched them while working the sail.

Kempe kept his voice low. "First, remember the name Diogo da Gama. Second, we can only save the children if we work together."

Zahra refused to look back at him. "You pushed me. I shall never forget that."

"In time, I hope to gain your forgiveness for that."

Was he being sarcastic? She snuck a look over her shoulder. The earnestness in his voice matched his expression. "You should know that they think you are my slave. You would do well to act like it. Start by not referring to me by my given name."

He nodded once. "Apologies. Mademoiselle Sabunde."

A touch of amusement tugged his mouth.

Zahra turned away, unsettled by his behavior. Was he different? And had he ever spoken her name? She could not recall ever telling him her name. She must have.

"The third thing I need to tell you is that Hadiza is not here yet. She will arrive on the *Sagrados Inocentes* in seven days."

• • • • •

Zahra had an urge to crumple to her knees and kiss the hard-packed sand of Marbella. Instead, she dug her toes in it. Monsieur Kempe stood beside her, surveying the majestic mountain range that framed Marbella.

She refused to give him the satisfaction of asking the obvious questions. What was that fire? How had they gotten here? How would he know anything about where Hadiza was? Her current theory was that she had been drugged to forget the long trip here.

Biko strapped a scalloped lamellar tabard over his hips and torso. He pulled a spear out of the boat and jumped onto the dock beside Zahra. "*Bialnajah*, brother." *Good luck.* His Arab fishing partner grunted, pushing the boat off the dock.

Biko gestured for her to walk. "Let us go see what the *malik* has to say about our *huriat aalma*." *Mermaid.*

She rolled her stones behind her back. How would she explain her arrival to Jabir? She eyed her good-natured escort. "Are you a soldier?"

Biko's broad smile almost made her forget the danger she was in. "I lead a squadron in the palace army. I catch bass and crab to sell when I can."

"Are you not paid to be in the army?"

"I am, but I have five children and a wife. She works the market. She always knows exactly what we need to sell to feed everyone for the week. All this, and she also cares for our wonderful children."

The reverence with which Biko spoke stirred her heart. Monsieur Kempe strode along with them, but some inches behind her.

Eight soldiers carrying round steel shields marched out in front of the magnificent, wooden gate. Many were bearded Arabs in ruby turbans. Biko ordered them to stand down. They bowed and stole glances at Monsieur Kempe towering beside her.

A loud crank clattered, and the polished teakwood gate opened behind the soldiers.

Biko gestured. "Welcome to the *malik's* humble home."

The thick forest hugged the palace's limestone walls. Everything looked much the same as she remembered it; sienna and cream, with hundreds of arched windows and elevated lookouts spilling with sheer fabric undulating in the warm breeze. Vibrant purple jacaranda trees filled every space, like the palace in its entirety sat in mother earth's palms.

They entered the grounds, soldiers marching in formation behind them. Fragrant citrus nut trees lined the swept pathway, reminding her of her care-free youth. Servants they passed cared for the livestock, swept, and carried buckets of water to fill the fountains and baths. Each one of them stared. Biko greeted them all, seeming to enjoy the attention.

Monsieur Kempe spoke quietly behind her. "You would not have come. You were afraid. You needed a push."

"Into a blazing fire?"

"It did not harm you. Do you not wish to save Hadiza?"

His use of her name disconcerted her, instead of 'your girl.'

"Of course, I do. You lack an important piece of information, Monsieur Kempe. My family here hates me. Especially the king. We would be lucky to survive the night."

The butt of a spear banged, echoing. At the top of the palace steps stood an Arab with olive skin, his meticulously groomed beard hovering stiffly over his chest. His gold turban flowed with fabric.

Uncle Yusef, the prince of Marbella.

The whirring stones halted, digging into her tightening palm. Zahra had planned to be strong when she faced him, but a tremble started deep within her body.

The soldiers bowed deeply, including Biko. "Your royal highness, *amir* Yusef. We found this woman and *uroubi* in the middle of the ocean, near to drowning."

Yusef's forehead scrunched, eyes on Kempe. He traversed the steps in an easy gait, his leather sandals scuffing the soft stone. Even 10 years ago, Yusef had been an accomplished warrior, having developed his combat skills from an early age. His brawn was visible even through his heavy royal robes. Brother to the king, her step-uncle, had been in line as heir to the throne should Jabir never sire children. She wondered if that was still the case.

Yusef halted in front of Kempe. While himself a tall man, Yusef still had to tip his head back to make eye contact. The long silence seemed designed to intimidate the Englishman.

But Kempe remained neutral. That in itself could be interpreted as contempt.

Yusef's beautifully crafted spear had sharp metal wings used for controlling an opponents' weapon. He shifted it to his side, a deceiving position; it looked casual, but in fact, it could penetrate an enemy's ribs in a split moment. And despite his advantage in height, she doubted Kempe could disarm Yusef, who had served in the Granadan army, where men raided, fought warring tribes, and slayed the occasional jaguar. Never breaking eye contact with Monsieur Kempe, he spoke in a threatening voice to Biko. "If nearly drowned, why are they now in my palace, wetting its floors?"

Biko bowed. "This woman claims to be the daughter of the late *malika* Ghaliba."

Yusef jerked his gaze to Zahra. Recognition flickered in his eyes. "Little Zahra?"

Though her pulse pounded, she returned his gaze.

As Yusef looked over her, she stiffened to obscure her shaking. Her wet gown clung, revealing more of her figure than she would ever wish a bunch of soldiers, villagers, or Monsieur Kempe to see. Least of all, Yusef.

He smiled, his eyes lacking any emotion. "You are the vision of paradise we knew you would become."

"I wish to speak to *malik* Jabir."

Yusef burst into vicious laughter, and Biko flinched. "You, the bastard daughter of a Berber whore, demand I summon my dear brother, the *malik*? Little Zahra, who disappeared just days away from her marriage to him?"

Biko's eyes rounded like an owl's. "*Amira* Zahra?" *Princess.*

Yusef's upper lip twitched. "The betrayer. The *malik* will order your immediate execution. And you, *salibiyyun*." *Crusader.* "I do not like you. It was idiotic to bring him here, little Zahra."

Biko chimed in. "This man is her slave, *amir*."

Yusef snorted, gaze roving over Kempe. "Slave?"

The explanation she had given to Biko caught in her throat. Could Monsieur Kempe not slouch, bow his gaze, or do anything to appear more like a slave? The lie burned each time she went along with it.

Biko filled the silence for her. "Apparently slaves remain *intact* in Europe."

Yusef shook his head. "You brought with you a *uroubi* slave who is not a eunuch? I recall you being smarter than that, little Zahra. He must become *khasahu*."

Heat crept up along her throat. Yusef spoke of a procedure that would make Kempe a eunuch. She snuck a sideways glance to the

Englishman, who would not know what was being said. She swallowed, grasping for anything she could think of. "He would not survive such a procedure."

Yusef smiled. "Either way, he will not survive here."

Panic welled inside her at the thought of Monsieur Kempe being subjected to such a thing. She stumbled over the lie. "This slave—his only value, well, he is a large, valuable slave that could—you understand. I would require generous compensation should you have this done to him without my permission."

Yusef looked dead level upon Zahra. After a long stare, he uttered a horse-like snort, and shook his head. "Still slipping mischief with your *lisan fudhayy*." *Silver tongue.*

She could not bring herself to look him in the eye.

Yusef stepped away, gesturing to one of the soldiers. "Take the *uroubi* to be processed. For now, he can remain intact... unless the *malik* says otherwise."

The soldier bowed deeply, and pointed his spear at Kempe, gesturing for him to move along. Kempe turned to Zahra, his eyes fierce. "Remember what I told you."

Yusef's voice cut in. "No English."

The soldier thrust the sharp, glinting spear toward Kempe, forcing him to take a step back as he spoke. "Do not part with the cloth."

Zahra inhaled. How did he know about the cloth?

"No. English." Yusef's voice was dangerously low, his beard shifting as he ground his teeth.

Monsieur Kempe was forced to take another step back. "This is not the first time you have come back to Marbella."

Yusef jabbed the butt of his spear into Kempe's side, causing him to double over and groan. Although Zahra was no fan of Kempe, she tensed at the sudden violence taken against him. "I see you still treat people well."

"People?" Yusef snorted again. "Biko, escort her to the *malik*."

Several palace guards surrounded Kempe, spears out. They forced him to move toward the *alfiz* archway, shaped like a horseshoe, beneath the palace stairs. Kempe sent Zahra a furtive glance before disappearing down the wide hall.

Zahra quashed her guilt, recalling that he had thrown her into a fire and chosen to follow her here. He could deal with the consequences.

CHAPTER 7

With each corner they turned, Zahra's limbs grew heavier. Biko guided her along the private stone pathway that led to the tower built for the king, his wives, children, and concubine. Although, as far as she knew, *malik* Jabir had sired no children, nor had he entertained concubines after marrying Ghaliba.

Quran verses intricately interwove the cream walls of the walkway. Sweet pea lathyrus hung in troves of berry pink. After some time, Biko cleared his throat. "Is it true that *amir* Yusef claimed you as his own years before your betrothal to *malik* Jabir?"

Zahra's abandonment had likely appeared a betrayal to everyone. The true reason she'd fled was too shameful to speak aloud. She recalled the awful night before her mother's funeral, when Jabir announced he would marry Zahra. She had naively run to Yusef for comfort.

"One year before." The stones rolled, playing a soft sonata as they strolled.

Biko did not seem to be in any hurry. "It is a topic of great musing: why your betrothal switched from Yusef to *malik* Jabir."

"It was not unusual for him to take another wife since the *malika* had passed. And I am not his blood."

Biko shook his head and sighed. "How strange it must have been to think of a man as your father, and then become betrothed to him."

Zahra eyed Biko. It was true. She had been devastated and sickened.

He looked around as if the sweet pea were listening to their conversation. His voice grew quiet; their gait slowed. "Many of us wondered why he insisted on marrying a Berber *qayna*. And then moved on to her daughters. Some have whispered that he believed Ghaliba to be the goddess Manat in the flesh."

A memory sprang to mind of Jabir on his knees, bowing deeply while kissing Ghaliba's feet. Zahra had always thought he acted like that because he was madly in love. As a child, she had thought it endearing. Recalling now, it seemed bizarre.

Still, she had trouble accepting he had believed Ghaliba was a goddess in the flesh. "*Malik* Jabir is of the Islamic faith—he believes in one God. If he practiced anything else, it would not be tolerated."

"You might be surprised what is tolerated nowadays, *huriat aalma*." Biko smiled as they entered the garden. It had a narrow fountain, its water running into a pool that reflected the rich foliage. "Some still practice the old religion, believing Ghaliba was Manat, you are al-Uzza, and al-Lat is embodied by *malika* Raha."

The title preceding her baby sister's name caused her chest to constrict. Although Jabir might order Zahra's execution, she most dreaded facing Raha. She wished at least for the chance to explain why she left. Hopefully, Raha would forgive her.

"And you, Biko? Do you believe that?"

"Not at all, *amira*."

Their stroll ended in front of enormous doors that could accommodate Goliath. A man appeared at a window overlooking the garden. "Who is that?" he called out but disappeared.

Was that *malik* Jabir? An instinct to run overtook her. She looked at the lodestones clinging together in her palm. Her fate could involve imprisonment, public humiliation, and even being pelted to death by rocks. Her only hope at that point would be if her sister spoke up in her defense.

The *malik* emerged at the far end of the garden. Female servants chased alongside him like baby ducklings. He appeared older and heavier. Otherwise, he looked the same. His olive skin was speckled with sunspots and his groomed black beard had two gray stripes at the chin. He covered the distance between them, gold and silver threading on his turban sparkling.

Did he intend to barrel directly into her? She braced herself.

Instead, Jabir swung her several inches off the ground into a tight hug. After a moment of shock, she relaxed and stretched her arms to return the embrace. His laughter bellowed. The sound brought back fond memories.

He set her down and she took a step back, shaking. Tears twinkled in his eyes. "Allah is good. My daughter has returned home."

Her throat tightened. She could not speak. She lowered her gaze.

His palms opened as he gestured to her with a grin. "You are still damp from your dip in the ocean."

She peeked at him. "*Malik* Jabir, I must speak with you."

"We have much time to speak. First, we shall celebrate your return with our finest meat, wine, and entertainers. All of Marbella shall attend."

Zahra opened her mouth, then closed it.

Jabir laughed, a deep, infectious sound. He turned to the young servant woman nearest to him. "Prepare a feast. Alert the people of Marbella of the joyous return of their *amira* Zahra."

The woman bowed and departed, taking along several of the other servants.

Jabir gestured to one of the remaining women. "Take *amira* Zahra to the Lynx."

The Lynx was one of the newer towers that she was rarely allowed into as a child. They entertained their royal visitors and guests there so they would spread the word about the lavishness of Marbella.

Zahra did not wish to be treated like royalty. She planned to find Hadiza and return to France. The thought sobered her. "I would prefer just to stay in mother's tower."

"That tower has no windows. It is best for storage."

"The Solar has a terrace—"

"You will stay in the luxury of the Lynx, dear daughter. I have asked Raha to pick the chamber. She is going to be overjoyed to see you."

Anticipation bubbled in Zahra's chest at the thought of seeing Raha again. To laugh with her again, hold her again, and tell her she was sorry.

• • • • •

The striking entry foyer of the Lynx Tower lived up to Zahra's memories. The vases were taller than she was. Wide, scenic windows framed the mountainous landscape to the north and the cobalt ocean to the south. Male servants wore maroon sashes to show they were eunuchs, pumping water from the walls into buckets. The warm air smelled fresh and salty.

Inside the bedchamber provided to her, servants bustled, whipping linens over the bed, filling the washbasin with steaming water, and tying open the veranda curtains. The chamber looked like a painting. The balcony revealed a sprawling view of the ocean and beach in strokes of aqua and gold. Orange honeysuckle draped the granite banister. Silk in sunset hues hung from a huge, four-poster bed.

Maids tugged at the laces on the back of her dress. She jumped aside.

"If she wishes to remain in her dirty French gown, let her."

In the doorway stood a dark-skinned woman holding a goblet of wine. Her full cheekbones and thick, luscious hair swept up high in a style fit for a queen, seemed familiar.

She wore a vivid ruby *takchita* gown, dripping with precious gemstones and twinkling fabric. She brought the goblet of wine to her full lips, weighty rings adorning her fingers. She watched Zahra with soulful dark eyes.

Zahra put her hand to her chest. "Raha?" She started forward.

"It is *malika*."

Zahra stopped and lowered her arms. Raha's eyes drifted over her damp dress. "Do they not have food where-ever you were?"

Raha, only sixteen, had sumptuous curves emphasized by the waist of her butterfly sleeved gown. Her hard gaze was a striking contrast from her youth.

Zahra, heart aching, couldn't look anymore. She knew she should explain why she had disappeared without a goodbye. Why she did not tell Raha she was leaving. Why she let the wolves have her.

Why she had sacrificed Raha to save herself.

"Are you a mute, now?"

Zahra could barely believe the harsh tone coming from her baby sister. Her lips went rigid to hide the tremble. "I heard you chose this chamber for me."

Raha's dark gaze roved over the luxurious accommodations. Zahra had a feeling she thought it too good for her. "Your companion has created quite the stir among the slaves. Rumors have already started."

A correction of the word 'companion' got stuck in Zahra's throat. Would she really just spew lies as her first conversation with her sister? "What kind of rumors?"

The queen pursed her full, moist lips into a smirk. "That man is no slave. He is clearly your lover."

Her own sharp inhale took Zahra by surprise. "Nonsense! I have never—never known a man."

"Yet you stutter." The biting laugh that erupted from Raha felt like a slap.

Zahra grit her teeth. "I do not care if you—or they—believe me."

"You do not care?" Raha's dark eyebrows rose toward the delicate gold crown that nestled among her magnificent onyx locks. "There is a surprise."

Her sarcasm lanced with the precision of an expert marksmen. Zahra clutched her hands behind her back, to conceal their shaking. "Do you stay in mother's bedchamber, now that you are…"

Fury flashed in Raha's eyes at the mention of their mother, but then her eyelids fell half-mast like a jungle cat's. "Tower al-Garbu has been given to our Portuguese benefactors."

Zahra did not understand. "Given?"

Sipping her wine, Raha shrugged. Her eyes wandered over the extravagantly decorated bedchamber, which put any room in her mother's tower to shame. Perhaps Raha thought it was too good for her. "They can have the whole palace, as far as I am concerned. Diogo da Gama sells the best wine."

Zahra blinked. It was the name Kempe had mentioned. That could not be a coincidence. And how did he fare at the moment, under Yusef's processing? Before she could worry, she reminded herself that if the situation were reversed, he would probably let her rot.

Raha threw back the last of her drink and shoved the glass toward one of the nearby servant girls. "We are sufficiently caught up; wouldn't you agree? See you tonight, to celebrate the return of our long lost *amira*."

Raha turned and left, her maids scurrying after her. The door clicked shut, and Zahra bit her lower lip, her eyes growing misty. It was treatment she deserved. But it hurt far worse than she had thought it would.

It was undeniable: Raha had no love for Zahra anymore.

• • • • •

A servant girl picked up Hadiza's ratty cloth.

Zahra called out, "Careful with that—place it out to dry, please."

The girl bowed and draped it on the back of the vanity chair.

Zahra lowered into the bath, biting back a groan of pleasure. A hot bath. In France, she used the public bath house. Unfortunately, she could not relish the luxury because her thoughts kept straying to Monsieur Kempe being led through the *alfiz* archway. As a child, Zahra was never privy to whatever 'processing of slaves' entailed. The way Yusef had ordered it, it did not sound pleasant.

The Arabic maidservant who attended to her had warm, smiling eyes, her dark hair covered by a delicate burgundy veil. Rich clay squelched as the woman gathered a handful from a jar and caked it into

Zahra's hair, massaging it into her scalp. Another maidservant shook dried herbs into the steaming water.

Zahra smiled. "That is a beautiful veil."

The corners of the maidservant's eyes crinkled. "I wore it for you, *amira*. It was a gift from your mother."

Zahra twisted to look closely at the woman, who must have been in her teens when Ghaliba was alive. "What is your name?"

The woman smiled and shook her head. "You would not remember me, *amira*. I was one of many servants who loved the *malika*. My name is Sukayna."

Zahra settled back into the water, the steam fragrant with lemon balm and white lilies. "Sukayna. Have you heard anything about the *uroubi* who arrived with me? He was escorted to be 'processed' at *amir* Yusef's orders."

Sukayna's strong hands worked the creamy clay into Zahra's scalp, with utmost care not to break her hair. "*Amira*, the word '*uroubi*' is on everyone's lips."

Two of the other maidservants suppressed smiles.

Zahra sank so her chin dipped under the hot surface. "His processing entailed what?"

"*Malika* Raha oversaw. Checking for weapons, disease, bugs, anything like that." After a hesitation, she grinned. "He was judged, by all present, to be quite well."

Despite the insinuating phrasing, Zahra was satisfied with the report. She rested her head back on the alabaster bath rim. Hopefully now she could enjoy herself.

Just as in her childhood, she was scrubbed, cleaned, dried, and dressed. She stood at the mirror and drew in a breath. With her umber skin and curls shining like onyx silk, she looked just like her mother. Her full lips had a ruby sheen, and she had the same enigmatic eyes. She remembered their last hug, in the garden under a fig tree.

The dress was like nothing she had ever worn. Sleeveless, cream silk flowed to the floor, cinched at her waist by a wide, soft leather belt. Sukayna rested a plum pashmina over her shoulders, which draped between her elbows and warmed her bare shoulders. "November evenings can become crisp."

Zahra resisted the urge to blurt, 'It is November?' She did not want to appear out of her wits. She and Stephen had gone into the woods the day after he testified, which was the seventeenth of October. Her suspicion was confirmed: at least two weeks had passed between France and today. It supported her theory that she had somehow been medicated and kept in a stupor until arriving here.

It might also explain how Kempe had known about the cloth. Zahra glanced in the vanity's direction where the scrap of fabric draped over the back of a small chair, dried out from her dip in the ocean. The men who abducted Hadiza had been demanding a 'relic.' Was this silly little cloth the 'relic' they had killed Isabelle for? She secured it under her wide leather belt, next to the attached pouch holding her lodestones.

One of the servants presented a gold headdress. It looked like a crown but rested across her forehead. These quiet, hard-working maidservants had transformed her from a scholar's daughter into a Marbellan princess.

Sukayna lifted her eyebrows. "Allah be praised, you are *jamila*." *Beautiful.*

Zahra averted her gaze from her reflection. "Sukayna, what happened with the Tower al-Garbu?"

The woman's eyes widened. She hesitated before answering. "It is the tower now in use by the Portuguese traders."

Zahra frowned. "Why would Jabir simply give mother's tower over to European traders?"

Sukayna straightened her veil. "The *malik's* gift ensures our protection."

"That is a high price to pay for protection."

Sukayna bowed. "Rest before your celebration, *amira*."

She and the maidservants hurried out in a respectful line. Just across the hallway from her bedchamber was an arched opening to the sentry bridge leading to the Tower al-Garbu. As a child, she used to hoist herself onto the stone railing and climb into a gutter. From there, she knew how to sneak inside, undetected. Looking at it now, it seemed like a dangerous climb.

The last maidservant in the line stopped in front of Zahra to tuft her locks and straighten her pashmina. Zahra grasped her arm. "I wish to see my mother's bedchamber in the Tower al-Garbu again. The Solar."

The girl's brow furrowed. "No one dares to go inside. Those who have do not come back."

After the maidservant scurried after the others, Zahra nodded. It was decided. The Tower al-Garbu was the first place she would look for Hadiza.

• • • • •

The Tower al-Garbu had several false entrances. Time had worn the tower's stone, having been built by *malik* Jabir's great-great-grandfather. It was designed to house the main food stores. If they were invaded, the construction allowed them to easily burn the tower down, forcing raiders to move on.

Cream marble stairs led to the north entrance, where a single guard stood before faded beechwood doors inlaid with intricate metallic details. How could Kempe possibly know whether Hadiza was here? The thought of Kempe lodged a knot in her gut. Had he come to harm in her absence? If Hadiza were here, along with Kempe's niece, Zahra could get this whole thing sorted now, retrieve Kempe, and they could all head back home to France. The idea of it lightened her steps and spurred her toward the tower entrance.

The guard lifted his hand to shield his eyes from the afternoon glow, watching her approach.

"I am here to see Diogo da Gama."

"Who are you?"

"The returned princess you may have heard about. Direct me to Diogo da Gama, and perhaps I will not mention how disrespectfully you addressed me."

The man cocked an eyebrow. The Portuguese guard rested a hand on the hilt of his sword. "No one may enter."

He was not a novice like the *gros valet* guarding the prisoner cells had been. What could she do at this point? She recalled something Monsieur Kempe had said. "Tell him I wish to speak about the *Sagrados Inocentes.*"

The guard frowned. He knocked on the door. It cracked open. He leaned in and murmured in Portuguese. "The woman here wants to talk to da Gama."

"So?"

"Says she has information about the *Sagrados.*"

"What could she know?"

"I have no clue. Tell the master."

"You tell him!"

So, a ship by that name existed. That was two of Kempe's details proven true.

The door opened further. "*Senhora.*"

With a strong sensation of foreboding, Zahra stepped inside the Tower. She stopped short, blocked by what appeared to be a huge wooden shield that emanated a resinous scent. It had not been here ten years ago. A Portuguese coat of arms emblazoned the gigantic sculpture. Past the shield, sunlight streamed through clover-shaped windows, illuminating languid specks of dust. Those were the last windows one would see in this tower until reaching its apex, the Solar, where her mother's bedchamber had been.

From behind the shield, metal-heeled boots clacked. Two men appeared.

One wore a velvet doublet and sleek leather shoes. The corner of his thin-mustached mouth tucked into an unimpressed smile. Beside him hovered a bald Arab in expensive white robes.

Zahra tipped her chin, careful not to bow. "You must be Diogo da Gama."

Instead of respond to Zahra, he turned to his impeccably dressed manservant. "Sohrab?"

The fellow then enunciated a crisp interpretation of her French into Portuguese. Sohrab must be his interpreter.

Diogo da Gama turned back to Zahra—and he also did not bow to her. "And this must be the prodigal *princesa.*" *Princess.*

Zahra glanced at the shield sculpture that dwarfed them all three times—at least. "This is new."

The men craned to look at the gigantic shield. Diogo clasped his hands behind his back. "Commissioned by Abdul-Rahman himself."

"Is it meant to dissuade prying eyes?"

"How… uncivil." Diogo frowned. "It symbolizes protection. To Christians, nothing is more important than protecting the world from evil. What we do here achieves just that."

"What do you do that protects the world from evil?"

Diogo's cheeks creased into a smile that didn't reach his eyes. "Something that I need to get back to, presently. You had a question for me?"

Zahra's pulse quickened. "Your ship, *Sagrados Inocentes,* has very special cargo."

Diogo da Gama's eyes bugged. "How could you possess knowledge of the cargo on my ship?"

She spoke over the interpreter. "Am I right in assuming you do not wish the king's guard to conduct a search of the vessel upon its arrival?"

Da Gama adjusted his ruffled cuffs. His interpreter added, "This woman may be called a princess, but she has no real power."

Zahra's teeth clenched. The nebulous nature of her title had been her only leverage in this conversation.

Diogo twitched his fingers in a small beckoning gesture. Two Portuguese guards approached her from behind. The soft scrape of metal on leather sliced through the air as they eased their swords out of their sheaths.

He offered her a bland smile. "Am I right in assuming you do not wish the *malik* to know that you trifle in his business relationships?"

CHAPTER 8

Zahra did not turn; the guards might seize her the moment she did.

"Take the *princesa* to a holding chamber until I can speak to the *malik*."

Sohrab chuckled. "Perhaps you can ply her with wine, master. It worked on the drunken *rainha*." *Queen.*

Thump thump.

That sensation again! Energy gathered and radiated from her midsection. She pressed a hand to her stomach, raising her voice. "*Quem semeia ventos, colhe tempestades.*" *Whoever sows winds, reaps storms.*

Sohrab's face turned a bright shade of red.

She closed her hand over the pouch holding her stones, but feigned confidence. "You should find a competent interpreter, *senhor*."

A fat horsefly buzzed around Sohrab's bald head. He waved it away. Diogo straightened and nodded to his soldiers. The interpreter slapped at another large fly weaving around him. She did not turn but heard the guards approaching her.

Sohrab cried out in pain, slapping his neck. Blood spotted his throat. His features twisted in fear at the arrival of several more horseflies. They were so large, she could see their iridescent green eyes from several feet away.

"What are these vermin?" Diogo stepped back, waving his guards over. One of them whipped at the flies with a handkerchief. They seemed to multiply, undulating only around Sohrab.

He cried out to Allah, swiping at the air.

Zahra backed up. The fierce beasts clung to Sohrab's flesh even as he slapped them. Blood sprinkled over his white robes.

A guard cried out, "What did you put on your skin, man?" and another suggested they throw him in the fountain, and yet another had a tremor in his voice as he said, "Where are they coming from?"

Sohrab fled beyond the shield statue. His screams, like a young boy's, pierced the air. Zahra turned and ran back out the doors. She scraped her fingers under her belt, yanking out Hadiza's cloth. The pulsing sensation at her midriff ceased. She dodged behind a large granite column. The swarm of flies surged out through the doorway in a rippling mass. She ducked as they whizzed past her head.

Just before a soldier closed the Tower al-Garbu doors, through the sliver, she caught sight of Diogo da Gama's eyes on her.

• • • • •

"Why would traders be given an entire tower?" Zahra stood before *malik* Jabir in the golden throne hall.

Jabir drummed his ringed fingers on the golden arm of his throne. "I told you not to go into that tower, daughter."

Sohrab's vicious horsefly attack flashed in her mind. The idea the cloth had caused it was absurd. Though at this point her concept of the absurd had become more malleable.

In the huge, gilded hall, at the bottom of the stairs leading to the altar of thrones, Zahra stood, insignificant. Expansive, open-air windows revealed a deep violet sky. Palace warriors lined the walls and Jabir's female servants hung by, waiting. An empty throne sat beside him.

How could she explain she had returned to Marbella to save a random Moorish girl, who, by the way, claimed other children were trapped in this palace somewhere? She needed proof, lest she be considered mad, or worse; an imposter posing as the long-lost *amira.*

Speaking of mad, she had returned to rolling the lodestones behind her back again.

"I wished to visit mother's chamber."

Jabir rubbed his graying beard. "After your mother died, Marbella declined. So, I gave the tower to the traders in return for protection."

Jabir had allowed a serpent to slither into their garden. She took a step forward. "Respectfully, *malik,* I believe the traders are hiding something."

Mirthful wrinkles formed around Jabir's eyes. "You are just like your mother. Always on a mission. You look just like her, too."

Zahra suppressed a smile. "Why did Marbella decline?"

Jabir gestured to Raha's throne, an expectant gleam in his eyes. Zahra cast a quick glance around the large hall. Should she sit in Raha's throne? She couldn't argue with the king, could she? She traversed the steps and perched on the edge of the gilded chair, placing her hands in her lap, hiding her stone rolling habit.

Jabir leaned into the armrest. "Do you remember the day I married your mother?"

Zahra tried to remember when she was three. "There was a heavy rain. They had to rush everything inside the palace."

A fond smile spread across Jabir's face. His eyes glistened. "That rain marked the end of a seven-week drought."

"You believe your marriage was responsible?"

His dark eyes settled upon her. "Allah blessed our union many times over since that day. Supernatural wealth and strength flowed from Marbella."

Zahra recalled their mother teaching her and Raha the history of caliphates, the precursors to their failures, and strategies for quelling a rebellion. "Wasn't mother well-versed in military tactics and imperial leadership?"

Jabir tipped his head back into a hearty laugh. "Daughter, do you think your mother's education explains our prosperity?"

Her mouth opened and closed again. Why insist on arguing? To what gain? The throne had a hard, uncomfortable edge.

Jabir chuckled. "Your mother was well-educated but also anointed by Allah."

Zahra swallowed, thinking of what Biko had revealed—that Jabir believed a Moorish prostitute and her two illegitimate daughters to be the three goddesses venerated by some of the Qurayshi people.

Though she would not dare accuse him. "Then why did Allah allow her to die?"

Jabir twisted the wiry beard hairs at his chin. His gaze drifted across the empty hall, as if he imagined the ghost of Ghaliba bowing to him the day he met her. "It was time for a new era to begin. A new birth."

Zahra's breath left her. "Are you saying that Allah killed her?"

"He kills us all, daughter. I wish it had been me. But he had other plans."

His gaze landed on her, full of longing. She sprung to her feet and bowed. "*Malik*, where was my slave taken?"

Jabir leaned back at her sudden rise. He chuckled. "I wish you would not be so formal with me. Call me what you used to."

"*Baba.*" It relieved her to say it. That was how she remembered him.

"It is good to hear that again." Jabir's eyelids creased as he smiled. He gestured with a ringed hand, and a young maidservant poured wine into a goblet from a dull gold pitcher. "Drink with me. We shall discuss why your slave does not belong here. First reason: he is *uroubi*."

The servant poured wine into a second goblet. Zahra shook her head. "*Baba*, I acquired him through great effort, and do not wish it to be in vain."

Jabir sipped, analyzing her. "Could he fight off a lynx?"

"I do not plan to enter the forest."

"Sometimes they wander out where they do not belong." Jabir dabbed his beard with a fine white napkin. "And they need to be put down."

Her heart seized. Had Kempe been harmed? Was he 'processed'—and buried? She was supposed to detest him, but the very thought that she had watched him walk through the *alfiz* archway to his death made her feel ill.

Jabir ran his fingertips up and down the neck of his goblet. "Out of respect for you, the *uroubi* was taken to the slave wing. He cannot roam in towers where our women are."

Zahra hid her relieved exhale by bowing. "Thank you, *Baba*."

"Daughter, I warn you. Should the *uroubi* misstep, I would not hesitate to have him executed. One mistake. That is it."

Zahra nodded. Jabir flicked his fingers, and two of his warriors stepped forward. "My finest shall accompany you until your celebration at moonrise. There, we shall drink to the tale of where you went, and how you returned."

Dreading the prospect of making up some elaborate lie to cover up an impossible truth, she bowed, yet again. "I know where the slave quarters are. I do not need an escort."

"They are not escorting you, daughter. They are keeping an eye on you."

• • • • •

The watchdog warriors followed her through the *alfiz* archway. A broad staircase led them to the depths of the palace where slaves dwelled. She strode ahead of them as if they were her lapdogs.

The labyrinthine slave wing had not changed in the last decade. As a child, Zahra often hashed together broken sentences in the slaves' native languages, which had earned her easy praise.

They ended up at a small chamber, a thick textile serving as a door. Inside, a man prayed quietly. It was Kempe's voice, but the words were humble, reverent, and grateful.

She should probably thrust the curtain open and order him around like a slave. Instead, she could only bring herself to clear her throat.

He stopped praying. The textile slid aside. Kempe filled the doorway, a tinge of scarlet just under his nose. A cut on his cheekbone had bruised. His clothes had dried, but his hair still appeared damp. He opened his mouth to speak but stopped.

Heat rose to her cheeks. How must she look to him in this skimming silk gown, her glossy hair free? She lifted the pashmina to cover her bare shoulders. "Yusef beat you?"

"We had a non-verbal exchange." He eyed the two soldiers standing in the narrow hallway behind her.

Zahra frowned. If Kempe had laid a finger on Yusef, he should not be standing here. "He could have easily killed you."

His gaze settled on her like a weight. "I am surprised to see you here."

She shrugged, not wishing him to know she had been worried. "Some things happened."

"Some things?"

Zahra sighed. "I paid a visit to Diogo da Gama. Now Jabir has given me 'escorts.'"

His eyes flashed with anger. "You could have gotten yourself killed. Is Diogo aware you are looking for the children?"

As he said it aloud, Zahra realized how reckless she had been. Still, she had the urge to defend herself. "I employed courage. That was what you asked of me in France, was it not?"

As Zahra's voice rose, the warriors shifted, bristling. Kempe seemed to calm, though his tone remained strained. "You should have thought before acting."

It was not the first time she had heard such criticism. She turned to the broad-faced Arab warrior with the fixed stare of an ox. "Get some appropriate clothes for this slave."

The man's nostrils flared, even as he bowed. "*Amira*, we are the king's warriors. We do not do such tasks."

"Do you think if I asked, the *malik* would not demote you to slave?" After he did not move, she snapped, "Find someone else to do it, then."

The warrior's lips pinched. He marched down the hall, spear in hand. The other warrior stood straighter.

Kempe slid his gaze to Zahra. "Settling into the '*amira*' role rather quickly."

Zahra just shooed him inside the small chamber. Let people think whatever they liked about her setting foot in here. As far as they knew, she was having a discussion with her property. She extracted her rolling stones from the small pouch on her belt. "Marbellans respond to strength."

Kempe just watched her. She pretended not to notice, instead eyeing his pantry-sized chamber lit by a bright lantern. A stiff wool quilt draped over a rope bed. She perched on the edge, and he settled down on the other end, its lattice of taut ropes creaking under his weight. Guilt tugged at her—but she needed only to reach into the recent past to ease it. She would never forget his furious expression as he hurled her into that blazing fire.

She stopped turning the stones in her palm. "Wait a minute. Before you pushed me, I had cut you."

Fingers laced loosely in his lap, he nodded. "You did. Quite deep. I bled a lot."

Another irritating knot of guilt formed in her stomach. "I should say you deserved it."

The silence that unfolded between them was so complete, she heard the warrior's leather armor shift just outside. She refused to express interest in how his hand had fared these last several hours. It was devoid of gauze, or dressings, or anything of the like. What had he done to staunch the bleeding?

"I could have a medic come take a look at it."

His mouth pressed into a smile. "Thank you. But no need."

Zahra openly scoffed. He knew she was curious but did not volunteer more information. She would not give him the satisfaction of asking. "What did you wish to tell me?"

Monsieur Kempe's gaze grew measured, as if readying for a dangerous stunt. "This is not the first time you have come back to Marbella."

"I am aware. I grew up here." She shifted on the hard edge of the bed.

He shook his head slowly. "No. I mean you have come *back* before. You have done all of this once already. You tried to save Hadiza, and you failed."

Heat flushed through her. "How dare you say that to me?"

Kempe sat forward, his eyes clear and urgent. "I do not mean you will fail. In fact, I believe you will succeed. This is your second chance."

She closed her eyes a moment, trying to reason through his statement. A delicate whirring arose from the lodestones. "Are you saying that I lost my memory of being here before?"

"That is not what I am saying, Zahra."

"Then out with it, Stephen!"

Her heart fluttered. Using his given name felt too personal. Although she noticed her name fell off his lips rather freely.

He scooted to face her. "When I followed you into the fire, I did not end up in Marbella like you did."

"Why *did* you follow me?"

He frowned, as if the answer should be obvious. "I needed you to have any chance of surviving here."

Zahra swallowed. She longed to retract her question because his answer made too much sense. She did not wish to let go of her resentment.

More quietly, Stephen added, "It does not excuse how I went about it. I am not the same man now that I was then."

She searched his gaze for deceit. The Stephen Kempe she remembered had cold, shadowy eyes that never looked upon her more than a passing glance, and in doing so, conveying disdain. Right now—these were the determined eyes of a man who cared.

Zahra still could not trust him. She almost stood, but Stephen slid next to her. He tugged back his sleeve and held out his palm. She drew back—but curiosity stopped her.

A jagged, white scar line ran from the base of his middle finger over his palm, and into the edge of his wrist. She set aside her stones and took hold of his hand, running one of her thumbs over the scar line. This could not possibly be the cut she had made only hours earlier, in France.

"Show me your other hand." She lifted her gaze to his, finding him closer than she had thought. She gave him his hand and drew back.

Stephen cleared his throat, flashing her his other palm. Unscathed.

She whispered, "How?"

"Time. I spent a lot of time in between France and Marbella."

Zahra shook her head. "It was only minutes."

"Not for me." He showed her his healed hand again.

Her heart palpitated. Perhaps he already had that scar. Had she actually cut him? She recalled the moment; the sensation of the blade sinking into his flesh, and his harsh reaction. His blood had flowed freely. Tension mounted in Zahra's chest. She stood.

Stephen sat straighter. "I have much more to tell you, Zahra."

"There is a gathering on the beach tonight, at moonrise. Until then, rest."

"I should take a nap?"

His sarcasm irked her. "If you are caught among our women—well, if you do anything that could be misconstrued or seen as offensive—the *malik* has informed me it will not be tolerated."

Stephen stood, filling the space in front of her. "We must find time."

"If your claim that Hadiza would not arrive for seven days is true, that gives us the luxury of time." Her voice sounded panicked. She turned to leave.

"*Amira.*" Stephen's voice stopped her at the doorway. A familiar soft clack rang out. He came up beside her, presenting her lodestones in his scarred palm. "Marbellans respond to strength."

She sent him a glare as she scooped up the stones. Was that amusement that shone in his eyes? She didn't wish to stare, so she whisked past the warrior down the hall.

CHAPTER 9

In the lush Lynx Tower, Zahra sank into her bed, a far more luxurious situation than what she had in France. Every bone found relief as she fell into a deep sleep.

When she awoke, the sun had set, and a beeswax candle flickered on the vanity. The drawn balcony curtains revealed a twinkling black sky. Arabic music pounded in the distance. With a sinking feeling, she realized all that had happened had not been a nightmare.

When Stephen had shown her his healed scar, her rationalism had taken a hit. She had rushed out to hold fast to her sanity. But that was not the only reason, was it? Twelve hours ago, she had been certain he despised her. Now, at a mere glance from him, nervous tension built inside of her.

Standing in the mirror, she arranged her tresses and the simple gold headdress. Hadiza's cloth remained secure under her fitted belt, the worry stones pouch dangling on her hip. Her soft strappy sandals cushioned her steps. She reached for the plum pashmina but paused. Her sleeveless ivory dress had a high neck. Why encumber herself with fabrics and layers, as in France? She left the pashmina behind.

The ox-faced warrior stood outside her chamber door. He escorted her to the gleaming palace foyer where servants raced about completing last-minute tasks for the celebration. Several maidservants scurried alongside her, touching up her lip color and massaging apricot oil into her hands and forearms.

A decorated camel cart waited for her at the bottom of the stairs. The knobby kneed camel truffled its lips, decorative knits draped over its hump. She climbed in and sat on a large damask pillow. Sukayna joined her in a simple gown and the burgundy veil her mother had given her. She found herself roving the villagers who had come to the palace entry way to see her off. Had Stephen's nap run long?

A young Moorish boy held a short black camel whip and bowed to Zahra. She had planned to tip her head magnanimously but yelped instead as the cart angled dramatically downward. The camel had crouched to its knees, allowing the boy to jump on. The people standing around laughed good-naturedly as she clung to a corner post. Sukayna grinned. The cart straightened and they set off.

The cart bumped past the palace gate and ran smooth over packed sand. Marbella's foliage passed by in a rush until the beach came into view. The stars glittered and the half-moon hung low in the sky. The scent of seasoned meats and the sound of sizzling vegetables drifted on the salty breath of the sea.

Marbella's celebrations were legendary, but had she ever seen quite this many people? She rubbed her moist palms on the pillow. Would they jeer at her? Call her a curse upon Marbella? Act indifferently?

An elaborate scaffold constructed on the beach came into view. The *malik* and *malika* perched in golden chairs with lofted backs, and a damask tent with multiple peaks rose behind them. Carpets and hundreds of lounging pillows sprinkled the platform and the sand beyond. Several torches created the boundaries of the event. Warriors guarded the shoreline, should any neighboring nations decide to show up during their very visible celebration.

Some noticed the arrival of the camel cart and ran toward it.

Although everyone grinned, she could not shake the sensation that it could be a set up for Jabir's revenge. Perhaps he would have her publicly dragged to the sand and humiliated or stoned.

Her hand shook as she accepted a warrior's assistance down the ladder. Marbellans surrounded her, crying out.

"Joyful return, *amira!*"

"You are as beautiful as the ocean!"

"I knew your mother!"

"Allah's glory to you, *amira*!"

"Welcome home!"

Three men sitting on the sand in front of the stage pounded a jubilant beat on *darkbouka* goblet drums. A beaming, elderly woman tapped a *taarija* on her hip, and two singers ululated in harmony. Several other musicians lounged barefoot on embroidered cushions, plucking at lutes and *rababs*. Each note resonated in Zahra's chest. She did not deserve this.

Maidservants threw geranium petals in the path ahead of her. The smell of burnt wood hung on the air as a fire burst to life down the beach, signifying that the guest of honor had arrived. Cheers rang out over the music.

Zahra stepped onto the royal scaffold and bowed to Raha and Jabir. Jabir lit up when he saw her. Raha took a sip of wine instead of acknowledging her. She wore sunset hues and mulberry rouge colored her full lips. Zahra had loved Raha more than anything in the world, and now they were like enemies—or worse, strangers.

Standing nearby, Biko bowed to Zahra. His contagious grin was overshadowed by the sight of Stephen in Marbellan garb, whose eyes were on her. The firelight cast him in a warm glow, and he had never looked so fresh. She forced her gaze away; afraid she had looked too long. This beach, this firelight, this music—and this man—were dangerous.

"*Amira* Zahra." Jabir announced. Cheers erupted. The moment she took his hand, he lifted her arm up and addressed the people. "We are overjoyed to have our *amira* back after all this time. Enjoy Allah's blessings on his beach. Celebrate his greatness with dance, laughter, and love."

Delighted shouts rang out. Jabir guided her to sit on the opposite side of him. The spot was only on the end of a long bench, but being placed beside him was a notable gesture. Zahra swallowed.

"I have met your *uroubi.*" Jabir's voice was low as he took his seat and leaned toward her. "He does not seem like a slave."

Zahra's teeth grit. Could Stephen not play the part better? She snuck a glance at him standing several feet away. He returned her gaze, his eyes reflecting the glow of the bonfire in the distance. "In Europe, slaves are not as they are here."

Jabir sipped from his goblet and did not respond. It unnerved her. Did he think she was lying? Her fingers flexed. She resisted the urge to fumble in the pouch for her lodestones. A bead of sweat trickled down the back of her neck.

She added, "They are not traded or sold like goods, as they are here. They are bound by land or domestic duties."

"Tell me, daughter." Jabir's eyes bore down on her. "Where exactly did you go all those years ago? And by what means did you return?"

Zahra's neck muscles tightened. "France."

"Who took you there?"

This was not a conversation. It was an interrogation. Her fears resurfaced—the ones she had the night Lord Raymond had helped her escape Marbella. If Jabir discovered his identity, he could send someone to assassinate Lord Raymond.

She accepted a goblet from a passing servant, if only to distract from Jabir's stare. "I was a resourceful nine-year-old. It was a long time ago. Those details do not matter, anymore."

"There is one detail that bothers me, daughter. You, in the middle of a shark infested ocean, with that man." He pointed to Monsieur Kempe. "With zero evidence of a shipwreck. For the sake of my life, I cannot solve the mystery."

Though Zahra had not planned to take to drink this evening, she took an especially long sip. The tangy wine was difficult to swallow. With a fingertip, she dabbed a droplet off the corner of her lip. "Honestly, *baba,* I have been trying to figure it out myself. I may suffer from lost memories, caused, perhaps, by hitting my head. Such events exist on record."

She almost began chattering about Lord Raymond's various medical studies but thought better of it.

He sent her a sidelong stare. "Lost memories?"

She tucked her shoulder. "Just a theory? It is a mystery to me, entirely."

"And did your 'slave' have a lapse of memory, too?"

Zahra glanced at Stephen, who was focused on something. She followed his gaze, and there was Yusef, cutting through the crowd like a bull shark. His turban flowed, his extravagant robes rivaling the king's. He had a cut on the bridge of his arched nose, from which purple bruises splayed under each eye.

If Stephen had done that, how had he not been executed?

"*Malik. Malika.*" Yusef ascended the steps of the scaffold. He held a rope connected to a baby goat shaking its head playfully. "I present tonight's first sacrifice in honor of our returned *amira*."

The people cheered.

Alarmed, Zahra turned sharply to Jabir. "Sacrifice?"

"It is our custom, daughter. Surely you remember that much?"

She sank back, avoiding his gaze. The goat had a tuft of fanned fur between its lopsided ears. She could not hold back. "Is this celebration not for me? I would prefer to feed, care for, and raise the goat to be free and be happy."

"Ha," uttered Raha, immediately burying herself in a long sip of wine as everyone looked in her direction. Zahra had the sudden urge to thrust her own wine upon her sister. The feeling passed. She deserved the jeer from Raha. And worse.

The goat bleated. Her step-uncle's eyes were on her. "We express our gratitude to Allah when we sacrifice a pure creature."

Yusef gestured to a servant, who plucked up the small creature and took it away.

Nauseated, Zahra gripped the goblet until its jewels pinched her skin. The sound of galloping drew everyone's attention.

Twelve camels hurtled toward the beach wearing white hoods with red crosses. They pulled a cart emblazoned with the Portuguese coat-of-arms.

Anyone sitting stood, including Jabir. The camels rounded to a halt, and they sank to their knees as if in worship. The riders hopped down, marching around to open the cart.

Diogo da Gama stepped out in a flowing wool cape lined with ermine fur. A wide-brimmed hat cast half his face in shadow. He raised his hands to greet Marbella. The people cheered, lifting their mugs and lamb legs into the air.

Who was this man?

After a flick of his fingers, his men withdrew items from the cart—wineskins, flasks of oil, troves of vibrant colored silks, and what looked to be small coin satchels. The people descended, receiving the gifts with cries of excitement.

The drumbeat resumed. Raha slid back into her throne, but Jabir remained standing. Zahra's senses tingled at a presence at her back. Stephen now stood behind her on the scaffold, watching the traders approach.

Da Gama made his way through the crowd. Marbellans stooped reverently as he passed, like he was a living deity. Yusef's upper lip curled in a poor attempt at a smile as he watched the trader's approach.

Malik Jabir bowed. "Master Diogo da Gama. We are honored."

Da Gama jumped onto the scaffold, the corner of his mouth tweaked in a perpetual expression of indifference. He bowed, but not deeply enough, in Zahra's opinion. Why would Jabir stand for this man? Why was he allowed on the platform at all? He addressed them in Portuguese. "Sohrab cannot assist me tonight."

An awkward silence descended. Diogo da Gama's eyes landed on her, expectant.

Zahra frowned. "Certainly, you do not wish to demote me to 'interpreter' at my own celebration, *senhor.*"

"Of course not." He smiled, turning to Jabir. "I shall take my leave."

Zahra waved farewell.

"Daughter." Jabir's voice was like gravel in her ear. "If you speak his language, I ask that you tell us what has been said."

Diogo paused in his retreat.

She wished to refuse. But what was she to do? All eyes were on her. Her face grew warm. She clasped a hand over the pouch on her hip, feeling the hard lodestones inside. "He said his interpreter is not present."

The smile that stretched across Diogo's face revealed his thin, lizard-like teeth. He turned to Yusef nearby. "*Amir*. What in God's name happened to your face?"

Zahra relished relaying that particular message. Yusef shot a deadly look in Stephen's direction. "It had nothing to do with God."

Diogo cast a glance to Stephen, seeming to catch on. "Is whoever did that to you dead?"

Yusef scowled. "Unfortunately, not."

"Then that man's God might have had something to do with it."

Gripping his spear, Yusef's knuckles whitened. "He was protected only by the order of the *malika*."

Zahra stuttered on the final word, 'queen,' and looked to Raha. Her sister lifted her chin, hooded eyes upon her step-uncle, Yusef. "The *uroubi* did nothing to provoke your brutality—his hands had been bound." Each of Raha's clipped words cut. "If you should ever become *malik*, you are free to allow violence to run rampant."

While interpreting, Zahra suppressed a smile. An amused snort burst from Jabir, but he sent Raha a warning glance. She raised her goblet, looking at Zahra. No—the look went above Zahra. To Stephen.

Cheers erupted from down the beach. Agile dancers moved in unison around the bonfire. Rosemary wafted on the cool, festive air. A young maid served Jabir a large platter of food. He bit into a leg of lamb. Zahra caught a glimpse of Sukayna exiting the tent with a plate.

"Has your mistress had you convert?" Diogo spoke across the scaffold to Stephen in accented English.

Although Jabir was known to rule with tolerance for other religions, she worried the topic could serve as an excuse to condemn Stephen.

Everyone's expectant gazes weighed on her. "Master da Gama asked if I allow him to practice his chosen religion."

They looked at Stephen, who remained silent. Chewing, Jabir motioned to him with his bejeweled hand. "Do answer, *uroubi*."

Stephen tipped into a respectful bow. "I am Christian."

Diogo's eyes crinkled in a smile. "We are lucky *malik* Jabir is a tolerant leader. I have even seen some villagers worshiping the goddesses of Mecca."

Jabir nodded magnanimously to Diogo, who snatched something from one of his men waiting on the sand. He produced a crafted bow tipped in silver. "I love a good dueling gods game."

Zahra stumbled over her interpretation of the strange comment. Sukayna crept over, presenting Zahra with a platter of delicately chopped lamb, warm bread, lentils, and grapes on the vine. Not hungry, she considered offering it to Stephen, but struck the idea. He could eat when they got back to France.

Zahra cast her a grateful smile but shook her head. Sukayna's eyebrows rose.

Jabir hummed a chuckle as he suckled meat off the lamb bone. "Master da Gama, here, we do not put gods to the test."

"Did I ask you?" Master da Gama's bulging eyes shined, the corner of his mouth tucked deeply.

Straightening, Jabir passed his plate off to a servant. After a long, tense moment, Jabir offered a reconciliatory smile. "How could arrows tell us whose god is most powerful?"

Diogo took a sideways step to block Sukayna from stepping off the scaffold. Holding the platter, she bowed, not looking up at Diogo. "This slave is Muslim, is she not?"

The tension was thick like smoke. Zahra did not wish to continue, but Jabir nudged her.

Diogo pointed the bow at Stephen. "And this slave is Christian."

Stephen stared upon the trader whose name he had foretold this morning. Why had she lacked the presence of mind to ask Stephen more about that earlier?

Zahra leaned to murmur to Jabir, "Why do we allow this trader to mock us, *malik*?"

Jabir did not acknowledge her. Yusef appeared more amiable toward the trader, pantomiming pulling an arrow back. "What do we shoot?"

Diogo tossed the bow to Yusef, who reflexively caught it in mid-air. "Them. And they pray to be spared."

"Tell us what he said, daughter."

Jabir would surely shut down this foolishness. She leaned toward him. "To see whose god is more powerful, the slaves shall pray the arrow misses them."

Those within earshot inhaled gasps. Sukayna's shoulders caved inward. Even Yusef cocked an eyebrow. Some of the chatter faded as people began to notice something happening.

Diogo's gaze roved from person to person, as if he relished their shock. "We shoot. They fervently pray. If the arrow lands true, their god is false. Belomancy."

Zahra's voice rose. "That is not how belomancy works."

"It is today," he snapped. His soldier produced a leather quiver full of arrows. He withdrew a black one with feathered fletching. Its metallic point glinted. He held it out.

Yusef closed his fingers over the arrow. "Mine is for the *uroubi*."

Raha sat up straight. Diogo turned and called out. "Put them before the fire."

Diogo flicked his fingers, and two of his men crawled onto the scaffold like a pair of roaches. One of them grabbed Sukayna, who dropped the platter of food and screamed.

Everyone turned to *malik* Jabir. They awaited his word on whether this should be allowed. He rested his mouth on his fist, saying nothing.

Zahra's stomach sank. "You are to allow this?"

A shadow fell over Zahra. A soldier approached.

Stephen stepped out from behind her, towering over him and shooting him a sharp glare. "I shall go willingly."

The soldier edged back. Stephen dropped off the stage and the crowd parted as he strode toward the fire. Sukayna's body was taut as they hauled her, her dragging feet leaving two stripes in the sand.

Raha stiffened, her eyes alert. She had stopped Yusef from harming Stephen earlier, yet she did nothing, now. Zahra turned to Jabir. "*Baba*, she was given as my maidservant, and he is my property. I shall not have them harmed."

Yusef tested the tautness of the string. "If you did not wish him to be harmed, little Zahra, then you should not have brought him."

Still resting his mouth against his knuckles, Jabir slid his eyes to Zahra. Tacit agreement. She could not stop this. Again, without power among men.

Or was she without courage?

Yusef nocked the arrow just as Stephen turned to face them, the fire blazing behind him. Zahra was reminded of the forest in France. At that time, she had hated him. Now, knowing Yusef's skill with weaponry could have only improved in the last decade, nausea swept over her at what she was about to witness—the execution of a changed man at the hands of the vilest of them.

Yusef called out, "Pray to your false god, *uroubi*."

The soldiers stepped out of the line of fire. Stephen must have gathered the prince's meaning, as his reply carried easily across the beach. "No need, if your aim is as weak as your fist."

Diogo snorted. Though Yusef did not know what Stephen had said, his lips pinched. He raised the bow and arrow and tilted his head to aim. In her utter powerlessness, Zahra had a sudden urge to pray. But to what or whom?

He roared, "*Allahu akbar!*" *Allah is great*. The shaft of the arrow scraped the belly of the bow and flew. Zahra pressed her hands to her mouth. Stephen stood still, a strong breeze rippling his tunic.

It hurtled past him, disappearing into the fire. Legs shaking, Zahra sat back on the bench, relief washing over her like a chilly rain.

Yusef cursed under his breath. Stephen turned and helped Sukayna draw to a stand. He spoke to her out of their earshot, and Sukayna nodded, her eyes full of tears. What could he say to her that she would understand?

Diogo extracted the bow from Yusef. In Portuguese, Zahra asked, "Why are you doing this, da Gama?"

The trader smiled and nocked his arrow, raising it to eye level. "I need you to know who you are dealing with. These people are mine. And I do not wish what is mine to be taken from me. This is all for you, *princesa*."

Her limbs grew heavy. Jabir had a hard line between his eyebrows.

"Please stop him, *baba*," she whispered.

Jabir's gaze darted between her and Diogo, whose torso was straight as he drew back the arrow. Sukayna clenched her hands together, her back hunched, shoulders tucked inward.

Stephen knelt in the sand beside her, bowing his head.

Whispers rippled across the crowd.

"What is he doing?" Diogo's voice rose as he switched to English. "That is not how this works!"

With his eyes closed, Stephen's forearm rested on his uplifted knee like a knight receiving honors, lips moving in what appeared to be prayer. Sukayna pressed her forehead into her laced hands, tears trembling off her jawbone. Her burgundy veil, the gift from Ghaliba, fluttered in the wind.

"It changes nothing. It means nothing." Diogo raised the bow again. Stephen was near enough to Sukayna that a misfire could easily hit him. Her veil whisked off and flowed on a gust straight into the fire. It burnt to a crisp in seconds.

"I have an announcement." Jabir drew to a stand, his voice commanding. The people turned to him. He held out his hand to Zahra. Shaking, she took it. He pulled her to a stand.

"It is time we bring back the prosperity we knew when Ghaliba was our *malika*. I have decided to make her eldest daughter Zahra my queen, as she had once been destined. And our progeny shall be anointed."

The crowd erupted into cheers. The sky spun. Jabir's grip on her hand tightened. He still wanted to marry her? Even though he called her 'daughter?' Even while married to Raha?

Diogo let his arrow fly.

CHAPTER 10

Women laughed. Mosaic globe lamps flickered. Thick smoke floated in an assortment of colors. Sweet odor burned from a smoldering hookah. A half-dressed woman draped over Zahra's lap. When Zahra moved, the woman slumped over, passed out.

Where was she?

"*Amira*, where are you off to?" A different woman called out.

"It is yet your wedding night. Do not seek the *malik* tonight."

The women laughed from their bellies. A breeze lured her. She crawled toward it, navigating around various lounging women whose eyes rolled as they attempted to focus upon her.

"Have a draw, *amira*." Someone shoved the saliva-glistened tip of the hookah pipe in front of her. She knocked it aside and stumbled to a stand. The women dissolved into laughter. Zahra gripped the trunk of wood that supported the leather tent. She saw a sliver of light leading out of this infernal hookah den. She staggered toward it, splitting the lynx furs with her arms. She sucked in a deep breath of fresh, beachy air that had a hint of burnt firewood on it.

The half-moon winked as a cloud passed by. The rolling tide thundered in the distance. Chatter filtered from the dining tent, its taut canvas rumbling under a stiff breeze.

"Zahra."

Stephen Kempe emerged from beyond the throne scaffold, his tone urgent and somewhat reprimanding. But his rich, pleasing voice also held a note of relief, in the way a perfume might hold a hidden base note of rose or vanilla. As if gently pushed by the wind, vertigo swept over her. Then Stephen was beside her, his warm hands providing solid support. For a moment she leaned against him, unable to help but notice the sheer breadth of his chest and within it, a strong, beating heart. She exhaled and turned her gazed up to his face.

She tried to say, "How do you do that?" but instead, a raspy sound came out of her dry throat.

"You need water. Come with me."

She attempted to stand on her own as she cleared her throat obnoxiously. She pushed him back, waving him off. "Where are my watchdogs?"

"Took to drink." Stephen seemed reluctant to release her. He gestured for her to walk. The sand was soft underfoot. She tried to focus on Stephen's face. She wobbled, placing her hand on the nearest thing—a wooden beam on the back of the throne scaffold.

What had happened?

"Will you bring me the water? I will wait here." She took a deep breath, willing her senses to clear.

Stephen shook his head. "I will not leave you."

"Will you carry the future queen of Marbella?" Her tone came out harsher than she had intended. "I am sure Jabir would love that. Get me the water, or I will find an obedient slave to do it."

Ire flashed in his eyes, jaw tight. He bowed in a mockery of his supposed position as slave. He emphasized each word: "Stay right here."

As he jogged away, Zahra stole a glance at his loose-fitting Moroccan tunic and slacks. It was the simplistic garb of the slave class, yet somehow it looked pleasing on him. She huffed a breath, trying to clear her head. Muted chatter came from inside the hookah tent.

A seashell crunched under foot as someone approached her from behind. "Fitting I should find you here among the whores, intoxicated by *hul gil*."

Yusef. Dread tingled over her back. She did not turn. The last thing she recalled was him shooting at Stephen and missing. Then Diogo had let an arrow fly. Had Sukayna been hit? She recalled Jabir's announcement to marry her. A memory flashed to that terrible night ten years ago, after a similar announcement. Jabir had declared his marriage to little Zahra, usurping Yusef's claim on her. After that, Yusef's gaze had turned mean and covetous. She peeked over her shoulder, and found he had the same look on his face now.

"Leave me." Her voice held no power.

"You must feel very satisfied with yourself. The bastard daughter of a *qayna* has accomplished the impossible."

In a visceral response to his nearness, she began to tremble.

She stepped away, but he cut her off, drawing her into an embrace. Anyone observing would think *amir* Yusef was welcoming the long-lost princess. But she was bound by his embrace, unable to pull away. His heart hammered against her ear. He smelled like rosemary lamb and sweat.

Her voice wavered. "Let go of me."

His stiff beard rubbed her face, his humid breath coating her ear. "I have tried."

She shied away, pushing her hands against his ribs. Her heart raced like that of a hunted hare.

Sand scuffed over their feet and a deep voice burned. "How is your nose, *sahibu alsmu almalaki*?" *Your Royal Highness.*

Stephen spoke entirely in Arabic. He stood mere inches from them, holding a copper mug. Yusef released her and she stumbled backward.

The men stared each other down. Yusef's stained teeth flashed. "Your time is short, *salibiyyun*." *Crusader.* "I shall offer your rotting corpse to Allah."

Partygoers seemed sparse, but some had stopped to watch. The warrior prince departed with an arrogant swagger, greeted by several women. Zahra smoothed her hands over her dress, feeling dirtied by his touch.

She approached Stephen. "Is that for me?"

He did not seem to hear her, his attention still tight upon the retreating prince, his pulse visibly pumping on his throat. She peeled the mug of water out of his hand. After swallowing all the liquid, she handed it back. "I cannot remember anything after Jabir's announcement."

Stephen looked at the empty mug in his hand. "You tend to lose your memory when inebriated."

"What do you know of what I 'tend' to do?" Zahra rarely drank and she certainly did not approve of taking other substances, as they limited one's capacity to reason. "Is Sukayna well?"

She swayed, and Stephen's hand on her back steadied her. He nodded. "The arrow missed. But she is shaken."

Levity rose in her chest, causing her to smile. "Oh thank—thank you. For telling me."

She had almost thanked God. But that would play right into Diogo's sick little game, wouldn't it?

Stephen gestured toward the palace. "I shall escort you back. You need to rest."

Zahra nodded, experiencing an unusual sensation in her chest. Was she pleased Stephen escorted her? She lifted the hem of her ivory gown. Numbness coated her skin, and her muscles weighed her down. She released her hem for the work it took to hold it.

Celebrations always put the servants into loose moods. They could enjoy themselves. Turn in earlier. Sleep in longer. Praise Allah for the life he had given them. If Yusef were king, he would likely not be so lenient with his people. He was a man willing to play a killing game for entertainment. What kind of kingdom would Marbella become under his rule?

Although Jabir's cowardice with the trader, Diogo, was inexcusable.

What kind of difference could she make as *malika?* Although the idea of marriage to her mother's husband sickened her, she was tempted by the idea of having the queen's power. It would certainly make it easier to access the tower and find the children. She could request the Portuguese traders be cast out as a wedding gift. She shook the very thought.

They ascended limestone steps. Passing villagers bowed to her. Their reverence drummed up feelings of guilt because she planned to abandon them again. Didn't she? Zahra reached the top of the staircase and turned around, looking out over the beach. The moon had risen high, and the bonfire had dwindled. A few people still lounged on the beach, smoking and laughing. A longing entered her heart at the sight of her beloved Marbella. Could she leave again?

Stephen moved into her view. Even though he was two steps down from her, they were eye level.

Zahra lifted one eyebrow. "I will not fall down the stairs."

Something in his gaze made warmth pool in her chest. In a low tone, he said, "Just to be safe."

She turned, and they walked in silence for a time, passing under archways and through breezy, outdoor hallways. They strolled through a starry, fragrant garden. They arrived at the side entrance of the Lynx Tower, which was connected to the main palace by a bridged walkway.

Stephen unlatched the wrought iron gate and pulled it open. The hall had open-air windows and oversized décor. Her bedchamber was just around the corner at the end, where a lone torch burned.

"Monsieur Kempe, you cannot go past this point, or Yusef will..." She made a snipping sound and her fingers mimicked spring scissors.

The corners of his mouth tucked disapprovingly. For some reason, this pleased her.

Zahra put her hands on her hips. "Where are the guards? Someone could raid this tower, and nothing would be done."

"Everyone took to drink."

"Well—*you* could raid this tower, all by your sober self."

A smile touched his lips. Her pulse raced.

"Stop." She pointed. "Stop that. Whatever that is."

He only smiled more.

"What is your game, Stephen? As far as I know, you are a sorcerer. You contact spirits, demons, and other things."

A line formed between his eyebrows. "Not anymore. Those things are evil."

"You were evil."

"I was."

His bold admission made her lean back. She caught herself, her balance still tenuous. She gestured behind her. "I regret that you cannot walk me to my bedchamber."

Another smile, more pleased than the last, crossed Stephen's face. "As do I."

Her cheeks burned. Did *hul gil* cause one to abandon their reserve? She cleared her scratchy throat. "That is, I feel like such a commoner walking by myself."

Stephen chuckled.

Zahra gasped. "You can laugh?"

"Good night, Zahra." His gaze was as clear as verdant quartz.

She took a few steps backward. "Why are you looking at me like that, Stephen Kempe?"

"Why did you agree to wed Jabir?"

"I did not agree. I did not know. However, being queen would put me in a considerable position of power."

"Would it?"

She chuffed, an un-lady-like sound. "Can you imagine if I were to turn him down?"

Stephen shrugged. "You would lose whatever perceived status you have here."

His phrasing made her hesitate. Did he suggest she had no actual status? Beloved stepdaughter of the king and potential future queen? She was more than a commoner. Certainly more than a slave. "I would also lose any chance of gaining access to the tower. And perhaps be stoned by the people. Or be fed to the forest."

Stephen held her gaze. "'The Lord upholds all who fall and lifts up all who are bowed down.'"

She was pretty certain that was one of the Psalms. She paused near the end of the hallway. Why did she dawdle? "Have you thought of a better plan?"

"A few."

"Tomorrow. You shall tell all." She turned, attempting to keep her gait steady. Why was it so difficult to resist looking back? She wouldn't. Or perhaps she would when she moved around the corner. Only for a moment.

Zahra tsked herself—all this make-believe in her mind, and he was probably gone already, exhausted from the dueling gods game and shadowing her all night. Zahra rounded the bend and glanced back.

Stephen still stood at the gate, his eyes on her.

• • • • •

After rounding the corner out of Stephen's line of sight, Zahra leaned against the stone wall and closed her eyes. She still felt hazy. How had she ended up in that den? Another thing she should have asked Stephen. She never seemed to think clearly around him.

She opened her eyes. In front of her was the archway leading to a sentry bridge that ran alongside the Tower al-Garbu, where the roofs of two coned pillars converged. Perhaps it was the effects of the *hul gil,* but the climb did not seem so dangerous at the moment.

With the sky dark and most of Marbella asleep or inebriated, this could be her last chance to sneak into the Tower al-Garbu. Should there be a legion of Portuguese traders waiting inside, she would be helpless. But she could take a look, couldn't she? And if she were caught, surely they would not harm the woman Jabir had announced as the future queen of Marbella.

The bridge overlooked the ocean. During the day, Zahra would be plainly visible inching along the short railing. She found a hand hold in the curved wall of the tower, and, with earnest effort, pulled herself up. Once she hoisted her torso over, she swung her leg up. She ducked behind the gutter wall, out of sight once again.

The crevice smelled of mildew, having collected leaves and other unnamable muck. She swept away leaves on the stone floor to find the iron grate.

When this tower was built, Granadan tribes had been at war. Tower al-Garbu was intended to house their most valuable assets: treasures, women, children, and food. It had several false entrances, hideaways, and double walls. When young, Zahra would surprise her mother by showing up in random places. She wondered if the passageways had been discovered by the traders since they claimed the tower.

The rusted hinge of the grate squealed. She paused, looking behind her. She lay the grate open, lowering herself into the narrow passageway. It would be wise to close it behind her, but she could not stomach doing so.

The effects of the *hul gil* must be fading because her blood burned with dread. She would just find out if the trap door still led inside the tower, have a look, and leave. See if she could learn anything new that could help Hadiza—and the other children. Perhaps even Mary was here. The possibility spurred her forward.

The tight passage grew narrower until dead ending. She crouched and ran her hand over the dusty ground. She caught ahold of a metal ring and lifted the weighty wooden trapdoor. It slipped out of her grip, slamming closed and reverberating through the walls.

Breathless, she waited. If she were discovered, she would likely be taken to Diogo. After a long silence, she tried again, successfully opening the hatch and easing down into it.

She no longer had the luxury of standing. As she crawled, sullying her silk dress, a man's voice susurrated at a distance. She paused. It was the wee hours of the morning, yet this man chattered away. She continued, noting the voice came from the chamber directly beneath her. It was a Russian man. Odd—Stephen the European's arrival had been big news, but no one ever mentioned a Russian being in Marbella. Let alone inside the palace walls.

The glowing border of a trapdoor appeared ahead. She knew it opened into the ceiling of a bedchamber. She pressed her ear to the wood, listening to the Russian man's voice.

"—hate it when you call for God. Do you understand me?"

"*Tak, moy gosudar.*" *Yes, my lord.* A young boy spoke in Russian, but with an accent. Zahra pressed her hand to her mouth.

"Do you think if God were real, you would be here?"

After a long pause, the boy's voice cracked. "*Nyet, moy gosudar.*" *No, my lord.*

"Do not be sad. I will tell you a little secret, yes? These things—ghosts, angels, demons. They make me uneasy. So, I choose not to believe it."

Her muscles turned leaden at a distant scraping sound. If anyone found the open grate, she would be trapped. Still, she pressed her ear harder to the wood.

"Now be good."

"*Tak, moy gosudar.*"

More silence followed. Did the traders run an orphanage of some kind? Or perhaps they were being used for labor. Zahra knew these scenarios were irrational.

But any reasonable explanation was unthinkable.

Should she drop in to help the child? She could fight, but even if she had a dagger, going head-to-head with a man was incredibly risky. Especially if any guards came to his aid. The most likely result of entering this chamber now was that she would not make it out alive.

She was just about to draw away, but a sound caused her to pause.

The child had begun to cry.

• • • • •

Zahra slept off the effects of the *hul gil*, but her rest was fitful. She had chaotic nightmares about Hadiza and the crying boy. She woke up often, clutching her lodestones in her palms, checking the sky for daylight. At the first glow, she flung off the covers and bathed, scrubbing the events of the rough evening off with myrtle soap. She dressed in an airy, dove-gray dress fitted to her torso with a high neckline. She pinned the front of her swept hair to keep the curls from falling into her eyes. She tucked Hadiza's cloth in a silver brocade sash tied around her waist, the frantic buzzing of her lodestones wrapping around her as she left the bedchamber.

Jabir's watchdogs were nowhere in sight. Though many slept, several servants already hustled to prepare for the day's work. They looked twice as she rushed past the *alfiz* archway leading into the slave wing.

Stephen's curtain hung open, his small chamber empty. A coarse wool quilt lay folded on the rope bed, as if he had not slept. A thread of fear tickled through her stomach. Had he made it back after they parted ways? Or had Yusef made good on his threat?

A passing servant bowed, offering a morning blessing.

"Where is the *uroubi*?"

"He is causing a stir in the servant kitchen, *amira*."

Zahra hoisted her dress-hem and set off, imagining other servants brandishing blades against the 'crusader.' One of the first things Stephen had said to her when they arrived in Marbella was that they had to stay together. Yet she continued to cut their discussions short and leave him at the mercy of Marbella.

She pivoted around a corner, hastening down the narrow hallway. The doughy scent of fresh bread signaled she was close. The arched brick entrance leading into the slaves' kitchen came into view.

Zahra slowed at the sound of laughter—and a familiar voice. She clutched her stones to silence them.

"In England, food is bland like dirt."

Stephen. But he did not speak in English. Zahra remained out of view and gaped at Stephen Kempe speaking in Arabic.

"This is like food from the sky."

Several men and women laughed.

"You mean 'paradise,' *uroubi*," said a woman.

Zahra dared to peek. A hearth fire blazed as a cook slid in loaves of bread on a wood peel. Those eating were standing and plucking morsels off large, shared trays.

"Yes— 'paradise.'" Standing a head above most of them, Stephen picked up a flat bread at the end of the serving counter.

A Moor spoke with his mouth full, hunkered over a bowl. "Do you mean paradise for Europeans, or Marbellans?"

Those gathered snickered. Stephen replied in Arabic, "If food is this good in Marbellan paradise, I choose to go there."

They thought that was hysterical. A man in a sleek white turban threw up his hands. "Why did we ever fight the *salibiyyin*? We could have just fed them tasty food, and they would have bowed five times a day to Allah!"

Another wave of laughter compounded from the last. Stephen laughed, too. His genuine, uninhibited smile was arresting. He looked tired, but his eyes sparkled.

Her jaw set. Stephen understood every word spoken. This confirmed that he was not who he claimed to be. She stepped out from behind the wall. "Monsieur Kempe."

Those gathered looked up. Stephen stopped mid-chew. Servants bowed, snatched morsels off the counter, and dispersed in different directions. She recalled how she must look—regal in gray with sheer sleeves, silver appliques glittering in the firelight. The cook in the back continued his work, oblivious.

Stephen resumed chewing, observing the hasty retreat of his new friends. "Trouble sleeping?"

"Please, do not speak English on my account."

Stephen cleared his throat and gestured to a large dish holding a medley of nuts, meat, and dried fruit. "Have you tried this?" He still spoke English.

Zahra crossed the kitchen, her eyes hard upon him. "You knew Arabic this whole time?"

"It is lamb, eggplant, dried grapes, figs—"

"I know what is in *al-sikbaj*."

"—almonds. Honey. Cinnamon." He scooted the bowl toward her.

Zahra widened her eyes, switching to Arabic. "I am hungry only for an explanation."

Stephen dropped his gaze. "I have been meaning to tell you…"

She shook her head. This man was not to be trusted. If he could hide such a thing, then surely his motives with her—his kindness, protectiveness, warmth—were not pure. What was he after? "Been meaning to? If you ever had any interest in gaining my trust, Monsieur Kempe, you would have told me immediately."

His focus sharpened, eyes narrowed. "This is just one of many things you have not given me the time to tell you."

That was his excuse? He could have spoken in Arabic to her at any moment, or to anyone else, for that matter. He had greeted Yusef in Arabic and he had appeared to speak to Sukayna. Zahra hadn't put the pieces together. Still, he had not mentioned it. She had even translated for him several times. She measured her breathing. "Fine. Now is your time."

He dipped the flat bread into creamy ground chickpeas soaked in golden oil. "You taught me."

Zahra stared at him, but did not press him, because she knew that was what he wanted. He pointed to his mouth as he chewed, as if it could not be helped. She clenched her teeth. He picked up a pitcher and poured himself a glass of *limonana*, a drink made of mint, lemons, and sugar. After tipping some back, he offered it to her. She crossed her arms.

He set the glass down. "Not here."

She threw her hands up.

"Why did you come here, Zahra?" Stephen kept his voice low, concern evident in his tone.

Recalling the reason—what she had heard in the Tower al-Garbu—made her chest feel heavy. She did not know how to begin. She clicked the stones excessively.

Stephen stepped around the table. "What happened?"

A maidservant stepped in, stopped short, and turned to leave. This area was meant for the servants to dine out of sight of the royals. Zahra turned and left the kitchen, and Stephen followed.

"After we parted ways, I did something stupid."

As they walked, she did not need to look at him to know he was frowning.

"I found a way into the Tower al-Garbu, and heard…"

"What?" He stopped in the middle of the narrow hallway to face her. He spoke quietly through his teeth. "I told you we had to work together."

"Am I to blindly believe everything you tell me? As I recall, you threw me into—"

"A fire that did not burn."

"It burned!" She blinked several times and continued walking.

Stephen caught up with her, his tone softer. "What happened?"

Zahra glanced at him, unnerved whenever he showed kindness. Was it kindness? Or was he a great performer? "I am… uncertain. I heard a Russian man's voice. There was… a child."

Stephen's jaw flexed. They made their way through the *alfiz* archway into the main palace entry, where dawn light spilled across the marble floor, shadows cast by pillars.

The child's cracking voice rang in her mind. She could not bring herself to describe it. "All I know is the child should not have been there."

"Those women were paid to lure you into the tent."

She halted and faced him. "Lure me?"

"One of the traders paid them in gold, promising double if you did not wake."

Zahra's blood drained. Diogo da Gama wanted her dead?

Stephen's voice held a tone of finality. "It is time for you to learn everything."

CHAPTER 11

Zahra took Stephen to her childhood refuge, which was at the top of a winding, plaster staircase. The width of each step narrowed until they came to a slender door embellished with iron flowers. Stephen grabbed the handle before she could, looking her in the eyes as he opened it.

Tangerine glowed on the horizon, the promise of dawn. Zahra turned in a circle, taking in the familiar sight. It was as she remembered, except her head reached the height of the wall. In the north, the mountains lay like sleeping giants. Toward the east, the thick forest rustled. To the south, the Alboran Sea calmly reflected the sky like a sheet of black glass. "This used to be an enemy lookout."

Stephen stood beside her and pointed to a black vessel sailing not too far off the beach, its white sails emblazoned with red crosses. "Why do the Portuguese caravels lurk?"

She had to step onto a stone stool wedged against the wall to see over it. In the distance, the small silhouettes of sea crafts drifted. "Perhaps as part of the deal for protection Jabir made with them. How did you know of Diogo da Gama?"

When Stephen looked at her, she realized how near he was. An orange blossom petal fluttered on a breeze, landing on his shoulder. The shadows of dawn toyed with the contours of his features. "When we went through that fire in France, it was to separate places. But where I ended up—you were still there. A different you. You—in the future."

Zahra could no longer resist—she plucked the slim petal off his shoulder. "Your attempt to sound sane is making it worse."

Stephen glanced at her hand as he if he had expected her to do something else with it. "This other 'you' taught me Arabic."

This was his story? That he went to a place where a different version of her awaited him? It was farfetched and ridiculous. How could she possibly believe such a tale? This was why she cut their conversations short—he kept making absurd claims. The urge to dismiss him itched.

Resisting that itch, she glanced at his hand. "Did this other 'me' have magical healing abilities?"

Stephen splayed his palm open. "That healed itself, over time, like any wound. You got the big one, here." He pointed to the end of the white scar, which trailed over his inner wrist.

Triumph surged in her chest. She caught him in a lie! She pointed at his hand. "If that were true, you would have died within minutes."

Without missing a beat, Stephen replied, "Good thing you hurried."

She flicked the petal over the stone barrier. "Nicely saved."

Stephen smiled. "It is true."

"It healed like any other wound? How long did you spend in this place with the 'other' me?"

When he did not answer right away, she was sure she had him. It was an impossible story.

"I spent a long time there with you." His voice caused a shiver to course through her. To hide her reaction, she flicked him a dismissive glance, stepped down from the stool, and strode to the opposite end of the lookout. "You know I do not believe any of this, right?"

"That is why I told you those things when I arrived. Diogo da Gama. You confirmed *Sagrados Inocentes* is real. And I am fluent in Arabic. Who else could have—or would have—taught me?"

He had traveled with his mother in the Holy Land throughout his childhood—perhaps he picked up Arabic along the way. And he could have learned about Diogo da Gama and his ships while imprisoned by Francois Prelati.

Zahra burned to pull out her stones. Instead, she settled on the bench. Stephen sat on the opposite end. "The other you had already been through the fire, arrived in Marbella, and failed to save the children."

Perhaps Stephen had been the one to hit his head. "What am I to do with this information, Stephen?"

It was a simple enough question, wasn't it? If he had come here with knowledge of the future, shouldn't he know how to use it? He looked to the sky. "The first time, you hated me."

"I find your use of past tense interesting."

He smiled. "Do you hate me now?"

"I sympathize as you deal with your delusions."

"The first time, she had me put into a prison." He showed his healed palm. "I died from the wound."

She straightened. "Yet here you are, alive."

"The 'other' me died."

A gruff sound of frustration escaped her lips. "With respect, perhaps you dreamed all of this? I would never let a man die, however much I hated him."

"Apparently, there was not much you could do about it."

"What do you mean 'apparently'?"

Stephen sighed, lacing his hands in his lap. "I do not understand it myself, Zahra. All I know is, we both came here, tried to save the children, and failed. And by the grace of God, I was given a chance to meet that Zahra and learn of her mistakes."

She closed her eyes.

Stephen added, "And mine."

Zahra looked at him. It grew more difficult to hold onto her mistrust. She thought of how he had been in France, but the memory seemed to be of a different man. Just as she had followed a criminal into the forest, would she follow a lunatic in Marbella? "So, you—this 'other' you—died of blood loss?"

Stephen hesitated imperceptibly. "Something like that."

She couldn't shake the feeling that she was being duped. Whenever he got what he wanted out of her, he would remove the kind, protective persona. Tell her what a gullible idiot she was. Maybe push her into another fire.

"Then do it again. Do your little ritual and we can travel to fix the problem at its source."

"I do not trifle in the demonic anymore."

"Come now! Not even once, to save the children?"

Stephen exhaled, bowing his head. "That is not how it works. I do not jump between times. What happened in the forest had never happened to me before."

"You did not intend to conjure that thing?"

Stephen shook his head. "The most I had ever 'conjured' was a voice, which revealed secrets to me. That was far more than a voice. And it was interested in you. Remember?"

The memory still haunted her. It was only a day ago.

He looked at her brocade sash. "It was interested in you because you had the cloth."

She trembled at the memory of the thing in the forest springing for her. "You said it tried to go inside of me."

Lines etched into Stephen's brow, his voice quiet. "I knowingly endangered you. For that, I am sorry. And deeply grateful you were not harmed."

Sunlight sparked behind a coastal outcropping. His apologies were healing salve on the wounds of her hatred. Soon, there would be no more wound. What then? They would link arms and laugh as they navigated the death trap between her royal family and the Portuguese traders? No, there was no room for her to warm to Stephen, just as there was no room for her to act upon his ludicrous claims.

"What do you think happens next, Monsieur Kempe?"

"We make a plan together."

"Here is a plan. I can become *malika*. With that power, I expose Diogo, have him executed, and find the children."

Stephen went still. "Your plan is to go ahead with marrying your father?"

"He is not my father!" It humiliated her to have Stephen know things about her history she had never told him. A small voice in the back of her mind said, *further proof of his claims*. "My mother had both of us before he married her. It was through his mercy that she—"

Stephen held up a hand. "You do realize you will be expected to consummate the marriage?"

The air went out of her. She had avoided thinking of it. The very idea sickened her. She did think of Jabir as a father. But what other choice did she have? She had tried demanding her way into the tower. She had tried to tell Jabir the traders were hiding something. Diogo had displayed his power at the beach celebration. She had even snuck inside from the roof.

"If I could save the children, it would be worth it."

"No, it would not." His nostrils flared. "You did it before, Zahra. It destroyed you."

She stood and pressed her hand to her stomach as she approached the wall. Had she truly carried out wifely duties with her stepfather in a past… a past what? A past iteration of an event? It was too strange to have been made up. Yet she could not bring herself to accept it.

Zahra's voice trembled. "It is rather trite that you can just say 'you did that already and it failed' to whatever I propose."

Stephen approached behind her, his tone gentle. "Think of it as rather helpful to know what would not work ahead of trying it."

"Monsieur Kempe, the problem is this: I do not believe you gained knowledge from a different 'version' of me. So, I cannot factor that into my strategy."

He uttered a breathy sound of disbelief, his tone incredulous. "You still do not believe? Look!" He held open his palm, revealing his long-healed hand. He gestured around them. "Look where we are, in an instant."

"It is sometime in November. So at least two weeks have passed."

Stephen approached the wall, tall enough to look out. The people of Marbella had begun to awaken. Voices chattered. A cart rattled. "It is the fourth day of November, to be exact. I do not claim to fully understand the mechanics of traveling through fire to appear in other parts of the world. You are right; time has passed. My claims still hold true."

She could not deny the evidence supported his claims. Whenever she had debated Lord Raymond over the supernatural origins of Jesus, he always argued, "Just because it never happened before, does not mean it did not happen."

But this was happening now, not 1400 years ago. And if she were to accept it, her understanding of reality would crumble. She could no longer be who she was.

Stephen stood at the opposite end of the lookout, his eyes closed as dawn's light shone upon his face. "I have given so much proof, and still, you refuse to see the truth. Lord, what else can I do?"

Her heart quickened as she witnessed Stephen entreating his God. He opened his eyes and caught her staring. A breeze picked up around them.

Biko's distant voice traveled on the wind. "...looking for the *amira*."

She drew in a sharp breath and hopped up on a step stone to peek over the wall. Biko, in his lamellar tabard, conversed with a palace worker. If she and Stephen were discovered alone here, questions would fly. Jabir might seize the opportunity to have him arrested.

"Our time is up." She turned, finding Stephen close. She thought he planned to reach past her, perhaps to rest his hand on the barrier, or pick up something—but instead, he slipped his fingers through hers, grasping her hand as he leaned in to kiss her.

Well, he tried. She turned her head, so his lips landed on the corner of her mouth.

She leaned back and slapped him.

Stephen stilled; head still turned away. His jaw clenched as he turned back to her. "Let me explain."

Her voice was a harsh whisper. "You men, you take what you want, when you want it, don't you?"

A line formed between Stephen's eyebrows. "Zahra—"

"No number of ruses, elaborate lies, or, or, or different personalities will give you power over me."

Stephen stepped back. "I am not trying to gain power over you."

She did not allow him to finish. "When men accost women, that is all it is ever about. Power. You make yourselves feel big by making us feel small. And this—" She jabbed a finger toward the ground. "—is my territory."

Frustrated, Stephen looked about to reply, but pressed his lips, appearing to think better of it. What did she expect? For him to apologize? To explain? No. She did not care for one of his bizarre explanations right now. She straightened and tore around him, heading for the door.

"Zahra."

She shot him a look that could cut. "If I need you, I will send for you."

• • • • •

Zahra fell into step with Biko. Chest tight, she struggled to catch her breath. Her stomach twinged as she recalled her harsh reaction. She did not believe Monsieur Kempe—sorcerer, outcast, and fugitive—had any genuine feelings for or attraction to her. It was a ploy, and nothing more.

The corner of her mouth tingled where Stephen's lips had touched. She rubbed the spot.

Although Biko offered her a grin, he was not as talkative as usual—perhaps foul of drink from the festivities. As they walked in silence, she pulled out her stones, finding immediate comfort in the soft glassy trill.

Their walk led to the *hujratu mushamasat*. Solarium. Sunlight streamed into the architectural beauty, its angular ceilings and walls all glass connected by lean wooden slats. Being in here gave one the experience of standing in the forest yet protected from its dangers. Weaved rugs overlapped on the venetian marble, pinned down by sateen chaises and floor cushions. Zahra had seen her mother and Jabir enjoying breakfast here many times.

Jabir sat on a cushion beside a low-set table. He pushed a dull blade through Manchego cheese. Velvet robes pooled around his crisscrossed legs. She perched on the cushion across from him and curled her legs under her. She discreetly rubbed the corner of her mouth again. Did he somehow know what had just happened on the lookout?

Only after Biko left did he finally look up at Zahra. He gestured to a small cup of frothy black liquid, sipping on one himself. She leaned to inhale the robust aroma. It was deeply pleasing.

"Try it, daughter. It is called coffee." Amusement glimmered in his wrinkled eyes. Perhaps he was not upset with her. The drink steamed as she took a sip. She drew back sharply—it tasted like distilled cigars. "What is this?"

Jabir chuckled. "The Sufis recently discovered these beans. They roast, crush, and steep them to make this drink to get them into a higher spiritual state."

She almost it spat out, setting the cup down with a clack. "The traders drugged me last night with *hul gil*. They wish me dead."

The muscles in Jabir face slackened, his eyes widening.

"Your ally, Diogo da Gama, does not like me, *baba*."

Veins throbbed at Jabir's temples. "The traders have grown too powerful."

"When did that become clear? When they took over Mama's tower, or when they shot at one of your loyal servants with your blessing?"

Jabir's eyes pierced her, his voice low and deadly. "I was certain Sukayna would be well."

"You believed Allah would save her?" It was impossible for her to keep the derision from her tone.

Malik Jabir looked outside. A spray of nettle trees swayed. Gray clouds gathered in the distance, the morning sun lost inside of them, rays of light angling over the mountain peaks.

"Allah has seen to it that you returned to me at just the right time."

She tightened her hand around her stones in her lap. "What do you mean?"

"When you left, I thought you had disrupted Allah's perfectly laid plans. But *this* was his plan all along."

"What plan, *baba*?"

"In the past several years, we have grown to power with help from the traders." His gums showed, so broad was his smile. "Now, following my union with you, we can oust them, allowing Allah to show his mighty hand."

Even as a child, it felt odd to be betrothed to Jabir. But now—especially after her conversation with Stephen—it chilled her bones. How could he act as if it were normal? "*Malik*, I am the illegitimate daughter of a *qayna* you married. What power could I possibly lend the kingdom?"

Laughter erupted from Jabir. Zahra clutched her hands together under the table. "Daughter, you still do not see? You are a third of the divine. I have been told Raha is al-Lat, ruler of fertility and wild beasts. I thought she and I would make half-god children together. But I realize I was not supposed to create children with the goddess of fertility herself—I am to make them with you, blessed by her divine power."

Primal fear gripped Zahra's spine. 'You still do not see?' Jabir said, insisting she was a goddess in the flesh. 'You still do not believe?' Stephen had said, telling her outlandish stories of skipping time and supernatural second chances. She was surrounded by men who insisted she adopt their dangerous beliefs.

"*Malik*—I am not suited to be a mother."

"Enough. I grow weary of your incessant argumentation. We marry in the light of the next full moon."

A wave of dizziness hit her. Less than a week. "Grant me access to the Tower al-Garbu. I wish to reclaim Mama's chamber."

After a long pause, Jabir nodded. "You shall have whatever you desire."

He climbed to his knees, placing a hand on the table. The wood creaked as he leaned toward her. She could smell the coffee on his breath. It did not smell the same as in the cup. Jabir pressed his mouth to hers, his wiry beard tickling her chin. She did not rebuff him as she had Stephen.

CHAPTER 12

Zahra rolled her stones more in the next two days than ever before. The wedding drew near, and Jabir continued to assure her he would grant her access to the tower. Whenever alone, Zahra jumped at noises and watched over her shoulder. She constantly swatted the nagging desire to go tell Stephen of her apprehensions.

But he had given her the space she had demanded.

Occasionally she had spotted him doing fieldwork alongside other servants. Although thankful he managed to stay out of trouble, something about the people warming to him irked her. Perhaps because he should be worried about the children, not doing manual labor.

Laughter erupted in the distance, somewhere near the shoreline where a string of boulders curled into the water like the spine of a sleeping dragon. She could not see beyond the pampas grass on the dunes, so she strode to the opposite end of the walkway and shielded her eyes from the glaring sun.

Stephen, Biko, and several other male servants were in pursuit of fan mussels hidden in the shallow sea meadows of the cove, their pants wound up to their thighs. When young, she had often accompanied the workers to help find them. The soft threads that anchored the mussels produced the finest silk in the world. One mussel could provide pounds of meat, and the iridescent shell served as decorative material. She had loved swimming, excited to spot an eel or a loggerhead turtle.

The sun bore down on Biko's ruby turban as he slapped Stephen on the back in a congratulatory manner. Stephen cradled a large mussel about two feet long, shaggy with algae. Zahra blew out a breath. Why were they in Marbella for him to be playing around on the beach? She was equal parts outraged and envious. The water looked rather tempting.

Zahra maneuvered through less traveled hallways to dodge her maidservants. Once outside, she summoned a camel cart. Within minutes, she arrived at the cove where the mussel hunters poked around in the shallows. Some waded chest-deep, flinging hemp lines to reel in bass. Stephen and Biko sat with their backs to her under the shade of a palm, eating dates piled on a banana leaf.

"I will teach you how to swim like a Moroccan." Biko flung a date peel. "Then perhaps you will stand a chance racing me."

Stephen chuckled as he chewed. His light hair was midway to drying—perhaps from this race Biko spoke of. What fun. She halted near a large mound of mussels next to an iron oyster shucking blade. As she stood waiting for them to notice her, she thought of the sight she would be: a navy chiffon day robe cinched by a wide leather belt, dark skin kissed by sunlight, her shiny curls banded back by a delicate tiara.

"Do all your people swim like that?" Biko scooped his arms in unison in front of him and devolved into what appeared to be silent laughter that pained him.

Stephen deadpanned as he watched Biko fall sideways into the sand. He caught sight of her. "Z—*Amira.*"

As Biko lay catching his breath, Stephen stood, working the rolled linen of his pants back down his long, muscular legs. He circled behind the base of the palm, his eyes never leaving her as he approached. Her heart paced like she was prey.

She feigned a confident tone. "I see you are making the most of your time here."

He bowed but kept his eyes on hers. "Waiting for you."

"And making friends."

"If I have to do this without you, I could use some friends."

The truth of his statement hit the air like a clear note played off a single harp string. She looked down at the sand as she realized how bitter she must seem. "I am sorry, Stephen."

"I should be the one apologizing." His sincere tone coaxed like warm cider.

Zahra nudged one of the mussels in the pile. She slipped her leather sandals off to feel the damp, grainy sand between her toes. She dropped the two lodestones beside her shoes and stepped around Stephen to avoid his unwavering gaze. "Biko, have you ever seen a woman pull up a mussel?"

"I dislike watching women fail, *amira*." Biko called out, brushing sand off his tunic.

"But you do not call me woman; you call me *huriat aalma*." *Mermaid.*

The men went still while she wound the front of her gown up between her legs, tying her skirt hem into a knot at the small of her back. She did not dare look at Stephen as she exposed her lean legs, wading barefoot into the temperate shallows. The men sloshed in after her. Seagrass tickled her ankles. She stopped when the water reached her knees, wiggling her toes in the squishy sand. Her foot bumped into something hard and slimy. She dunked her hands to grip the base of the mussel, yanking at it. She wiggled it back and forth to tear at its silken roots. It wouldn't budge.

Biko called, "Having trouble, *huriat aalma*?"

Her glare made him laugh.

Ripples of water rolled in as Stephen slid in beside her. He bent to grasp the mussel, too. Except, instead of helping her, he gripped her hands, stopping her progress. Their shoulders touched, arms underwater. "The other Zahra told me she believes the cloth holds powers. We must figure out how to harness it."

She released the mussel, but he caught her hands under the water, his thumbs pressing into her palms. He had once restrained her similarly before throwing her into a fire. Shouldn't she feel afraid?

She felt something. But it was not fear.

She glanced at Biko, who poked around the meadow further off. She kept her voice low. "The cloth does seem to have performed feats before. Chapeillon's spontaneous skin disease—I suppose that was me."

Stephen nodded. "It was the cloth."

"Sohrab being attacked by horseflies."

Stephen hurried to add to the list. "And the broomstick turning into a snake."

A shock coursed through her. She recalled the snake but had not considered that the broomstick had had anything to do with it. She remembered that the knight with the crooked mustache had found the stick down the hall. In a direction she had not taken it. The direction the cobra had chased the men. The stick had turned into a snake. How had Stephen worked that detail out on his own?

He hadn't, had he? He had worked it out with *her*. The other Zahra.

As belief crashed into her reality, she realized all of Stephen's wild claims had to be true. In this moment of clarity—and absurdity—she grabbed for the mussel again and yanked it loose. Triumphant, she held the stringy, foot-long mussel like a trophy over her head. Biko turned and shot his fists up. The other servants cheered.

Breathless, Zahra laughed. She trudged toward the shore, and laughed more because she wore her skirts tied up around her thighs like a fisherman's wife. Weak, she placed her mussel into the pile on the beach. She plunked down on the sand, looking up at Stephen, who stood blocking the sun, a smile touching his mouth.

She reached behind her to work out the knot of her skirts. "I thought about it—what happened on the lookout. You have never seen me in traditional Granadan clothing. It is vastly different from what is worn in France. Some might say our garb is more provocative."

Stephen's eyes narrowed. "Is that what you think?"

Her face grew hot. She had been certain his reaction to seeing her dressed for the celebration had been one of appreciation. Perhaps he had just been surprised to see her hair free. In Europe, wearing it like that got such a strange, sometimes negative reaction, that it was preferable just to keep her hair smoothed and bound up in braids or a bun. She recalled the statement he had made in France: 'Plenty of men would fancy a Moorish woman.' Perhaps Stephen Kempe did not even find her attractive compared to the European girls likely after him. Her temples throbbed from the rush of heat to her face. She wished to swim to that Portuguese caravel anchored about half a mile from the shore. Hopefully she might drown along the way.

Stephen crouched beside her, speaking quietly. "When I saw you, I was not shocked by how beautiful you were."

"Very well, then!" She pretended the sun was too bright, shielding her face.

"On the contrary, I am incredibly well-acquainted with your beauty."

She meant only to look at his face a moment, but her gaze lingered. Sunlight reflecting the sparkling water illuminated his eyes, which matched the color of the sea as it foamed green at the shore. His features were masterfully sculpted with the care of a gifted artist.

She swallowed. "I may believe what you have told me is true. But you could still be duping me into thinking you—you—" She gestured both palms at him, unable to finish the sentence: *into thinking you have fallen in love with me.*

Stephen suppressed a smile. "For that, I can be patient."

Her heart stirred.

"Caleb? Caleb!" Biko's voice sounded strained. He swung around, raising his hands. "Caleb was just throwing a net for bass. Did you see him leave, *amira*?"

Their eyes darted around the empty cove. Biko uttered a choked gasp as one of the servants floated to the surface, face down. Another servant, deeper out, uttered a cry that cut short as he sucked under water. Biko dove toward him. Stephen swept into the water to help. Was it a shark?

Motion caught the corner of her eye. Was that a sea turtle? No—it was a man dressed in brown, crawling through the shallows under the surface.

Toward the shore.

Toward her.

A scorching sensation shot through Zahra's veins. She stumbled backward several steps. Water cascaded over the man as he broke the surface, taking in a deep breath. He stood, wiped his face, and advanced on her. Blade in hand, he obviously had a clear aim: kill.

She snatched the oyster blade, its hot metal searing her palm.

The man ran at her. She put the large pile of fan mussels between them. He cut around it, lunging—but Stephen appeared behind him and slung his arm around his throat. The man swung his blade. Stephen flipped him face-down into the shallows.

Another man burst out. More ripples signaled another swimmer nearby.

"Run Zahra!" Stephen shouted.

She ran the only way out of the rocky cove—but a man cut in front of her. He had a hairy chest and a short sword. She froze, her wet skirts like chains wrapped about her legs.

Stephen grabbed her and backed up toward the water. He brandished a dagger he'd taken off the man, his muscles rigid against her back. Remembering her oyster shuck, she jerked it up too. Three breathless traders stood on the shore, advancing into the shallows.

Water sloshed around their feet as Stephen drew her backward.

Behind them, Biko cried out, "More are coming!"

The Portuguese caravel anchored a half-mile out looked like an active anthill, traders using rope to splash down, disappearing under the water. The remaining servants caused waves in their attempt to swim to shore. The traders outnumbered them, erupting from the water. Biko dove on one and fought him beneath the surface.

The cove was well enough hidden that the stealthy nature of this attack could go unnoticed. She, Stephen, Biko, and the servants could vanish without a trace.

Stephen pulled her deeper into the water. "They plan to kill us and make our bodies disappear."

A hard shiver coursed through Zahra. The men closed in.

His voice was low against her ear as the water rose around them. "Can you swim like Biko?"

Her voice trembled. "Yes, but not in a dress."

Stephen loosened the knot of her belt. "Take it off."

"I beg your—"

"Die in your dress or survive in your knickers."

Now waist deep, Zahra's dress fell loosely around her shoulders. She snatched Hadiza's cloth before it could float away, clutching it to her chest to hold up her dress. She called out in Portuguese. "Have you no shame?"

The hairy-chested man had eager eyes, but remained cautious because they had weapons. "Only children feel shame."

Thump thump.

Zahra gasped. That familiar energy spiked into her hand that held the cloth against her chest. Blood billowed into the water.

One of the traders pointed at her. "The princess is hit!"

Crimson spread through the water, surrounding them in a dense cloud. Biko swam in long strokes toward them. Stephen's arm loosened, his hand groping for some kind of gaping hole in her stomach to explain the amount of blood.

"Stephen, it is the cloth," she whispered.

The hairy-chested man surged toward them. Stephen yanked her backward. She could no longer touch the sea floor. He pressed his lips to her ear and whispered, "Go with God."

He let her go. The hairy man lowered on his haunches and lunged.

Zahra sucked in a breath and dunked under the surface. The men clashed above her. Her gown pooled at the surface. She pushed against the sea floor. In the blurry distance, shadows of swimmers encroached like a herd of hammerhead sharks. Crimson poured out of the cloth as she swam. The dark cloud shrouded her escape.

Wearing only a *rifada*, a taut band of linen supporting her chest, and pantalettes tied by a simple drawstring, she was able to pick up speed. She swam toward one of several lighthouses in the distance. She circled around a colorful reef. A bright yellow moray backed into the coral. Her lungs creaked with pressure. She grabbed onto one of the large rocks that made up the dragon spine. She pulled herself along, getting behind it. Hidden by the large black boulder, she poked her head above the surface, gasping for air as quietly as she could.

The men grunted and sloshed in the water beyond the boulders. She dared not peek over. A sinking sensation pooled in her stomach. It was unlikely that Stephen or Biko would survive, outnumbered as they were. She bit her lower lip, her eyelids fluttering closed.

Both Stephen and Biko were willing to die for her. Zahra did not deserve it.

A trader shouted—he sounded much too close. She took a deep breath, ducked under water, and pushed off toward the lighthouse.

• • • • •

Zahra sat against the curved wall of the lighthouse, arms over her knees. The sky dimmed as the sun withdrew. She held the oyster blade in one hand, and the damp cloth in the other.

The lighthouse smelled like soot and sea. Its fire basin sat on a wooden table in the middle of the dusty circular room. Someone should come by to light it, soon. She was too far out to be able to see if anyone lay dead in the cove. Jabir's warriors had combed back and forth in fishing boats, but their numbers thinned as it grew dark.

The blood that had seeped from the cloth had spread all the way to the deep. Even now, the glassy ocean glimmered maroon in the diminishing light.

The disastrous scene played over and over in her mind. If she had run sooner, she could have gotten help. If she had escaped, they might have abandoned the murderous mission altogether. She was, after all, the main target. She clenched her teeth whenever a wave of shivers came. It was early November, and she wore next to nothing.

The sky turned auburn. Tremors rolled through her body. Although she could step out on the veranda encircling the top of the lighthouse and remain invisible, she decided to wait. Though she and

Stephen had had a questionable beginning, she had grown to respect him. She touched her ear, remembering their last moment together. He had whispered as if saying goodbye.

Warmth clouded her eyes as she bowed her head to her knees. Perhaps what she felt was more than respect.

The lighthouse door rattled.

CHAPTER 13

Zahra scuttled under the bolted table and clutched the oyster shuck. Footsteps ascended. She hoped it was the lighthouse servant, but if it wasn't, she planned to stab their throat and push them down the stairs. Her cruel imagination conjured the hairy-chested trader, his sword sullied by Stephen's blood. She tightened her grip on the shuck and stared hard toward the lighthouse staircase.

A man's bare feet crested the top step. In one fist, he held a bundle of lavender fabric.

"Zahra?"

Her breath caught. "Stephen!"

The shuck clanged to the floor as she scrambled from under the table. They both hurried toward one another but halted a couple of feet away. His gaze searched her body. "Are you hurt?"

She shook her head, and he exhaled, relieved. She was painfully aware of her state of undress—thin pantalettes and a *rifada* banded across her chest. He straightened out the bundle he brought: a lavender tunic dress with decorative stitching, worn by maidservants.

Without asking, he helped pull the dress over her head. She burned with embarrassment. No man had seen her like this before. He had changed into fresh clothes—what he had been wearing before had likely been stained by the mysterious blood that filled the ocean now. And the blood of those who died today.

"Is Biko well?" The dress settled over her, falling to her ankles, warming her chilled skin.

"He was injured but will be fine. He fought well for you."

Zahra blinked back tears. The laces of the dress remained loose at her back. She did not dare reach back to attempt tying it herself, for the struggle would draw his attention. Asking him to perform such a task would be akin to propositioning him. "How did you know I would come here?"

He opened his palm, revealing her two lodestones. "I know you very well."

A strange feeling gripped her heart. Retrieving the stones, she allowed her fingertips to linger over the scar she had given him. His hand curled over hers, but she withdrew.

Zahra was filled with the certainty that he would lean toward her, as he had days ago on the lookout. Instead, he said, "I can think of two times in the historical account that water turned to blood."

Zahra inhaled, and dutifully nodded. Perhaps her heart could calm while distracted by this puzzle. She rolled the rocks in her hands compulsively. She shut her eyes and dug through her Biblical knowledge. "Revelation—what does that mean? The apocalypse starts in Marbella?"

"Also, Exodus."

The story of Moses unfolded in her mind. He had turned the Nile to blood. "It was the first of Moses' plagues."

"God's plagues." Stephen's eyes shined. "The flies on that interpreter might be a small 'plague,' but a plague no less."

"The snake! The stick turned into a snake, just as Moses' staff had. How did you and the—the 'other Zahra' not figure this out?"

Stephen looked toward the veranda of the lighthouse. The ocean glittered crimson as the horizon swallowed the sun. "The sea never turned to blood."

Her mind spun like a watermill in stormy winds. Did that mean her choices were changing events? They were also coming to understand the power they dealt with. It seemed similar to what Moses had access to in the Exodus account. She widened her eyes. "Do you think… I could part the sea?"

He cast her a sidelong glance. "The thought had crossed my mind."

She ran onto the veranda, stopping by the short stone railing. She tucked the cloth under the taut linen of her *rifada*. "Stephen, if I believe all that you are saying, does that make me—one of you? A Christian?"

Stephen leaned against the frame of the door, watching her from the shadow of its arch. "What do you believe?"

She had battled her whole life against the notion of a creator. Especially the Christian God, which she had been raised to detest. She had rarely prostrated herself for Mohammed, and certainly never for Jesus. But now she had to decide who—or what—gave her this power.

"I suppose I believe that there is a Creator."

The statement settled like a weight on her chest. Millions of leaves rustled in the distant forest. The silhouette of a bird crossed the sky. The stars winked to life in the navy tapestry above. All these things seemed far less trivial, somehow.

"That is good." Stephen's voice held a note of promise that thrilled her. "But it is only a small part of the equation."

Not wishing to expose her state of awe, she asked, "Equation? Did the other Zahra teach you mathematics, too?"

Stephen smiled. Every time he did, she warmed. A breeze caught her hair, and she shot a hand to smooth her wild curls. She had lost the tiara during her swim. "Oh, my hair must look—it does not do well in saltwater."

"It is perfect." He had grown nearer. A tickle touched her back. She turned sharply, her heart racing.

"Your dress is unlaced."

Closing her eyes, she chided herself. This man had saved her life and repeatedly risked his own for her. Even his one 'misdeed'—throwing her in the fire—had not actually harmed her. She faced her back to him and peeked over her shoulder. "Thank you. I would appreciate it."

The look he gave her put her pulse to the test. She turned away so he wouldn't catch her flushing like a green farm girl. Tingles sprang over her back as the leather strings tightened, and he tied them off near her nape. She tipped her chin by way of thanks but neglected to look him in the eye. The stones circled in her palm.

Now might be a suitable time to get the cloth to 'work,' as Hadiza had put it. She set the stones down and closed her eyes. A breeze fluttered through her lashes. She pressed her hand to her chest, where the cloth nestled, with the intention of 'wielding' its powers.

So, God.

She cleared her throat, trying to forget Stephen nearby.

Now I believe You exist. I also believe You want me to save Hadiza and these other children. So, what do You say we part the sea?

She opened her eyes. The retreating sun cast a crimson stripe over the glassy ocean, which remained calm. Stephen watched the water. Another breeze carried on it the scent of mint, lemon, and sugar.

Her stomach growled. "You had *limonana*? What else did you eat?"

Stephen looked down at her. "Should I have fasted for you?"

Zahra shrugged. "It would not have killed you."

"My apologies, princess." The sound of his chuckle pleased her. The waters sloshed around the rocky base of the lighthouse. "Do you recall what Moses said to the people before parting the sea?"

Zahra flipped through her memories of the scriptures she had often read with Lord Raymond. "Something about standing firm and not fearing."

Stephen hummed in agreement.

She remembered more. "The Lord will fight for you. And you only have to be silent."

Seemed simple enough. She remained silent. Cleared her mind. And pressed her hand against the cloth. She willed the waters to part as they supposedly had for Moses. She narrowed her eyes, urging the waves to grow violent. Her shoulders sagged. She implored the ocean to ripple, at least?

Feeling ridiculous, Zahra turned to Stephen. "It seems to 'work' only when I am in danger."

He leaned to examine the distance to the rocky shore.

She shot him a playful glare. “Do not even think of dangling me over the edge.”

He raised his eyebrows. “I could.”

Zahra took a step back. “You wouldn’t.”

Stephen’s eyes lit up with amusement.

She dug her teeth into her bottom lip, holding back a smile. A shiver stole through her. “It works when I need it to. Suppose I forge ahead trusting that?”

“Yes. And we forge ahead into the Tower al-Garbu, together. You know it well.”

She rested her fist on her hip, tilting her head. “And fight off a hundred soldiers, the two of us?”

Stephen glanced at her body language. “Trust. Remember?”

“I can trust but still make wise decisions.”

“Zahra.” His gaze captured hers like a snake charmer. “You cannot marry Jabir.”

She set her jaw. “I have considered it at length. There are no other avenues. Being queen will give me the power I need to save the children.”

“*Ya rohi.*” *My soul.* She held her breath as he reached behind him and unfastened from his waistband a small pouch used for coins. “I did not say you should not wed him. I said you *cannot*.”

She exhaled as he turned the pouch over, something metal clinking into his palm. “Are you—are you proposing to me?”

“No.” One of his fingers brushed a weighty gold band aside, revealing a delicate, shimmering circlet. “We are already married.”

Zahra stepped back. Both gold posey rings had inscriptions delicately carved, but she could not bring herself to examine it. “This is too much.”

“I had not planned to tell you, unless you were going to try to wed Jabir again.”

“Again,” she parroted.

“I cannot let you marry him. Again.” Now he was just goading her.

"You cannot *let* me? Does marrying some 'future me' give you possession of me?"

He hesitated. "Yes."

Zahra let out a puff of air and turned away. Stephen sighed. The rings clinked as they dropped back into the pouch. She craned to see the palace in the distance, nestled among the foliage. A palace that she could exert some influence over if she were to become Jabir's queen. But the wedding night…

"Wait." She turned back to him. "You say you married the 'future' me. Does that mean you… did you lie with her?"

Stephen stilled. They remained like that for several seconds. Finally, his eyebrows rose.

The air went out of her. She crossed her arms. Could he have been with her in such a way? She felt exposed.

"I spent years there. With you, Zahra." His eyes were heavy with burden, imploring. "I was in love with you."

Zahra's cheeks flushed at his stark admission. His fingertips nudged her palm. She uncrossed her arms so he could grasp her hand.

His adam's apple dipped in a swallow. "I still am."

A strange sensation kindled inside of her chest. She shook her head slightly, her hand trembling in his. "Perhaps you love her. But you cannot love me."

"Yet, I do."

Zahra shook her head again. "You do not know me, Stephen. I am not—"

"You don't need these anymore, *ya rohi*." He scooped the lodestones out of her other hand, which she had grabbed without noticing. He set them down on the banister. "You have me. And Him."

Stephen did not treat her like a conquest. He did not use her. Nor harm her. In fact, it seemed he would do anything for her. And right now, amidst all this chaos, she realized she only wanted a single thing.

Afraid he would see desire plain on her face, she dropped her gaze. He touched her chin so she would look back up at him. Her heartbeat drummed in her head. His thumb ran over her wrist. Even in the dark she could see a broad spectrum of emotions in his eyes, ranging from sorrow to joy. He did not move closer, though. And why should he? She had slapped him the last time.

"Stephen." After a long, expectant pause, she added, "I wish to apologize."

"For?"

"For hitting you." She was glad her voice had sounded calm, because truly, at this moment, a signet could press her down like hot wax.

Stephen smiled, a beautiful sight. Zahra could now see all the things she had willfully ignored before: how much he cared for her. His ever-present concern. His open adoration.

By her wrist, he drew her toward him and bent down. He radiated warmth. First his lips brushed hers, as if he relished each touch. Then he kissed her, tender. She returned it. An unfamiliar sensation coursed through her—of being known and wanted. Time slowed and their troubles lost meaning as he lured one kiss into the next, and another.

Her hands slipped over his shoulders and crossed behind his neck. Zahra realized she had been pining after Stephen Kempe a lot longer than she cared to admit. Even when he had testified in Nantes, she had been captivated by him, drawn by his integrity. Even his last act in France had shown that he would do anything to save his niece, Mary. Love like that was rare. And now she was the undeserving recipient of it.

Knees weakened, she sank into his supportive embrace. A small prayer floated out of her, unbidden.

Thank you for letting him survive this time.

Survival. They had survived this long in large part due to the good graces of the king. And what would *malik* Jabir think of this clandestine entwinement at the lighthouse?

As gently as she could, she unwound her arms and broke the kiss. Unable to look up at him, she could only muster a breathless whisper. "We cannot do this."

His heart knocked beneath her palms. He wrapped his hands over hers. "We will find a better way."

"Stephen." Her hands trembled in his grip; her voice pitched higher than she had intended. "We are in Marbella. The men we are up against are powerful. There is no solution that involves us being together."

His nostrils flared, his anger quick to boil. "Why do you think I came here? To watch you wed Jabir, fail, and destroy yourself all over again?"

She withdrew her hands. A chill curled between them.

"Zahra, I need you to understand that after all that time—" His voice grew quiet. "By the end, I did not wish to get home. I did not want to come here. It meant leaving her. —You."

His correction was like a strike. He had tried to convince her they were married, but truly, he was talking about a different woman. 'Her.' The future Zahra. The one she had yet to become.

She stepped back. "Whatever world you were in is not this world. I am not bound by vows I never made."

Stephen looked down, appearing stricken. "You are right."

His easy agreement hurt. But she assured herself that marriage meant captivity and abuse without recourse. It required offspring. And considering how easily she had abandoned Raha, she would make a terrible mother.

She rubbed her chest bone with her fingertips to soothe the pain in her heart. "You got to survive this time around, did you not? I shall work with the cloth myself. I will figure it out. I will not fail."

A line formed between his eyebrows; perhaps as he realized she was trying to get rid of him. "We can still work together."

Her emotions were like a herd of wild horses. "If you can, you should—you should try to go back to that place." She choked on the words. "Get back to her. If Mary is here, I shall return her to James and Merla."

Stephen's jaw tightened as he turned away. Zahra opened her mouth to say more, to convince him it was better this way, but she was instead overwhelmed by the desire to embrace him and try to make it work like he wanted.

But she did not do that, because she knew it could not work.

So, she said nothing.

CHAPTER 14

Hundreds of dead fish washed onto the shore, paving their return to the palace. Stephen prowled silently alongside her. The unguarded gate hung open. They made their way onto the grounds, wind kicking up dust on the wide limestone pathways lined with citrus trees. It was deserted.

Voices filtered from up ahead. They came to the edge of a crowd packed into the Court of Wolves. The agitated people fought for a view. They cried out for answers about the bleeding ocean. It looked to be most of Marbella crammed outside the assembly hall where the king judged on civil matters. Slender white columns supported the awnings framing the courtyard.

A man's Portuguese shout caught on the wind. "We searched far and wide for the *princesa*."

"Da Gama," whispered Zahra as they approached the back of the crowd spilling around the corner. They could not yet see Diogo, but Sohrab interpreted loudly in Arabic.

"We all mourn her loss."

Stephen gripped her arm before she could barrel between the people and announce her presence. She shot a sharp look up to him. He shook his head. Perhaps she owed him a moment to think, for all the hasty judgments she had made in recent days.

Men in the crowd called out, angrily.

"If it is answers you seek, then that is an easy task." Diogo crooned. "Prosperity? It is yours."

She could only see Diogo's black hat and Sohrab's fly-bitten scalp. Stephen tipped toward her and whispered. "His men are passing out wineskins."

The angry voices dissipated. Several cheers rang out. Diogo's tone changed, deepening with warning. "A solution to the blight on the Alboran Sea? That might prove a bit more difficult."

A woman at the back bobbed a sleeping baby against her chest. Her husband spoke to her in hushed tones. Then he caught Zahra staring. He spared her a brief glance before noticing Stephen towering beside her. He shook his head and murmured to his wife, "If the *amira* is dead, why is her slave still allowed to roam our village freely?"

Zahra had forgotten how she looked. Her untended locks, lavender maidservant dress, and bare feet. Patting her baby's back, the woman gave Zahra a small smile, and a wary glance to Stephen. A wineskin passed over head to the man, and he asked for a second one for his wife. Wine vapor drifted on humid exhales.

"Let us show our gratitude." Jabir's voice rose above the exultation of the people. Zahra could only see his gold crown, inlaid with rubies—one he wore only for ceremonial purposes. "As we grieve, take solace in knowing Marbella's future is safe. Master da Gama has promised that he can cure our ailing ocean."

The people cheered and held up their wineskins. Diogo's voice rang out. "As the ocean bleeds, drink this wine to remember the day that I saved Marbella."

Zahra looked to Stephen, whose brow furrowed.

Jabir raised his hands high above his head. "Allah has inspired me to give Master da Gama heirship, should anything happen to me or my brother, Yusef."

The people gasped.

"He cannot do that!" Zahra's shouts were drowned by the outcry from others. Many people cheered with their wobbling wineskins.

Diogo spoke and people quieted. "As your new *emir*, I promise to double the presence of protective guard throughout the palace walls and beyond. My second promise is that these strange occurrences will never happen again. I only need one thing of you: a sacrifice. Who is willing?"

Whispers arose like the low wind before a storm. Heads turned; murmurs hummed. Someone called out, "I sacrifice my flask." Another called out, "I offer my finest lamb." Several others chimed in with similar offerings. Zahra pushed to her tiptoes, trying to see between the heads of the hundreds of people.

"Those are all well and good offers." Diogo paused for Sohrab. "But for extraordinary circumstances such as these, we need to think bigger. The king has sacrificed his daughter, much like Abraham. Who is willing to pay a true sacrifice to save Marbella?"

The voices of the volunteers died away. The husband of the woman holding the baby turned suddenly and reached for his child. Confused, the woman allowed the father to take the baby.

"I offer my baby girl!" He thrust his child into the air. The baby's eyes fluttered open, face contorting into toothless anguish as she released a stuttered cry.

"No!" The mother's scream pierced the night sky like that of a slaughtered calf. The crowd's uproar drowned out all of Zahra's attempts to shout that she was not dead. The man holding the baby up was allowed to pass through the crowd. Pressure from the front caused the back of it to surge. Stephen blocked a man from knocking into Zahra.

"I am not dead!" she screamed, but it was a mere squeak among the roars. The metallic slice of unsheathing swords pierced the air.

The mother was gone, lost in the sea of people. Zahra whipped to clutch Stephen's tunic. "Pick me up."

His indecision lasted only a fraction of a second. He dropped to one knee and wrapped his arm around her hips. Their hands clasped, and he pushed her high into the air, perched on one of his shoulders.

At this height, Zahra could see everything. The crying baby being paraded to the front. The mother clawing her way after. The people divided between outrage and acceptance. A mix of soldiers and warriors protecting Jabir and Diogo. Jabir slumped in a gilded chair, his pale face sagged over his jawbone. Diogo's mustache drawn into a noble smile.

Zahra sucked in a breath—but before she could utter anything, Stephen's voice boomed above the discord. "*Inzir*!" *Behold*. "The *amira* is alive and well!"

Those around them turned. Recognition flickered in their eyes.

With that, a ripple effect of gasps and cries began—people dropped out of the way as Stephen carried her through the crowd. She trembled as she held onto his hand, his supporting arm hooked securely over her thighs. The shouting abated, and Jabir thrust to a stand, a hopeful sheen in his eyes. Diogo's smile faded.

The people formed a wide path for her and her towering slave. Zahra spoke loudly so Jabir could hear her. "No such sacrifice will heal the ocean's wound. I know because I am the one who caused it."

Those who heard drew in air. The man with the baby turned, lowering the child. The mother shoved between two people and grabbed the baby out of her husband's hands. Tears shined on her cheeks as she clutched the wailing child. She backed away and struck her own chest three times, a gesture of deep pain and disappointment.

Diogo da Gama stood straight in his fitted vest and ermine cape, the corner of his mouth tucked inward, unimpressed. Once at the front, Stephen lowered her to the ground. She traversed the steps and spoke loudly to Diogo—but in Arabic. "Know this: I have caused the oceans to bleed. I have set a horde of vicious flies upon your interpreter. Cobras have attacked at my word. I have made a man's skin erupt with disease at my will."

The people covered their mouths, and shared glances with one another. Diogo's eyes bugged as Sohrab repeated her words in his ear.

Zahra never let her gaze stray from Diogo da Gama. "Set the children free, and you shall be spared my wrath."

"What children?" Diogo placed his hands on Sohrab's arm. "If I had any, I assure you, you would never lay eyes on them."

Thump thump.

Her chest burned with the energy from the cloth tucked against her heart. Her blood rushed with that familiar burn. Shadows fell around them. Eyes turned up to see black clouds billow and cover the clear night sky, like ink filling a pool. It looked otherworldly. An eerie silence fell over the crowd as a misty pattering of raindrops began to fall.

Diogo adjusted his hat and spread his arms. "Rain from God—both yours and mine—signifies prosperity. Let us rejoice."

Many hesitated while others cheered. A soldier near Diogo sent her a savage smile and let out a triumphant roar, throwing his fist into the air. A ball of ice the size of an anvil swiftly crushed him. A woman standing behind him shrieked as the slush exploded around her shoes, intermixed with blood and flesh. Diogo clutched his hat, ducked, and ran.

The screaming began. Icy boulders hurtled from the black clouds. One grotesquely decimated a soldier behind Diogo. One after another exploded, cracking the tile, as if it chased him in his race toward the cover of the awnings.

Strangely, Zahra felt certain she could stand in the middle of it all and not be struck.

Stephen slung his arm around her, her body jolting with the force of him dragging her toward the entryway. Jabir stood under cover of a stone arch leading inside. Stephen got her to safety, and she breathlessly watched her people flee the courtyard. With frightening precision, the monstrous hail dispatched Diogo's men until they were strewn about as if boneless.

The people piled inside the assembly hall and surrounding domiciles. Jabir stood watching as the ice shattered the statues of wolves lining the long courtyard. He backed up as the slush from an exploding hail slid across the tile toward him. He turned to her, his eyes rimmed red with tears of joy. "My daughter, you truly are the embodiment of al-Uzza."

The sky cleared, but the people still rushed to get inside. Jabir approached her. Instinctively, she stepped back, bumping against Stephen. But Jabir grabbed her and pulling her into a tight embrace.

He whispered in her ear, "Forgive me for doubting you, daughter of Allah. Tomorrow, we wed, and you shall have your mother's chamber as your own."

• • • • •

Jabir begrudgingly thanked Stephen for finding Zahra. Since his warriors and servants had scattered from the chaos, Jabir reluctantly lifted Stephen's ban from the Lynx so that he could escort Zahra safely back to her bedchamber.

Before they departed, Jabir locked his eyes on Stephen's. "This will not save you if you misstep, *uroubi*."

Stephen seethed in silent fury as they walked toward the Lynx.

The hallways were empty. Everyone had been at the Court of Wolves when the hail rained down. By initial counts, the only deaths had been among the Portuguese. Diogo remained unharmed, however. And it seemed Jabir planned to cast out the traders after they said their vows before Allah. The thought made her feel ill, especially considering the overwhelming desire she had right now to reach over and hold Stephen's hand.

Only when they reached the gated side entrance to the Lynx did Zahra speak. "You are angry because Jabir—"

"You are descending into corruption." He drew open the iron gate, facing her, his eyes ablaze. "You claimed the power as your own, and you have allowed Jabir to believe you are a goddess."

Zahra threw up her hands. "How am I to know the source of the power? I seem to be causing it."

Stephen nodded, his expression taut. "Even worse. You yourself believe it."

She growled and stepped through the gate. "I did not say that."

"This is the path you followed before."

Rounding the corner toward her bedchamber, she waved a finger without looking back. "Not exactly. You did not die this time. The ocean never turned to blood for her. And what about the ice?"

She stopped beside her bedchamber door and turned to face Stephen, who was not far behind. He said, "A specific event caused the cloth to stop working for her. If you keep following this path, the same may occur to you."

Her shoulders sagged, exhaustion gripping her like the weight of the sea. "What happened?"

Stephen hesitated. "Something happened with Yusef. I cannot say more."

A flash of fear shot through her veins. Something was to happen with Yusef? She had hoped she would not have to look at him again before she found Hadiza and went back to France. "Stephen, when are you going to tell me the whole story?"

"When we are married again."

Zahra bowed her head, covering her eyes with one hand as a wave of emotion overtook her. How long had she been certain she could not be loved?

"Again," she whispered.

"Again," he repeated. His fingers slipped under her palm to pull her hand away from her eyes. She closed her fingers over his. His persistence weakened her resolve.

"Here is what we will do." He glanced down the empty hall, then pulled her toward him. "I have been told da Gama has had specialized locks installed throughout the tower, to reduce the need for guards on the inside."

She drew near enough that she had to tilt her head back to look at him. His determination was irresistible. "You know how to move through the tower, undetected. Show me the way. I will take care of any opposition."

She found the idea compelling—but with far too many flaws. "And what of the children? We form a long chain as we move through the tower. And somehow, they would let us leave?"

"When we get to the Solar, we climb down using the rope ladder from the lever room."

She had forgotten about that. She had only laid eyes upon it once, many years ago. He must have worked out this plan with the other Zahra. She allowed him to pull her closer, their bodies almost touching. As if without her own permission, her free hand lifted to rest upon his chest.

Her body wanted one thing, but her mouth ran contrary to it. "Do you not think Diogo would notice his men being 'taken care of' as we abscond with the children?"

Stephen ran his thumb over her cheekbone. "What I think is that God is on our side."

Just as she was sure he would lean down to kiss her, a clatter sounded inside Zahra's bedchamber. They drew apart. A voice from within said, "Who is there?"

Raha.

They went inside and found Raha on the floor beside an empty goblet. Eyes bleary, she struggled to focus.

Hastening to her side, Zahra helped her stand. "What happened? Are you hurt?"

Raha took a few moments to recognize Zahra. Swaying, the smell of wine strong on her breath, Raha placed her hands on both of Zahra's cheeks. Her eyes sparkled. "You are alive."

Zahra smiled, her heart aching. She pressed her palms to the backs of Raha's hands.

Raha withdrew. She stumbled toward the stone washbasin, where a pitcher of wine sat. "What was it then? You just disappeared to make everyone go crazy?"

Zahra dropped her hands to her sides. "Why would I do that?"

"I do not know why you people do what you do."

Raha's slurred words cut. The shimmering jewel-tone kaftan complemented her hickory skin. She stumbled on the small step leading to the washbasin. Stephen jumped and caught her, casting Zahra a disquieted glance.

Raha pushed off him and dropped to sit down next to the pitcher. "For example, why did your slave hide the fact he knew Arabic?"

In English, Stephen said, "She said some things when she did not know I could understand."

Raha's eyes narrowed. "Do not speak in the language of the *salibiyyin.*" *Crusaders.*

Zahra stepped toward her. "Raha, it is not the language of—"

"*Malika*!" Raha's eyes were like smoldering coal. "You most of all shall refer to me as *malika.*"

Zahra bowed her head. "Forgive me."

Raha exhaled a bitter laugh. "You cannot even bring yourself to say it. Why? Because *malika* is your coveted title?"

Zahra was unable to look at her sister. Stephen's shadow engulfed Zahra as he stood beside her, hands behind his back. He addressed Raha in Arabic. "You do not have to be embarrassed, *malika.*"

Raha uttered a 'ha!' rebuke, cradling the pitcher of wine in her lap. "Commenting on the worthiness of a slave's physique is common. Tell him." She ordered Zahra. "We are not overly prudent, as I have heard they are in Europe."

Although Raha's skin was dark, it was not as dark as Zahra's, so the young queen could not effectively hide the blush in her cheeks. Zahra hurried to nod. "It is a common topic when processing slaves."

Raha tipped up her chin, gazing at Stephen past her nose. "You should show more respect to me, *uroubi.* I am queen. And I am also the *woman* who stopped Yusef from beating you to death."

Stephen bowed. "I am grateful to you."

His tone was genuine. In fact, Zahra detected fondness.

Raha observed him with a pensive gaze. "Many wait for you to make a mistake, *uroubi.* At which point, you will be sentenced to be eaten by the forest. And my long-lost sister would be forced to watch."

Zahra recalled the forest sentence—it was the worst of the worst. The criminal was tied to a tree, covered in pig's blood, and ultimately eaten alive by whatever wild animals discovered them first. It was thought to desecrate you, condemning you to hell for eternity.

The last time Zahra had seen her, Raha had been six years old, with braids and a rosy-cheeked grin. Now she drank excessively and hated the person who had once been her best friend. Longing ached in Zahra's chest. She wished to explain what had happened, to justify why she'd left. She wanted nothing more than to beg her forgiveness.

But Zahra was too afraid. Instead, she said, "You were relieved I was alive."

Raha stared for a several seconds. She stood unsteadily, tossing the pitcher behind her into the washbasin. It plunked deep into the water. "The only reason for my relief is my wifely burden shall be significantly lessened, starting with your wedding night."

Zahra grew hot, Raha's words like a punch to the stomach. Stephen's jaw tightened. Raha shoved between them, her drunken gait so off-kilter, she bumped into the doorframe on the way out.

"Would you escort her?" Zahra whispered.

Stephen hesitated, noticeably reluctant to leave. He exhaled and then followed Raha.

"And Stephen?"

In the oversized doorway, Stephen turned back to her.

Zahra spoke past a lump in her throat. "Please do not return. Rest."

Stephen watched her for a long moment. He closed his eyes as he turned and left. The wine in the bath water billowed, and the pitcher sank to the bottom.

• • • • •

Pre-wedding grooming rituals transpired amidst the fishy stench of decay.

As the sun rose, Zahra soaked in hot water infused with eucalyptus and sweet orange oil. Maidservants caked her hair in creamy coconut paste and cleansed it. They scrubbed her skin and massaged her. They palmed hot castor oil over her curls. None of it was pleasing while plagued by the impending wedding to her stepfather, the abducted children still trapped, and the brokenhearted look on Stephen's face when she had told him not to come back.

She stood before the mirror in a traditional, three-piece *takchita* wedding gown. Her under garments shimmered, silver *kafkan* tunic and matching pantalettes that skimmed to her ankles. The maidservant held up the sumptuous cream and silver *takchita* robe, which glittered with thousands of precious stones. Silver and gold leaves embroidered the silk. The ivory sleeves contrasted her dark skin. A fitted, white gold belt pinned together all the layers at her waist.

"This belt is familiar."

"It belonged to your mother." Sukayna smiled.

The idea that her mother wore this when she married Jabir made Zahra's stomach queasy. Could she go through with this? She thought of Hadiza, Stephen's niece Mary, and the other children. All she had to do was say the vows. Then Jabir's warriors would storm the tower. Then she could produce some excuse to delay being alone with him and abscond with Hadiza and Stephen back to France. The loose plan strengthened her resolve. She was so close.

Two maidservants worked at clasping the hundreds of tiny hooks running from her asymmetrical neckline to the floor. They adorned her with various pieces of jewelry; a delicate gold leaf necklace, thick-banded bracelets, several rings, and a crown that tickled her forehead with pearls. She gazed upon her reflection.

"So much metal. Am I gearing up for war?"

Sukayna plucked fastidiously at Zahra's curls. "We each have a battle to fight, *amira*."

That was an unusual thing for the docile Sukayna to say. Perhaps the near-death experience at the celebration gave her some grit. Zahra could use some of that.

She opened a small vanity drawer, picking up Hadiza's neatly folded cloth. She tucked it hidden under the tight belt and fastened the pouch with her lodestones as well. Sukayna lifted her eyebrows. Zahra gave her a look that dared the maidservant to say she could not wear those to her own wedding.

Zahra crossed the bedchamber toward the balcony terrace.

"*Amira.*" Sukayna's tone was urgent. "The humidity is not good for your hair."

Zahra stepped out anyway, hit by the scent of rotting marine animals. The beach looked like a gaping wound, its waters deep burgundy like old blood. But Zahra did not notice any of it—only a docked black ship with white sails and red crosses. According to Stephen, the ship Hadiza was supposed to be on would not arrive for another two days. But Zahra's stomach dropped as she read the large name painted across its hull.

Sagrados Inocentes.

CHAPTER 15

Despite her maidservants' protests, Zahra demanded to be taken to the pier. She did not care if she ruined the dress. This could be her last chance to intercept Hadiza. If she hadn't missed it already.

As the camel cart lurched forward, Zahra called out to Sukayna. "Tell Biko to meet me there with his squadron."

Low-hanging clouds sped over Marbella. Narrow and deep, the *Sagrados Inocentes* was the type of vessel that could carry a large capacity while cutting impressive speeds. Choppy waves slapped the pier posts, staining them red. Marbellans often greeted unloading crews, but today only Portuguese soldiers stood along the dock.

Somehow, Stephen had been wrong about when it would arrive.

Two by two, Portuguese traders carried chests off the ship. She spilled out of the camel cart and lifted the hem of her heavy gown. A Portuguese soldier stood at the end of the dock, his hand on his sword. Zahra expected the stony stare she usually got from Diogo's men—but his eyes darted away.

"Allow me to pass."

His hand tightened on the hilt of his sword—and he bowed, taking a step back. He did not lift his eyes again. She strode past. The next soldier peered sideways at her, his body straight. As she approached him, he lowered his hand from his weapon and bowed his head.

Zahra smiled.

She dropped the hem of her gown and stalked the length of the dock. Each soldier stood down. They must have heard about or seen what happened at the Court of Wolves.

The ramp leading into the ship skated back and forth with the lapping of the waves. Zahra was half-way up when a shadow rose over her.

"Look who it is, Gordy."

Pierre. Sweat dotted his tanned flesh, lips peeled back to reveal teeth like wayward tombstones in a sinking cemetery. He eyed Zahra's gown and planted a boot at the upper end of the ramp. Zahra backed onto the dock as memories of Isabelle assailed her.

Gordy appeared beside him, peering down at her. His eyes bugged, emphasizing his resemblance to his father, Diogo. "How did the snake charmer make it here before us?"

Another pair of traders passed between them down the ramp, carrying a chest.

Biko and several palace warriors galloped up on lanky camels. She held her hand out to stop the men with the chest. "Open it."

The ramp creaked.

"The long-awaited *Sagrados Inocentes.*" Diogo's voice made her pulse race. He wore a blasé smile under the shadow of his wide-brimmed hat. He walked the length of the ramp and dropped onto the dock. He pointed to the chest and his men set it down.

Diogo flipped his cape up and sat down upon it, as if it had been a proffered throne. "I finally put the pieces together, *princesa*. The child you seek is the innocent Hadiza. And you possess my relic, correct?"

Zahra swallowed, her fingers itching to roll her stones. Now that Diogo knew she had the cloth, he could have her searched. Biko headed down the dock toward her. Pierre trundled down the ramp, attention trained on the Moor. His fingers caressed the hilt of his sheathed blade. Biko came to a halt beside her, spear in hand. At the neckline of his armor, a bandage strapped over his collarbone. It must be the injury he sustained at the cove. She surmised he would be quite ready to put these traders in their place.

Biko spoke quietly to her. "*Amira*, we cannot go to battle at your word. You are not yet queen."

Zahra held her breath. He would not fight for her? She hoped no one had understood him. His warriors lined the beach beyond the crimson sand, merely the appearance of a threat. Perhaps that was all she needed.

A shuffling sound emitted from the chest Diogo sat on. Biko reached for his sword, his eyes wide.

Zahra's heart raced. Was Hadiza in there? "Release the girl now and leave our home."

Diogo drummed his hands on the chest beneath him, the pale skin on his face drawn taut. "Anything could be in here. We sell wine, black pepper, cloves, cinnamon, silk, mustard seeds. 'One need only the faith of a mustard seed to move mountains.' Do you have that, *princesa?*"

Since she could not order Biko to launch an attack, she had no choice but to play along; distract him until the cloth decided to work. "Have what? The 'relic' your men killed Isabelle for?"

Diogo's eyes flashed, his thin mustache pulling into a smile. "Do you know what the relic is?"

"According to Hadiza, it belonged to Jesus."

"Oh, no. He only touched it. It is said to have been the blindfold Romans put on Him on his walk along the Via Dolorosa."

Zahra curled her lip in disgust. "Let me guess. You believe this 'relic' has magical powers."

Diogo laughed—a strange, mirthless sound. "I know it does."

She pointed. "Open the chest!" The traders who had been carrying it flinched, as if at her word, hail might dispatch them.

However, Diogo seemed unconcerned. "What is in this chest is worth ten of you, *princesa*. Even your unholy hailstorm cannot dissuade us from our cause."

Zahra huffed a sound of disbelief. "You believe Jesus touched this cherished item of yours, yet you still call its power unholy?"

He shrugged. "It performed for me once when I was young. Made me invisible. Who knows the source of its power? The Via Dolorosa was the most triumphant moment in Satan's history."

Switching to Arabic, she turned to Biko, her voice harsh. "A child is in there!"

Biko gripped his spear and twisted to look back at his men on the beach. Rattling chains caught their attention. The ship's winch cranked on a rope and pulley system, swinging its cargo over the edge.

The large hook carried Hadiza, her wrists bound above her head. Her powder-blue dress was dirty from travel, her springy hair tossed by the wind. She kicked her bare feet.

Zahra's throat hurt as she cried, "Hadiza!"

"*Anisa!*" Hadiza's frightened eyes met hers, voice raw with terror.

Biko bristled but did not call his men. Diogo stood and flicked his fingers, at which his men picked the chest back up. Zahra worried about what was in it, but far more so for Hadiza. Her heart felt like it might burst. But no thrumming energy from the cloth.

God, is this not the right moment?

Diogo gestured to Hadiza. "*Princesa*, I did it this way so you would know that I do not fear you, your soldiers, the king, or the people. My power here is absolute."

Zahra trembled and growled to Biko, "*Hujum.*" *Attack.*

Hadiza looked up at her own wrists straining in the rope binds that held her on the hook.

The camels shifted restlessly. One of Biko's soldiers called out, asking what they should do. After a long hesitation, Biko called back, "Stand fast, await orders."

Tears threatened to spring. She wished to call him a coward—but he had risked his life for her. Why would he fail a child?

Biko's brow creased. "*Amira*, we have been told not to follow your commands. The king would have our heads."

They were told that? By whom? And why?

Diogo observed the tension between her and Biko as a conductor observed his orchestra. "*Princesa,* you know I could just have your gown torn from your body to find my relic."

A shiver snaked up her spine. "You would not do that."

Diogo widened his eyes. "Why not?"

"The people of Marbella would see. The king would hear."

"Tedious threats."

Zahra swallowed, ashamed of the tremor that shook her voice. "What do you fear, Diogo?"

At her question, Diogo's eyes flicked erratically over her gown, down the beach, and to the sky. He composed himself with a throat clear. "I fear only God. He brought my relic all the way from France. I am favored."

Zahra willed the cloth to work. *Hail! Leprosy! Snakes! Anything!* Hadiza clung to the hook, tears streaking her cheeks.

Diogo turned to Hadiza as if examining cargo. "Know that I am not upset with you, *princesa.* This is all part of the learning process for you people."

Zahra's knees trembled, threatening to buckle.

"Your sister and I bumped heads a few times, early on."

Thump thump.

The ship creaked. "She soon learned that my wine tasted better than her freedom."

Thump thump.

The creaking intensified. The whole ship tipped as if Hadiza's weight on the hook were pulling it down. Gordon released the winch lever as he stumbled to the edge of the boat. "*Pai!*"

The pulleys unraveled, chains whipping loose. The hook swung. Hadiza sailed toward the dock. She dropped several feet, shrieking. Biko leapt and caught Hadiza before she rammed into a dock post. He ducked and rolled with her.

"Get the girl!" roared Diogo. Pierre lunged for them.

Zahra sprang forth as well, but Gordon jumped off the boat, landing in front of her. She backed up. He seized her, grappled her around, and pinned her arms behind her back. Pierre wrenched Hadiza out of Biko's arms. The ship continued to tilt, the pier posts gutting its hull with a deafening crunch. Diogo backed up, staring.

"Something is in the water!" Biko's soldiers cried out. A shadow pooled around the ship. The crimson water appeared to boil. Something oozed its way out of the surf.

Frogs.

The innumerable slimy creatures hopped, flopped, and climbed over the *Sagrados Inocentes*. The entire portside hull broke open, crimson water rushing into the vessel. Frogs spilled over. Thudded onto the dock. Leapt over their heads.

What had begun as gasps turned to battle cries. The warriors on camels broke into a gallop toward the palace. Biko stared in horror as he climbed to a stand. Hadiza bounced under Pierre's arm like a rag doll as he raced off the dock, onto the beach.

Zahra struggled to draw a breath in Gordon's tight grip. "Biko, get the girl!"

Biko appeared unable to tear his gaze from the impossible multitude of amphibians growing like fungus out of the water. "I cannot leave you, *amira*!"

"You are a father, Biko. You must!" Her voice was raw. Biko turned and sprinted after Pierre and Hadiza.

Gordon growled into her ear. "*Bruxa!*" *Witch.* He dragged her away from the sinking ship, holding her like a shield against the amphibious onslaught. "I should have killed you in France."

A slippery sonata of croaking and wet slapping surrounded them. One of the frogs tucked its thick haunches and launched. It cleared Diogo's head, arching straight for them.

Gordon uttered a high-pitched sound, ducking back. She wrenched free and cracked her elbow into his nose. His head snapped back. She spun and shoved him. He toppled off the dock, swallowed by the blood and frog stew.

Zahra ran the length of the dock and dashed into the sand. In the distance, Biko ran, but she could not see Pierre or Hadiza.

Gordon crawled out of the ocean, blood seeping from his hairline over his face. Her gown weighed on her as she moved as fast as she could. He rammed into her, covering her in blood as he tackled her. She clawed at the sand. He held her down with his knee, reached for a sharp rock, and reared it above his head.

"Gordon, stop!" Diogo's voice carried. The wind caught his cape as he approached, his hair slicked back from his tall forehead. "Get off her, you brute."

The boulder thumped to the sand beside her head. Breathless, she squinted. Diogo and his son stood over her like crows ready to peck out their prey's eyes.

She had nothing to say; no threats worked on Diogo, and he did not even seem perturbed by the act of God that just destroyed his ship.

"If you are to be queen, I would like to show you what we do inside the tower."

She pushed to a sitting position. "How do I know this is not a trap?"

"How about this, *princesa*." Diogo offered her his hand. "When you get there, you can ask your slave, the Englishman, if it is a trap."

• • • • •

Zahra stalked through the entryway of the Tower al-Garbu as if she were escorting Diogo in. She should have known Stephen would try something without her. She could have refused to go with Diogo, but he had shown himself capable of grave harm. He might just kill Stephen.

The huge shield towered before Zahra. The stench of manure hit her.

"We brought our livestock inside, in case there was more hail." Diogo took the lead, strolling around the shield and down the long entry foyer. The gray sky shined through clover-shaped windows near the ceiling.

One of the Portuguese guards muttered to himself, "The smell is even worse in the portrait room."

Portrait room? As Zahra recalled, the adjoining chamber was a sitting parlor where her mother had met with other women in royalty. Zahra and Raha had often enjoyed mint tea and crispy *krichlate* cakes there.

Diogo engaged a metallic gold lock which clanked loudly. The next chamber was indeed the sitting parlor, its floor a puzzle of colorful flagstones. Bright oil lamps lined the walls, casting shadows on the ceiling carved in the intricate *mocárabe* pattern, which looked like thousands of pods in a massive wasp nest.

All the chaises and benches had been pushed to the far end of the parlor, forming a sort of fence where sheep clustered, chickens flapped, and goats bleated. The musky odor of the animals hung because there were no windows.

A heavy door strapped with iron sat in the shadows, with another one of those strange locks installed, reflecting gold.

A white-haired man clung to a lean wooden podium, poring over a thick text. He looked up as they entered. He choked when he saw Zahra—her elaborate wedding gown drenched in blood. Diogo had sent Gordy, she assumed, to clean himself up.

Diogo gestured with a palm. "Sir Drake, show our guest what we do here."

Deep creases formed in the man's forehead. After a long, probing stare, he withdrew a black journal and flipped through it. "Patron's first and last name?"

"Skip the sign-in." Diogo snapped and pointed. "Just show her the portraits."

Sir Drake's eyes widened. Zahra noted that the elderly man was English. He closed the journal and withdrew a weighty leather satchel used by artists to transport their work. He pulled out poplar panels and mounted each upon an iron hook. Zahra stepped closer. A gifted artist had sketched charcoal drawings of a child on each panel. The sketches were innocent enough, but something felt very wrong about it. The portraits depicted children ranging from four to eleven or twelve, the oldest of which appeared to be a boy with long dark hair and fierce eyes.

"Hassan." Diogo spoke from just behind her. "The artist has captured his strong spirit. Which is a good thing—until it becomes a problem."

"You sell artwork of children?"

Sir Drake snorted. Diogo shot him a sharp glare. The man cowed as he hung the last portrait. Her gut seized. The drawing was of Hadiza, and in it, she looked back over her shoulder, her black eyes large and dewy.

"What do you do here?" Zahra demanded.

"*Princesa*, have you ever heard of the river Brue, in Glastonbury?"

She looked between the men and nodded.

"About a century ago, it flowed naturally across the moors, through a gap in the hills between two small towns. But river engineers rerouted it for faster travel and better trading opportunities. Now it flows west from Glastonbury and on to the sea at Highbridge."

Zahra clenched her teeth. "Where are Stephen and Hadiza?"

"Now, instead of a river, imagine the flow of evil."

"An evil river?"

"I learned today that you were the interpreter at the trial of the disgraced commander Gilles de Rais. So, you understand the destruction that can be caused by a man who answers to his whims. His evil single-handedly drowned the city of Nantes."

Zahra had a sick feeling in the pit of her stomach. A pair of goats got into a scuffle, sending chickens flapping in a spray of feathers.

Shadows moved over Diogo's sharp features. "These evil men devour our little ones, destroying families. They are Satan's finest foot soldiers."

"So, you protect children?"

"Exactly." His upper lip tugged into an expression somewhere between a smile and a snarl. "My family was destroyed by one of these men. We tried to recover. But my father killed himself, and my mother took to drink."

She imagined Diogo as a boy, hiding from an abuser.

"Do not pity me, *princesa.* I was able to take my vengeance. That man gnashes his teeth in hell as we speak."

She began to think something terrible may have already happened to Stephen and Hadiza.

"After I ended his reign of terror, another man popped up in his place. Then another. And another. Imagine how helpless I felt."

Diogo settled his eyes on her.

"That is when I understood evil rushes like a river, destroying everything in its path. It cannot be extinguished."

She whispered, "It must be redirected."

His trembling mouth drew into an emotional smile. "It is my calling to redirect the flow of evil *away* from those happy families."

Zahra looked at the wall of portraits. "What are you doing in this place?"

"These children are my innocent sacrifices."

Zahra voice pitched high. "Tell me!"

Diogo jerked his gaze to her. "No need to be uncivil, *princesa.* My innocents do not come from families."

Zahra's eyes burned. Her hand pressed against her waist where the cloth hid. "Hadiza is my family."

"Not by my definition. But I offer this." Diogo bowed slightly. "The world is better for your sacrifice."

Silver stars filled her vision. "How many of those men do you bring here?"

Diogo looked away, appearing to do mental math. "One could argue that my work saves many cities each year."

Her legs weakened. She sank to her knees.

Diogo sighed. He flicked two fingers at Sir Drake, who approached the heavy wooden door with the iron straps. "Unfortunate. I had hoped to have another ally on the throne."

Zahra mustered the energy to speak. "Where are Stephen and Hadiza?"

"I have grounds to execute him. He tricked my men to get inside."

Sir Drake turned a key in the lock and dragged the door open. Pierre emerged first, followed by Stephen, hands bound behind him. He was escorted by the threat of a double-curved *yatagan* blade.

Held by Biko.

CHAPTER 16

It stung to see Biko holding a blade to Stephen's back. They had formed an alliance, the three of them. She should have guessed he was a rat when he would not call the warriors to help Hadiza.

Zahra stood as Stephen's gaze settled on her. His hands were bound behind him, the embroidery of his tunic stretched across his chest. Pierre stepped through the door, chewing something small between his front teeth. Shoulder gripped by Biko, Stephen looked tense and ready to spring.

The corner of Diogo's mouth tucked in disdain. "*Princesa*, your man here is not who he seems. He was not here for Hadiza, but he sought another innocent."

Zahra nodded. "Mary."

Diogo's eyes bugged. He looked at Pierre, speaking in accented English. "Pierre, I am surprised to learn that there is a man here looking specifically for little Mary."

Zahra gasped. Did that mean Mary was here? Pierre cleaned his dagger with his sweat-stained tunic. He looked eager to bury it into Stephen's gut. Stephen now craned to look behind him at a particular panel coaled of a girl with light hair and clear eyes. The artist had captured in her expression a mixture of fear and rebellion.

Stephen turned, veins in his eyes visible. "Where is she?" he roared.

Pierre seized a fistful of Stephen's collar and pointed his blade near his ribs. Biko struggled to hold Stephen, pinning the double-bladed *yatagan* tautly at his back.

"Who is she to him?" Diogo stepped back. He cast a quick nod to Sir Drake, who disappeared into the iron-strapped door again.

Pierre shrugged. "He was in jail alongside Gilles de Rais. You think he wants that girl for any good reason, *patron*?"

Zahra stepped forward. "Mary is the daughter of Stephen's brother James, who is the son of John and Margery Kempe."

Diogo snorted. "I do not know who these people are."

"Perhaps this will help: *your* river of evil drowned Stephen's entire family."

Diogo closed his fingers into a fist, but otherwise, appeared perfectly calm. "What is rule number one of our operation, Pierre?"

Still holding the blade treacherously close to Stephen's ribs, Pierre said, "Orphans only."

He grinned.

Stephen bucked forward, butting his head into Pierre's skull. The Frenchman sprawled to the floor. The blade clattered. Biko clapped a hand to Stephen's shoulder, jutting his spear up into his back. "Stay back, *uroubi*!"

Stephen stood straight, the tendons of his neck pronounced. His chest rose and fell rapidly, blood dribbling at his ribs. Pierre rolled over and held his nose, blood pouring over his mouth and chin.

Diogo glanced impassively at Pierre. "Correct. Orphans only. We live and die by this rule, *princesa*. Pierre, stand down."

The Frenchman had snatched up his blade and scrabbled to a stand. At Diogo's word, he stilled, fixing a murderous stare on Stephen. His bloody nostrils flared.

"*Tonton*?" *Uncle.* A clear voice rang out from the iron-strapped doorway. Two children emerged ahead of Sir Drake: Hadiza, and a young girl with blonde hair and sea green eyes. She bore a striking resemblance to Stephen. Her nose wrinkled fitfully several times, her head shaking.

Stephen sank to one knee.

"Rabbit." The nickname caught in his throat.

She dashed forth, her arms out.

"Mary."

She stopped abruptly at the sound of Diogo's sharp voice. Hadiza wrapped her arms protectively around Mary's shoulders.

Stephen stood and turned to Diogo. "You're dead."

Biko's weapon must be digging into Stephen's back now—blood sprinkled on the floor at his feet.

"Biko, *tawaqaf!*" *Stop!* Zahra's shrill voice cut through the tension.

Biko struggled to get a firmer hold of the Englishman. Pierre gripped and regripped his dagger, waiting for his moment to use it. Diogo took another step back, standing between two soldiers. They withdrew their long swords, as if Stephen were a bull about to break out.

How could she possibly save all three of them? She could only think of one way that did not end in bloodshed.

"I have the relic."

Diogo cast her a heavy-lidded glance, his cheeks creasing as he smiled. "Hand it to me very slowly."

She lifted her chin. "You will allow all of us to go."

Diogo smiled. "Fine."

"*Anisa* Zahra, no!"

Zahra's heart jumped. Hadiza did not speak Portuguese, but she seemed to understand some negotiation was under way. What would it mean to give up the cloth? That she was abandoning its power? Or the good graces of the Creator? "Why do you want it, da Gama?"

Diogo looked at Mary and Hadiza. "To remind the children who holds the power in this place."

"You cannot claim power greater than whoever caused the ocean to bleed."

"Nonsense. That was some natural phenomenon."

"The plague of frogs?"

"The frogs fled the tainted water."

"The ice?"

Diogo's teeth flashed. "Strange weather events occur all the time. Each incident you attribute to the relic can be explained."

Zahra curled her fingers under her belt, withdrawing the cloth. "But this explains all of them."

The soldiers stepped back and Sir Drake disappeared through the iron-strapped doorway. Now would be an ideal moment for the power to work. Zahra envisioned a legion of flies attaching to Diogo. Disease erupting over his flesh, like the prosecutor in France. But no energy surged.

Diogo stepped forward, his palm up. "Well? Show us your power."

Stephen shifted in Biko's grip. Pierre stood close, his dagger poised near Stephen's stomach. Both Mary's hands gripped Hadiza's arm around her. Her eyes remained steadfast on her uncle. Hadiza inched backward, pulling Mary with her toward the door they had come through.

What was she doing? Zahra called out in Arabic, "Hadiza, come here."

But she kept drawing Mary back, tears gathering in her eyes. "You must come back for all of us, *anisa* Zahra."

"Mary!" Stephen's voice reverberated.

"Hadiza, come here!" Zahra gripped her gown and dashed forward. The shadows of the hallway swallowed them. Hadiza reached for the handle. Knowing she could not get there in time, Zahra halted. "Hadiza *ammughen n 'Isa, tazwara nnegh.*"

Hadiza, daughter of Jesus, our Savior.

Hadiza stopped, appearing stricken. The animals scuffled as tension mounted.

Stephen shot one fist after the other into Pierre's mouth. Pieces of frayed hemp dropped to the floor.

Pierre's eyes rolled as he staggered backward.

Biko must have cut the ropes!

Stephen hooked a blistering jab to Pierre's temple with the full weight of his shoulder. The Frenchman crashed like a tree.

Zahra held her hands out to Hadiza. "I came all this way for you."

Hadiza's grip on the handle loosened. Stephen sprinted straight for Mary. Eyes wide, Hadiza threw her weight back to yank the door shut with a reverberating boom.

Her voice echoed. "Come back for all of us!"

CHAPTER 17

"Mary!" Stephen roared.

Zahra ran, the door still vibrating from being slammed. Stephen reached it first, but its handle did not budge.

"Rabbit, open the door. Please, open the door." Stephen's tone was raw, desperate.

"It auto-locks." Diogo's lips pursed in a tight smile of delight. "A key is required on both sides. Beautiful, is it not? Engineered in Greece."

Stephen turned. "Open it."

"Only Sir Drake has the key on the other side for this very reason—"

"Open it!" Stephen took long strides toward Diogo, not seeming to notice as Zahra grabbed him by the crook of his elbow.

His arm was like stone as she tried to drag him to a halt. "Stephen, don't! We will die!"

The soldiers crouched in the defensive, weapons drawn. Stephen stopped, quivering with rage. Beads of sweat clung to Diogo's brow. Pierre lay unmoving next to the wall of portraits.

Something rumbled in the distance.

Diogo straightened. "*Princesa*, your slave has grievously harmed one of my men. What do you think his sentence will be?"

The accusation alone was an easy excuse for Jabir to order Stephen's execution.

"Our trade, then." She held out the cloth, her hand shaking. "Give us the girls."

Diogo just smiled. The rumbling sound grew louder. The door from the entry foyer burst open. Gordon strolled in, still caked in dry blood. Soldiers poured in behind him. Chickens clucked and the sheep crowded against the wall, ululating. Biko stood beside Stephen, clutching his *yatagan* blade anxiously.

Diogo stepped forward, as dozens of men lined up behind him. "I think I shall just take what is mine and keep the innocents."

"Mary has a family. What about that rule you live and die by?"

"I see a man obsessed with a child. Quite commonplace in my line of business."

Zahra was grateful Stephen did not speak Portuguese. She released his arm and stepped forward, her voice raw. "She calls him *tonton*. Uncle."

Diogo sniffed. "I do not know French."

"Zahra wields the power of God." Stephen issued the threat in a low tone.

Diogo's eyes darkened. "Or the power of Satan."

Zahra shook her head. "Would evil cause a young boy to become invisible to his abusers?"

His eyes widened for a moment—then the corner of his mouth quirked into a contemptuous smile. "God has always looked after me. Why do you think those innocents slipped through your fingers just now? Back to where they can do a world of good."

Thump thump.

As a surge of energy spiked through her hand where she clutched the cloth. She let forth a war-cry.

The goats screeched and stumbled to their knees. The sheep fell silent, crumpling, their wool shedding to the floor. The chickens collapsed, wings splayed. All the animals began to shrink and rot.

Swords drawn, the soldiers backed away from the invisible enemy. The animals' fur fluttered away, replaced by scaly flesh and crusty blisters. Their skin peeled back, teeth exposed as if they had been left too long under the sun.

Pestilence.

She locked eyes with Diogo and saw fear. Swords and shields clanged to the floor like trash. The soldiers fought one another to escape the chamber.

She commanded in Portuguese, "Let the children go."

"Never!" Diogo ducked down among his frenzying men.

"Get him!" Stephen roared, plowing forward through the horde.

But both Diogo and Gordon disappeared like ghosts.

• • • • •

Frogs had finally made their way into the palace. One flung and landed with a heavy slap on the swept stone walkway. Others rustled in the shrubbery, jowls undulating.

Zahra followed Stephen, who chased after Diogo's men. Anyone he snagged by the collar cowered, afraid of his threats and her presence.

They all said the same thing: only Diogo had a key to the iron-strapped door.

Their pursuit took them through the high garden. It had several tiers overlooking Jabalu Mountain, the gray stone mass that blocked their view of the sky. As a child, she often played here, slithering among the watermelon vines and dancing with dangling wisteria. Her dress snagged on a bramble, and she ripped it free, making a gruff sound of frustration.

Stephen grasped her arm. "*Ya rohi.* Breathe."

My soul. A nutty, fruity aroma cocooned them, pink flowering loquat trees hanging low. They stood before one another in the shade of an orange tree dangling with underripe fruit.

Zahra covered her face with her hands. "We almost had them!"

He pulled her against his chest, his heart beating wildly. "God has a plan."

She gripped his tunic in her fists and looked up at him. The whites of his eyes were tinged pink. How hard was it for him to say that, after almost having Mary in his arms, only to have her retreat into the belly of the beast?

She clutched his tunic, gazing up at him. "I want to do your plan, now."

He did not look encouraged by her declaration, in fact, his shoulders sagged.

Zahra put her hand in Stephen's, squeezing it. "Together we are strong. Alone, I am too weak."

With the gentlest of touches, he caressed her cheek, a smile on his angelic lips. "His power is made perfect in our weakness."

"*Amira!*" Biko's voice rang out from the bottom of the garden. He ran up, his slacks sliced open across his thigh.

Zahra sucked in a breath. "Your leg!"

"I am fine, *amira*. It is a shallow cut." Breathless, Biko briefly glanced at their clasped hands.

A row of cypress trees rustled under a strong gust of wind. Stephen spoke in Arabic. "*Akun.*" *Brother.* "Thank you. You saved us."

Biko shook his head. "Why did the Moorish girl take your niece?"

Stephen cleared his throat. He was unable to speak for several seconds. His fingers flexed around Zahra's hand. His voice was rough. "She thought we wouldn't come back for the others."

"Others?" Biko bowed his head, covering his mouth with his hand.

Stephen grasped Biko's shoulder. "Do not risk yourself anymore. Go against us if you have to."

Moisture gathered in Biko's eyes. "I cannot do that."

He shook the warrior's shoulder. "You have a wife, and children. Do what you must to protect them."

A tear broke free from Biko's eye.

Beyond the lowest garden tier, the large door handles rattled. Stephen withdrew his hand from Biko's shoulder. The doors creaked open. Zahra tugged her hand free from Stephen's, an act which stabbed her heart.

Several people emerged, led by *malik* Jabir. Behind him marched Raha, Yusef, and palace warriors. A few parched frogs hopped through.

Jabir halted next to Biko and glared across Stephen's blood-stained clothing. Zahra spoke first. "We discovered grievous wrongdoing being perpetrated against children in the Tower al-Garbu. I demand the traders be banished from Marbella, immediately."

"Did I not tell you I would take care of this in proper time?" Jabir's paternal good humor had been replaced by a king's fury.

"I had no choice. They took Stephen captive."

"He trespassed," said Jabir through his teeth. He flicked his fingers at Stephen, and warriors surrounded him cautiously, their spears glinting.

Zahra raised her voice. "To help the children, *baba*."

Jabir snapped, "*Malik*."

She flinched. Yusef stepped forward, his turban causing him to tower over Jabir. His bearded smile belied the seriousness of the moment. "The man he attacked was a Frenchman. And your slave is... English."

What story was being believed here? That Stephen hated Pierre because their two nations were at war in Europe? "He attacked Stephen first. Tell them, Biko!"

Biko squared his shoulders. "*Malik—*"

"Is the Frenchman dead?" Stephen cut in, speaking in Arabic.

Jabir lifted his bearded chin, narrowing his eyes. "He survived."

Stephen's gaze was as she remembered them in France—dark and cold. "*Safaqatan*." *Pity*.

"Take him," ordered Jabir.

Several warriors closed in. Stephen turned to Zahra. "Trust God. And do not sin in anger."

A bottomless well opened up inside of her. How had it come to this? Zahra had made all the same mistakes again. She extracted the cloth from her waistband. "You will need this." She tried to sound authoritative, but her voice trembled. Jabir's arm stretched to block her path.

"Where he is going, he will have no need for possessions." His aging teeth showed as he spoke in a measured tone. Stephen walked at the prodding of sharp spears, turning his back to her.

"He is an innocent man, *malik*."

He looked over her ruined wedding gown. "That is for Allah to decide."

In a moment of tragic clarity, Zahra realized it didn't matter what they said, how they said it, or when. Stephen could not escape Jabir's eager judgment. And any fervent protests would make her look hysterical—or worse; attached. So, she kept quiet, willing herself to remain emotionally distant and calm.

Just like Raha.

Jabir turned, his maidservants skittering after him. "Biko. Take the *amira* back to her chamber, where she shall remain until the ceremony tonight. Our union will be a private affair under the full moon."

Raha's murky eyes connected with Zahra's for an instant before she sauntered off. Yusef strode behind the men escorting Stephen, batting a frog out of his way with the butt of his spear.

She wished Stephen had looked back at her once more before disappearing through the darkened doorway.

• • • • •

Biko escorted Zahra to her chamber. He asked for her forgiveness. She told him, "There is nothing to forgive. Go be with your family."

Sukayna and several other maidservants buzzed around her, correcting what was in disarray from her disastrous day. They removed her bloodied *takchita* robe, but left the airy, sleeveless tunic and pantalettes, which remained unscathed.

Memories haunted her. Hadiza pulling Mary out of reach. Stephen's haunted resignation. The sound of crying boy. The portraits.

The maidservants stepped away, revealing her reflection. It repulsed her. Her black gown hugged her torso, onyx seed pearls shimmering. Multiple layers of filmy skirts rippled to the floor. Her lips were bold red, her dark cheekbones rosy. A wide, rippling scarlet sash cinched her waist, pooling down her hip as if she had been cut in in half. A wounded warrior queen.

Black was an unusual wedding gown color in Granada.

Not that she could refuse to wear it. She was merely the *malik's* property.

Was there a difference between a concubine and a wife? Between a slave and a queen? All were the toys of men to be passed around until no longer useful.

Stephen had been different. The last thing he had said to her was not to sin in anger, and to trust Him. Hadn't she been doing that so far? Doing right by the cloth? She imagined what Stephen might have replied to that. "The cloth is not the Lord."

But Stephen was not here. And the cloth was all she had left.

The faded moon hung in the late afternoon sky, as if arriving early to make sure Zahra didn't miss her appointment.

She wished to sleep. Having just styled her hair in regal plaits and pearls, her maidservants insisted she not lie down. They settled her into a woven chair on the balcony terrace and promised to return in an hour to take her to the ceremony. Thousands of deceased frogs were a blight on the golden sand. The crimson ocean glinted as if winking at her.

Once alone, she held up the cloth. She had an urge to rip it in half, to show God how she felt. Imagining it, a twinge clenched in her gut. Perhaps that was the fear of God—understanding the consequences of turning against Him.

In moments of desperation, she had made small prayers, but she had always kept her mind open to who it could be. This time, she did it differently.

"Right now, I am—I pray specifically to You." She whispered. "Jesus. The Christ. The Jewish Messiah." She cleared her throat. "And… our savior." Her cheeks burned with embarrassment. But why? No one was watching her. "Please, help me. Help the children. It is all that matters."

Moisture collected on her eyelashes.

When the snake had appeared, Isabelle had just been murdered. When Chapeillon had contracted leprosy, he had just informed Stephen he was to hang. When the flies had attacked Sohrab, the soldiers had just blocked her from leaving the Tower al-Garbu. What was the common thread?

She tried to empty her mind. Cruel images of Stephen's inevitable execution played out instead. A shiver coursed through her body.

When the ocean had seeped with blood, Stephen had just pulled her into the water at the fan mussel cove. Their twilight moment in the lighthouse made her pulse quicken. She would never forget the way he had gazed at her, enraptured. She shook off a wave of grief that burned in her eyes.

When the frogs had overtaken the beach, Hadiza had just been dangling from the winch hook. When the animals had rotted away, Hadiza and Mary had been just within her reach. Zahra had failed yet again.

Unbidden, her mind tripped and landed on the memory of her conversation with Merla.

"What child are you looking for?"

"Raha."

Hadiza and Raha occupied the same space in her mind—a child she had failed to protect for her own selfish reasons. The Creator had made each of these children—and He had created Zahra, too. How displeased He must be with her.

"I'm sorry," she whispered.

Thump thump.

Her vision went black. She was no longer in her bedchamber, but in a humid cell. Stephen sat on the floor nearby, his hands bound behind him. His head rested back against the wall, his eyes closed. Yet she knew he was not asleep, because his brow was slightly furrowed. She reached to touch his shoulder, to comfort him.

Her hand passed right through him. She must be dreaming. A breeze rustled the hem around her ankles. She peeked, and saw she was still on the woven chair on the balcony, the cloth thrumming with energy in her grip.

Closing her eyes, she was alone with Stephen in the cell again. Her breathing quickened. What was happening?

Metal clanked. Stephen opened his eyes and looked past Zahra.

Raha carried a lantern, a thick braid draped over her shoulder. She pulled the prison door shut behind her. She was alone. She looked simple. Young. And beautiful.

"Everyone is preparing for the reception." She spoke in a sweet tone Zahra had not heard her use. It reminded her of when she was a child; humble and heart-melting. "The ceremony itself is to be private."

Stephen's jaw flexed. In his accented Arabic, he asked, "Is she aware of what will occur during this ceremony?"

A smile tugged Raha's full, bare lips. "I do not think so. She believes she is so smart, but she is naïve to the ways of the world."

Stephen stared at her. "And you feel nothing?"

Raha placed the lantern on the floor beside him. "Just as she felt nothing for me, *uroubi*."

A lump wedged in Zahra's throat. She was right.

Raha untied her silk evening robe and shed it into a pile around her feet. A ruby night shift showed her shapely calves. The lantern light revealed the sheer nature of the fabric, and perhaps more notably, that Raha quivered from head to toe.

Stephen's eyes widened. "What are you doing?"

She scooped her long braid off her shoulder. "You have lived in my mind ever since I first saw you. This is the only way I can cleanse myself of you."

He sat straighter.

Zahra pressed her hand to her chest. She knew her sister had taken to drink, but was she capable of such depravity? Zahra bitterly recalled Raha's opportunistic personality. It seemed she had lurked until Stephen was captured to be disloyal to the king.

As Raha knelt beside him, Stephen found his voice. "Such a thing would harm you, *malika*."

"It is my only desire." Her eyes trailed over him, as if uncertain what to do. She reached a trembling hand toward his leg.

Stephen avoided her touch, his eyes intent. "It would not help you."

She rested her hands in her lap. "I shall remove your binds. And leave this prison unlocked."

Zahra inhaled. Raha would allow him to escape. He could possibly survive this ordeal. Would Stephen consider it? Did Zahra even want him to?

"I will not do this."

Raha's nostrils flared. "Then I will tell everyone you tried."

"I love my wife, *malika*."

She looked down, brow furrowed. "What difference does that make?"

"I… do not want you." He did not seem eager to say the words, his tone gentle.

Raha's eyelids fluttered as if he had dealt a physical blow. Lines of anguish formed in her brow.

"But the King does want you."

Raha shook her head sharply. "He does not want me. Only an heir."

"Not Jabir. Our King, Jesus Christ, wants you."

Raha reeled back. "How dare you say that to me?"

Shackled in a death cell, Stephen Kempe proclaimed Christianity to a Muslim queen? Was he bent on meeting his end? "He allowed your desire for me to grow, so you would come to me. Now He wants you to know that He loves you, and cares for you. Seek Him, and you will find rest."

Raha spoke through her teeth. "I seek no one but Allah."

"Did you choose that path?"

She pushed back into a crouch like a cornered bobcat. "Did you choose yours?"

Stephen nodded. "After I learned of His son, Jesus, who came to be among us and show us His heart. Your heart can be like His. You can purge your hate, lust, and sin, and find joy."

She struck him. It wasn't the mother hen slap Zahra had given him days ago. Raha belted him across his jaw with her fingers curled. He huffed an exhale. But he had seemed to expect it. He turned his gaze back to her. "Raha, do you know why Zahra left Marbella? The whole story?"

Her teeth showed. "What do you speak of?"

"The day she left, the day after your mother died, she had just learned that she would not be marrying *amir* Yusef as planned, but the man she called *Baba*."

"It is a feeling I know well."

"That night, she ran to Yusef for comfort."

Heat swept over Zahra's body. The other Zahra must have told Stephen all of this. Dread filled her chest.

"And he did comfort her. For a moment."

Zahra's closed eyelids trembled. She had an urge to get up, walk away—but fearing she might lose this connection, she remained still. Her fingers flexed, and she tightened her hand over the lodestones pouch instead of taking them out.

"He decided Jabir would not have what was promised to him. Zahra's purity."

"You lie."

"Yusef held Zahra down and stole her innocence. When she cried afterward, he told her to be glad her first time was not with her stepfather."

Raha swung her head side to side. "Not possible."

"He gave her two stones—lodestones—to remind her of what would happen if she told. That he would claim she had tempted him, and her sentence would be a brutal stoning."

The moment Yusef had placed the cool magnetic stones in her moist palm, she had wished he would use them against her. She had felt like a glass jar, its valuable contents emptied, no longer serving a purpose. He could have shattered her and swept her into the garbage.

After she abandoned Raha, she engraved them with the Latin words to remind herself that she could take control of her destiny.

Raha swallowed. "*Amir* Yusef would not do that."

"Just as you would not do to me?"

Raha's gaze dropped. The flickering lantern illuminated tears on her cheeks. They were silent for a long time.

Eventually, Raha lifted her gaze to him. "I merely wish to feel love."

"Raha." Stephen's voice was gentle. "You are just a child. You also had your innocence stolen. These burdens are not yours. Let Him take them from you. You will need no one but Him to feel love."

Raha shook her head, avoiding his intense gaze. "I would not know how to do what you are saying."

"Seek Him, and you will believe. When you believe, you will ask to be forgiven. When you are forgiven, your heart will turn from sin."

Raha glared. "I deserve to sin, just once. I can make up for it."

"Haven't you defiled yourself with me a hundred times before coming here tonight?"

Her eyebrows furrowed together.

"'You have heard it said, 'Thou shall not commit adultery.' But I say to you that whoever looks with lustful intent has already committed adultery in their heart.'"

The color in Raha's cheeks deepened.

"And haven't you murdered Jabir a thousand times?"

She gasped. "I would never!"

"'You have heard, "Thou shall not commit murder." But I say, if you are even angry with someone, you are subject to judgment. If you curse someone, you are in danger of the fires of hell.'"

Raha pursed her lips. She appeared to be losing patience for this conversation. "You people cannot think bad thoughts? That is not even possible."

"I know. That is why He made a way for us."

Raha gestured to Stephen, sitting bound. "It does not look like He made a way for you."

He smiled soberly. "'Whoever believes in Him shall not perish but have eternal life.'"

Raha curled her lip, unconvinced. "You say 'Jesus' is all I need to feel love. Does that mean you did not need your wife to feel love?"

Stephen appeared momentarily speechless. He looked down. "She is in a place I cannot get back to."

Zahra's heart skipped. Stephen was not talking about her. He clearly referred to the other Zahra. A dull ache pitted itself in her stomach. Jealousy.

The cell chamber disappeared. The bond was lost.

CHAPTER 18

Zahra clenched the cloth in her fist and sat straight. It was Raha! The mention of Raha seemed to make God's power work. Whenever something supernatural happened, Raha, or a child she equated to Raha, had been mentioned or threatened.

She stumbled over the hem of her gown on the way inside from the balcony. She had to get to Stephen. She pulled at her door, but it did not budge. She took a step back. The maidservants had locked her in? Was Zahra a prisoner in her own home, where she was to become queen, ruler of Marbella?

The truth hit her. What Stephen had been trying to tell her. She would not have any power as *malika*. She would be only another tool in Jabir's repertory. She would be used for power. And pleasure.

Her door shook. The wooden cross bar locking her in scraped aside. She stuck the cloth under her ruby sash and backed away as the door swung open.

Yusef.

Zahra's quick pulse filled her throat. "What are you doing here?"

Yusef smiled, strolling in and shutting it behind him. "I wish to congratulate you before your big night."

"Get out." A tremor snuck into her voice.

His expression darkened. "I do not take orders from you. Not now, not ever. It was unwise of you to come back."

"There are children trapped in the—"

"Ya, da da da da." He spoke over her like she was a noisy gong. "Allah, does she ever shut up? You yap, and you yap, and yap, and no one hears you, little Zahra. No one cares what you say. Least of all Jabir."

She bumped into the edge of the wash basin, then stumbled around it.

His path toward her remained unchanging. "Do you think he would react well to knowing that you are not innocent? If you do as I wish, I will not reveal it to him."

Memories of that night slapped her like relentless waves trying to pull her under. Yusef's dense body on hers. His hot breath on her ear. The searing pain. The moment her fear had been replaced by numb hopelessness.

Her voice pitched high. "I will scream."

"No one will hear. All are far off, preparing for the big reception." His eyes skimmed over her. "Afterward, you will face the same choice as before: follow through on your most important duties as *malika*, or… run away."

Yusef neared. He could grab her at any moment.

Her back hit the wall. "I blamed myself for what you did to me." Her voice trembled. "I thought I had confused you."

His upper lip curled. His hand slapped the wall beside her head. She flinched. He leaned in close. "It was that night dress you arrived in."

Heart racing, she braced herself. "It was not the dress, Yusef. You are just evil."

He grinned as his hand slithered over her ribs. "Allah decides who is evil."

Every muscle in her body clenched. "What happened to Raha after I left?"

Yusef leaned back. "She was betrothed to Jabir, to save him embarrassment."

"When did they actually wed?"

The corner of Yusef's mouth twitched slightly, as if trying to suppress a smile. "I heard she begged her maidservant not to tell the *malik* when she had her first cycle. She was nine."

Thump thump.

"She asked where you were for months."

Thump thump.

"Then one day, she stopped asking."

Thump thump.

Each of his words were like a blade twisting in her gut. Zahra had lived a better life with Lord Raymond, while Raha fended for herself among the wolves. Raha was right to hate her. Tears streaked down her cheeks, but her body thrummed with familiar energy. She pushed off the wall. Yusef jerked back, confused.

He froze.

He slapped his own hand, then his arm, and his face. A multitude of tiny bugs crawled over his skin. He stumbled another step and scratched at the collar of his tunic. He clawed his scalp under his turban, knocking it off. He scrubbed rough at his beard, his skin reddening.

"What is this?" He rubbed his eyes. Lice infiltrated every fiber of hair—his head, his eyebrows, his lashes. "*Sahirata*!" *Witch.*

Yusef turned and fled. He climbed into the washbasin, water splattering out. He shrieked, brow twisted. He looked down at his arms. Bleeding boils erupted on his flesh like mushrooms.

His anguish satisfied Zahra. It was justice for the pain he had caused her as a little girl. The sick plans he had for her today. He deserved all of this, and more.

She stood at the edge of the bath. He tried to climb out but sank back when his exposed wounds touched the stone. Patches of his skin broke away in bloody chunks. He thrashed like a lobster being boiled alive. His screams went unheard.

"All are far off, preparing for the big reception."

This would not stop. Not like with Sohrab and the flies. She knew, because she lorded over Yusef, willing it to happen. To worsen. She *wanted* to see him die. She wanted his punishment to be final. A smile tugged at her mouth.

Unbidden, she remembered a conversation with Stephen.

"A specific event caused it to stop working. If you keep following this path, the same may occur to you."

"What happened?"

"Something happened with Yusef. I cannot say more."

She recalled Stephen's final words to her.

"Trust God. And do not sin in anger."

Zahra knew what had happened with Yusef to make the cloth stop working for the other Zahra. She had let it kill him. *She* had killed him.

Zahra gasped. Yusef began moaning as his flesh disintegrated. She hurled the cloth to the floor. "Stop! Stop! Please, God, do not let this happen. Please! Make it stop!"

It did not stop. He would die by her hatred.

Yusef slumped, sinking under the surface. She raced around the pool, grappling his bloodied shoulders. She could not pull him out, but she kept him from slipping under water. His bleeding face tipped like a rag doll, his eyes sliding sideways to look at her. He did not appear afraid anymore—he only looked sad.

A tight boil on his cheek stopped distending. The blisters slowed to a halt, receding, leaving wrinkled pock marks. Yusef moaned. She repositioned her grip on his shoulders, keeping him afloat. The lice seemed to have vanished, leaving only vicious claw marks striping his skin.

He rolled his eyes to peer down at the water soiled by his own blood and flesh. He whimpered, tears leaking from his red-rimmed eyes. "You saved me."

She still feared him, but she was far more afraid of this power. She had almost killed a man; extinguished his life. With glee.

Yusef whispered, "How?"

Her voice shook. "I do not cause the power. This is—it is the power of the God Christians believe in."

He snuck a glance upward. He must be thinking about Allah, and damnation should he consider her claims. He bowed his head. "Could you ever forgive me?"

She remembered Raha as a child. Her growling laughter when being tickled. Resting her head on Zahra's shoulder as they planned the day after the funeral. She had had trouble understanding why their mother was gone, asking Zahra if Mama would be able to breathe underground. For years, Zahra tortured herself imagining Raha being alone in the huge palace. Her dimpled smile fading as she learned what she was to do on her wedding night. Zahra recalled how hollow Raha's eyes looked now, as she kept herself inebriated. Her tormented expression in Stephen's cell.

All of that was because of Zahra's choice ten years ago.

Yusef was a monster—and he now looked like a monster, erupted sores glistening red in the firelight.

"Now," she whispered near his ear. "I forgive you now, Yusef."

Yusef's shoulders shook underneath her arms. His cheeks slackened, tears running into his beard. His eyes remained closed as if sewn shut by shame. "Why? I deserve to be dead."

Zahra's voice was a mere whisper. "Because I wish to be forgiven."

• • • • •

Zahra sent for a healer and gave no explanation. She hastened along obscure pathways. After the encounter with Yusef, she felt closer to the Creator than ever before. She prayed He would help her free Stephen—again.

Then they could infiltrate the Tower al-Garbu together, the way they should have from the start.

As she rounded a corner, she rammed into a woman. A pitcher shattered at their feet. Black powder spilled around them. An eggy scent arose.

"Sukayna!" Zahra stepped around the mess. "Why do you have *mashuq aswadu?*" *Sulfur.*

Sukayna knelt to clean it up. "I was ordered to bring it to the *malik*."

Zahra crouched, helping Sukayna gather shards of clay. "This is used for explosive warfare. Why would he have need of this?"

"I do not know!" Sukayna ducked her eyes. "Forgive me, *amira*. I do not know what is happening. I am afraid."

Zahra took the broken base of the pitcher filled with its smaller broken pieces and set it aside. A large frog hopped around the corner, causing Sukayna to screech. Zahra pressed her hand to Sukayna's back, leading her away. "Can you help me enter the prisoner chambers without being detected?"

"Your slave has been relocated."

Zahra stopped abruptly. "Why?"

"*Malika's* orders."

"I must find him. I cannot marry the *malik*."

Sukayna's neck visibly tensed, her forehead puckering. "*Amira*, you must!"

Zahra had not expected such a reaction from Sukayna. "What is it?"

The maidservant gripped Zahra's arms. "*Malik* Jabir will not rest until he has wedded al-Uzza."

Zahra's skin prickled. "What do you know of this?"

Sukayna seemed to have trouble swallowing as she considered her answer. "He believes… that the goddess of fertility can be made incarnate through creation. Birthing. But your sister, Raha, was never with child."

Zahra uttered a sound of disgust. "Incarnate? He thinks he can bring the goddesses to life?"

Sukayna dipped her chin in a nod, not looking Zahra in the eye. "And he believes the virgin goddess, al-Uzza, can be made incarnate through consummation."

Zahra's blood ran hot. How long had Jabir harbored these fantasies? "Sukayna, did my mother know about this?"

The whites of Sukayna's eyes shone. "Yes, *amira*. Jabir performed a ritual on your mother ten years ago."

Ten years ago. Zahra's breathing quickened. "How—what did he believe about Manat?"

Sukayna seemed hesitant, her hands clenched together. "That Manat comes in the flesh… through death."

Zahra pressed her hand to a nearby limestone wall as a wave of dizziness hit her.

Tears fell as Sukayna fluttered her eyelashes. "It did not work."

"This cannot be true."

Yet it rang true. She had been too young to properly interrogate anyone about the details surrounding her mother's death. She had been told it was an illness she could catch. But there was nothing to catch.

It was murder.

"Jabir." Zahra's voice exhaled on a growl. "Take me to him."

Without an utterance of opposition, Sukayna led the way.

• • • • •

Zahra strode into the *Mashwar*, the ceremony hall. It was empty. Firelight bounced over the walls, the etched Arabic calligraphy dancing. The light came from between the spokes of a lofted entresol, where Jabir's shadow rose and stooped in the rhythmic prostration of prayer.

"Jabir," she called.

"Please, *amira*." Sukayna whispered urgently. "Do not tell him what I revealed to you."

Jabir emerged at the banister, peering down at her. "Allah be praised, you look stunning."

Zahra glanced down at her gown. When Jabir had said their ceremony would be 'private,' she did not think they would be alone.

"I shall not marry you." Her voice echoed off the polished mahogany ceiling.

Sukayna darted forth, disappearing into the stairwell leading up to the entresol. One of Jabir's eyebrows hitched. "Why have you decided this?"

Zahra had come to condemn him for her mother's death, but now did not wish to betray Sukayna. Jabir might not be merciful to the servant. "Your goddess fantasy is dangerous."

Behind him, the fire blazed in a brazier, a large metal bowl burning wood. Obscured by shadows, his cheeks pushed into a smile. "That is what I love about you. Your innocence. You have always believed you had a choice."

The urge to run surged through her. She took a step backward and bumped into someone. The ox-faced warrior grabbed her arm. A flicker of fear shone in his eyes, but his grip was like an iron shackle.

Zahra forced herself to relax. The warrior guided her up the small spiral staircase leading to the entresol. The bronze brazier blazed next to a table used for animal sacrifices. Blood stained the imperfections and cracks that ran through the marble. Jabir gestured to the table.

Zahra pushed against the warrior for a split moment. But she compelled herself to remain calm. She allowed images of Raha to wash over her, to activate the powers of the cloth.

But she could only conjure images of Raha's visit to Stephen's prison chamber, propositioning him. Even her mother, a *qayna*, although a concubine, had elite status. She would have never skulked through the palace looking for 'love.' Zahra tried to think of Raha as a child, innocent. But each attempt was transplanted by Raha's sheer night dress, her thick braid, her tears. Had they been fake? Where was Stephen, now? Sukayna said he had been relocated at Raha's orders.

Had he been relocated to her bedchamber?

Zahra tried to shake the bitter thoughts. She had been so confident she would be able to 'work' the cloth, as she had with Yusef. Now she found herself secured by rope onto the table like a docile lamb. The round mahogany ceiling looked like a bottomless pit. She craned her neck until she spotted Sukayna. She pled with her eyes, but the maidservant just ducked her gaze.

Jabir stood back, his anticipatory expression illuminated. "Do not be afraid of this ritual."

Zahra tested the ropes. They held fast like iron. "This 'ritual' killed my mother!"

Jabir looked in Sukayna's direction. She genuflected. He said, "That was an unfortunate accident that you should never have known about."

Her chest filled with pressure. Her breathing grew shallow. "Will tonight's accident be unfortunate?"

"You misunderstand. The ritual is different because you are different."

She closed her eyes. Apparently, her mother had been naïve enough to lie here. Zahra had been naïve enough to end up here. Or arrogant enough.

Jabir nodded to Sukayna. The maidservant approached, and untied Zahra's crimson sash, removing it along with Hadiza's cloth.

As understanding dawned, Zahra's chest rose and fell.

"And he believes the virgin goddess, al-Uzza, can be made incarnate through consummation."

"Do not do this, Jabir," she urged, her voice sharp. "I am no follower of Allah, let alone his daughter!"

Sukayna began unfastening the many clasps at the front of Zahra's beaded black gown. Jabir's eyes reflected the popping fire. "I loved Ghaliba. But you, daughter, are pure."

She sucked in a breath. "I am not! I am not pure. I am not—I have known a man."

Jabir glared in Sukayna's direction. The maidservant's eyes widened. "*Malik,* I swear she told me in confidence that she had never been with a man."

Jabir looked between the two women, and then smiled. He unfastened the embroidered ties of his royal robes. "Cunning. You were always so clever."

Her voice grew shrill. "Please believe me! It was Yusef. When I was young. Before I ran away."

Jabir paused again, staring hard into Zahra's eyes. He shook his head. Sukayna unclasped the final fastener and spread Zahra's gown open, exposing her linen under garments. A chill washed over her. Jabir approached.

Panicked, Zahra blurted the first prayer that came to mind. "'Bow down thine ear, oh Lord, hear me, for I am weak and need you.'"

Jabir countered her prayer with a haunting Arabic chant. "By al-Lat and al-Uzza and Manat, verily they are the most exalted, and their intercession is to be hoped for." His bejeweled hand tugged the drawstring of her pantalettes. Zahra clamped her eyes shut, seeking comfort by thinking of Stephen. But the thought of him brought only self-condemnation. He had warned her. Repeatedly.

A loud crack of wood on stone echoed up from the ground floor of the *Mashwar.*

"It is true." Yusef's strong voice came from the main floor.

Robes hanging open, Jabir approached the railing. "Guards!"

Panting, Zahra strained to see between the spokes of the entresol railing.

Jabir put his hands on the banister. His jaw fell slack.

Yusef said, "As you can see, brother, I can do no harm to anyone."

Jabir held up a hand to stay his warriors, gazing down at his younger brother. A tapping sound punctuated each of Yusef's footsteps as he struggled his way up the stairs. When he appeared in the entresol, he leaned on a cane. He was strapped in muslin, blood spotting his tunic and linen slacks. It looked like a hasty medical intervention.

Even his eyes had transformed; once arrogant and cruel, they were now humbled and determined.

Jabir exhaled the words, "*Ya raby,* brother, what has happened to you?"

Yusef's eyes locked on Zahra's, glistening. "What I deserved."

Jabir followed Yusef's gaze to Zahra. "Seems you now know that Zahra has been gifted the powers of al-Uzza."

Yusef's upper lip trembled. "I do not believe that is the source of her power, brother."

"The ceremony we shall complete now is said to plant the seed of Manat. With her powers at our disposal, Marbella would become a nation that could crush all its enemies."

Yusef looked at his brother, the king. "Who told you this? Certainly not Muhammad, *sallallahu alayhi wa sallam.*" *Peace be upon him.*

"Tell me the truth." Jabir stepped forward; his voice rising. "If you defiled her, you have ruined Allah's well-laid plans. And that is punishable by death."

Yusef dipped his chin in a single nod. "I accept responsibility for what I have done."

The *malik* wrinkled his nose and bared his teeth. For a moment she thought he might lunge at his brother. Instead, Jabir's cheeks drooped, and he sighed. "I had not cast out the traders in case the ritual failed. I must protect Marbella. I truly did love you, Zahra."

Past tense. Now that she no longer served a purpose, she was not '*amira*' or 'daughter.' She was only a tool for him to produce an heir.

"Jabir." Hatred burned through Zahra's veins. She knew she was doomed, and she wished to damage him in return. "You will never have children. You are likely infertile."

His eyes narrowed, the firelight stressing the deep lines in his haggard face. "Guards," he called out over the banister. "Escort the former *amira* to see the *malika* Raha."

A pinch of confusion formed between Yusef's eyebrows. "Why send her to see Raha?"

Jabir never took his eyes off Zahra. "To say goodbye."

• • • • •

Zahra had hastily closed her gown and snatched Hadiza's cloth as they escorted her out. The walk through the empty palace felt weighed down by doom. She pulled out the lodestones, turning them in her palm. She stopped. The soft buzz failed to comfort her.

They arrived at the *hujratu mushamasat*, the glass sunroom. When the doors opened, Raha remained still, lying in the shadows on a tufted lounge. Particularly eerie at night, sparsely placed lanterns burned dim. Anything brighter would attract animals. Raha still wore the loose braid and silk night robe Zahra had seen in her vision. She hugged a goblet against her chest and stared into the dark forest.

The trail of her black wedding gown flowed like a rippling stream of tar behind her. "You were right, you know. When you said I could not bring myself to call you *malika.*"

Raha turned, her eyes wide. She set the goblet down and stood.

Heat rose to Zahra's cheeks as she approached her little sister. "But it is not because I am jealous. It is because the title reminds me of what I did to you."

The queen stared back at her.

She took another step closer. "If I could go back and tell that little girl not to leave, I would."

Yusef had been brave enough to ask for forgiveness, despite all the evil he had committed. So would Zahra. She now stood just a few feet away. "I got a clean escape ten years ago. You were my bait."

Zahra could not look at her sister as she mustered a mere whisper. "I thought I was saving myself. But leaving you was like cutting out part of my heart. The part that was you."

She took her sister's bejeweled hand and pressed the lodestones into her palm, finally looking into her eyes. "I never let myself forget I deserved to be stoned for what I did to you."

The queen's features trembled, making her resemble the young girl she truly was.

"I'm so sorry, *shaqiyqati.*" Zahra squeezed her baby sister's hand.

Raha's eyes had grown moist, but her tone remained cold. "Apologies do not mend."

The rejection lanced Zahra's heart. This would be the last time she would hold her sister's hands. "Jabir sent me to say goodbye to you."

Raha jerked her hand out of Zahra's grasp to swipe a tear off her cheek. The stones fell to the rug. Zahra grappled for them with a fervor she did not understand.

"Goodbye to me? Or him?" Raha stepped aside. Through the glass, a flicker of light shone deep in the forest. Past their reflections and the swaying foliage, a lantern sat in a clearing, illuminating a man. He was kneeling, his head bowed, arms bound behind him to the crooked trunk of an olive tree.

Stephen.

Zahra uttered a cry, rushing to the glass. The wind caught dangling strands of his hair. His chest rose and fell—he was alive. His lips moved. He was praying.

Zahra whispered, "Please God help him." The cloth did nothing.

"Take her," said Raha, her voice hoarse.

A warrior pulled Zahra off the glass. She wrenched free and plunged to Raha's feet. She clung to the hem of Raha's robe. "*Sahibu alsmu almalaki, malika.*" *Your royal highness, queen.* "I beg you to stop this."

The palace warrior snatched Zahra up. She flung one of the stones. It smacked the glass, creating a small crack that grew in size several times before halting. The warrior twisted her arms behind her, dragging her out. She craned to see her sister. "Raha, please! Do not do this! Stephen is a good man!"

She locked eyes with her sister. "I love him, Raha!"

The lantern lights blurred to blobs in the dark as they hauled her out. Raha did nothing.

CHAPTER 19

In the entry foyer of the Tower al-Garbu, the palace warriors unceremoniously passed Zahra into the unforgiving grip of Portuguese soldiers. The remaining lodestone pitted itself in her palm. No comforting spinning, and no satisfying click of magnetic attraction. One stone; utterly useless.

Frogs lay rotting in every corner. The monstrous shield loomed. The clover-shaped windows winked the full moon. Would it be the last Zahra would see of the sky? The decomposed livestock in the sitting parlor had been swept, but the stench of death still lingered. The portraits of the children were gone.

The image of Stephen awaiting his demise in the clearing haunted her.

Sir Drake, the older Englishman, led them past the iron-strapped door she had last seen Hadiza and Mary disappear through. Zahra gained access not as a commanding queen, but as one of its prisoners.

Familiarity struck her. The winding hallways had low ceilings with wooden cross beams. Once majestic tapestries collected dust. Clay pots full of flax straw lined the floors. Where would they take her? Tower al-Garbu's cylindrical construction unfurled in her mind. It had only a single stairway connecting several floors: the grain storehouse, the prison chamber, the kitchen, a small library, the steam room with a copper boiler, the mosque, the infirmary, and dozens of bedchambers. The entire top floor was the Solar, where her mother had resided.

They stopped at the prison. A humid chill hung in the air. It had glossy tile floors and various dangling chains. Pierre stood in the shadows, wiping his short blade with a rag. Beside him, a man slumped in a chair, head hanging.

"Biko!" She lunged, but the guard tightened his grip.

"Let her." Diogo da Gama's voice came from somewhere in the dark.

She rushed to Biko and clutched his shoulders. A fresh wound oozed among the folds of Biko's scalloped tabard. She pressed her hands over it, unable to draw a proper breath. Recognition flickered in his eyes. "I thought I could help you. And those children. I failed."

Zahra closed her eyes tight. Amongst wet inhales, Biko struggled to smile. "*Huriat aalma.*" *Mermaid.* His lips trembled and his smile faded. "Do not try to fight him."

Blood spilled between her fingers. She fumbled for Hadiza's cloth and applied it to Biko's wound. She pressed her forehead into his shoulder and prayed.

You are the Creator of the universe. Heal him. Please do not let him pay the price for me being a fool.

Biko's chin drooped, his rough cheek touching her face. His inhales came in short puffs. "He is a god in this place," he whispered, sucking one last, short breath. He went still.

Zahra clutched him and let out a rough cry. "Why?"

"To show you I can." Diogo's tone was upbeat. "Bring them in."

Lantern light poured in from the hallway, accompanied by jangling metal. A string of children shuffled in, their eyes averted, wrists strapped in bar-shackles. Each one interconnected to the other by rusted chains.

An olive-skinned boy with dark circles under his eyes clung to a thin Arabic girl with a jagged pink scar across her face. A tall girl with frizzy blonde locks stared at the ground. A boy had freckles and wide-set blue eyes. A tan girl with wild brown locks and delicately flared nostrils held hands with a pale girl whose hair resembled fire. A terribly young boy with a broad face and pitch-black hair sniffled. Another girl had Moorish features but light skin and eyes. The youngest, perhaps four, was a boy with mysterious brown eyes and dark, curly hair. The tallest was the long-haired boy with the fierce gaze that Diogo had called Hassan. Hadiza and Mary crept in last.

Hadiza caught sight of Zahra and her face lit up. Mary's eyes widened, shining the pure green of the Alboran Sea just before a warm rain.

Hot tears blurred Zahra's vision and she looked down at her hands, where lay the bloody cloth and one lodestone. How could she face these children, who had placed all their hope on her?

Diogo gestured to Zahra, speaking in Portuguese. "Innocents. Meet your 'savior.'"

Several children merely darted their eyes in Diogo's direction, then down again.

He approached Zahra and held out his hand, long fingers outstretched. She looked at the crimson-stained cloth. It had not saved Biko. It did not seem to work for her at all anymore. She had no leverage.

Was God here at all? With His power, all this could have been resolved by now. Whose power was it? Did anyone know for certain?

She held out the cloth. Hadiza drew in a sharp gasp, her eyes filling with tears. Diogo wrinkled his nose as he plucked it out of her palm.

"And in exchange." Diogo untied a leather pouch from his waistband. He overturned it, spilling a multitude of tiny seeds over her black gown. Mustard seeds.

He discarded the pouch and laughed. "That is a specific amount—thirty. Instead of thirty pieces of silver."

Thirty—as many coins Judas had accepted to betray Jesus. Thirty to signify that she had betrayed the children by giving him the cloth. She bowed her head.

Diogo circled the children. "Do you know what is most dangerous for you? Hope. Hope has made you believe you can escape your God-given destiny."

The dim lantern light reflected on Hadiza's tears. Some of the children cowered when Diogo passed by. Hassan watched the man furtively.

He stopped beside the lantern. The expensive embroidery on his cork-soled shoes gleamed. "*Princesa*, please know that no one is more pained by my innocents' suffering than I am. It is my own sacrifice in all this."

Those eyes, as dark as chasms to hell, glittered in the flame light.

He turned and addressed the children. "The purpose you serve far outweighs the pain you endure. You suffer just as Jesus suffered."

"They cannot understand you!" Zahra's scream cut through the room like a javelin, bouncing off the walls. The children covered their ears, and the youngest one buried his head against a girl's back and cried.

"How uncivil." Diogo smiled. "Perhaps they will understand this."

He held the cloth over the lantern's flame.

It caught on fire.

"No!" Zahra dove toward Diogo, but Pierre snatched her back, twisting her arms. Pain spiked through her shoulder blades.

Smoke rose as the flame devoured the bloody cloth. Diogo dropped it to the tiled floor. Hadiza wept and pressed her cheek into Mary's head.

Diogo splayed his hands in an apologetic gesture. "As much as I relish these small successes, clients await. Guards, leave Hassan; he shall be visited in here."

The plume of fire turned to cinders, leaving a pile of steaming ashes. Zahra's legs slackened. Pierre was all too happy to drag her out of the chamber amidst the wailing sound of broken hope.

• • • • •

Pierre shoved her into a bedchamber. She spun around as he slammed the door, plunging her into darkness. The lock engaged. She banged on it until her fists were sore.

Unable to see, images of death surfaced to give her company. She pressed the heels of her palms to her eyes, trying to unsee all that she had witnessed. Stephen's grief when forced to leave Mary behind. Biko's empty eyes as he died. Raha's cold neutrality as Zahra begged at her feet. The children's elongated faces as their final thread of hope snapped.

Zahra's temples throbbed. Without windows, she would soon lose track of time. This feature of older Islamic construction worked well to hide Diogo's wicked operation.

A creaking sound stopped her cold. What if one of those men lurked in here? She remained still, listening to her pounding heart and raspy breathing. Creaks, crackles, and bumps emanated through the walls.

Time passed. She slumped against the door. She had believed she was some savior to these children, sent by God Himself. A hoarse giggle bubbled out. To think—the Creator of the universe had chosen her, a cowardly shrew, to overcome powerful men. Another chuckle burst forth. Had she truly come to believe that God had not only decided she would set these children free, but had deigned to give her a miraculous second chance at it? She erupted into laughter. The joke was on Zahra for believing any of it.

Her laughter dissolved into a raw cry.

Sinking to her knees, she pressed her forehead to the floor. "I don't care who saves them. Allah," she cried, her throat hurting. "Manat? Al-Lat? Al-Uzza!"

The names echoed in the black.

"Make no mention of the names of other gods, nor let it be heard on your lips."

A lump formed in her throat. "I am weak."

"His power is made perfect in our weakness."

The memory of Stephen's voice was both a salve on her wounded heart, and a blade that twisted in her gut. She whispered, "I am sorry."

Who was the apology for? Stephen, perhaps, for getting him killed—again. Perhaps Biko—or Isabelle. Hadiza and Raha deserved apologies, as Zahra had pursued her own desires at their expense.

No. The apology was for God. For refusing to give Him a fair chance. For trying to do everything her own way. For using His power as if she herself were a god. For not being willing to trust Him.

But why had He allowed all this suffering in the first place?

"His power is made perfect in our weakness."

She opened her eyes. Zahra sat up, took a deep breath, and wiped her cheeks dry. She crawled across the gritty wood floor, feeling around. She caught hold of the bedpost, and then felt her way along the quilt toward the nightstand. She imagined a man in the bed, ready to grab her. Her body riveted with tension. Her knuckles bumped into the side table, fingers closing over the drawer pull. She felt around.

She got ahold of what felt like a dusty tinderbox. They were oft kept in night tables. She pried open the lid and let her fingertips run over the items: waxy candles, rough flint stone, and cool metal. After several attempts directing the sparks toward the wick, it burned blue and then bright yellow. The flame grew, reflecting a brass candle holder in the box. She mounted it and held it out. Heavy, ochre quilts blanketed a four-poster bed. A jaguar skin lay in front of the dormant hearth.

Zahra knew this chamber. Just as she knew all the chambers within this tower. This was where she had grown up, a little princess, burning restless energy by exploring.

Her plan had been to become Jabir's queen, get access to the tower, and save the children. It wasn't a bad plan. But it wasn't based on the truth. The cloth was gone, but she was still able-bodied. A woman alone was not a formidable adversary for the men that ran this place. Despair tugged at her heart. Then she recalled Paul's letter to the church in Corinth.

But He said to me, "My grace is sufficient for you, for my power is made perfect in weakness." Therefore, I will boast all the more gladly of my weaknesses, so that the power of Christ may rest upon me.

Zahra whispered into the empty chamber. "Is Your word a promise?"

She approached the door. These new, heavy-duty locks engaged automatically. Diogo had said a key was required on either side. She peeked through the hole but saw nothing. Of course, these chambers would be well proofed against escape. But Zahra knew something that Diogo may not.

Every room had a secret space, like a cupboard, a hatch, a nook, or a crawlspace designed to appear to be for storage, but upon closer inspection, each one led to a different room. None of the rooms were independent; all were interconnected. It was one of the ways that the lever mechanism worked, allowing fire to spread easily, destroying the whole tower more swiftly.

Using the meager flame, Zahra searched for this chamber's hidden compartment. Sometimes they were beneath a rug, inside an armoire, or hidden in plain sight as a hatch in the ceiling. She pulled open a beechwood cabinet. Bed linens, blankets, and extra cushions piled inside. She set the candle down, scooping them off the bottom shelf. There it was—a small hole hidden in the shadows. She stuck her finger in and worked at it, worried it had been nailed shut. The wooden panel creaked as it popped loose, sliding sideways with a grating sound.

Cool air gusted out of the opening. A puff of dust arose, and with it a musty draft. She closed her eyes and exhaled the words, "Thank you."

She stood and removed her red sash. It hit the ground, weighed by the pouch holding her lodestone. She unfastened her shimmering black *takchita* robe, shedding it like a thick snake skin. Left in only her under garments, a sleeveless *kafkan* tunic that flowed over a pair of matching pantalettes, she gathered up the pile of clothing.

She shoved it all into the washbasin, peeling off her bangles, earrings, rings, and even her pearled accent crown. Everything that gave her value in Marbella. It all went in, except the sash, which she tied back around her waist, pouch still attached.

She pulled the stiff jaguar skin across the room and wedged it into the washbasin. Tugging the candle from its holder, she set the open flame on the iridescent gold jaguar fur. The crusty hide caught fire, searing her nose with the stench of burning flesh. The thousands of sewn-in precious stones fell away as the flame swallowed the fabric. She would never trip over its hem again.

She would also never marry.

As a sense of loss lodged in her throat, one of Stephen's most prescient declarations echoed in her mind. *"Die in your dress or survive in your knickers."* A small smile trembled on her lips.

The smell of this fire would be noticed. She dropped the candle in and hastened to the hidden opening in the wardrobe. After crawling in, she was able to sit up inside the wall. She lifted her knees and turned, casting one last look at the growing flames in the tub. She reached out and gathered the linens back onto the bottom shelf. Pulling the doors of the wardrobe shut pinched her fingers. Finally, Zahra hooked her finger in the hole and slid the little secret door closed. The flickering of the fire shined between the cracks. A house spider the size of a pence scuttled nearby.

She crushed it with her fist and began crawling down the corridor.

• • • • •

Zahra reached a hatch with an iron rung. This one would look down into a bedchamber. The ceiling hatches blended with the wooden bridging joists. The maze of passageways did not connect in order—sometimes they led up or down a story, or across to the opposite side of the tower. She pressed her ear to it.

Hearing nothing, she pulled the small iron rung, taking her time so the long-unused hinge wouldn't screech. When she could, she slipped her fingertip under the flap and ducked to peek through the crack.

Lanterns lit a bedchamber similar to the one she had come from. The long-haired boy, Hassan, sat on the floor, his wrists bound to a bedpost with rope. He appeared to be sleeping, his head resting on his uplifted arms. A man lay in the bed, his bare back facing Zahra.

Zahra closed her eyes. Was there some Christian scripture that called for the brutal punishment of the unrighteous?

"It is mine to avenge. I will repay," says the Lord.

She clenched her teeth. She could not kill this man while he slept.

Easing the flap open, her heart thudded against her chest. She had few options, considering her size and strength compared to a man's. She scanned the room for anything she could use as a weapon. Perhaps Hassan's ropes—or that iron shackle resting on the table. It was two circles for the wrists connected by a bar.

The hinge squeaked. She stilled, holding her breath. The man did not move, but Hassan's eyes opened and locked on hers. His mouth fell open. She put a finger to her lips.

Zahra eased through the opening, stretching to hang as close to the floor as possible. She dropped the remaining few feet into a crouch, emitting a thump. She crawled over to Hassan, who stared as if she were an apparition. His hands were purple from the rope binding his wrists. She clawed at the knot with her fingernails.

She whispered in Arabic close to his ear. "Once untied, get dressed and hide."

"There is nowhere to hide."

She bit the knot to loosen it, and the rope finally fell away. He began dressing himself.

When he stood, Zahra was surprised he was her height. Although only perhaps twelve, he held himself like a warrior. In Granada, many boys his age began training for war.

She pantomimed turning a key, and Hassan pointed to a pile of clothing on the side where the man lay sleeping. She whispered, "Hide."

But he did not hide. Instead, he approached the man's clothing, crouched, and searched for the key with trembling hands. He glanced at the sleeping man several times, who had a manicured beard and black hair striped with silver. He had his hand tucked under the pillow, where something glinted—perhaps some kind of jewelry.

Moving slow as if in a dream, she picked up the bar shackle, testing its dense weight in her grip.

A clink made her jump. Hassan loomed over the sleeping man, a rusty chain strung between his fists. Where did he get that? She tiptoed over and gripped Hassan's arm. She shook her head. He never broke his gaze from the man, his nostrils flaring.

Zahra pulled Hassan, his body rigid. He took a step back. She held the shackle up like an axe. She had hit no one before. What amount of force was necessary to render someone unconscious? And what amount of resistance to prevent his demise? She swallowed.

The man startled awake and sat up. Upon seeing Zahra, he blurted a Spanish curse word. From under his pillow, he withdrew a *cinqueda*, a civilian short sword. "Who are you?"

Her heart stopped in her chest. She regripped the iron, holding her breath.

"Identify yourself, *berberita*."

Behind her, Hassan spoke in Arabic. "She is your angel of death."

The man laughed and swung his legs off the bed. The drawstring of the man's long underwear cinched his soft midsection. "With a shackle?"

Zahra weathered through a strong desire to run, regripping the shackle in both hands. "You deserve death."

The man snorted, dropping to his feet on the floor. "Everyone has forbidden desires. Even you."

"True." She nodded. "I desire to kill you."

Zahra lunged and swung the bar. The iron connected to his face with a satisfying crunch. Blood leaked from his mouth over his chin.

He roared and slammed into her. She flew off her feet, landing on her back. He twisted the shackle out of her grip and flung it. Crouched over her, he bared his bloody teeth. "Tonight, I shall beat death."

As he reared his blade back, she braced her arms in front of her. A chain whipped around the man's throat and cinched. The man gurgled and thrashed his blade at Hassan behind him, who held the chain taut. Zahra jabbed her foot into the space between the Spaniard's ribs. He buckled onto his side. Hassan crumpled underneath the man but held fast to the chain. Zahra scrabbled to retrieve the shackle.

"Do you enjoy choking?" Hassan growled in accented Spanish. She stumbled over and cracked the bar on the Spaniard's hand. His sword clanged to the ground. He lumbered to a partial stand, grappling at the chain digging into his throat. He dropped back to his knees.

Zahra picked up the sword. "Hassan, you must stop!"

Every muscle taut in his wiry frame, Hassan jerked the chain tighter. The Spaniard wheezed and his arms fell slack. His face turned purple.

She grabbed Hassan's tunic and yanked him. He did not budge. "Hassan, you cannot kill this man!"

Eyes narrowed to slits, Hassan held fast—and released the chain. The Spaniard slumped to his side, motionless. His face returned to a normal color. His chest rose and fell.

"Bind his hands with the rope."

Hassan kicked the Spaniard to a facedown position and tied the rope so tight, the veins in the man's hands stood out.

After he finished the sixth knot, Zahra touched Hassan's shoulder. He yanked it and stood, wiping the sleeve of his tunic across his sweating brow. He panted, nostrils flaring. She kept her hand on his shoulder and squeezed. He looked at her, his eyes no longer hard and haunting. They were young and afraid.

His lips parted, but his voice cracked, and nothing came out. It was as if he wanted words to help, but he knew they would fall short. They always did. So, Zahra reached out to him, pulled him toward her, and wrapped her arms around him.

After several seconds, he lifted his arms around her. His body shook. His embrace tightened. He rested his head on her shoulder, his silent tears wetting her tunic.

CHAPTER 20

Zahra closed the ceiling hatch she had come through. She led Hassan to a chest at the foot of the bed. It was bolted to the floor. They pulled out the musty bed linens and pillows. He gasped as she slid the false bottom open, revealing a gaping hole in the stone below.

They crawled through the narrow, winding passages. Hassan kept the chain tied around his waist. The next opening led them to an empty bedchamber. They felt through the dark to find the tinderbox and light a candle. With only a single entry and a single exit in each chamber, they painstakingly camouflaged the hatches behind them in every empty bedchamber.

As they progressed, Zahra whispered questions.

She learned the children were kept separate except at meal and bath times—each only once a day. Most of the bedchambers remained unoccupied because Diogo kept only twelve innocents at a time. Hassan did not know why. She learned one man kept the company of the youngest boy in the chapel, the steam baths were often occupied, and the dungeon was a common place for clients to request.

With this information, she formed a plan. She would go to the chapel, the baths, the dungeon, and as many bedchambers as possible along the way. Whoever she had, she would lead them to the Solar. There she would open the lever room, retrieve the rope ladder, and they would climb out of the tower. It was unlikely to succeed, but having a plan gave her hope.

They heard a man's voice. They froze inside the walls. The exit of this passage was on the side, which meant it was probably inside the bottom shelf of a wardrobe like the first one she had found. Her slick palm tightened around the hilt of the Spaniard's short sword.

Hassan whispered. "I know this man. He is Russian. And big."

Hassan, a wiry twelve-year-old, was no match for a burly man. The two of them could work together—serve as distraction—but against a man who knew how to fight, they would likely fail. "What else can you tell me about him?"

Hassan was quiet. He shrugged. "I only know his name is Milosh."

Zahra shook her head. She may just have to move fast with her blade. She did not want blood on Hassan's hands, but she would kill if there was no other choice. "Stay until I give a signal. Understand?"

He hesitated, then nodded.

Zahra did not stop to think, lest fear sneak in and hold her back. She tugged the finger hold and the wooden door scraped. The Russian man stopped speaking. Heart pounding in her throat, she continued despite the noise.

His voice sounded nearer. "Does this place have rats?"

A pile of towels sat in front of her. She pulled them inside. Hassan used one to wipe the sweat from his face. They waited.

Movement darkened the crack of the sagging wardrobe door. "It came from over here."

She crouched, ready.

"From this cabinet." The door popped open, revealing thick, hairy calves.

She buried the blade into his leg. The man roared and stumbled back, her weapon still lodged inside the sinew near his ankle. He crashed to the ground, slithering backward in his nightdress.

Their eyes met. His were like ice.

She climbed out. He groaned and examined his wound. He cursed in Russian. "Woman, why do you hide in there?"

A child whined from the bed. Zahra saw movement under the quilt.

"Quiet, you." With a sickening squelch, he dislodged the blade and stood. He winced as he put weight on his foot. He tested the blade in his hand. Only a small trickle of blood leaked out of the wound.

Zahra's stomach dropped.

The Russian limped over to the bed, muttering to himself. "A ghost I cannot fight. A small woman hiding in cabinet, not such a problem."

He rummaged in the bedside drawer. She stole a look at Hassan in the shadows. She mouthed 'stay' and moved to put the bed between her and the Russian. An olive-skinned boy, seven or eight, lay in the bed. His eyes struggled to open.

The boy mumbled in Italian. "*Polvere.*" *Powder.*

The man held up a small glass vial holding a white substance. He dumped some onto his hand and beckoned Zahra. "Come. I will show you how it works."

That fear finally grabbed her heart and squeezed. She spoke in trembling French. "Small men use potions on children."

The man's jovial mien fell away like a mask being torn off. "It is good for women, too."

He sprang forth with terrifying speed. She stumbled backward but he caught her arm and yanked her like a rag doll. He blew the powder into her face. The room spun and went black.

• • • • •

Whenever fear snaked its way into her heart, she thought of Stephen. Remembering his strength gave her more faith. Or was it his faith that gave her strength?

The strange thoughts faded. Nausea teased at her innards. She struggled to open her eyes. The room jerked to-and-fro like a buoy on rough seas. Her arms lay immobile at her sides. She lay in a feather-stuffed bed.

"Are you awake yet?" The Russian man's voice sounded near.

Zahra tensed. Her eyelids slitted open. He stood beside the bed. Her eyes rolled back. Zahra hoped Hassan had remained in his hiding spot.

"Can you feel yet?" A sharp prick pierced her throat. She breathed harder. The Russian man chuckled. "Good. You hear and feel but cannot move. That is perfect time for sport."

"Please wake up, *Signora.*" The boy's speech was not slurred like before.

"Do not speak to her."

"*Tak, moy gosudar." Yes, my lord.*

This was the same boy she had first heard when she snuck into the Tower al-Garbu. Her determination renewed. She forced her toes to wiggle.

The blade ran over her collarbone, accompanied by a pinch and a wet trickle. "You stuck me good with this thing. Now I return the favor, eh?"

Zahra was only able to utter a moan. If she could speak, it might distract him while she figured out how to survive. The man chuckled. Cold, rough metal ran over her arm.

"You have this black rock with Latin on it. I had to think hard to remember the meaning of '*Faber.*'"

Artisan. The tip of the blade scraped her throat, where another tickle from a droplet of blood ran to the back of her neck. She began to shake.

His breath touched her ear when he spoke. "It means Creator. Why do you have this? Who is your Creator, woman? Allah? Mohammed? I do not know what you people believe."

She realized the Latin phrase *Suae Fortunae Faber* was 'artist of your own fortune.' But *Faber* on its own could be interpreted as 'creator.' It was typically used to describe those skilled at creating or crafting things, like blacksmiths or carpenters. But Milosh had interpreted it as *the* Creator. An idea took shape in her mind.

She was finally able to utter whimpered words in slurred French. "Please stop shrieking."

The Russian grunted. "You are able to speak already?"

Zahra held her heavy eyelids open for a few seconds. "The creature… it won't stop shrieking."

"The stuff had bad effect on you."

She focused her eyes on the space past his shoulder. She pitched her voice high. "I will tell him whatever you wish. Just stop shrieking!"

The Russian man twisted to look. He held the blade to her throat. "I do not shriek."

"Not you, monsieur. The thing that follows you." She found she was able to flex her fingers.

The Russian snorted and looked over his shoulder again. "I will not fall for this trick."

"You do not see it? It speaks in a strange language."

He uttered a mirthless laugh and his teeth showed. "Nice try, woman."

Another prick of the knife made her cry out. She spoke in hurried Russian. "'I am waiting to take you, Milosh.'"

The man froze. Her Russian pronunciation was strong, and he probably considered it very unlikely that she should know his native tongue. Russia was isolated from Europe, its language written in the Cyrillic script.

She asked in French, "What does it mean, monsieur?"

The Russian spun to observe the chamber, blade brandished. "You cannot trick me."

"There! On the bath. Do you see it?"

She was now able to focus. The young boy sat beside her, his eyes wide.

She winked.

The Russian man neared the bronze tub. He gripped the blade, knuckles white.

"It tells me to say this to you. 'Kill yourself so you can join me.'"

The Russian roared, "How do you do that, woman?"

"Do what? What does it mean?"

He rushed over to her. She braced for a blow.

"Prove it!" He held the blade to her cheek, his hand shaking. "What does it know about me?"

She craned away, panting. "It says—it says— 'A woman hiding in a cabinet is not such a problem. But you cannot fight a demon.'"

A clatter erupted from the empty wash basin. The Russian whipped around, uttering a panicked sound. She pushed up and strained to see the dark space at the bottom of the cupboard. Where was Hassan?

"What is this?" The Russian withdrew a rusty chain from the bathtub. The whites of his eyes showed.

Zahra swallowed. "Monsieur, I do not understand—"

The man's face reddened. "Tell me!"

She flinched. "It says—'This will chain you down in *peklo*.'" *Hell.*

The blood drained from his face. He dropped the chain and ran. He grappled up a pile of clothing as he swung the blade at the empty air around him. The walls trembled from the force of the door slamming behind him.

Zahra dropped to her elbow, too weak to hold herself up.

Hassan stood from behind the tub. "Benny."

"Hassan!" Benny swung off the bed and ran to hug Hassan.

Zahra slid her legs off the bed, and crumpled. The boys rushed to her side. Benny gazed up at her. "You were sent by God."

Lips trembling, she smiled and combed his shaggy hair off his forehead. She did not argue with him.

Hassan picked up the chain, wrapping half of it in his fist. "I wanted to kill him."

Zahra shook her head. "That would make you no better than him."

"You do not know the things he does to us, *anisa*. He is evil. It would be an honor to purge him from this world."

Zahra commiserated. But she would not allow a child to shoulder the responsibility of murder. Look what had happened to Diogo, who admitted he had killed his abuser at a young age.

Benny picked up the bottle of powder. He glared at it. Zahra softly closed her fingers over his, speaking to him in Italian. "Can you find the cork? This *polvere* might come in handy."

He paused—and smiled.

Once they found it, Zahra stopped up the small bottle and placed it in her pouch, attaching it back to her belt. She found the lodestone on the floor under the bed and looked at it. *Faber.*

Creator. Emotion warmed her eyes as she thanked Him.

She turned to Hassan. "We must move. 'Milosh' will likely return with a guard."

Hassan nodded. "Or worse. The master himself."

• • • • •

Weaponless, the three crept like rats through the crusty tunnels. They came upon a rung and Zahra crouched near it, having developed a silent method for cracking open the wooden hatches. Peeking through the crevice, she went still, blood pounding in her ears.

Diogo sat at a desk across from Sukayna.

Zahra's mother's library of books lined the walls, but a Portuguese coat of arms gleamed over the blazing hearth. A small girl with a jagged scar across her face stood near the desk, her head down.

Diogo's stringy black hair fell thin around his neck. He held a small spatula of gold wax over a candle flame. "The situation has been handled."

"Handled? I am no longer in his majesty's good graces." Sukayna spoke in what sounded like native Portuguese. Her lips pursed in a sour expression.

Diogo shrugged, holding spatula over a vellum envelope. The creamy wax oozed onto the flap. "You told the king his goddess was pure. You were wrong."

Sukayna's arms slithered crossed, her eyes cold upon Diogo. "You think this does not affect you? Now you have no one on the inside to whisper into the king's ear. And what of *amir* Yusef?"

Diogo snuck a quick glance at Sukayna. "Yusef has no power."

Glinting gold filaments floated in the hot wax as it settled.

Sukayna shook her head. "As the *malik* declines, Yusef will rise in power—and conviction."

A smile formed lines in the thin skin around Diogo's mouth. He replaced the spatula in the wax jar. His delicate fingers peeled out a silver seal from a velvet-lined box. "Is this how you sound when soothsaying for Jabir?"

Zahra's lips parted. Sukayna was Jabir's soothsayer? Feeding him lies about the goddesses, his step-daughters—and Ghaliba? Was Sukayna responsible for Ghaliba's death?

"Listen to me." Sukayna leaned into her hands on the desk. "Yusef has changed. If he finds out what goes on here, he will not tolerate it as Jabir did."

Zahra clenched her eyes shut as they watered. So, Jabir knew. It explained why he never took her accusations seriously. He was in on it.

With great care, Diogo pressed the seal into the semi-hardened wax. It flattened, rising around the edges. "And what exactly do you propose I do about it?"

"Start again in Ceuta. Get rid of this place."

Diogo pulled back the seal, revealing a Portuguese emblem emblazoned with his initials. "Why did you wait to tell me about this all-important 'lever room?' I could have had the door removed when my servicers were here doing the locks. As it is, I fear even a battering ram could not open it."

A reverberating bang caused Benny to whimper. Hassan clamped a hand over the boy's mouth.

"*Pai*, there was a fire!"

The bang had been Gordon bursting the library door open. His face was flushed as if he had been running. Diogo's eyelids narrowed in irritation as he set the seal aside and drew to a stand, observing his son calmly.

Gordon spoke breathlessly. "The *princesa* lit a fire in the washtub. While she...was inside of it."

Diogo shared a glance with Sukayna, who placed her fingertips to her mouth.

Gordon looked pale. "An—Another thing, *Pai*—Milosh says he was visited by a demon or a ghost. Says a Berber woman attacked him in his room."

Diogo's eyes narrowed. "Are we certain she killed herself?"

Gordon swallowed. "Smelt rancid like burnt flesh in there. After we doused the fire, it was a mess of bits of what she was wearing when we threw her in. Smelled like—"

Sukayna groaned. "Please, spare us the details."

"Sounds like the *princesa* lost all hope." A small smile appeared on his lips. "Milosh is eccentric. Still—have the guards search every chamber, just to be sure. Even if we have to interrupt the clients."

Diogo turned to the young girl whose dark hair hung around her plump face. "Stay here, Ja'ida. Root around in my office if you wish to receive a personal punishment from Pierre."

The girl with the scar cringed from him, her small shoulders curved inward. Diogo picked up his freshly sealed letter and headed after his son, but Sukayna stepped in his way. "You should order your men to distribute the sulfur into all the corridor pots."

Zahra pressed her lips to hold in a gasp. The black powder in the pitcher had been for Diogo!

After a moment, Diogo raised his eyebrows. "I suppose they can perform both tasks simultaneously."

Sukayna smiled. "We start again in Ceuta."

Diogo held up his letter. "Ahead of you on that one, *senhora*."

After they left, Zahra closed the hatch to catch her breath. She pressed a hand to her frantic heart.

"*Anisa*," whispered Hassan. "What is it? What did they say?"

"Diogo plans to burn the tower down with us in it."

CHAPTER 21

The three of them dropped from the ceiling, and Ja'ida hugged Zahra as if she had known she were coming. When they found a key in the desk drawer, she and the children had a muted celebration. But the threat of death still loomed. Although Diogo did not have access to the lever room, he may yet find his way in.

The angular, iron key clinked against glass as Zahra dropped it into the leather pouch. The four of them scuttled through the next opening. They reached an arched hatch that looked like a brick oven door. She knew it would led into the gatehouse, which had a maze of false entrances and hallways leading to dead ends or endless circles, designed to discourage a ground siege. The entrance faced the mountains. Which meant it was also an exit.

Just underneath the gatehouse was the dungeon, where Pierre had stabbed Biko—and where Diogo had burned the cloth. So much had happened since. A mix of emotions churned through Zahra. Hope that she might be able to save these three. Fear because Hadiza, Mary, and the others were still somewhere inside. Wonder that the Creator of the universe may be directing her steps like a composer.

Shame for not paying heed to Stephen.

An ache pierced her chest. Had Stephen endured his heinous execution yet? She briefly prayed that he would survive the ordeal. Could God reverse his death if her prayer had come too late? How did it work, exactly?

"*Anisa*, what is it?" Ja'ida whispered, her hand resting on Zahra's back.

Zahra blinked, the onslaught of emotion abating. She must be strong for the children. She shook her head. "Nothing, *saby*. Stay here."

Twisting the metal handle, a sensation overcame her—a foreboding, as if they were stepping into a giant furnace. She paused each time it squealed. The children panted behind her. Once it popped open, she peeked out. Torchlight flickered from somewhere.

When she opened the hatch door, it bumped into a flagstone wall that was part of the maze. They need only pass through the short maze, unlock the gatehouse exit, and the children could run away and hide. She would stay to find the others.

She crawled out and peeked around the bend. A row of spears of varying lengths hung on the far wall. A door opened beyond the labyrinth. Zahra flattened against the flagstone, bumping into Hassan. She shot him a frown. He held the chain against his body so it would not make a noise.

Shackles rattled, and the door slammed closed.

"*Patron* told me to teach you a lesson for what you did." Pierre's gruff voice echoed.

The idea of fighting that beast of a man made her bones ache. He was certainly the strongest of their foes so far, and perhaps the cruelest, seeming to enjoy inflicting pain.

"I prefer to die, not to be alone with that man." Hadiza spoke hoarsely in accented French.

Zahra closed her eyes, her heart hammering in her throat.

Pierre laughed. "I will not kill you. What is the fun in that?"

She stole another look. Pierre perused the spears, perspiration glistening on the back of his neck. Hadiza's hair was loose, her crisp white night dress dangling to her bare feet, a bar shackle between her wrists.

Her eyes cast down. "What you do to me?"

Pierre plucked a short spear and prodded Hadiza with it. She yelped and hopped backward. He forced her toward the iron-studded door that led down to the dungeon. "I will beat you and make you mop up your own blood."

Zahra clenched her fists. A clear goal took form: Zahra would sooner die than let Pierre touch Hadiza. The gatehouse maze unfolded in her mind. Its curves, dead ends, and outlets.

Shoulder to shoulder with Hassan, Zahra pointed to his chain and pantomimed heaving it down the hallway.

Hassan hesitated but did it. The chain clattered into a dead end.

Pierre whipped to face the noise, his spear cutting the air. "Who is there?"

Zahra's blood rushed. She closed her eyes, letting the feeling wash through her.

Take my fear. Please, God, give me strength.

Pierre's shoes creaked. He was on the move. So, too, was Zahra.

Just as his back disappeared down a maze corridor, Zahra crept out. She shot toward Hadiza, whose shackles rattled when she clapped her hands over her mouth. Zahra snatched an Ottoman spear off the rack, clutched Hadiza's arm, and yanked her behind a different wall. Pierre's voice rang out.

"You hide, I break more bones. You'll end up in the infirmary with the redhead."

Hadiza's bar shackle clicked as she trembled. Zahra closed her fingers over it. It silenced.

A bump and a scuffle sounded from the opposite end of the gatehouse. Pierre's heavy steps pounded—and stopped. Zahra held up a hand to urge Hadiza to stay, who nodded several times.

Zahra looked past the wall. Short spear at his side, Pierre craned around a corner several yards away. She slipped across the opening into another corridor. She clacked the dull end of her spear twice, so the sound would carry to him. He moved in her direction. She slipped down a different bend.

Someone scampered noisily across the stone floor.

Pierre hummed a voracious chuckle. "I see you, *garçon*." *Boy*. "No use hiding. You know you cannot escape this place."

Zahra spoke in loud, enunciated French. "*Qui vivra verra.*" *Whoever lives will see.*

Silence followed.

"I knew you would never put yourself to fire." He sounded much nearer.

Heart in her throat, she stood her ground. "Perhaps I am haunting you."

Silence. He could advance on her from either direction. She pressed back to the wall, watching both sides peripherally. She strained to listen, holding the spear ready.

A scuffle sounded. She dipped around a bend. Pierre sidestepped as Hassan whipped the chain. The Frenchman grabbed the boy's throat. He cracked his short spear on Hassan's hand, causing him to cry out and drop the chain. Hassan attempted to gain purchase on his tiptoes, his face turning red.

Zahra stalked over, jabbing toward Pierre's back. But he swung Hassan around, causing her to stumble to avoid stabbing the boy instead. Pierre laughed and threw Hassan aside. He hit the ground, gasping for air.

Pierre advanced on her, tapping his temple. "Think, woman. Not allowed to kill the boy."

Zahra called out in Arabic. "Hadiza, get to the exit with Hassan. Run!"

Shackles jangling, Hadiza darted by. Somehow, Zahra had to distract Pierre and give the key to Hassan. The Frenchman swung his fist. Zahra ducked and jutted the spear at his chest. He blocked with his own spear.

She staggered backward, fumbling for the leather pouch.

He swung his short spear like a club. Zahra shot hers out and blocked it. Sparks filled her vision as he struck her temple with his fist. Her long weapon clamored to the ground. When she opened her eyes, her cheek was pressed to the cold flagstone. The key lay among broken glass and white powder. She lifted her head. The room rocked.

"There are more of you?" Pierre strode away. Benny and Ja'ida shrieked. Zahra scooped up the key among the glass and powder. Her legs shook as she climbed to a stand. The floor seemed to tilt.

"Pierre, I have a key." Her voice was raw. "Come and get it, you coward; you *enfant batteur*." *Child beater*. "You pedophile lover."

He stopped, his beefy back facing her. Deliberately, he turned. His nostrils flared. "You shall regret calling me that."

Pierre burst into a sprint. She receded to reduce his impact. He slammed her into the wall. She wheezed as all her air exited her lungs. He clutched her neck with both hands. Her feet rose above the floor, pressure building in her head. Her tendons and bones strained under Pierre's grip.

She clapped a hand onto his face. The broken glass dug into his eyes. Along with a generous dose of the white powder.

He snuffed like an angry bull. He jerked his head. The shards of glass pinged as they hit the ground.

He let go and she crumpled. She crawled away, heaving, trying to draw a breath. Black spots pulsed in her vision. Behind her, Pierre hit the ground like a felled oak, his head cracking the stone. He lay still.

"*Anisa* Zahra!" Hadiza ran to her side, shackles clacking.

"Stay back! Do not touch that white powder." Zahra choked out, her voice rough. She climbed to a slow stand, fighting off a wave of drowsiness.

Hassan crouched over Pierre. "He is not dead."

Zahra delicately brushed her hands off. "We must hurry."

Hassan picked up the short spear, angling it toward Pierre's palpitating throat.

Zahra cried out. "Stop!" She snatched the spear from Hassan, unafraid of his piercing glare. "You cannot kill people, Hassan."

"He tried to kill you!"

"We are not them."

He spoke through his teeth. "He shall wake soon."

Pierre's chest rose and fell. Any moment now, those eyes would flick open, and the paralysis would wear off. He would bear down on them like a tusked boar. An image of Stephen, strapped to the gnarled olive tree flashed in her mind. Were he here, he could have protected them.

Pierre's body twitched. They all jumped. Hadiza pointed her chained hands toward the dungeon doors. "Let us lock him down there."

The five of them looked at each other. Tentative smiles sprang up.

They removed Hadiza's shackle so that all five of them could work together to drag his heavy body over to the dungeon doorway. By the time they finally got him through the door, he groaned, eyelids flickering. The young ones, Ja'ida and Benny, raced to a corner, watching from a distance. Zahra got behind Pierre in the stairway and gripped his tunic to pull him down four or five steps into the dark. She squinted into the shadows. A motionless figure sat hunched in a chair. They had not moved Biko, yet.

When she looked down, Pierre stared up at her. Lacerations marred his face, bleeding freely. The whites of his eyes sprouted veins.

She bent over him and hissed, "Now you shall spend the night with him."

They slammed the dungeon door.

Footsteps pounded in the distance. Perhaps it was the guards searching for her. Zahra guided the children through the maze. They came to a large wooden door that led to freedom.

Everyone looked at Hadiza. She accepted the key from Zahra and stepped forward. Hadiza shoved it into the lock and twisted. It spun without effect.

Hadiza lifted wide eyes to Zahra. Ja'ida whimpered and buried her face in Benny's shoulder. Hassan's features were drawn as he said, "The outer doors must have different keys."

Hadiza covered her face. Zahra pulled her close, hugging her—to comfort herself as much as the girl. "We will carry on. God did not bring us this far for us to fail."

"Which God trapped us here in the first place?" Hassan's tone burned like acid.

Hadiza wiped the tears off her cheek. "God did not do that. Master Diogo did."

Ja'ida sniffed. "I will follow whatever God *anisa* Zahra follows."

A rustling sound came from inside the dungeon.

"Pierre is stirring." Zahra brushed a tear from Ja'ida's cheek. "Follow me back into the tower."

• • • • •

Once inside, the door closed as heavily as Zahra's heart. No longer obscured by the passageways, they crept down the hallway. The beechwood door leading into the stairwell sat at the end of the hall, its German-made lock glinting in the dark like a tiger's eye.

Despite Hassan and Zahra both wielding spears, they could be easily overcome. She scanned the ceilings for openings disguised by lighter stone. These nooks were designed as hiding places for women and children during sieges. As a child, Zahra would throw persimmon seeds on people passing by and duck out of view. None ever discovered her.

Zahra unlocked the stairwell door. She craned inside to peer up the spiral staircase. It seemed empty. Holding the spear carefully, Zahra took two steps at a time. The children followed her like a gaggle of ducklings. Hassan guarded the back of the line.

A door slammed. They halted. From several flights up, a guard called out in Portuguese. "They could be in the granary."

"Maybe they are hiding in the dungeon." Several men laughed.

Another man barked, "Move it, unless you wish to be inside when it comes down."

Hand shaking, she unlocked the nearest door. They hurried out of the stairwell, and she eased it closed. Unfortunately, the mechanized lock clanged, echoing. A man called out. Zahra rushed the children along. The soldiers would burst from the doorway any second now. They would be trapped.

Zahra caught sight of one of the camouflaged openings in the ceiling. "Hassan, help me!"

Together, they hoisted Hadiza up. She grasped the edges of the opening and pulled herself into the nook. From there, she reached down to help pull up Benny. Zahra lifted Ja'ida up by herself. Pounding boots and clacking weaponry in the stairwell grew louder. The children ducked out of view. It was as if the break in the ceiling healed itself, bathed in shadow.

Hassan sprinted and rammed his shoulder against the stairwell door, holding his spear at the ready.

"What are you doing?" Zahra cried. "Get up there!"

"There is no more time, *anisa.* I will distract them. Go!" He yelled. The lock clanged.

She ran and grabbed his arm. "Hassan, we cannot beat them!"

The door rattled, and Hassan braced his feet, shoulder pressed to the door.

A soldier called, "It is stuck!"

Another said, "I hear the boy."

Hassan locked his dark eyes on hers. "Go. Do not make this be for nothing."

Her stomach dropped. He knew he would likely die fighting. Someone inside the stairwell shoved the door. It popped open and Hassan pushed it closed again, its lock automatically engaging. The soldier cursed.

Hassan yelled, his eyes watering. "Please go, *anisa!*"

Zahra fished in her pouch for one of the keys. She planted it in his palm.

"Hassan—Go with God." Her voice broke. The lock clanged again.

Several heaving groans punctuated a stronger shove against the door. Hot tears flowed as Zahra rushed to where the children were. The door sprang open. Hassan levied a devastating strike with his short spear to the nearest soldier, who he kicked back inside. His legs planted in a warrior stance, Hassan roared and leapt into the stairwell, mounting a single-man attack.

Zahra was unable to put on a strong face for the children who peeked down at her from the hole in the ceiling. She wept as she yelled up to them. "I will come back for you."

"No *anisa!*" Ja'ida cried. Hadiza put her arm around the young girl, chin trembling.

Zahra wiped her face. "Stay. Hide. Be quiet. And pray."

She ran so Hassan's sacrifice wasn't wasted.

• • • • •

Zahra fumbled to unlock the double doors leading into the bathhouse. The slam echoed. Steam encircled her as she pressed against the door and wiped off her face with her shaky hand. It was futile; the tears kept falling.

"What is all that commotion? I have the baths to myself for the day." A man yelled from the back in Italian. Zahra sniffed. The fog diffused light from flickering torches. A long, rectangular bath trickled with running water kept hot by a furnace.

The figures came into view as she drew nearer to the source of the voice. A young boy sat at the edge of a bath, his forearms crossed over his lap. A slightly older girl bobbed in the water next to a man, her shoulders hunched.

Gripping and regripping her spear, Zahra had no plan. Only the mounting pressure of wrath in her chest. She spoke in breathless but perfect Italian. "Enjoying your evening, *signore*?"

The man whipped around. His gaze flicked between her and the spear. The children exchanged wide-eyed glances, seeming to recognize her.

He waved her off. "I am already aware of the evacuation orders. I will be done soon."

Still forcing a smile, Zahra's heart hammered against her breastbone. The boy's hair was blonde, and the girl had Moorish features but pale skin. Zahra took a chance that the girl might know Arabic. "Children, get out of the bath."

They exchanged glances with one another but did not move.

"Begone, Berber! I am a Cardinal from the Vatican. I shall leave when I am ready to." The water sloshed around the Italian man's sagging pectorals.

The boy said something in his native language. She caught 'dansk' and 'fransk.' Danish and French.

Zahra did not know Danish. She would have to say it in French, which the Cardinal certainly knew. "Children, out of the pool now, and go to the stairs."

The girl sloshed toward the edge. The boy jumped to a stand and reached to help her, but the man grabbed her ankle. As she fell back into the water, her shriek bounced off the walls.

The Cardinal glared up at Zahra. "What kind of emergency has the help wielding weapons and ripping my innocents from me?"

Zahra pushed the boy gently toward the stairs, but he remained close to her. "*Signore,* how long might it take you to drag yourself out of this pool? Five seconds? Perhaps three?"

His nose wrinkled.

"But it would take only a split second for me stab this spear into your heart."

His eyes widened. The young girl cried out in pain as he squeezed her arm. "How many seconds to injure her?"

Zahra raised the spear. "Release her now, or this pool becomes your grave, *padrone.*"

The Cardinal hesitated, then loosened his grip. The girl scrambled out of the pool. The children held hands and dashed toward the stairs.

Zahra called after them. "Get dressed and wait at the top."

The Cardinal's mouth tilted into a haughty smile. "Your life as you know it is ruined."

Zahra stood in a defensive stance. The moment he climbed out of the bath, he would become dangerous. "It was ruined the moment I set foot in this place. So, I thought I might save some children along the way."

"Save?" He spoke the word on a laugh. "Their lives are not worth the food that is cooked for them. If by some miracle you get them out of this tower, which is nigh impossible, they will be damaged beyond repair. At least here, they serve a purpose—to protect children out there."

"*Sì*, they are throwaways. I have heard this speech before."

"It is not our fault. Many believe it a worthy cause to open places like this up all over the world. It gives purpose to orphans who would otherwise be neglected or die."

Zahra understood why Hassan wished to kill these depraved men. It seemed justified in the face of such evil. Her gaze strayed toward the two children. They had dressed and now watched from behind a column at the top of the stairs.

The Italian shot his hand out toward her ankle. Anticipating this, Zahra pivoted and buried the spear into his hand with a sickening crunch. His scream echoed. He grabbed the spear with his other hand. She abandoned it rather than stay and fight him.

She bounded up the steps. "The door!"

The children raced toward the exit.

The Italian roared, "You shall hang!"

She fumbled for the key. The Cardinal had already climbed out of the pool. Zahra's hands shook with such intensity, she had trouble lining the key up.

A trail of blood followed the Italian as he bore down on them, grunting up the stairs like some swamp beast. The young girl clutched Zahra and screamed. The lock disengaged, and she dragged the door open. After they poured through, she whipped around to pull it closed.

The Cardinal caught the handle, and it inched back open.

CHAPTER 22

Zahra pulled with all her weight, but the Cardinal continued to gain. He roared.

Arms enclosed around her—the two children clung to her, adding to her weight and pulling. She planted a foot on the wall and threw herself back.

The door slammed, followed by the clang of the lock engaging. They crumpled to the floor in a pile. They shared breathless smiles. A large pile of red and white fabric with ornate embroidery lay beside the boy.

The Cardinal's clothes and belt, hung with several leather purses.

Zahra grasped the boy's cherubic face between her hands. "Good boy."

His grin caused his pink cheeks to shine. Her heart ached at the sight of him. How could anyone see these children as damaged or worthless?

"What are your names?"

The young girl smiled, her light eyes shining. "I am Agnes. This is Varyn. I am French. My daddy was from Mali."

Parents, again. "Nice to meet you, Varyn and Agnes."

"Da Gama! Get me out of here!" Banging punctuated The Cardinal's words.

"We must hurry." Zahra ushered them down the hall where they would find the *Dar al-Shifa*. House of Healing.

"Please, no!" Agnes clutched Zahra's arm. Her eyes shined with tears.

"What is it, *ma chère*?" *My dear.*

"It is a terrible place, mademoiselle. It is where we go to die."

Zahra brushed damp hair out of Agnes's eyes. "Let me show you something."

She retrieved her lodestone and held it out to the girl. Agnes accepted it, a crinkle forming between her eyebrows. "Fa-bair?"

At her sweet French accent, Zahra smiled. "Yes. In Latin, it means Creator. Hold tight to that, for comfort. For I now believe He is with us."

• • • • •

As they entered the *Dar al-Shifa,* it reeked of eggs. Under each torch sat a clay pot that appeared decorative. But her mother had explained that if the lever got pulled, the mounts would fold and drop each torch into the pots. The charcoal, flax, and sulfur mixture would explode, compromising the integrity of the walls and floors.

The *Dar al-Shifa* had once been a shining example of medical advancement staffed with expert physicians. Now the counters were splattered with unknown substances. Cabinets with sagging shelves surrounded a brick hearth. Blood-stained linens piled on a soapstone surgery table.

The pile shifted, followed by a soft moan.

Zahra hurried to the table and pulled aside the linens. There lay a red-headed girl around seven, so pale she looked gray.

"Emily!" Agnes took the girl's hand. Emily did not awaken. Zahra peeled back the sheets. Blood-soaked bandages wrapped around Emily's hips. Zahra clenched her teeth.

The curtain leading into the pantry shifted. A pair of large, black eyes peeked out from the shadows. Zahra was deeply disturbed for a moment before she recognized who it was.

Sukayna.

"*Amira*, I am so happy to see you." Sukayna slipped out from the curtain. She wore a blue headscarf and embroidered kaftan dress.

"No need for the ruse."

Sukayna's lips parted. "Whatever do you mean?"

Zahra measured her words. "Why did you do it? Trick Jabir into killing my mother?"

Sukayna's lips pressed. She reached up and removed her head covering, freeing her silky black hair. Her hunched shoulders straightened. She switched from Arabic to Portuguese. "It was not like that. How did you get in here?"

The dramatic change in her maidservant was unsettling. "What happened to this girl?"

Sukayna shrugged. "She was here when I arrived. It happens sometimes."

"The stench is a lot like the black powder you had in the pitcher earlier."

"I know!" Sukayna blurted. "And the pots are too heavy. I could not pull them out of the way."

"They are bolted down, Sukayna." Zahra made a sweeping gesture. "There are hundreds of them throughout this tower. When he pulls that lever, the whole thing will crash down on our heads within minutes."

Sukayna's chin trembled.

"I take it you cannot leave this chamber."

The woman lowered her gaze.

Zahra smiled, her fist clenched at her side. She had a powerful desire to strike something. "When you suggested he destroy the tower to hide evidence of this operation, did it not cross your mind that *you* were part of that evidence?"

"Stop," whispered Sukayna, her features pinched. "What is your plan to escape, *princesa*? I will help you."

"Tell me what Diogo knows."

"He believes you are dead." She sent a glare to Varyn and Agnes, who cowered. "He thinks one of his little ones stole a key."

Zahra stepped to block Sukayna's view of the children. "But it is no matter, since he intends to destroy the tower, kill us all, and start over in Ceuta, right?"

Sukayna's eyes widened. She would now realize Zahra had somehow heard them in the library. Stephen would have disapproved of how forthcoming she was with this information. She imagined him sending her a chiding look. She would give anything to be scolded by him once more.

Zahra turned to the unconscious child and touched her cheek. The girl's skin was burning. She could not leave her behind, but they could not carry her through the passageways. They would need to take another route—and trust Him.

"You will carry little Emily for me."

Sukayna's forehead wrinkled. "She will slow us down. She shall die soon any—"

Zahra stepped toward the woman. "Do an honorable thing, for once. Or I shall leave you in here."

The woman's eyes glistened as she nodded. Zahra did not trust this serpent, but she had no choice. Hopefully, Diogo's betrayal was motivation enough to help them. "First we go to the chapel."

Sukayna's eyebrows shot up. "*Princesa*—"

At Zahra's blistering glare, Sukayna closed her mouth and approached Emily to scoop her up. Stepping outside the infirmary, Zahra peered down the empty hallway. Had the soldiers stopped searching after finding Hassan? She closed her eyes and asked God to protect him and the others she had left in the ceiling nook. She still felt presumptuous speaking directly to the Creator of the universe—while also chiding herself for not asking Him earlier.

They crept back toward the stairs—where the door clacked and pushed open. Zahra's heart seized in her chest. The children huddled behind her.

An older maid with bushy black hair stepped out carrying a pitcher. Seeing them, she clutched the pitcher to her chest. Zahra held out her hands. "Please, listen to me—"

Sukayna dumped Emily against Zahra and pawed at her waist, ripping the leather pouch from her sash. Zahra stumbled to catch the girl.

"Sukayna!"

Sukayna flew past the maid and disappeared into the stairwell. "The *princesa* is alive! *Princesa* Zahra is alive, and she is taking the children!"

• • • • •

This would be their undoing. In a devastating single act, Sukayna robbed them of their only two advantages: their keys, and Diogo's belief that she was dead.

The maid froze, her eyes darting between them.

"Go back," she commanded. Agnes grabbed Varyn's hand, and they rushed back inside. Emily flounced limply as Zahra hastened in and slammed the door with her foot. Now they were trapped inside.

"Go to the hearth."

The children raced toward the brick alcove. Beside it, billets of brittle firewood filled a recessed nook.

"Take all that wood and pile it in front of the door. Show me how fast you are!"

The children got to work, racing back and forth carrying wood. Zahra placed Emily back on the surgery table. The girl's head rolled to the side. Zahra gathered the linens back over her.

"It happens sometimes."

Zahra's eyes burned. She had grown up believing all quarrels among men could be worked out with a sincere effort at communication. It was her trade. But she had stared into the face of evil. It desired only to destroy. How naïve she had been.

She bowed over Emily. "I do not... know how to pray, but..." She pressed her mouth into her clasped hands. A hot tear dropped to Emily's sheet. Long silences stretched between each of the girl's inhales. "You brought me this far. I ask humbly. Protect her until I can return."

"*Mademoiselle* Zahra." Agnes's sweet voice was tentative. "Emily is not coming with us?"

Zahra brushed Emily's hair back over her ear. "We have to leave her behind. For now."

Agnes' clear eyes were sad but wise. Even as young as she was, she probably knew that escape was unlikely. Varyn, about six, stood with his fists on his hips, observing their pile of firewood. He muttered something in Danish, shaking his head.

Zahra exhaled a laugh and wiped her eyes. "Come here."

She ushered them over to the hearth and knelt beside the empty firewood nook. She brushed away slivers of wood and craned to look inside—and upward. A familiar wooden hatch sat in the nook's top. It was not the damper, which was in the hearth itself. This little doorway connected to the network of passages. Thank God for whoever took the time and care to hide them so well.

A bang followed by muffled footfalls sounded in the distance.

The hinges of the hatch screeched loudly from lack of use. No instruction needed—Agnes and Varyn scrambled in. The infirmary lock clanged.

"*Tais-toi.*" *Be quiet.* She pushed the hatch closed just as the main door swung open. Firewood blasted across the room. She ducked behind the stone surgery slab Emily lay on.

A soldier snorted and murmured in Portuguese. "Did they think the firewood would hold the door?"

"They are still in here."

"Check the pantry."

Three separate voices so far. How many crawled like wasps over their nest? As one rounded the surgery table, Zahra drew to a stand.

Startled, he unsheathed his sword with a metallic slice, stepping back. "Where are the children?"

His voice tremored. There were three men in total.

She spoke in Portuguese. "That is a lot of weaponry for one little woman."

The soldier closest to the door regripped his sword. "This little woman can do big things."

Zahra smiled. "In that case, you should not have come at all."

The men looked between one another. "Come with us, *berberita*."

She lifted her chin, eyes settling on the man who spoke. "Do you know what happened after your Master Diogo refused to release the children?"

Leather armor creaked as they shifted.

"Does Diogo's interpreter, Sohrab, still nurse the bites of those bloodthirsty flies? Or did the hail crush him that night? Have you yet heard of the lice and boils that consumed the Prince of Marbella?"

The soldier near the pantry swallowed.

"Did Diogo's son, Gordon, tell you about the twenty-foot cobra that bit Pierre's leg? It showed him mercy, letting him keep his limb—and letting him live. Do you think that mercy shall endure for you?"

Now she could see the whites of their eyes. None advanced.

"And what happened when da Gama refused to release the children for the fifth time? The Lord rotted all your animals in seconds. He could do that to you. Just… like… that." She snapped. They each flinched.

The one who had spoken so bravely now had a foot out the door.

How must she look to them, speaking in bold Portuguese with her sleek silhouette in dusky linen; bruised and scraped up yet holding a proud posture.

The soldier's voice cracked as he stepped backward out of the room. "Boys, this chamber's as good as any to hold her in, wouldn't you say? She's got no way out."

The others eased backward.

Zahra took a step forward. "When you see Diogo, tell him I have asked—yet again—that he set the children free."

One of the men, pale and sweating, blurted, "*Não brincando com isso*," and knocked against his comrade as he ran out.

Not trifling with this.

Another stumbled backward and nearly slipped in his retreat. The last man's brown-tinged teeth bared as he scowled. The door slammed, its lock clanging into place.

• • • • •

After kissing Emily's hot forehead, Zahra climbed into the passageway. They crawled a brief time before coming upon the next opening above them. She slid it open, and linens fell around them. She continued pulling in the sheets and towels to empty what appeared to be a large chest, likely sitting at the foot of a bed. Zahra put her upper body through the opening, crouched half-way inside the chest. She was just about to push the top when it suddenly flung open.

A girl about ten with a curly mane of chocolate locks stared down at them.

"Marta!" Agnes squeaked. The new girl helped them climb out of the chest, marveling at the passageway below. The girls hugged. Zahra scanned the bedchamber. They were alone.

Marta wore a white linen dress with a square neckline.

"You came for us," Marta said in Portuguese. When she smiled, dimples appeared on both of her cheeks.

As Zahra stared into Marta's fierce eyes, gratitude swelled in her chest. Eight children in total. Although Hadiza, Benny, and Ja'ida waited in a dark hole to be retrieved, Emily lay dying, and Hassan had sacrificed himself to save them. Her eyes stung.

A distant thump from another chamber startled them. If they found the hearth hatch in the *Dar al-Shifa,* they would find their way straight to this chest. "Find heavy things to put inside it."

The children were productive. They lined the bottom of the trunk with framed paintings, a heavy brass vase, a statue of Saint Jude, and half-burnt firewood from the dormant hearth. When all the heavy things ran out, they began stuffing it with pillows and linens. Closing the chest required Zahra to sit on the lid.

She led them to the next hatch hidden between two cross beams in the ceiling, which was low enough that she could stand on a chair to help each of them get inside. By the time Marta climbed in, Zahra's arms trembled with exhaustion.

"Wait, *senhorita.*" Marta pointed to the wardrobe cabinet. From up here, she could see a curved sword resting on top of it.

Zahra shook her head. "Too large. It would be loud—and dangerous to carry through the passages. You cannot bring it, *namorada.*" *Sweetheart.*

Marta flicked a curl out of her eyes and nodded. "*Vamos.*" *Let's go.*

The next hatch they came to was shaped oddly. Then she remembered—this one led up and into the chapel. Each time they ventured up a level, further from Hadiza and the others, the pit in Zahra's stomach tightened. By now, they awaited her return three floors down.

A scream pierced her ears—it came from inside the chapel.

Varyn said something in Danish, his voice high with fear. He mentioned the name 'Leo.'

Zahra whispered, "Where is Leo from?"

They exchanged glances. Marta said, "Keterlyn often tries to get him to eat more. He yells 'den fayito.' Something like this?"

Agnes whispered excitedly. "'Echo fah yeeto.' 'Den echo…'"

Zahra perked. *'Den echo fagito'* meant 'I do not have hunger' in Greek. She reached and squeezed Marta's shoulder. "Good."

Zahra cracked open the flap, which was itself the top of an altar step. It squeaked, but the boy's shrieks drowned it out.

Pews divided into two sections, the aisle running from the altar steps. A single torch lit the room, mounted on a pedestal table. The domed ceiling was pocked like a gilded lotus pod. Atop the pedestal table sat an Islamic *wudu* water bowl—perhaps now used for holy water in mass. Did Diogo conduct mass, here?

Movement caught her eye.

The boy, Leo, shrieked again as he ducked between the pews. He narrowly escaped someone.

Or some *thing.*

A large, beaked creature perched on the pews, letting forth an unnatural screech.

The harpy was actually a slight man in a black cape and a beak-shaped mask. His bare feet clung on the backs of two pews.

Leo ran. The birdman hopped along the pews. He crouched and pecked the boy's head with the beak. Leo tripped and crumpled to the marble floor, skidding several inches. The man laughed.

The shocking scene compelled Zahra to crawl out of the hatch. If the birdman looked in the direction of the stairs, he would immediately see the gaping hole with a dark woman climbing out. But he was too engrossed.

Zahra closed the hatch and hid behind the *wudu* pedestal table. From this angle she could now see hanging on the altar wall a realistic sculpture of the crucified Jesus Christ, eyes half-mast and sunken.

In her shock, she must have uttered a sound because the man hissed something in Hebrew. His bare feet slapped to the marble floor.

In one swift motion, Zahra stretched to grab the torch off its mount and dunk it into the *wudu* bowl. The fire hissed, and the room plunged into darkness. The man rammed into the pedestal, water sloshing out. As she sprang away, she hit her hip on a pew. Holding in a cry of pain, she hobbled as quickly as she could.

"The darkness does not worry me, whoever you are." The man's voice was melodic. Footsteps pattered in her direction. Her pulse ran wild. She ducked down between the pews. Leo's whimpers echoed.

Zahra slithered down several rows. Her hand hit what felt like a leather shoe. She flung it as far as she could. It whacked against something which thrummed a metallic tone.

The man padded with eerie rapidity in that direction. Pulse in her throat, Zahra coasted toward the front where she had seen several large candles on thick gold stands. One of those could make a formidable weapon. She waved her hands in front of her. Something busted her face and clanked to the marble floor, followed by a muted shatter of dry candle wax. His footsteps advanced toward her as if he were flying. She dropped to the floor, searching until her fingers closed over the cool candle holder.

She stood and held it like a spear. It was much heavier than she thought it would be, with an awkward weight distribution. But she could do some considerable damage with it. Other than Leo's whimpers, the chapel was silent. She blinked several times, desperate for her eyes to adjust. A clink sounded from the far end of the chapel. She worried the man had gone for Leo instead of her. His whimpering made him an easy mark. What might he do to the boy to force her compliance?

Going head-to-head in the dark with a man would almost certainly end in her demise. But Zahra couldn't stomach anything happening to Leo. He was her boy, now.

"Monsieur, are you Jewish? I have always wanted to know something."

A pew creaked and Leo whined.

She blurted, "Was Jesus not everything the Jewish people could have wanted in a Messiah?"

The man chuckled, his voice echoing like a song. "A false prophet who caused great harm to my people."

Her throat was dry, but she dared not swallow. All she could hear was Leo's high-pitched panting. She must keep him distracted. "Rising from the dead was proof enough, wasn't it?"

His sinister voice danced on the shadows. "'Those who say that the dead will rise again are mad, and the truth is not in them. For they do not understand that this is like saying that a stone which has been dissolved in water will come together again and return to its former state.'"

It sounded as if he were quoting something. Her eyes watered in the effort to see. Was that a shadowed shape moving? She blinked, and it was gone. She strained her ears but could no longer hear Leo. She crept into the main aisle, moving toward the altar. She leveled her candlestick with slick palms. "Can't the Creator do anything?"

A shadow appeared in front of her. She swiped the candle stand and made contact. He grunted, grabbed her hair, and wrenched her face down on his knee. The stand hit the marble with a deafening knell. Next, she was flat on her back.

He clutched a fist full of her hair and dragged her. "You may yet make a believer out of me, woman. He delivered you right into my hands, didn't he?"

CHAPTER 23

"Are you the reason they are evacuating us? But why? I can take care of a little Berber pest."

Pain ripped through Zahra's scalp. She gripped his wrist as he dragged her toward the altar. Each step scraped over her back.

He stopped at the landing and leaned close. "Can I tell you a little secret?"

She did not wish to provoke him further, so she did not reply.

"I do not believe any of it." He swung her across the altar stage. She slammed into what was likely the stone lectern. Its corner jabbed into her spine. She curled up and groaned.

His voice receded as he walked away. "I concluded long ago that it was all made up by men with quills seeking control. Quite ingenious, if you think about it."

A familiar mechanized clang echoed. Light shined from a door tucked underneath the angled staircase leading to the mezzanine level.

A sharp ache spiked through her back as she crawled away, scanning the pews for Leo.

The man returned with a torch. He slammed the door behind him. The black bird mask still obscured his face. His cape flowed behind him as he advanced on her.

She stumbled down the altar steps and caught herself on the pedestal table. She whipped around to face him. Then she saw it.

At the base of the steps, out of his view, lay a lean falchion sword. One of the children—probably Marta—must have crawled back to get it from the previous chamber. With this weapon, she might have a chance.

Zahra took several steps forward. He drew to a sharp halt at the top of the altar stage. "That is a lonely belief, monsieur."

Beneath the mask, his mouth stretched into a smile, teeth snaggled in such a way that his incisors protruded like fangs. "Quite the opposite. It is very freeing."

Zahra held her aching spine straight. She dared not look at the sword.

His eyes glittered in the depths of his mask. "I am curious. Why are you not running?"

A rush of energy surged through her body.

"Because we are two against one." She peered past his shoulder.

When he twisted to look, he would have laid eyes on the statue of Jesus.

Zahra lunged for the sword and slashed at his legs. She felt it slice into the flesh of his calf. His roar echoed. He stumbled and collapsed.

Zahra ran, shouting in Greek. "Leo! Leo! Get up! Stand up where you are!"

She raced down the aisle. The boy stood in the middle of the chapel. She raced toward him. Despite his injury, the man recuperated like a flapping crow. He still held the torch as he gave chase.

The boy shrieked and dove again. Zahra dove to slide underneath the pews, her sword clanging on the marble. She grappled for Leo's ankle. The birdman swept past her, arms outstretched. She yanked Leo out of his reach.

The man laughed. "You are much wilier than the children ever are."

She pressed her palm to Leo's mouth and whispered in his ear, "*Menei.*" *Stay.*

Her sword scraped the marble with a metallic ting as she stood. She stepped into the aisle. The man turned, only three pews away.

She was still catching her breath. "How did you open that door? I thought clients could not have master keys."

The man eased into the aisle, exhibiting a minor limp. Blood soaked his pant leg. "I could buy your king and the surrounding kings thrice and put them in a ring to fight one another to the death."

A shiver stole through her body. "I propose a trade. My sword for your key."

The man eyed her. "What use would a key be for you, under threat of blade?"

Zahra held the falchion blade out, her arm trembling under its weight. "Then it is a deal?"

His torch flickered, eyes glowing deep in the mask. He unlaced the front of his tunic, where it split open, revealing a pale chest bone. With a snapping sound, he popped out a black leather pouch. A memory sparked of the relic she had kept tucked under her belt. Her heart skipped a beat. For a moment, it felt like it was still there.

The man produced the blunt iron key. She eased into a crouch, pain spasming up her spine. "We slide them across simultaneously."

A jubilant chuckle tumbled out of him. "You are a strange one. Who are you?"

"A nobody."

"Sad." He held out his open palm with the key in it.

She placed the sword on the ground. "Throw it."

He nodded. "When you slide the sword."

Pulse pounding in her ears, Zahra pushed it toward him. "Throw it!"

He clamped his bare foot on the sword's hilt and regripped the key in his palm. He dropped it into the pouch and snapped it back in his tunic. He picked up the sword. "Somehow, I had hoped you were cleverer."

Zahra stood and shook her head. "Should I be surprised you have no honor? You are a man who believes in nothing."

His expression darkened, his grip on the sword tightening. He raised the blade. It would only take three steps to cut her down.

Zahra drew in a sharp breath and bellowed. "Marta! Varyn! Agnes! Come out!" She repeated the command in French and Portuguese.

The man swung the blade as he whipped around. The hatch in the steps popped open, and the children poked their heads out.

His back to her, he stared as they hesitantly climbed out, their expressions uncertain.

He stalked toward them.

The children screamed and huddled into one another. Zahra had not expected him to give her the key. She only needed to know where it was. She gave up the sword so he would lower his defenses. It was the only way the Gourmelon might work on his injured leg.

Zahra sprang forth, swiping her foot out to hook his stepping leg behind his shin. He crumbled hard to the floor, cinders spraying. His mask skidded.

Zahra dove onto his back. He growled, rising off the floor. She hooked his arm and wrenched it behind his back. He dropped, growling. Gripping his wrist with both her hands, she pulled his arm up between his shoulder blades. He screamed. Her elbows anchored into his sinuous back. Her feet grappled for purchase as he bucked underneath her. He swung the sword. She hunkered down, ducking to avoid his rearing head.

At this angle, his shoulder blade poked out of his tunic like a bird's wing. He uttered a high-pitched sound. "You will break my arm!"

"Better to lose your arm, than for your whole body to go into hell." She heaved it upward.

A sickening crunch sounded from his shoulder. He shrieked like a child. He bucked. She tumbled to the floor but hung onto his cape. She jerked him off balance, climbing onto his back again. He dropped to his chest and swung the sword back at her. She ducked and began ringing his cape around his throat. A slice from the blade stung her shoulder blades. She uttered a cry but held fast to the cape.

Cinders flew—Marta snatched up the torch and now ground the fire into the man's sword-wielding hand. He let out a strangled sound as his skin sizzled like burnt pork. The sword clattered away. Marta snatched it up, her voice frightened. "Do not move!"

Flat on his chest, the man curled his burnt hand in, his broken arm hanging limp. He panted. "Spare... me. I will give you... riches you cannot even imagine."

Zahra shot her hand into his tunic, tearing the pouch out. "Children—go to the mezzanine staircase."

Marta passed Varyn the torch and grabbed Leo's hand. They ran toward the steps leading to the chapel's mezzanine level.

The man's face turned an unsettling shade of purple. Zahra got a good grip of his graying hair. Disturbed by what she was about to do, she hesitated. When he bucked, she slammed his head against the floor. Once, twice. The third time, he went still.

She stood, legs shaking. Her back stung, liquid dribbling under her tunic. The children gathered at the top of the staircase overlooking the chapel. Zahra limped toward them.

Tears trembled on Leo's eyelashes, but he was obviously trying to be strong. After she reached the top of the stairs, she brushed the backs of her knuckles against his round cheek. In Greek she said, "You did very well, Leo."

Chin trembling, he nestled against Agnes.

Zahra pressed her ear to the door at the top of the stairs. She unlocked it and cracked it open. The eggy scent of sulfur seeped through. Had Diogo figured out how to open the lever room, yet?

The Solar was three floors up. Hadiza and the others were four floors down. After getting them, all eight of them would have to travel seven floors undetected to make it to the top. It was seemingly impossible; but she could not leave the children in the chapel with him. At least not while he was alive.

She looked over the railing. He lay motionless in the aisle between the pews. Shadows shrouded the statue of Jesus. He had brought them this far. She would trust Him.

She tensed at the distant sound of boots pounding. Zahra began to pull the door closed—but paused at the cuffing sound of bare feet.

Four children emerged from around the corner in a full sprint, arms pumping. Hadiza, Ja'ida, Benny—and a girl with bright red hair and a bloody dress.

Emily.

• • • • •

Zahra held the chapel door open. After they were inside, it took great restraint for her to close it quietly. Boot steps rumbled like thunder around the corner and down the hall.

Heart knocking in her throat, sweat trickled down her temple. Muffled voices of men called out to one another. "They could have gone into any one of these chambers."

The men seemed to pivot near the chapel door. The children stilled. Zahra clamped her eyes closed and prayed.

The men spoke to one another. "Why do we give chase? They cannot get out of the tower before it comes down, can they?"

"Orders."

"*Orders* going to get us killed while the defilers get evacuated."

"Not evacuated yet. Master Diogo's got most of them in the kitchen. The Cardinal was found stark-naked."

"The king's warriors are in formation outside. We are about to go to war for these pederasts."

"By the saints! I wash my hands of this!"

Their voices faded from earshot, and the door slammed at the end of the hall.

Zahra released her breath. Diogo's men were abandoning post. The tower grew increasingly empty. Jabir's warriors gathered outside. For what purpose? To help them, or to protect the dark secret within?

Zahra turned to Emily.

The girl's eyebrows were like two stripes of sunset paint. Zahra reached to cup her face between her hands. "Are you well?"

Emily smiled. "*Estoy sana.*"

I am healed.

Zahra blinked several times. Healed?

Hadiza whispered in Arabic. "We came upon the *Dar al-Shifa* door open. Emily was trying to tell us something."

Zahra spoke to Emily in Spanish. "What were you trying to say?"

"Master da Gama's son went inside the hearth."

Zahra's eyes widened. "Gordon found the hatch?"

Emily looked between Zahra and the children, speaking timidly. "After he went inside, I closed the little door. I put the billets back so he could not come back out."

Zahra knelt beside Emily and combed her hair behind her ear. "That was an extraordinarily smart thing to do, *mi corazón.*"

"God healed her." Hadiza wrapped an arm around Emily's shoulders.

The Jewish man groaned. With his grievous injuries, she and the eight children could likely take him. Eight! Zahra marveled at what she had accomplished. Stephen's voice in her head reminded her that God had done it—not her.

He lumbered to standing, clutching his limp arm. Leo buried his face in Agnes's neck and began to cry.

"The Solar," she whispered to the children. Her brain struggled. For Greek, she just said, "Top floor."

The man uttered a gruff chuckle. "What keeps you?"

The children huddled by the door. Zahra approached the railing. He looked like a specter risen from the underworld. "Monsieur, I spared you, as you begged. Where might I retrieve my unimaginable riches?"

Sweating profusely, he stalked toward the stairs. "I may have a lame arm, but you are merely a woman. And it appears you all are trapped in here with me."

"Wrong. You are trapped in here with Him."

• • • • •

"Berber!" The man roared.

The chapel door slammed. The emotions that broiled within her were a strangely harmonious synergy between her newfound trust in the Creator, and a willful determination to act.

The best word for the feeling was hope.

She took the falchion blade from Marta and led them toward the staircase. Stephen sprang to mind—how much he had sacrificed to return here and save his niece. Would Mary and the others she had yet to find perish? She felt sick to her stomach at the thought.

Their bare feet scuffed as they hastened up the steps, occasional lanterns mounted. The tower was ominously empty. Seemed the ants had flooded outside the hill.

A heavy door banged from the top floor. Zahra put her hand on Benny's chest to stop him. They all cascaded to a halt. Someone rushed out of the Solar and down the steps.

Sukayna. She drew up short at the sight of Zahra and the eight children lined along the curved stone wall.

Her black hair was disheveled underneath her bright blue veil. Why wear that? Who was she tricking? The whites of her eyes framed her dark irises.

Zahra lifted the blade to point it at the woman, speaking in Portuguese. "What were you doing in the Solar?"

Sukayna darted her gaze toward the top of the stairs. "How do you plan to get out of the tower, *princesa*?"

"Why? Did Diogo not elevate your status when you betrayed me?"

Emily stepped up, standing beside Zahra. "Trust nothing she says, *soltera.*" *Miss.*

The color drained from Sukayna's face at the sight of the girl with the bloody dress. "How… how are you—"

Marta climbed up and held Zahra's hand, as if to give her strength. "This woman is a snake."

Sukayna ignored the many glares upon her. "I have news of the *uroubi.*"

Zahra's heart skipped. What could she know of Stephen while trapped inside the tower with them? Had he somehow survived? Could Zahra believe anything the woman told her?

Zahra lowered the blade. "Tell me."

Sukayna's eyes filled. "The king's warriors surround the tower. All of da Gama's soldiers are in the foyer. You will never get out. He will bring the whole thing down before he lets you out." Her voice broke as she added, "Or me."

"You brought this on all of us, Sukayna."

Sukayna drooped her head, and tears fell. "I do not want to die, *princesa*."

Zahra clenched her teeth—in truth, she had no choice but to allow Sukayna to stay with them. She had no wish to help the woman, but the alternative was to cast her out and have her try once more to get in the good graces of Diogo by betraying their whereabouts.

Zahra held out her hand. "Give me your key."

"*Princesa*, I no longer have your keys." Sukayna gestured with a hand toward the Solar door, which was out of Zahra's view. "The *uroubi* got me into the Solar."

Zahra inhaled. She crested the landing. In the hallway leading up to the ajar Solar doors, a man lay unconscious. Zahra recognized him as the white-haired Sir Drake who oversaw the portraits of the children. Several black journals lay strewn around him. Some splayed open, revealing the scribbled signatures of the men who had harmed the innocents of Marbella. A bloody gash marred his forehead.

Sir Drake was English and could thusly also be referred to as *uroubi*. *European*.

Of course, Sukayna had known what using the term *uroubi* would mean to Zahra.

She snatched the blue scarf out of Sukayna's hair. The woman flinched. The head scarf was a symbol of piousness, Godliness, and this serpent was neither. Sukayna shrank back, as if Zahra might strike her. And what if she did? It was the least of what she deserved after all she had done to her, her family, and the children.

Before the emotion ripped Zahra under, a sound rang out from inside the Solar. The sound of curtain rungs raking over a steel bar. And a child's voice.

"What are you doing?"

Speaking in English.

Mary! Zahra burst past Sukayna and leapt over Sir Drake's legs. The bright morning sunlight streamed in from the wide balcony, briefly blinding Zahra. Shielding her eyes, she made out the familiar hanging tapestries, tile wading pool, and shimmering fabric streaming between the four posters of the large bed. The children piled in behind her.

Mary's back was to them in ivory linen and soft blonde waves. She stood near a large man at the far end of the room. He roughly jostled the handle of the locked lever chamber. In his other hand, he held a Dane-axe. Zahra's blood drained—they had stormed in without a plan and might face off with the largest of their foes who carried a formidable weapon.

At the sound of the children's gasps, the man turned, gripping Mary at his side. The girl's nose wrinkled once, twice, and she shook her head.

The children shrieked. The man looked grotesque, drenched in dried blood. He stepped forward out of the glare, his eyes the color of the Alboran Sea as it foamed green at the shore.

CHAPTER 24

Zahra's gut seized as if she were witnessing a phantom. Was this a gift from God, a final wisp, perhaps an echoed word, before he scattered like dust on a warm breeze?

But Stephen Kempe looked as shocked as she; his Dane-axe clunking to the rosewood floor. He exhaled, a cautious smile touching his mouth. Emotion warred over his angelic features, his eyes clouding with emotion. "You survived."

His voice warmed her ears like a rich, mulled wine. The reality of his presence—his being alive—hit her. She dropped her sword and ran, colliding into him with an embrace. He lifted her off the ground, holding her aching body so tightly, she could scarcely breathe.

But she could breathe enough to say near his ear, "In my knickers."

A wondrous smile formed as he set her down, cradled her nape, and kissed her. She reveled in his strength, his warmth, his love. The sun seemed to halt in its path. She clung to him.

Reality resumed its course as Mary cried, "Hadiza!" and dove into the Moorish girl's arms. Stephen held onto Zahra as he looked over the children she had amassed against all odds.

Hadiza grinned as she held Mary. Varyn lofted the torch with a purpose. Agnes and Leo held hands. Emily serenely smiled in her bloodied dress. Benny and Ja'ida panted, tired and sweaty. Marta plucked up the falchion blade, and dutifully stood guard by the door. Sukayna remained in the hallway next to Sir Drake, who was still unconscious.

Near tears, Stephen looked over the children. He squeezed Zahra and she groaned. He loosened his hold and looked at her, alarmed. "You are injured."

"And you are not?" Dried blood marred his tunic.

His eyes held the promise of a smile. "Boar's blood. A story for later."

The sentiment of 'later' with Stephen warmed her like a hearthside mug of cinnamon cider. Thoughts of 'later' made her more determined than ever to get these children out of the tower with Stephen and herself. A weight seemed to grip her muscles as a thought occurred to her. She loosened her arms and gazed up at him.

"Stephen, there are still two more children. You will need to climb the children down safely, while I remain to look for them."

• • • • •

There was no time to argue over who would stay and look for the ones still missing. They got to work in silence. Stephen informed her that Sir Drake's key did not work for the lever room. An iron grid strapped the heavy oak door, marred by his axe-marks.

Zahra approached Agnes and crouched in front of her. "Do you still have that stone I gave you, *ma chère*?"

Agnes looked down at her fist and peeled open her fingers. Among the dirt-crusted lines in her palm sat the black lodestone. "It helped me be strong."

"May I borrow it a moment?"

Zahra took the stone to her mother's bed and knelt beside one of its four posters. Sightlessly, she ran the stone over the wood underneath. A quiet click sounded, and she poked her fingers inside a small hidey-hole that had a magnetic mechanism. She pulled out a tiny gold key that looked different from all the others. She held it up, marveling that such a tiny thing would save them all.

Sukayna clapped her hands together. "*Alhamdulillah*!" *Praise be to Allah.*

Zahra shot the woman a severe look. "You should thank my dead mother."

Sukayna swallowed.

Stephen frowned at the interaction between them. An image flashed in her mind of sitting with Stephen by the grandiose hearth in the safe great hall of the *Manoir des Cieux*, while she told him her whole side of the story.

They opened the lever room door. Relief weakened her knees. She pointed to what appeared to be a large clump of tangled ropes. "That is a rope ladder that reaches all the way to the ground."

The children shared excited expressions and embraces. Zahra gave the key to Marta to watch over. The girl had proven herself.

Stephen carried the heavy pile out to the balcony. Gray mountains surrounded them. The crimson ocean lapped against the black rocks. It felt surreal to watch him kneel and fasten the rope to the stone spindles of the balcony. She crouched to work at the opposite side, a smile twitching her lips. She set the stone aside so she could work with the rope, uncertain why she continued to hold onto it. Was it because it said 'Creator' on it? Or did she feel attached to it? It had been essential to their ultimate escape, after all.

Marbellans gathered below, yelling at the Portuguese soldiers guarding the tower's perimeter. Palace warriors stood in an organized formation, their blades glinting.

"Stephen, do you know why the king's warriors are involved?"

He yanked one knot secure and gently took over for her, his eyes dancing with warmth. "You will require the long explanation, for which we do not have time."

Perhaps for the first time, Zahra was not annoyed that Stephen seemed to know her better than she knew him. "Nonsense. I shall applaud your brevity."

He smiled as he worked. "Your sister got me into the tower. Then she called on the palace warriors to raid it. They have not done so yet. Why, I do not know."

Zahra grit her teeth. He was right. She needed to know more. How had Stephen gotten out of his punishment? What had caused Raha to call a raid? And what was Jabir doing about all of this?

Stephen tightened the knot and yanked upward, testing the strength of his work. "My question is, why hasn't Diogo tried to pull the lever, yet? Seems like an easy out at this point."

Zahra replied without thinking. "He does not have the key."

Stephen faced her. A powerful feeling of dread washed over her. Without fully understanding why, Zahra recalled the moment she had produced the lever room key—Sukayna had cheered. Why would Sukayna wish that room to be accessed if she were to be trapped in here with the rest of them when the lever was pulled? She had not learned of the rope ladder yet.

"Where is Sukayna?"

Zahra rushed back into the Solar. Several of the children jumped up. Hadiza had gathered Sir Drake's fallen books. The Solar door was still ajar.

Both Sir Drake and Sukayna were gone.

Zahra knew Sukayna had gone to inform Diogo that all the children were in the Solar. And that the lever room was now accessible.

"Listen." Stephen spoke behind her. Zahra's ear perked at a distant rumbling sound.

Boot falls.

"Marta, lock the door!" Zahra screamed. Stephen slammed the lever room closed. Marta's face turned white as she fumbled for the pouch. "Then cast the key off the balcony!"

Stephen grabbed the axe on the way and pushed the Solar doors closed. They could hear the multitude of soldiers ascending. Stephen picked Mary up with one arm, ushering the other children behind the bed.

The doors shuddered as they swung open. Marta locked the lever room and Zahra snatched the key from her. She made a break for the balcony. Soldiers marched in bascinet helmets and lamellar armor.

"Zahra!" Stephen's voice sounded distant as she sprinted. The children screamed. A broadsword sliced through the air. She crumpled to her knees and elbows. A soldier collapsed in a cacophony of armor beside her on the floor, blood pooling around him, his eyes wide. Dead.

Stephen had axed the man down. He swung around to face the next advancing soldier. Zahra scrambled forward.

"*Princesa*."

Diogo's voice was both a command and a warning.

"If you deny me that key, you rob the children of a quick death."

Her fingers clenched around it, along with her lodestone. She had not noticed that she had snatched it up too. Stephen growled and swung the axe, blocking a blow. He narrowly jumped back, but the soldier's sword still sliced Stephen's chest near his collarbone. Several men closed in.

"*Tonton*!" Mary screamed.

Zahra whirled, her hands out. "Stop them, Diogo! I will give you the key."

"*Alto*." *Halt.*

The soldiers jerked to a standstill. They lowered their weapons, panting. Stephen's chest rose and fell, blood seeping from the shallow wound splitting open his tunic. The children huddled behind the bed.

Sukayna moved aside, and Diogo stepped into the Solar. The wide-brimmed hat cast his face in shadow, dark circles under his eyes. "Relinquish the axe."

The corners of Stephen's mouth turned down. He gripped the axe tighter, his nostrils flaring. Zahra grasped his arm. "We are gravely outnumbered."

At least ten soldiers spread out in the chamber alone, and seemingly more lurked in the stairwell. Jaw flexing, Stephen raised the axe and punted it at the nearest man. The soldier fumbled his own sword to catch it. His pearly blue eyes flashed, threatening.

Diogo strode between the soldiers, like Moses parting the sea. "*Princesa*, I am no longer amused by your presence in Marbella."

"Where are the other two children?"

A line creased between Diogo's eyebrows as he looked over the children. They shrank back. "I thought you had all of them. We cleared all the chambers. Including the chapel, where you left our richest patron injured and quite angry."

"You should have left him in there."

Diogo's eyes were dull and haggard. Where was his usual banter? Why did he not seem more triumphant? He pointed to the blue-eyed soldier. "You. Cut that ladder down."

The soldier trotted out like an obedient dog. He swung the axe at the base of the balusters until the stone chipped and the knots burst asunder, pieces of hemp catching on the wind. Tossing the axe aside, he picked up the pile of ropes.

And threw them over.

As the ropes splayed in the air and disappeared from view, the children wailed. Leo and Agnes bent into one another and cried. Hadiza clung to Mary, petting her hair. Zahra must have stumbled because Stephen steadied her.

Stephen's voice was a cold burn. "It is a terrifying thing to fall into the hands of the living God."

Diogo's black eyes narrowed. "The key."

This was it. She was about to hand the lever room key over. The small gold metal stuck to her lodestone. Once she gave it to him, she would lose the tower, lose Stephen, and lose the children. She hesitated, as if prolonging the inevitable might give God more time to save them.

The blue-eyed soldier approached, holding out his hand. Stephen bristled. She dropped the key into the man's hand. He shot a smirk to Stephen before walking it over to Diogo.

Zahra's blood rushed knowing what was about to happen and there was nothing she could do to stop it. She clutched the back of Stephen's tunic, and he wrapped his arm around her shoulders.

Then Diogo pocketed the key.

Zahra held her breath. What was stopping him from pulling the lever now? Or having someone pull it after he escaped? Distant shouting filtered up to them. It sounded like the crowd was growing angry.

Ermine cape swishing, Diogo crossed onto the balcony and looked over the railing. "Nice work stirring up the royals." He spoke in English. "Seems a couple of them have had a change of heart on who should rule Marbella."

A faint smile touched Stephen's mouth. Was Raha one of the 'royals' Diogo spoke of? Who else? Perhaps Yusef. His heart had changed after his brush with death. Did the unrest outside keep Diogo from pulling the lever?

Zahra called out to him. "It is over, Diogo. You do not have to murder the children."

He whipped around, standing in the balcony opening. "Did God murder Jesus?" The sun reflected off his brocade hat as he adjusted its rim. "It does pain me deeply. These innocents are my sacrifice."

Was Diogo delaying for remorse? Or the pain of ending this lucrative operation?

Zahra leaned into Stephen, perhaps for the last time. "I believe the relic stopped working for you as a child because you started killing people."

Diogo cast her a hard glare. "When my wife bled out giving birth to little Gordy… when it let her die, I knew the relic was not of God."

Diogo's eyes grew misty. This struck Zahra as odd; how could a man willing to sacrifice a dozen children without batting an eye grow emotional over the memory of his wife and baby?

A realization dawned on Zahra. She knew why Diogo had not pulled the lever yet. She released Stephen and stepped forward. "I know where Gordon is. You will not find him without my help."

Diogo removed his hat. Red veins streaked the whites of his eyes. He spoke in Portuguese through gritted teeth. "Men, at my word, kill the Englishman."

The soldiers lifted their weapons.

Stephen crossed his arm in front of her, guiding her backward. Zahra spoke in bold Portuguese. "At least one of you shall die trying to kill Stephen. Just like your brother here, in a pool of his own blood. Are you ready to die today? I have freely offered da Gama the information he wants. Yet he sacrifices you."

The soldiers snuck glances to one another.

Zahra pressed on. "Da Gama, a brawl between all of us will take time. Precious time. Gordon does not have much of that. He suffers. Let the children go now. Gordy can be in your arms in minutes."

Diogo seemed gripped with indecision, eyes jumping between her and the children.

Stephen spoke in a low tone. "What is going on?"

She kept her focus on Diogo. "Gordon's air supply will be getting low by now."

Diogo grimaced, teeth showing. "Yusef has asked that I spare you. The balance of power shifts in Marbella as we speak. You are free to go."

"If even one child remains, I will not leave."

"Blast you! You and your Englishman and his niece may go. Live out your lives."

A sharp sensation of longing tore through her. The prospect of suddenly being free from this nightmare—to walk out alive—struck Zahra in the chest. If Yusef had taken power and had requested her freedom, perhaps they could work together to save the children. Outside these walls, she would be in a better position to make a difference. She find Yusef and tell him everything before Diogo could pull the lever and escape with the clients.

Stephen would be by her side. And when this was all over, they could have a future together. The possibilities blossomed in her mind. Mary would return to James and Merla. Zahra and Stephen could make a home together. Perhaps even have children together.

Stephen's whisper cut into her paralysis. "What did he say?"

Zahra looked up. Stephen's eyes were like the circle of the earth, rife with oceans and wildlands, inside them, their future suspended in stasis.

But what of the futures of the rest of them?

If she left to make a life for herself, sacrificing these children on the altar of her desires and comfort, she would be no better than Diogo, who sacrificed them for riches. Stephen touched her cheek where a tear had fallen. She gritted her teeth and stepped away from his side, his warmth, his protection.

She faced Diogo. "All the children must be freed."

His teeth flashed, his impatience flaring. "Not a chance! If they are released, my cause is over. I cannot have that on my conscience."

Zahra's face grew hot, her voice rough. "Allow the children with families to go. There are several of them. Mary, Agnes, Leo, Hadiza."

Diogo's face reddened. "That is not possible!"

Zahra took another step toward him. "You have been deceived, Diogo. Your operation is Satan's work."

"*Cala a boca*!" Diogo roared. *Shut up.* "I shall not let the innocents go!"

"It is four children, you coward! I hope your son is still alive!"

Sweat sheened on Diogo's brow. "Only those you named." He turned to the guards, "Step aside you fools. Let them pass! Hurry!"

Zahra drew in a sharp breath and swung toward Stephen. "Take Mary, Agnes, Leo, and Hadiza. I have negotiated your freedom."

Stephen clutched her shoulders. "What have you done?"

She gripped his forearms. "Stephen, this is your only chance to get Mary home."

His eyes clouded and he bowed his head. He pulled Zahra against his chest and held her. She clung to him, his heart knocking against her ear. She bit back a wave of grief. She needed to show strength for her children.

"Get out!" Diogo's voice was raw.

Stephen leaned to kiss her, pressed something into her hand, and turned away. He did not look at her again. "Rabbit. Leo. Hadiza. Agnes."

Mary scrambled into his arms. Leo stood as if in a dream. Zahra grasped Hadiza and Agnes up to hurry them. "Agnes, take care of little Leo. Hadiza, go with Stephen! *Saby*, you are free!"

Eyes wide, Hadiza walked a few steps until she noticed not everyone was joining. She dropped to her knees and clutched Zahra. "No, *anisa*, it must be all of us!"

Zahra hugged Hadiza, and her voice broke. "We must stay."

Stephen peeled Hadiza off Zahra. Hadiza cried, "I cannot leave them behind again!"

Unable to watch Stephen and the children leave, Zahra gathered Marta, Ja'ida, Varyn, Benny, and Emily. Hadiza's raw cries followed them out of the chamber.

Diogo's eyes bugged. "He is free. Now tell me."

"What is the point if you can just apprehend them again? I will tell you when I see them safe outside."

Diogo panted, roaring down the stairwell. "Escort them out as quickly as you can."

Zahra wrapped her arms around the remaining four children and unfurled her hand. Along with her dusty black rock, there sat a gold band. The posy ring. She turned it to read the inscription.

I found the one whom my soul loves. Song 3:4

• • • • •

The children gravitated around Zahra on the balcony, watching for Stephen and the others to emerge. An apology hung at the tip of Zahra's tongue. But she resisted the urge. It would be an admission that all hope was lost.

She thought of the two children she had not found. She thought of Hassan's sacrifice. She wondered if the Lord would welcome him. He had been only a child.

And would she be welcomed? Feathery clouds floated against a deep blue sky. She was ashamed by how she had lived her life for herself. She prayed the children would be safe with Him after all this was over.

The lodestone burned in her palm. She had neglected to give it back to Agnes before she had left. Why? Zahra had thought the stone had been their liberator—but it was their destruction. It was the reason Diogo now had the power to bring the whole tower down. She gazed at its familiar smooth but dull surface, the engraved Latin lettering. Then she realized why she kept it.

She believed in it.

In a startling moment of clarity, she realized that none of these items—the cloth, the stones, the keys—had saved the children. Only One had that power.

Zahra approached the railing and looked down at a clutch of flowering pink myrtle trees at the base of the tower. She let the stone fall from her palm. It clinked off her delicate wedding band and arched the long way down. A puff of pink blossoms erupted where it landed.

She stared where Stephen and the children should have emerged by now. Part of her had hoped something miraculous would happen when she gave up the stone.

Villagers had begun to throw things at the traders; a basket; a handful of dirt; a boot. Something glinted in the corner of her eye. *Malik* Jabir emerged from the North tower in his crown and robes, flanked by several of his warriors. He strode toward the restless crowd.

Amir Yusef stepped out as well, still strapped with bandages. Though supported by a cane, he stood straight, as if at the front lines of a battle. His army, the angry villagers, rerouted toward Jabir.

The king stopped and backed up. He bumped into his warriors and whipped around. They stared down at him. The villagers descended upon him. One man ripped the crown off his head and swung it as a weapon. Jabir defended himself with uplifted arms, crying out to his men.

The palace warriors stepped back. The villagers ripped off his robes. Jabir stumbled to his knees. They kicked him until he lay crumpled. Crimson splattered in the sand. She ushered the children away.

"Da Gama." Zahra gestured to the commotion. "The king was struck down by the villagers. Do you think you will ever walk safely in Marbella?"

Diogo, eyeing the stairwell out in the hallway, turned to look at her. "My clients and I shall escape as Marbella witnesses the collapse. We will go unnoticed amidst the destruction."

It could work. Especially with a padding of soldiers and a fleet of vessels ready to sail.

The villagers dispersed, and Jabir lay unmoving. Still no Stephen. Something was wrong.

"*Princesa*, remember my loyal servant, Pierre?"

Pierre emerged, settling his bovine stare on Zahra. Angry cuts stippled the flesh around his eyes. He yanked someone up the stairs behind him, holding a short blade near her throat.

Zahra sucked in a breath as she locked eyes with Raha in a ruby *takchita* gown. Her thick braid lay tousled over her shoulder as though her crown had been torn from her head.

Tears streaked Raha's cheeks.

Zahra recalled the moment she had resolved to leave her sister: the morning of their mother's funeral. Having the night before endured Yusef's assault, Zahra had felt nothing for her grieving sister. Zahra had felt no remorse deciding to leave Marbella, leave the pain, and leave her baby sister. Emptiness had hollowed her.

Pierre dragged her into the chamber. Everything she should have felt then swept over her now. Guilt snaked around her like the liana vine that choked the life from a tree. Zahra had come here to save Hadiza and the children. Now even Raha's life was forfeit.

Raha's chin trembled. "*Shaqiyqati.*" *My dear sister*. "Forgive me. I understand. You did not know. You could not have known." She shook her head as tears ran over her face. "I forgive you."

Zahra's heart cracked open like a fan mussel. That crushing weight lifted away as if God had plucked it from her shoulders. A profound joy poured into that emptiness. Not only had Raha forgiven her; she realized that He had forgiven her, though she did not deserve it. He loved her when she had not earned it.

Her shame was replaced by belief.

Thump thump.

CHAPTER 25

The balcony ground seemed to tilt as a wave of dizziness rocked Zahra. She leaned into the railing. That wonderful thrumming sensation rushed through her. It was not concentrated anywhere—instead, it radiated from her toes to her fingertips to the top of her head.

In that instant, she understood. She understood why the power of the cloth would never react to Zahra's need for help. God's power had never been in the cloth. The cloth had just been a symbol that stirred up the tiniest bit of faith within her.

God's power had worked through her faith—and her repentance.

"*Princesa*? Do you understand what is happening, here?" Cock-eyed, Diogo spoke through bared teeth. "I have the queen, your sister. If you do not tell me where my son is, I shall cut her down before your eyes. Next, I shall move on to the innocents. Do you believe you have the strength to watch all of them die before you tell me?"

Zahra's dizziness faded. She wiped her hands over her wet cheeks. She pushed off the railing and stepped inside. "He is trapped in a hidden compartment within the infirmary's hearth. It has been hours—I would hurry."

"*Senhorita*!" Marta darted inside. "The others are not outside yet!"

"Find him," roared Diogo to the soldiers in the doorway. Two men turned and pounded down the stairwell.

Zahra pushed Marta behind her. She faced Diogo. "Release the children."

Diogo tucked his wide-brimmed hat back upon his head and smiled. "You have told me what I needed to know."

Pierre chewed something small between his browning teeth, eyes on Zahra. The tendons in Raha's neck protruded in avoidance of his blade.

The thrumming coursed through her body, a steady stream of God's power. She stared into the faces of evil. Pierre, with his lust for violence. Sukayna, with her cowardly self-preservation. The many soldiers who blindly followed orders. Master Diogo da Gama, willfully illiterate in God's truth, so he could continue his sinning. His arrogance.

Pressure built inside of her. "I shall ask only one more time, Diogo."

Diogo stared back at her, his upper lip trembling.

She repeated quietly, "Release His children."

Diogo jabbed his finger at her, his eyes contorted into black slits. "God's wrath be upon you! For relentlessly disrupting our peaceful operation. My poor innocents and your Englishman shall be crushed and burned in this tower! Because of your actions, *princesa!* If Gordy is dead, I shall slit the queen's throat myself!"

Zahra lifted her chin. "How uncivil."

Diogo's eyes flicked wide. "Throw her over."

Marta covered her mouth. Hesitation rippled through the twenty men, shifting glances among one another.

"Do it!" bellowed Diogo. The blue-eyed soldier lurched to snatch Zahra by her arms, dragging her toward the balcony.

"Unhand her!" Raha shrieked in Arabic, straining against Pierre's bruising grip.

Pierre grunted. "Were the order given to me, the harpy would be catching the wind by now."

Several of the children began to cry. Zahra craned her neck to look at them. "Do not be afraid," she said in Arabic, and again in Italian, and last, Portuguese.

Zahra marveled at her absence of fear. Did God protect her from it? Unbidden, a verse in Isaiah that Lord Raymond loved came to mind.

Do not fear, for I have redeemed you; I have summoned you by name; you are mine.

The soldier shoved Zahra into the stone railing. Pain shot up her injured back. She held back a groan.

Diogo had a wild sheen in his eyes. "Throw her over now!"

A shadow fell over them. The soldier's blue eyes squinted in the sun's direction. He removed his helmet. Zahra did not need to look. She already knew the Creator would show Himself.

Everyone inside stilled, looking to the sky. A deep sound resonated in the distance, like the reverent humming of monks.

"What is that?" Pierre backed up a step.

Sukayna disappeared down the stairs in a frantic patter of leather shoes. Pierre released Raha, turned, and fled after her. In his retreat, he pitched past a flushed Gordon ascending the steps.

The children encircled Raha, steadying her.

Gordon's matted hair framed his blotchy face. His scuffed clothes hung torn in some places. He swiped a dirty sleeve over his brow. "What's with him?"

The soldiers tilted to stare at what had made Pierre run. Gordon approached his father, who only acknowledged his son's presence by clutching his sleeve.

Pressure built in Zahra's chest. "Diogo da Gama. God wants His children to be free."

Diogo struggled visibly to swallow, his eyes on the sky. "But—these children are sacrificed in God—God's mighty name."

Distant screams of terror erupted from those down below. Raha wrapped her arms around the children.

Diogo's shrill voice rang out. "Theirs is innocent blood, shed for *His* divine purpose! Just like His son!"

A shadow darkened the sun.

Zahra locked eyes with Raha. "*Asfal.*" *Get down.*

Diogo cried, "Hear Your humble servant!"

The blue-eyed soldier turned and stumbled inside.

An incalculable number of huge insects slammed into the side of the tower like a landing blow in a siege. Thousands swooped inside the Solar, striking the blue-eyed soldier down as if by cannon fodder. They merely breezed by Zahra, sweeping near but never touching her, Raha, or the children.

The screams of a soldier choked to silence as the insects crammed into his mouth. He doubled over, gagging.

They had striped, chitinous exoskeletons. They emanated a mind-numbing buzz. Gordon dropped to his knees, slapping the bugs off of him. His voice pitched high. "*Pai*, they sting!"

One of them slipped into Gordon's mouth. He spat it out, beating it into the floor with his fist. He sealed his lips shut. Each man, in their own terrible way, fell prey. They swarmed the entire chamber, attaching to every surface, crawling and whirring in circles. The children peeked out from under Raha to look at the horrific scene from which they were somehow safe.

With his bottomless black eyes, Diogo watched her. He stood motionless, coated in the quivering striped insects, his lips stiffly closed.

The creatures never touched Zahra. "The power was not in the relic, da Gama. It was never in you. Nor me. The power is God's alone, working through us, according to His plan. This is your last chance: let His children go."

The veins under the flesh around Diogo's eyes pronounced as he strained, the creatures piling onto him grotesquely. Stings caused his flesh to spring open in places.

He shook his head.

In one swift motion, he picked up a fallen soldier's sword, and charged.

Not at Zahra—but at Raha and the children.

Fear stabbed through Zahra's gut, but she stopped herself from acting. Time seemed to slow as she relaxed her shoulders and closed her eyes. His promise was a certainty now.

Thump thump.

Diogo dropped the sword with a clang. His hands flailed. Gordon, still on his knees, shot his hands out, fingers splayed. His eyes were wide.

"Gordy! I've lost my vision!" Diogo's voice tremored as he clawed the clinging insects away from his mouth. Blood streaked his skin.

Gordon kept his lips shut. The bugs crunched under his boots as he clambered to a stand. She stepped back to avoid Gordon stumbling, arms outstretched, feeling his way forward.

"Where is my son?" A thread of fear entered Diogo's voice.

Gordon rammed into a post near the balcony, and stumbled to a crouch with a groan. Diogo crawled, his cape lumpy over the locusts that had made their way inside his clothes.

Zahra called out. "Da Gama, where are Stephen and the others?"

"In the kitchen with the clients. Lead me to my son!"

Her chest tightened at the thought of her children being anywhere near those monsters. Urgency spiked through her blood. They had to leave—now.

"*Pai*? Has God blinded us?" Gordon's voice pitched high. He swung his arms wildly. He stumbled onto the balcony.

"Wait!" Zahra cried out—but she was too late. He slammed into the railing and tipped forward, his arms swinging in wild circles. The weight of his torso toppled him over the edge. His scream followed him all the way down until abruptly stopping.

"Gordy," whispered Diogo. He blinked several times, his eyes focusing on her. His sight had returned. "Gordy, my boy?"

He clawed off the insects clinging to his face and staggered to the balcony. He gazed over the edge. He dropped to his knees, and then curled on his side at the base of the stone balusters. His arm covered his face as he cried in an anguished voice. "My boy! My boy!"

Zahra led the children and Raha toward the door. They weaved between unmoving soldiers and waded through a thick layer of crackling carapaces.

"Be gone! I wish never to lay eyes on you again!" Diogo bellowed. The children and Raha fled from the Solar, and Zahra did not look back once.

• • • • •

Zahra, Raha, and the five children reached down the stone spiral stairwell.

"We must get to the kitchen!" Her voice sounded sharp—panicked. A twinge fluttered in her stomach. She asked God for the trust she had experienced moments ago when her demise had been all but certain.

Dead locusts lined the stairwell. Ja'ida and Marta squealed in disgust if they stepped on them barefooted. They held hands as they ran. Varyn went ahead of the girls to kick the dead bugs aside, which made the children grin. Benny held Raha's hand, smiling up at her. Raha tentatively smiled back.

Once they had descended several levels, a peculiar clunking sound reverberated through the tower. They halted in the stairwell, exchanging looks. A repetitive pounding rumbled, each time growing nearer.

Zahra raced to unlock the nearest stairwell door. The stone walls vibrated, shedding dust. A sense of foreboding snaked its way into her heart.

Would Diogo pull the switch, even if he had nothing to gain from it? Even if he were stuck at the top, doomed to be crushed in the tower's destruction?

As if time had slowed, Zahra watched as the torches dipped mechanically in their mounts, folded down, and fell straight into the clay pots full of dry flax, charcoal, and black powder.

"Get down!" Zahra screamed, closing over the two nearest children. The pots began exploding one after another, shards of clay and fire spraying. Flames blazed. Tapestries caught fire. Wooden rafters smoldered. Her mother had explained when she was a child that these explosions would compromise the structural integrity of the tower one floor at a time. The whole thing would collapse in minutes.

They flew down the stairs. The stairwell insulated them from the explosions. If only she had taken the key from Diogo! She had overlooked that detail in her haste to get to Stephen.

When they reached the fourth level—the kitchen—Zahra grabbed Raha's arm. "Hold the door. If it gets too dangerous, get out."

Raha blinked back tears and gave Zahra a hug. "*Shaqiyqati,* may your God protect you."

Zahra squeezed her baby sister. "All of us."

When she opened the door, black smoke billowed out. Zahra kept low, dodging the licking flames and burning bits of destruction that littered the hallway. She raced toward the kitchen, where smoke seeped from the top of its doors. The hinges trembled as she unlocked and shoved one open. The men in the chamber caught sight of her and began crawling toward her. The Cardinal, wrapped in a Moroccan *djellaba* robe, lay with his mouth hanging open, obviously deceased. The Jewish man, clutching his bandaged shoulder with a burnt hand, locked eyes with Zahra. The burly Russian, his ankle bandaged, pointed. "The Berber woman!"

Stephen's black-smudged face filled her vision like a warring angel from heaven. He yanked her arm. "Run!"

Leo, Agnes, Hadiza, and Mary poured out of the kitchen like a herd of wild piglets. They raced down the hallway roiling with gray smoke. Zahra ran, Stephen close in tow. A wooden beam crashed to the ground behind them in a fiery spray of cinders. Her eyes blurred. Raha, crouched against the open door, ushered the children into the stairwell.

The first of their pursuers to climb the wood beam was the Spaniard who had abused Hassan. The Russian sprung over it next. Stephen and Zahra dove into the stairwell and Raha threw her weight into closing the door. It seemed to lodge unevenly in its frame, the lock not engaging. The tower trembled.

Zahra shoved the key into Marta's palm and repeated 'Go!' in several languages, aggressively shepherding the children. "Next floor down is the portrait room!"

Marta raced ahead, opening the stairwell door. Black smoke shrouded the end of the hallway. Raha sped to the front of the line, covering her face with the crook of her elbow. Last out, Stephen slammed the stairwell door behind them.

Chunks of burning wood fell. Firelight shined from cracks in the mortar below her feet. The floor shifted. A girl's scream erupted behind her. Hadn't all the children been ahead of her? As she turned to look, the stone beneath her feet fell away.

It all happened in an instant, but it was as if time slowed, revealing every detail of her last moments. She grappled for a handhold. The stone crashed a dozen feet below into the granary's chaff-pit. The smoke was light and sweet-smelling. Straw smoldered and disintegrated. Zahra spotted a woman's bejeweled hand among the chaff. Half-charred, Sukayna lifelessly rolled over, her mouth stuffed full of scaly wheat bracts. The unholy fire belched as it rose, as if desiring to snatch Zahra. With calm clarity, she knew that falling boulders would pummel her, break her bones, and she would burn to death.

A strong grip caught her forearm. With a hiss, time returned to normal. She locked onto the dark eyes of her savior. Shock coursed through her. "Hassan?"

With significant effort, the young warrior held her, his lips pressed, face strained and perspiring.

Stephen leapt and landed beside Hassan. Together, they pulled her to safety. Her legs wobbled as she flung her arms around Hassan. "You are alive!"

His body shook as he returned her embrace. Zahra saw Sukayna's body become engulfed by the sooty chaff.

Stephen called out across the chasm. "You can make it!"

Zahra turned. A blonde girl in an oversized brown tunic stood on the opposite side. Her red-rimmed eyes glistened with tears.

"*Quviasunga*!" A young boy cried out, clinging to Hassan's leg. Zahra did not recognize the language, nor the boy—about five years old with smooth skin and shiny black hair.

Hassan had found the other two children!

"Keterlyn, jump. Now!" Stephen's commanding voice carried.

"Berber!" Roared the Jewish man at the end of the hall. The stairwell door had broken open, and the men tumbled out. "These children cannot live!"

The girl Stephen called Keterlyn looked over her shoulder and shrieked. She ran about four or five steps before flinging into the air over the fire-breathing chasm. Stephen and Hassan caught her before she could slip at the edge, pulling her onto steady flooring.

The tower trembled.

The Jewish man supported his injured shoulder. The Spaniard had wild, panicked eyes. There were other men she did not recognize. They gauged the distance as they approached the edge.

Zahra plucked up the black-haired boy and Hassan grabbed Keterlyn's hand. Stephen held the rear as they ran down the hall. The portrait room door hung open. Inside, the children and Raha crawled on their hands and knees. Raha yelled over the deafening growl of fire. "It is worse in here!"

The iron-strapped door shook on its hinges as Stephen shut it locked behind them. Black smoke and red flames roiled like a beast above their heads. The children's portraits lay strewn, smoldering. A wave of dizziness hit Zahra.

"Stephen." She passed the boy to him, shouting in Portuguese. "Marta, the foyer has windows!"

Keterlyn shrieked as tile shattered beside her. The ceiling was coming down. Hassan slung his arm around her, keeping her moving. Ahead of them, Agnes collapsed with Leo in her arms. He cried at the impact, followed by a rough, chesty cough. Stephen helped Agnes stand, and then scooped Leo up in his free arm, crouching low as he ran. Mary and Raha grabbed Agnes' hands to help her keep up. Zahra raced ahead of the hobbling group.

Marta shoved open the entry foyer door. A gust of cooler air filled their lungs. Gray smoke swirled out of the clover-shaped windows in the ceiling. Cries of joy and laughter erupted as the children passed through.

The sounds of excitement died. Diogo's shield statue roared with flames that warmed her skin even twenty meters away. Pieces crumbled off, ashes sparking and swirling. The mountain of fire obscured the doorway. There was no way out.

A gruff laughed pierced the air. Pierre lounged on one of the tufted chaises, his arms folded behind his head. "A key won't get you through that."

• • • • •

"We shall all die in here today." Pierre threw his legs off the chaise and stood. He pointed at Stephen. "But before that, I shall have the pleasure of killing you."

The Frenchman produced a blade in a swift, practiced motion. Stephen lowered Leo and the black-haired boy to the ground.

Mary pulled at Stephen's tunic. "No, *tonton*!"

"Get them back," Stephen commanded Zahra. "Get out if you can."

Zahra did not tarry with fear; nor did she argue. She grabbed Mary's hand. She and Raha ushered all the children toward the fire. Heat baked their skin; it was like standing next to Sheol itself. For some reason, they had not opened the doors from the outside—perhaps Diogo's men continued to ward off the palace warriors. Perhaps the mechanism had melted. Surely her people had formed a water brigade by now.

She had no recourse. Except one. She dropped to her knees. "Lord. The All Powerful. Creator of the heavens and universe."

Pierre charged at Stephen. Raha restrained Mary as she screamed. Stones crumbled from the walls.

Zahra's voice grew strident, trembling. "Fear not, stand firm, and see the salvation of the Lord, which he will work for you today."

Stephen invited the impact, getting ahold of Pierre's wrist to fend off the blade. They hit the ground hard, grunting. A slab of charred wood fell from the ceiling, cracking the frame of the iron-strapped door, where a legion of depraved, desperate men worked to silence their voices before they could escape.

The tower would collapse any second.

"The Lord will fight for you, and you have only to be silent."

Zahra opened her eyes. She could see a path through the fire that was not as thick as the rest. If she could just open the door, the people with buckets of water may be able to give the children time to escape. It was the only thing, short of another miracle, she could think to do. A deafening crack spurred her forward.

As she launched forward, Zahra thought a short, simple prayer.

Lord, Your will be done.

"Zahra, no!" Raha's voice cut through the chaos.

Stephen cracked his fist to Pierre's jaw—again, and again. His attention shifted to Zahra, and his eyes went wide. Pierre struck Stephen and tore him down. Another slab of flagstone crashed near where they fought. The tower let forth a deafening groan.

Zahra called to the children. "Do not be afraid. When the flames are doused, follow me."

Then she whisked herself into the fire like a self-immolating monk. She stumbled over charred remains of the shield sculpture. Her flesh burned, and the voices of the children faded away. She struggled to keep her eyes open as her flesh flayed, puffs of fire bursting into being all over her clothes. She gritted her teeth to hold back a scream, tears steaming off her cheeks. For a moment she thought she had gone the wrong way, because a shadowy figure stood in front of her. She jerked back and turned. Then the door handle appeared before her, bright orange like a blacksmith's workpiece. She dove and clutched it, her skin sizzling. She screamed as she pushed out. With a laborious grating sound, the door cranked and popped open. The fire extended toward the sky.

She sprawled out on the dirt, her burning lungs soothed by fresh air. A man's voice cried out. She could not see, but she heard many footsteps approach. Several people clutched her and dragged her to safety. Her eyes watered as she struggled to see.

No one was there with water. No one neared the tower, from which large boulders tumbled. They only pulled her further and further away.

She wailed and fought. Then she looked down at her flesh and her gown—and all were untouched by fire. She had walked through it unharmed.

CHAPTER 26

One of the warriors helped her stand. Villagers surrounded her, gazing at the spectacle of the burning tower. Fire licked out of the doorway like the mouth of a dragon.

"Your queen is in there!" She tried to jerk free from the warrior's hold. "Let me go!"

A breeze cut through Marbella, wildly tossing everyone's clothing and hair. That would only stoke the flames.

"The fire didn't burn me!" She screamed the names of the children. She screamed Stephen and Raha's names.

The cold breeze did not let, as if a storm was rolling in. The fire belching out of the doorway whipped like a candle flame. It split open in half, the constant wind blowing it apart. She realized she could see the children inside.

"Run!" Zahra commanded in each of their languages, again—and again, and again. Raha swung Mary forward as she grabbed Leo and the new boy's hands and ran. As if a spell broke, the rest of them raced forth through the parting fire.

Diogo's clients appeared behind them. Perhaps they ran simply to pass the children and escape—or perhaps they ran after the children, to extinguish any evidence of what had happened in this wicked place.

Deep inside the crumbling foyer, Stephen stood and wiped blood off his face. He sprinted after the men, pulling the last two to the floor—the limping Russian and another.

The Jewish man led the group, his broken shoulder forgotten. Tiles rained down from the ceiling like blades. Agnes and Varyn emerged first, received by warriors who dared to near the tower. Hadiza clutched a black book and supported a limping Benny. Holding hands, Keterlyn, the new boy, Hassan, and Leo raced out next, followed by Ja'ida, Emily, and Marta.

In the back, Stephen grappled down another man, who grabbed the tunic of another, taking him down too. They collapsed with guttural cries, and Stephen leapt over them to continue his pursuit after the Jewish man and the Spaniard, who were closing in on Mary and Raha.

The Spaniard dove forward to snatch at Mary's dress—but Stephen tackled him. The Spaniard's bearded jaw cracked on the marble floor. Raha and Mary reached the exit. A large piece of the shield statue crashed down in a blaze of smoke and cinders. Mary emerged, crawling out from the dust and smoke.

"Raha!" cried Zahra. The warriors wrestled her back. The tip of the tower wobbled.

Raha appeared in the smoke-filled doorway just as the Jewish man clutched her braid and brought her down onto her back.

"Release me!" screamed Zahra. "Help the queen!"

Amidst the smoke, Stephen slung an arm around the Jew's throat, twisting his bad arm behind his back. The man let forth a horrendous screech. Raha crawled out and stumbled to a stand. Zahra wept—they would make it!

A thunderous sound split through the air as the tip of the tower sucked into the belly of its base.

Raha lost her footing as the marble broke apart beneath their feet. Stephen appeared behind Raha and shoved her. She soared, her arms flailing. Beaten and bleeding, Pierre appeared behind Stephen, jabbing him in the back.

The tower crumpled in on itself like a wad of parchment in God's fist. The people of Marbella ran to avoid the rolling debris and the harsh spray of dust and smoke.

Zahra broke free from the warrior's hold and raced over to Raha, who lay in a heap.

"Are you well?" Her sister's eyes opened, her dusty lips parting. Zahra laughed on an exhale and hugged her sister. The children broke away from the crowd and ran to Zahra's side, surrounding her. An airy laugh tumbled out of her as she touched their hair and their faces. All twelve! God had done it. He had done it! And Raha was well. And Stephen had made it out.

Hadn't he?

She gazed at the thinning dust pluming from the collapsed tower. "Where is Stephen?"

Raha's voice cracked. "He was right behind me."

"Stephen!" Zahra stood, scanning the wreckage. Despite the danger of drawing near to the fallen building, she began climbing the rubble. She had not seen him emerge. Could he be under there? Trapped? Dying? Dead? Her throat hurt. "Stephen?"

If God could part the sea, and if He could part a fire, He could part the stone for her, too.

"Please do it," she whispered.

Black smoke curled from between the stones. She climbed further, screaming down into the rocks where he might be buried and grievously injured. "Stephen, call back to me!"

She listened. She stooped and began throwing rocks aside. If all the people helped, they could get the stones moved. "Help me!" Her foot slipped on a loose rock, and her chin skinned on jagged rock. She gasped as her tears stung the new wound. She climbed back up and continued throwing stones aside. She reached a large one that would not budge. Her fingers blistered as she jerked at it. "Move the stones, Lord. Show the people Your power."

Villagers and warriors watched from a distance. Lightning cracked through the sky. Rain fell. Clouds hung dark and low. The drizzle increased to a downpour.

The rain washed away the blood in the ocean, leaving it cleaner than before. A cool wind swept out the dead locusts and frogs. The sin of this place washed away.

The rain also brought these twelve new children into Marbella. They had emerged from the tower broken but saved by the grace of God.

But however long Zahra sat next to the ruins of the Tower al-Garbu, the stones never moved. No voice rang out. And Stephen Kempe never emerged.

• • • • •

One Month Later

Stephen was not among the dead recovered from the ruins.

Zahra functioned in a strange place that fell between joy and sorrow. She could not deny God's liberating grace that brought her to the edge of Iberia to save twelve of His precious children. She still struggled to reconcile that with being shown what it was to love and be loved, and have it snatched away.

Raha and Zahra stood on the pier overlooking the sea. Yusef, healing nicely, ordered his men about, preparing Zahra's ship for departure. The children played in the sand, their shoes getting wet in the shallow waves.

"How long will it take to return the children with families?" In a bold yellow *takchita* gown, Raha's crown sparkled in her immaculately braided hair.

Salty air filled Zahra's lungs. "Could be a year or more. We have a detailed itinerary."

"Mary goes home first?"

Zahra nodded. "Ja'ida wishes to stay here, with Biko's family."

"I shall make sure they are well taken care of."

"And Hassan?"

Raha smiled. "He is old enough to train among the warriors. I shall keep a close eye on him if you wish."

"I wish for him to be well-loved." Zahra blinked back tears. He was her little hero.

Raha took Zahra's hand and squeezed. "I shall treat him as my own son."

She looked down at her sister's bejeweled fingers. "I wish I did not have to leave you again, Raha."

"*Shaqiyqati.* You are not leaving me. You are giving these children a chance. You do not blame yourself anymore, do you?"

Zahra's eyes grew moist. "When you forgave me, and when He forgave me, I forgave myself."

She bowed her head to hide the fall of tears. In truth, after a month of searching for Stephen in the wreckage, her heart could not take another morning breaking upon hearing the same news.

"We shall keep looking for him."

Hassan had promised Zahra he would not rest until he found Stephen. Nightmares haunted her—Stephen suffocating deep in the pile of stones, alone. For several weeks, in the middle of the night, she had visited the debris and prayed for one more miracle.

When it was no longer feasible that he had lived, she told herself that if God had wanted her to be with Stephen, He would have let him live.

"Is the gold we gave you enough?"

Zahra gave Raha a small smile. "Far more than enough, *malika.*"

Raha grinned. "Tell them you bumped into Mansa Musa."

They laughed, and Zahra had the urge to squeeze her sister's full cheeks. So many years she had lost with her. Now, she had overcome much and emerged stronger.

A line of worry formed between Raha's eyebrows. "Will you have trouble in France?"

Zahra shrugged. "If I am recognized, perhaps."

Raha cast her sister a cock-eyed look. "How will you not be recognized?"

Zahra loved seeing Raha sober and playful. "Remember the book Hadiza had?"

Raha pressed her lips. "I nearly threw it into the fire once or twice. She insisted on keeping it."

"It might help me with said 'trouble' in France."

Raha lifted her eyebrows. She looked down at her feet. "I will pray for you."

Zahra embraced her sister. "Thank you."

They held each other for a long time. The ocean sloshed against the side of the boat. Men stocked the ship. They drew apart and Raha sniffed, dabbing the corners of her eyes with her fingertips.

"Zahra, I did not want to ask. But it could be some time until I see you again." Raha bit her lip, hesitant. "The—Stephen. He mentioned he was married and could not go where his wife was. But then…"

Raha touched the gold circlet on Zahra's finger.

Zahra's throat tightened. "It is difficult to explain. But I assure you—I am the woman he spoke of. I am his wife." Stephen had believed that, so she chose to believe it too. Though part of her did wonder if the 'other' Zahra had truly been her.

"I accept this vague answer. For now. One day, you shall tell me everything."

Zahra succumbed to the urge to press her hands to Raha's cheeks. "Everything."

• • • • •

One Month Later

Their carriage wobbled through a rural village in Nantes, thick curtains warding off the icy December air. Last time she had been here, she had been traipsing into the woods after a hostile Englishman. The thought of him pinched her heart.

Her long-sleeved black gown revealeed her widowed state. Mary and Hadiza sat on the opposite bench, clapping and rhyming. Zahra's first stop had been *Manoir des Cieux*. When Lord Raymond had first lay his eyes on her, he had wept and praised God. He had to take a seat when she revealed the riches she brought from Marbella. Zahra chuckled at the memory of his expression when she asked him to watch after eight children for a few weeks while she returned Mary home.

Bernard, who seemed eager to be taking orders from Zahra and Hadiza again, hopped down from the carriage and poked his head in. "We have arrived, 'moiselle."

Mary's green eyes peered out of the carriage toward the wattle and reed home. "The weeds are gone," she said in a soft voice. Her nose twitched.

They approached it, hearing muffled voices from within. Hadiza hopped forward and knocked. When it opened, James first locked gazes with Zahra.

Then he saw Mary. Tears clouded his eyes. He sank to his knees, gripping his bearded face. Mary was a year grown since he last saw her.

His little girl's face turned blustery red. Her nose wrinkled several times—then she dove into his arms.

"Merla," he choked out, to get his wife's attention. He buried his face into Mary's hair and sobbed. Merla appeared, her forehead furrowed in concern. She clapped her hands to her face on a tender cry. She slid to her knees, staring. James pulled her into the fold. Merla whimpered, enveloping Mary and bowing her head.

Hadiza leaned against Zahra, smiling.

The Kempes pressed their foreheads together. They laughed quietly at something Mary said about her bed. James looked at Zahra, rubbing his fingertips over his eyes. "My brother?"

Zahra nodded once. "Stephen did everything possible to get her home to you."

James drew to a stand, scanning the terrain. Only Bernard stood by his carriage, hat in his hand. "Where is he?"

Zahra was unable to say the words.

"Where is my baby brother?" James' voice was rough.

Mary buried her face in her mother's neck. "*Tonton* is gone, Papa."

Merla's voice broke. "Oh, dear God."

James blinked several times. He hung his head, voice pitched high. "And I would not even give him my coat."

He pressed his hand to his face and wept. Merla cried against Mary's hair. Zahra struggled not to give in to the emotion, lest she be unable to recuperate for what she had to ask them.

Once inside, they gathered at the small table. Zahra learned that Stephen and James had not always had a contentious relationship. James had watched after Stephen when their mother did not want a tag-a-long on her pilgrimages. He taught Stephen whatever he knew—like fighting, farming, and flirting. They laughed tearfully as James described some of Stephen's early failures capturing the attention of girls.

"But he always loved fully that boy." James gnawed at his lower lip, fighting back tears.

Speaking about Stephen seemed to soothe their grief, but it worsened Zahra's. She was not ready to hear about him. She should have had the chance to learn it on her own. But she would not descend into these thoughts that defied the will of the Creator.

"James, Merla." Zahra placed her hand on the table, her ring sparkling against her dark skin. "Stephen and I... I am his wife. I am a Kempe, now. You are my family. I wish to care for you."

Merla placed a hand on her chest, and she and James exchanged glances.

"My father, scholar Lord Raymond de Sabunde, has need of a productive, God-fearing family for our village. Mary would have a big family there who loves her."

Sitting in James' lap, Mary strung her arms around his neck. "Please can we move there, Papa?"

He cleared his throat and shared a glance with Merla. She blinked back tears, nodding. He turned back to Zahra and gently placed his hand on hers. "We would be honored to accept, Zahra, wife of Stephen Kempe."

She recalled Stephen's beautiful smile.

• • • • •

While the Kempes packed for the move, Zahra asked Bernard to take her to visit the Bishop of Nantes.

The bishop could have her imprisoned on sight until her sentencing, which could amount to fines, flogging, or even execution. But she had to take the risk because there were still evil men out there harming children.

Zahra entered the Château of the Dukes of Brittany where the trial had taken place. They searched her leather satchel and returned it. It took little time for news of her arrival to reach the bishop.

The knight of the Château Guard with the crooked mustache retrieved her. She scratched her upper lip and cleared her throat. "I see your wife has improved her barbering skills."

His guarded gaze shifted to her briefly, perhaps still angry because he had been the one in charge of the English prisoner. "Can't imagine why you came back. Your head's gonna be on a block."

She swallowed. He escorted her to the Council Chamber with torches blazing at the four cardinal points. A wave of melancholy consumed her, recalling her dear friend, Isabelle, a lifetime ago, who had often told Zahra to trust Him. That was precisely why she had come.

Bishop Jean de Malestroit stood in the Council Chamber alone, his expression tight. "Mademoiselle Sabunde."

Zahra approached and curtsied, ebony gown brushing the floor. "It is Madame Kempe."

The Bishop's bagged eyes widened. After the shock passed, he said, "I see. You have nerve to swan in here like this. You broke a criminal out of jail—a man sentenced alongside the most notorious killer in history. Chapeillon seems to think you gave him leprosy. It is his desire to have you tried and burned for witchcraft."

Zahra's heart pounded in her throat. "Monsieur Kempe's sentence was handed personally by Monsieur Chapeillon, who was corrupt."

It was quite an accusation to make—and by a woman and a Moor, no less. He could easily throw it out and forget it forever. The fact the bishop remained silent surprised her. Finally, he removed his spectacles and placed them on the table. "Madame, there is little we can do about corruption without proof."

Zahra unhooked her leather pouch and withdrew a black leather book. She dropped it beside his spectacles. "Good thing I came with that very thing."

The bishop cocked a brow.

"Have you yet heard of the tower collapsing in Granada?"

Brow furrowed, the bishop said, "Who has not heard of it? Some trader's tower in a little Iberian village, wasn't it? Last I heard, the trader, along with several men, died in the collapse. Unfortunate."

Zahra's chin trembled but she smiled. "Bishop Malestroit, if you have ears to listen, I have a story to tell you."

EPILOGUE

"Whoever believes in me will do the works I have been doing, and they will do even greater things than these." John 14:12

Marbella, Granada
April, 1441
Hassan finally fulfilled his promise. He found the body of the *uroubi.*

Why did he feel so bad?

The rubble of the Tower al-Garbu was cleared, its victims recovered. They found Diogo da Gama, his son who had fallen to his death, all the child abusers, the maidservant, the cruel Frenchman, and at last, the Englishman. There were sixteen bodies total.

Five months of obsessive searching, for what? What if *anisa* Zahra just wanted to forget this place?

But it was not for nothing. It was for his guilt. That wonderful, terrible day, he had fought for hours. He found and rescued two of the other children, Tak and Keterlyn. He had been past the point of exhaustion by the time the torches had dropped.

When *amira* Zahra had almost fallen to her death into the granary, Hassan had grabbed her just in time. He had thanked Allah for this impossible moment because she turned out to be the one who had the power to save them all.

When Keterlyn had jumped, Hassan had all but slipped. But the *uroubi*, Stephen Kempe, had clutched Hassan's waist, too. He had seen

Hassan's exhaustion, and encouraged him in Arabic, "Almost there." The *uroubi* with intense green eyes.

In the portrait room, Hassan had huddled with the other children. He told himself at the time it was to protect them. But while searching in earnest for the *uroubi's* body, the truth became clear. He could have helped in the fight against the Frenchman. If he had, the *uroubi* might have lived. Instead, Hassan had rested. That was why he made the promise.

Guilt.

When he had found the body, it had lain in a crevasse of marble and stone. Hassan had had everything he needed—his *mihrab* to pray on, incense, and the golden egg he liked to pray with. But it felt wrong because the man had been Christian. Would Allah smite him as he prayed over a Christian? So, he had not prayed when he found the body.

The man had decomposed a lot. Hassan had removed his ring, should *amira* Zahra ever return.

Malika Raha had been pleased. She had held Hassan's hand and told him he should rest knowing that the *uroubi* was with God. The comment struck Hassan as odd. That was not how it worked according to the Quran.

Come to think of it, *amira* Zahra had not been reciting the *dua* when she prayed for them to be saved. It made him wonder. It made him wonder a lot.

Then there were the ashes of the relic. The relic that had been the source of all those miracles. After Master da Gama had burned it in front of all of them, Hassan had been left alone in the dungeon. He had gathered the ashes into the mustard seed pouch and kept them all this time.

But they were just ashes and seeds. Nothing more.

The *uroubi*'s funeral was held in the palace, overseen by a Christian priest. Word had spread of how Stephen Kempe had been vital in freeing the children. Many Marbellans attended. Even those whose hearts remained steadfast for Allah, like Hassan. The people honored the *uroubi* with simple garb, prostrated prayers, and mournful songs.

Some even brought candles and rosaries to place into the basket near the box the Christians put their dead into. Ja'ida had come; her tearful smile had encouraged Hassan, for a moment.

Hassan had only this little pouch with the ashes. He considered putting it inside the box, but it was closed because the man was badly decomposed. Hassan wished it were open. Why, he could not understand. Perhaps he had been possessed by *jinn* in his long, lonely search amidst death in the ruins.

After most people had departed, Hassan approached Stephen's casket and placed his hand on it. *Whoever you are, if this Jesus is the Messiah, let us know the truth and not be uncertain.* This seemed like a reasonable request. He had not known the man well, but his heart hurt as though his brother had died.

In a lapse of good judgment, Hassan unclasped the latch. The scent of cinnamon pinched his nose. He lifted the top and saw the emaciated corpse of the *uroubi* dressed in a pristine white tunic with ivory embroidery.

Jewels chinked behind him. "You are supposed to put your gift in the basket—not inside."

Hassan dropped the casket closed. "I am sorry *malika.* I—"

"Do not apologize." A sheer veil trimmed in gold shadowed her face. He bowed his head. She was only a few years older than Hassan, but she held herself like an elder.

He lifted the small pouch he had kept for six months. "These are the ashes from the relic."

Raha closed her jeweled fingers over the pouch. "Amazing what *amira* Zahra was able to do with it."

Hassan nodded. "It was said to have been touched by the Christian prophet, Jesus."

"To Christians, He is more than a prophet."

Hassan nodded. "I know, *malika.* It had already been destroyed when *amira* Zahra performed her final miracles."

Raha handed the pouch back, smiling behind the veil. "Then it was her faith in *Al-Qadir*, not the relic."

The All-Powerful.

It was a term they used to refer to Allah, but Hassan wondered about the way she said it. "*Malika*, if you approve, I would still like to leave it for the *uroubi*. It is all I have to offer."

Raha's eyes shined with tears. "You worked tirelessly to find him. You have given more than most."

Hassan shrugged. He lifted the lid again and placed the pouch on Stephen's chest, hastily closing it again. Grief overtook him. He bowed his head, embarrassed.

Raha placed her hand on his shoulder, but his urge to cry passed. Why did he not feel better after accomplishing all he had set out to do?

They remained quiet like this until the sun drifted away, taking its light with it. The sky streaked with colors. Only torches and lanterns lit the great palace.

The Christian priest approached with four acolytes in ceremonial robes. He bowed and spoke in accented Arabic. "We must take the body to be buried, *malika.*"

Raha nodded, and stepped back, running a handkerchief over her tears under the veil.

Hassan asked, "May I help carry him?"

Malika Raha gestured for Hassan to go ahead. He and the other young men each took a corner. Not practiced in casket carrying, it jostled as he lifted his corner and became unbalanced before he recovered. He recalled when Stephen had steadied him after they had pulled Keterlyn up. That reminded Hassan: he had planned to ask Stephen how he had known Keterlyn's name without ever meeting her. Now he would never know.

They carried the casket down the foyer toward the front of the palace.

Bump.

Hassan darted his gaze to the other carriers. But none of them seemed to notice the odd sound. Hassan dismissed it as perhaps normal; perhaps it was natural shifting of the body as they carried it.

Bump bump.

The casket noticeably jostled, causing one of the men to drop a corner. The rest of them bent their knees to rest the casket on the ground.

One of the acolytes puffed out air, his voice cracking. "Did someone put an animal in there? I felt something move."

The *malika* raised her eyebrows.

Bump bump bump.

The lid rattled. The men's cries echoed as they scrambled backward. Raha lifted her veil.

Pressure mounted in Hassan's chest. With a shaking hand, he neared enough to flick the latch, but stepped back again.

He waited. The men waited. The *malika* waited. The quiet was punctuated with the sound of their breathing.

The casket hinges creaked, opening by itself. Hassan fell onto his behind. The lid rose. The arm holding it open was in the pristine white tunic. The hand was strong, splayed fingers articulate and long; not decomposed as the *uroubi's* had been. The hand was fully formed.

Stephen Kempe sat up. Not a body, but Kempe himself, the man who had brandished a Dane-axe in the Solar. The man who had spoken words of encouragement in the infernal hallways of Tower al-Garbu. It was Stephen Kempe. Healthy. Healed.

Resurrected.

Malika Raha moaned and pressed her hand to her mouth. One of the acolytes crumpled, unconscious.

Intense green eyes settled on Hassan's, shining with excitement.

"Hassan. Raha." He nodded in greeting. "Where is Zahra? There is much to do."

ABOUT THE AUTHOR

R.C. Mogo is the pen name for Rebecca Claire Mogollón, who works as an e-learning developer in Spring, Texas. She is married to a Colombian hunk, and they have three happy, goofy, brilliant children. To connect with R.C. Mogo and receive a free prequel novella in the Unburning Fire Series, subscribe to her mailing list at www.rcmogo.com.

NOTE FROM R.C. MOGO

Word-of-mouth is crucial for any author to succeed. If you enjoyed *Innocents of Marbella*, please leave a review online—anywhere you are able. Even if it's just a sentence or two. It would make all the difference and would be very much appreciated.

Thanks!
R.C. MOGO

Printed in the USA
CPSIA information can be obtained
at www.ICGtesting.com
JSHW020031270624
65395JS00001B/5

9 781685 134822